FROM A
DEAD SLEEP

JOHN A. DALY

BQB

Alpharetta, Georgia

Published in the United States by BQB Publishing
(Boutique of Quality Books Publishing Company)
www.bqbpublishing.com

Printed in the United States of America

978-1-937084-54-7 (p)
978-1-937084-97-4 (e)

Library of Congress Control Number: 2013933400

Book design by Robin Krauss, www.lindendesign.biz

To my wife, Sarah, whose love and encouragement
helped me fulfill a dream.

To my children, Chase and Olivia, whose smiles and laughter
are constant reminders that anything is possible
in this world.

Chapter 1

S ean Coleman grunted at the mercy of an excruciating headache as he began to awake. His skull throbbed in anguish, as if it had been knotted tightly with a rope. With blurred vision behind flickering eyelids, he struggled to find clarity and discovered himself lying facedown on a bed of damp, coarse dirt. Blades of long, healthy grass, wet from morning dew, brushed against his cheek as he clumsily turned his head to the side. A roaring cough erupted from deep within his throat, contorting his face and prompting him to raise his muddied fist to his parched lips.

Fragmented events from the night before began to stumble through his mind as if a diary was being thumbed through. He remembered getting off work late and stopping by O'Rafferty's Bar for a drink. One drink turned into many, and he soon lost fifty bucks to Moses Jones in a game of eight-ball. Sean couldn't afford to lose that money. It was his lifeline, but he had beaten Moses in the past on numerous occasions and another Sean Coleman victory seemed like a sure bet. Moses must have been practicing.

That money was needed for rent—rent that was already two months overdue. His landlord's patience had been expended. He recalled the seriousness in that angry man's eyes while he threatened Sean with eviction if the amount due wasn't paid in full by the week's end. It was the story of Sean's life: always making the wrong decisions at the worst possible times.

"You stupid son of a bitch," he grunted. His voice was hoarse, barely audible above the clamor of river rapids. The words were hoarse, grating.

Birds chatted peacefully above, their song the only sound that resonated above the loud roar of moving water whose constant echo bounced off the towering trees and large, rounded, moss-covered rocks. Fresh daylight shined through narrow openings in the thick Gamble Oak and evergreens. A ray kindled a swaying glimmer off of an empty beer bottle that lay just inches from Sean's face. His stinging, bloodshot eyes glared hypnotically at it, as if he were staring through an open campfire.

He grappled with adjusting his eyes over what felt like an eternity, but was closer to a minute's time. Finally the world focused.

Among the muggy turf and the scent of pine, his nose intercepted a lingering, recognizable, but vile stench. Through narrowed eyes, he scowled at the large clump of vomit that nested intrusively on the ground in front of the beer bottle he barely recalled carrying in his hand the night before. The sight prompted him to hastily spin over onto his broad back, away from last night's penance. A wake of pain flowed across his skull from the brisk movement. His body flattened the grass beneath him, while small, underlying stones crackled from his movement.

His fluttering eyes soon grew large when a piercing sensation pricked into his chest. His hand hustled to his front shirt pocket, and his fingers quickly clenched the thin but heavy metal object that resided there. He grabbed it and raised it to his face. He examined the blemished badge whose securing pin dangled loosely in the light breeze. His thumb smeared mud and tiny grass particles from the front, exposing a smooth glimmering shield with an etched star at the middle. Above the star, in blue engraved print, read the word "Hansen." The lower half read "Security."

A whisper of moving brush and the snap of a thin twig spun Sean's head to the side like a weathervane through a sudden wind gust. A subtle smile formed on his lips as he welcomed the unexpected company of a large jackrabbit who glared back with beady black eyes. The critter was hunched timidly between two small shrubs; its oversized ears pointing straight upward, while its nose trembled erratically. The small animal's coat was nearly camouflaged against a dead overturned tree that lay in rot behind it. The rabbit examined him curiously, approaching within a few feet with a single lunge. Sean sneered back, engaging in a stare down with its lifeless black eyes that appeared to be silently judging him. The rabbit's eyelids clenched with an expression that could be best interpreted as a scowl if it were formed on the face of a human. After several seconds of neither giving in, Sean sighed in dismay.

His low, gravelly voice broke the stalemate. "I know," he stated in a hopeless, conceding tone.

Seemingly satisfied with the large man's confessional, the furry creature quickly lurched to the side and scurried off under brush and around trees. It soon disappeared from sight.

"I know," Sean repeated before his eyes slowly dropped to the ground.

He lay there in an almost relaxed state, tracing the contours of the shield with his eyes while using his fingernails to scrape the remaining filth from each and every groove. To Sean, it was a badge of honor . . . a dwindling reminder that he had a responsibility, a noble purpose in life, even though life hadn't turned out the way he'd imagined it. He craned his head forward; the action of which formed a double chin that displayed a day's stubble which looked prematurely gray for a man of thirty-seven years of age. He quickly used both hands to reattach the shield to the front of his pocket. He fiddled with it until he was certain it hung symmetrically.

From his reclined position, he couldn't help but notice his exposed stomach peeking out from under his untucked, gray button-up shirt. It crested over the top of his belt, no longer resembling the defined row of abdominal muscles of which he had once been very proud. His uniformed pants, accented with black pinstripes, were severely wrinkled and stained by grass, mud, and vomit. The tips of his brown, worn-out cowboy boots pointed upward toward the morning sky.

A straining groan slid from between his large, yellowing teeth as he crunched his body up into a sitting position. With his broad shoulders, he looked like a large lonesome tree stump, indigenous to the wilderness that surrounded him. He felt dampness on his back and butt, immediately accompanied by a brief chill going through his body that was now being exposed to the open breeze. The night's events flooded back to him. Wallowing in the familiar misery of his loss and convincing himself that there was no redemption for his mistake, the barrier of self-restraint crumbled down around him and he had found himself at the bar ordering a much-needed drink at O'Rafferty's. It was the first of many.

He also remembered Ted O'Rafferty himself limping outside into the parking lot after him and all those drinks and snatching his car keys away.

"You ain't driving anywhere tonight, Coleman!" the old man had lectured as he pressed the tip of his crooked wooden walking cane into Sean's chest.

Sean recalled he'd caused the kind of scene that had become expected of him over the years, but stubborn Ted would have none of it. The old man had too much respect for Sean's uncle to let his drunken nephew climb into his car and drive off. Hobbling back up the steps toward the front doors, Ted had screamed in his grainy, frail voice, "You can sleep out here in your car, but you ain't driving anywhere tonight!"

Now lying among the cool grass, Sean wondered why he hadn't taken Ted's advice rather than attempting to walk home. The last thing he remembered was stumbling his way down the roadside and marveling at the wicked lightning storm that had illuminated the night sky to the north.

"Yeah, this is much better . . ." he muttered wryly.

His legs burned when he reached for his knees, attempting to stretch out his wide back as his shoulders lunged forward. His hand went to the back of his head, where his teeth-manicured fingernails scratched a constantly irritated area at the base of his skull. A quarter-sized patch of hairless skin resided there, rubbed raw. The blemish was surrounded by an otherwise decently kept, short flat-top crew cut.

He noticed a collection of small dusty pebbles stuck to the bottom of his elbow. The same section of skin served as home to fresh scratches and scrapes. As he glanced up at the dirt road above the ditch he was nested in, he noticed his black plastic hair comb snagged on the thin limb of a small straggly bush. It was about halfway up the hill. Above and below the bush lay a wide vertical path of flattened and broken vegetation. Sean concluded that he had fallen down from the road above before rolling down the gradual embankment. He remembered none of it, but strangely enough enjoyed a touch of satisfaction at being able to reenact the scene in his mind based on the clues before him.

"Forensics . . ." he whispered. "They're the only true identifier to the mystery of an untold past." He grinned as he repeated the profound statement, which he remembered hearing William Petersen iterate from a recent episode of *CSI*.

With County Road 2 and Meyers Bridge residing so closely above, it was a wonder no early morning drivers had seen him lying down in that ditch. Maybe they did and just didn't care. Maybe the locals had all figured out by now that it was best not to ever engage Sean Coleman.

With his finger carefully scraping yellow crust from his eye, he raised himself up to one knee, yawning while peering out from behind the thin wispy grass that surrounded him. His gaze traced the tops of the low mountain range that sprawled familiarly along the northern horizon. He then glanced over his shoulder and along the road leading up the old wooden bridge—the same one he drove back and forth across most days.

That was when forced clarity suddenly grabbed Sean's attention, as if he had been shaken awake. His eyes focused in surprise as he beheld an odd site—the dark figure of a man, clad in a long trench coat, standing directly at the center of the bridge. Sean hadn't heard him approach. The black outfit cloaking the stranger's body couldn't have been any more misplaced; a foreign sight to the rural area far outside of any large cities. The man was leaning forward, peering blankly out in the direction of the river's flow. His knees pressed against the rusted steel guardrail that traveled along the edge of the bridge. It was clear that he hadn't spotted Sean in the ditch.

The man was average in height with bright blonde, well-kept hair that was short at the sides and back, and not much longer on top. His dark pants and shoes matched his trench coat.

The bags under Sean's eyes tightened and his mouth drooped open as he curiously examined the stranger. He noticed the man's chest was visibly expanding and contracting with large breaths. He watched him lean forward with his hands in his pockets, peering aimlessly down at the water below. His leather dress shoes, despite being scuffed and muddied, shined under a gap of sunlight penetrating through the trees.

Even from the distance, Sean could smell money. He fancied the man as a business executive. A big-shot city slicker. The stranger was thin but athletic, with a runner's build. He was clean shaven and appeared to have quite noticeable wide, red marks under his dark eyes, as if he normally wore glasses. Sean guessed they had to be large glasses, because the streaks traced well down to his cheek bones.

Without warning, the man's head quickly spun to the side.

Sean, out of pure instinct, ducked down low to keep from being seen. The long grass helped conceal him from view.

The man intently investigated the stretch of road to the west and then spun to the other side to check out the east.

Sean felt a little silly for hiding; he wasn't sure there was a point in it. He was a large and strong man who had little fear, a trait that often served as a detriment. But it was the pure fascination he was developing with the gentleman's foreign nature that kept Sean from revealing himself. As if observing a deer in the forest, he felt compelled to stay still and silent, to keep from startling the man.

The stranger on the bridge peered back and forth several more times in a paranoid fashion. This was all the more fascinating to Sean, whose large frame sunk lower onto his hands and knees.

As if he was suddenly being timed, the man quickly regained his composure and raised his hands from his pockets. A shiny gold wristwatch, now visible, danced in the sun, sending a beam of light directly into Sean's eyes.

Sean was forced to squint but kept his sight trained on the stranger's odd behavior. Once the glimmer vanished, Sean's face twisted in puzzlement. He now had clear sight of the man's hands.

His left hand was wrapped in what looked to be a gauze bandage or maybe a towel. The bandage wasn't clean; a crimson blemish stained the area over his palm.

"What the hell?" Sean whispered under his breath, struggling to decipher the display.

The man's head snapped quickly from side to side again before he lifted his left leg over the guardrail and stepped onto the narrow outer edge of the wood planking. His other leg followed. He was now in a sitting position, nested across the railing with his knees facing out and his feet dangling in the empty air.

Sean's nostrils flared as his eyes held a firm squint. Every now and then he had seen one of the locals perched in a similar position on that same bridge with a fishing pole. However, that was usually in the spring or fall when the water was moving slower—not this time of year. Either way, it was clear that the man was not a fisherman. A hint of concern flashed through Sean's mind; he was familiar with the merciless power of the river. If the man wasn't careful, he'd slip and fall in, and not likely make it back out.

He noticed the man's lips moving, deliberately, as if he were talking to himself. Whatever he said could not be heard over the rush of water pounding below him. The stranger's hand then crept into the side pocket of his trench coat. There resided a small bulge that Sean hadn't previously noticed.

As he arched his neck up a little in an attempt to analyze what would emerge, Sean's eyelids quickly opened to their widest extent. To his shock, a black handgun rose from the pouch.

"Jesus," Sean muttered softly, lowering back to his hands and knees. His heart began pounding.

The pistol appeared to be a Glock, but the barrel looked a little too long. Sean knew a little something about guns. A thousand thoughts raced through his mind, like lightning bugs bouncing off the inside of a glass jar. Upon closer examination of the pistol, he realized that it wasn't the barrel that made it appear disproportionately long; there was a silencer attached. He had never actually seen a silencer in his lifetime, but it looked just like they did on television and in magazines.

Sean's mind was cloudy, and the hangover wasn't helping his focus. He strained to form a sensible explanation. Then, a thought suddenly occurred to him.

Could this guy be a hit man? Had this lone stranger just *taken someone out*, and was he now about to dispose of the evidence?

Sean understood the ridiculousness of the notion but began to make a case for it in his mind. It would explain the way he was dressed and the style of the gun . . . or so Sean deemed reasonable. If he was a professional, however, why was he taking so long and acting so peculiar? And where was his car? How did he get there? None of it made sense. Sean felt the best course of action was to stay put and let the show play out.

The man's shoulders deflated. He sighed before his arm whipped behind his body where his fingers searched through his back pants pocket. Shifting his hips and tugging at his arm, the extended effort allowed him to remove a black leather wallet. With the flick of his wrist, he flipped open the sides of the trifold, and gazed at whatever was inside.

Sean wondered if he was looking at a picture.

The man set his gun down sideways on a wooden post beside him, one of many of that supported the guardrail.

The stranger's eyes drooped from what, up until then, had been direct intent. They now read a much less organized tale.

It was the same expression Sean himself had witnessed so many times—when looking in the mirror. Sorrow. Regret.

A hit-man with a conscience? he wondered.

The man's shoulders dropped lower, and he took another deep breath. After glancing back out along the river's path, he suddenly built up enough motivation to stand up straight. The bottom of his long trench coat spilled back to his ankles. He used his right hand to hang onto the guardrail, keeping himself balanced on the edge of the old wooden planking. The injured hand quickly shoved the wallet back into his pocket. It went in much easier than it came out, though the man's face seemed to twist in pain at the movement. He leaned to his side to retrieve the pistol.

Sean wondered why the man was making no immediate attempt to climb back over the railing to safety.

Instead, the stranger remained in an upright position balancing his heels along the edge of the bridge while his calves rested against the guardrail. Then, he held the butt of the gun to his chest with both hands.

"Hey . . ." Sean instinctively said to himself in a whisper before quickly raising up to his knees. Remaining hidden no longer felt important.

His focus shifted back and forth from the man's desperate eyes to the gun he held in front of his body in an awkward grip. It had suddenly become apparent that the series of actions unfolding before Sean were concluding something very different than what he'd originally thought.

The stranger shuffled the gun in his noticeably trembling hands before holding it in a conventional fashion with his right. He steadily raised his arm back over his shoulder and drew the gun awkwardly to the back side of his head, using his other hand to direct the barrel to the base of his skull.

The oddity and mystery of what he was witnessing was no longer Sean's concern. No more questions. No more observation. He was certain the man was about to take his own life, and he wasn't going to sit by and let it happen.

"Hey!" Sean heard himself call out in a voice loud and scary enough to gain the attention of anyone . . . unless that person was standing above the loud crashing sound of roaring water rapids.

The man didn't flinch or show any indication that he had heard Sean's call. He continued to hold the barrel in place with the metal tip resting against the back of his skull.

Sean's teeth clenched as he quickly scrambled up the short hill and onto the dirt road. His footing slid on the damp grass, but his persistence gave him the traction he needed.

"Hey!" he screamed out again, projecting his voice even louder than the first time.

There was still no reaction from the man who stood about forty yards away. The motion of his arms had come to a grizzly halt. His limbs contorted back behind his body with the barrel of the gun glued to its intended target.

"Stop!" Sean roared, waving his arms frantically back and forth above his head as if he were directing a grounded plane. He prayed his wild movements would catch the man's peripheral vision, but they received no response.

Sean engaged in an all-out sprint, something he hadn't done much of since his high school football days. The loud modulation of crackling gravel was soon replaced by the sharp groaning of wooden boards once he broke the plain of the bridge. Air pressed heavily from his nose and mouth. With a grueling red face, his chest thrust forward with each stride. Despite the great amount of effort he was extending, he felt as if he were running underwater in a dream. His body couldn't move as fast as his mind.

About twenty yards away now.

Sean's jaw lifted as he prepared to deliver another verbal plea, but before a syllable could leave his mouth, his eyes glared in horror at the image of the man purposely letting his body fall forward off the bridge. Sean's mind interpreted the scene in slow motion. Regardless of how fast his legs were pumping, there was no way of reaching the stranger in time. This curtain of helplessness was quickly replaced by numbing shock when a deep-red spray jetted through the air, just above where the stranger's body dropped from visibility. After hovering for a second, the red mist quickly dispersed into the breeze.

There was no sound of a gunshot. The silencer had done its job.

With a coarse gasp and a wrenching cramp in his stomach, Sean immediately altered his direction toward the railing at his side. He dropped to his knees and craned his neck over the edge, just in time to see the fluttering trench coat drop into the swirling water below with a loud splash.

Water flew high into the air, but the jetting rapids quickly replaced all disruption of the river's flow. The body disappeared into the violent churning; swallowed whole. All that was left was a burning smell and a red, discolored stream of water that dissolved into whiteness as it was quickly carried downstream.

Sean's chest heaved in and out as he struggled for breath. He felt as if he himself was drowning. The realization of what he had just witnessed quickly sank into the depths of his stomach.

Chapter 2

Breath was in short supply as Sean's feet fumbled briskly along the rocky edge of the river. He tried his best to keep his eyes on the black blob he'd thought he saw momentarily bobbing up and down as it shot downstream.

Thick pine branches smacked against his face, and his ankles repeatedly buckled under the weight of his body as he negotiated round, wet rocks and overturned foliage. He could taste sap on his lips. More than once his legs dipped down into freezing cold water, which drenched his pants. Yet, none of nature's obstacles hindered resolve.

Sean himself couldn't say where his persistence and motivation were coming from, but the helplessness he had felt while kneeling at the top of the bridge did not sit well. His heart wouldn't let him give up. Anger encompassed him as he briskly lumbered alongside the water. The anger stewed from his failure to recognize, until it was too late, what was transpiring right before him. He also felt intense guilt over the effect his poor decision from the night before was having on his body. If his head was just a little clearer, and his legs had moved just a little faster, maybe he would have been able to stop the stranger. Then again, if he wouldn't have gotten drunk, he wouldn't have been there in the first place. Perhaps he was being too hard on himself.

After a few more seconds, and one last possible appearance of the bubbled-up coat, Sean lost all traces of the stranger. The water was moving too fast. The body was gone.

He stopped and dropped to his knees, refusing to take his eyes off of the river. All was eerily tranquil again. A light breeze; birds singing. It was as if nothing had ever happened.

Minutes later, his side cramped with ferocity as he strove to keep up a jogging pace. A dry belch bellowed from deep within his stomach and he tasted hours-old alcohol in his mouth. His ankle ached from twisting on a rock along the river's edge. Still, even through straining muscles and painful panting, he lumbered his way steadily down on the dirt and gravel of County Road 2, headed toward town. Dense beads of sweat poured down the sides of his face. His drenched hair shone. Images of the horrific scene from the bridge were still fresh in his head, and the scent of a gun being fired still lingered in his nose. They all took a momentary backseat to the thoughts of what reaction he would face from the town's authorities.

Sean had a very complicated relationship with the chief of police, Gary Lumbergh. The two were engaged in what could best be described as a rivalry that was a secret to no one. In fact, it was often the local talk amongst the citizens of Winston, where gossip was as common as the fields of purple and white columbines that decorated the surrounding landscape.

He dreaded the thought of another encounter—especially one that would surely leak to the public—but he knew he hadn't a choice.

His heavy breathing and pounding feet hindered Sean from hearing the rattling frame and purring engine of the old, red pickup truck that approached him from behind at a snail's pace.

"Hey, Sean!" a gravelly voice sounded out, causing Sean's head to quickly spin.

The view of old Milo Coltraine's gray-bearded face, hanging outside the window of his 1972 Chevy pickup, was a welcome sight. Sean came to a relieved halt and doubled over to suck in air. His hamstrings ached, and his throat felt raw. With his chest mightily expanding and contracting, he scurried up to the driver's side door, his hand clutched at his side. He hadn't the energy for a drawn-out explanation of what had happened at the bridge, but Milo was certainly eager to talk.

"I hear Moses Jones gave ya quite a spankin' last night!" Milo hollered, following up with his trademark obnoxious laugh that resembled more of a howl.

The wide suede cowboy hat he always wore made Milo look like an old gold prospector from another era. At the same time, his weathered skin and the space at the center of his crooked teeth invited comparisons to a desert lizard.

Without wasting another second, Sean's large hand latched onto the outside handle and quickly yanked the truck's driver side door open. Milo's eyes bulged in surprise and his laugh disappeared, not expecting such an intrusion.

"Move aside, Coltraine!" Sean snarled before shoving his open hand firmly into Milo's shoulder.

"Hey!" Milo screamed, his voice reaching even a higher pitch as Sean shoved him effortlessly across the bench seat.

Milo was a very short, top-heavy man with little coordination. His legs kicked wildly in the air as he struggled to keep from being knocked to his back.

"What in the hell are ya doin', boy?"

The truck never even came to a stop. It coasted slowly as Sean lifted himself up into the driver's seat with a hardening grunt. The door closed behind him.

"Sean! Dammit!" Milo yelled, after managing to lean forward enough to latch his frail and freckled fingers onto Sean's wrist.

Sean effortlessly shook his arm free and stomped his foot down on the gas pedal. The sudden jolt of acceleration forced Milo's body to sink deep into his seat. Sean's legs barely fit around the steering wheel, and his knees dug into the dashboard. He felt like a canned sardine and quickly grabbed a side lever above the floorboard and yanked on it to slide the bench seat back.

"Jesus, Milo! How short are you?" Sean grumbled more in the form of an accusation than a question.

A cardboard air freshener, shaped like a pine tree but having long ago lost its scent, swung from the rearview mirror as wind and dust filled the car through the open window. Two empty boxes of cheap cigarettes fell off the dashboard and onto Sean's lap.

"I ain't playin' 'round!" Milo threatened after finally managing to sit up straight. "Pull over and get outta my truck!"

Milo's breath smelled strongly of corn chips, which was confirmed by the handful of crumpled-up Big Grab Fritos bags wedged into the middle of the seat cushion.

"I'm not playing neither!" Sean barked without taking his eyes off the road. "Listen to me! A man just died! I need to get into town and tell Lumbergh!"

Milo didn't immediately respond, taking a moment to let Sean's claim bounce around the walls of his head. "Whatcha' talkin' about, *A man just died?* What man?"

"Back at Meyers Bridge! Just now! He shot himself!"

Milo hesitated again before responding, glaring suspiciously at the side of Sean's face.

"Are you shittin' me, boy? There's a dead fella at Meyers Bridge?"

"Yes! I mean . . . No! He jumped into the river!"

Sean couldn't verbalize a coherent explanation and had little patience to. He was out of breath, his heart was racing, and his primary concern was reaching town.

Milo, however, wasn't about to let Sean off the hook with such a cryptic statement. He grabbed his shoulder and used his other hand to point an accusatory finger.

"Ya said he shot himself! Then ya said he jumped inta' the river! This story smells like horse-shit ta' me!"

Sean's head shook in frustration while a sour scowl twisted across his lips.

The truck tore around a sharp corner and onto the paved road of Main Street, leaving behind it a wide cloud of dust. Sean scratched the back of his head with one hand, causing small flakes of dried skin to drop to his shirt collar. His other hand stayed tightly glued to the steering wheel.

"Milo! I just . . . I don't have time for your shit right now!"

Milo didn't take kindly to the words. "Oh! Oh! I'm so sorry! Ya stole ma' truck! Whatcha think Lumbergh's gonna say about that? Huh?"

"Milo . . . I don't give a shit what Lumbergh says! When I'm done talking to him, you can tell him your whole life story. For now, just sit there and shut up!" Sean's head turned toward the old man for the first time, and a frightening glare finally earned compliance.

Milo was visually furious, but the look in Sean's eye scared the old man. Sean had a reputation for being a loose cannon, and Milo knew better than to light the fuse. He sat back in his seat and folded his arms in front of him, shaking his head in disapproval.

The engine roared louder as Sean picked up speed. Main Street was a straightaway right into town.

Peering at Sean from the corner of his eye, Milo spoke in a less fiery tone. "Ya know . . . All ya had ta' do was ask, and I'd a given ya a ride ta' town."

"Milo . . . No offense, but I could have jogged to town faster than if I'd have let you drive."

Chapter 3

E very morning, Chief Gary Lumbergh looked forward to that first cup of coffee. That day's flavor was Ethiopian Longberry.

Its rich aroma elegantly drifted up from the steaming ceramic mug that sat proudly on a coaster on top of the chief's redwood oak desk. It spread an ambiance of warmth and comfort through the small office, reminding Lumbergh of the big city. The chief had recently become a member of a coffee of the month club, which he had signed up for over the Internet. This was the premium stuff. Gourmet; much too coveted and high-quality to find at the local supermarket.

Clad in a neatly pressed, light blue dress shirt with rolled up sleeves and a sleek, navy blue tie, Lumbergh didn't fit the mold of the typical small town lawman. In fact, he was about as far removed from the laid-back and hospitable Andy Griffith–type anyone could possibly be.

While he was well respected by the citizens of Winston and neighboring communities, it wasn't Lumbergh's charm or demeanor that made him a hit with the locals. He had a name and quite a resume.

Unlike most of its citizens, Lumbergh hadn't grown up in Winston, Colorado. He hadn't even stepped foot inside the state until two years earlier, when he left a prestigious position as a police lieutenant in Chicago. There he'd been involved in numerous high-profile cases that spanned a range of crimes. Murderers, rapists, bank robbers—Lumbergh had worked them all. There, he had quickly become a seasoned veteran of law enforcement, receiving numerous promotions, all of which were earned before his thirty-fourth birthday. Back then, the sky was the limit for Lumbergh.

For the chief, those days seemed so long ago. A quickly fading memory. Now, his largest responsibilities usually involved delinquent high school kids, domestic disputes, or public intoxication—often a combination of the three. He regularly questioned his consequential decision to leave the big time . . . but only to himself. He had made a commitment, and that commitment left him as a big fish in the small pond of Winston.

Chief Gary Lumbergh's name was bigger than he was, at least physically. He was a short and thin man, standing at around five-foot-six and 135 pounds of pure, unadulterated confidence. Short, slicked-back, dark hair only partially covered the thinning area along his scalp, but Lumbergh wasn't self-conscious at all about how he looked. Always clean shaven and feverishly chewing on a stick of gum, he had a way of getting things done.

He was a certified workaholic, living in a world that never moved fast enough for his liking. For him, patience was not a virtue—it was a shortcoming. It wasn't uncommon for him to be seen snapping his fingers to hurry up the testimony of a complainant or feverishly writing down notes in a cryptic form of abbreviation that only he could decipher.

Cowboy hats and cowboy boots—Lumbergh never wore either. In fact, he despised them both so much that he forbade his officers from wearing them while on duty. The uniforms that he approved weren't much different than what he had worn proudly during the early days of his career: black shoes and a black tie over navy blue. If a subordinate wasn't professional enough to look professional, he or she had no place in Lumbergh's squad. The chief took his job extremely seriously and demanded perfection. Of course, perfection was a relative term when it came to the citizens of Winston. Still, he was persistent in striving for it.

It was a slow morning, like most mornings in Winston, yet Lumbergh was feeling uncharacteristically cheerful. Unlike most people, he enjoyed working on the weekends. What little crime that did occur tended to happen then.

Leaning back in his burgundy leather desk chair and clasping his fingers behind his head, he admired the numerous plaques and certificates that decorated his office walls. They made him feel proud. They made him feel legitimate. They let him remember. With a sly smile, he glanced down across his desktop at a large black-and-white framed photo of him with his arms wrapped around a pretty brunette with long hair, bright brown eyes, and a dazzling smile.

Lumbergh's office was extremely organized. Artwork hung symmetrically along freshly painted walls, the tile floor had been recently waxed, and all furniture was free of dust.

Outside his door, he enjoyed the sound of file cabinets being opened and closed, and keys being typed. It meant work was getting done, or at least sounded like it was getting done. He liked his people busy. In fact, as small as it was, his office often helped neighboring divisions with their workload. The unusual practice helped increase the chances that Lumbergh would be involved in more interesting work than could be found inside his own town limits. He also felt it somewhat of an obligation, considering his skillset.

Being from the big city, he was an automatic celebrity to the rural townsfolk. To them he was articulate, knowledgeable, and commanding. Many seemed to place greater value on him than they did themselves, and who was Lumbergh to argue? He won a landslide election victory over the previous chief, who couldn't compete with the big-time law enforcement experience a former police lieutenant could bring. The incumbent was so old and ready for retirement anyway that he later thanked Lumbergh for running against him. The voters always supported Lumbergh. His latest funding request for a new police cruiser won almost unanimous support from the public. In fact, records showed that only one person in the town voted against that initiative, and he had a pretty good idea who that person was.

The chief's eyes shifted toward his coffee mug, displaying an almost criminal longing. He had never experienced the utopia of Ethiopian Longberry, but message-board reviews claimed it to be exquisite. The wait was over. Anticipating the sharp, winy flavor and slightly tangy kick, he stretched out his small hand for a taste of heaven. The mug roasted in his palm as he leaned back in his chair and raised its rim gingerly to his lips. He wanted to savor the experience.

Without warning, the piercing screech of rubber skidding on pavement blared intrusively from the outside parking lot and through the thin walls of the police office. The hairs on the back of Lumbergh's neck stood straight up, and his body instinctively jackknifed forward. Hot coffee intrusively streamed down the sides of his chin and onto his shirt and tie.

"Goddammit!" he yelled without reservation. His voice echoed through the small room and into the outside hallway.

With his face twisted in anger, he sprung up to his feet and promptly scanned the room for a towel or napkin. There were none to be found in the neat office. His thin arms worked fervently, opening up every drawer in his desk until he spotted a large legal-sized envelope that he found to be empty. He snatched it with his fingers and stomped briskly to his door where he noticed the rest of his small squad curiously gathering in the narrow lobby at the front entrance of the building.

Holding the envelope to his chest and quickly recognizing its liquid-absorbing deficiency, he stuck his head out into the hallway. From there he could see his officer, Jefferson, who had just returned from patrol. He was peering interestedly out through a window at the top half of one of the dual front doors.

The muffled sound of two people arguing was just barely audible from outside, and the scent of Pine-Sol momentarily distracted Lumbergh's senses. Still he thought he heard a familiar voice, which compelled him to momentarily forget about his coffee-stained clothes.

"Tell me that's not who I think it is," he loudly said through narrowed eyes and a fuming scowl.

Jefferson whipped his head around. There was uneasiness in the officer's eyes. "Yeah, it's Sean. He's with old Milo. And neither one looks none too happy!"

Lumbergh's eyes rose toward the ceiling. His shoulders lowered as he exhaled an embittered grunt. "Everybody, get back to work!" he firmly directed. "Jefferson, you handle it! I don't want to be disturbed with his bullshit this early in the morning!"

An audible gulp lifted from Jefferson's throat. "Me?" he asked, hesitantly.

Lumbergh shot him a glare much like a parent would toward a child who had just spilled a glass of milk.

Jefferson quickly lifted his shoulders and broadened his chest, not wanting to disappoint the man whose approval he so often sought. Licking his upper lip and composing himself, he delivered a firm nod to his boss before turning his attention back to the window.

The chief ducked back inside his office and slammed the thin wooden door shut before retrieving a bottle of Evian water from a small refrigerator beside his desk. While the sound of footsteps shifting back to their cubicles drifted underneath his door, he dabbed water over the top of his coffee-stained shirt.

He knew this would be a good test for Jefferson. The officer had shown hints of promise in the past, but at times tended to lack the proper initiative that Lumbergh felt the job required. The two had spoken of the topic on many occasions, and he had made it clear to Jefferson exactly what was expected of him.

Sean and Milo ranted back and forth like an old married couple engaged in a spat. Their colorful, quickly traded insults grew louder as they neared.

The tall and lanky Jefferson extended his long arm along the door and pushed it open wide for the two to enter.

From behind his desk, Lumbergh could hear Coltraine wildly scream out, "Jefferson! Jefferson! He stole ma' truck! He kidnapped me!"

Lumbergh's eyes widened and his fists clenched. He was nearly tempted to immediately dash out into the hallway and launch a verbal assault on Sean—the man who seemed hell-bent on extending as much complication into life as possible. He fought the urge, deciding to give Jefferson a chance to prove himself. Lumbergh rested his elbows on the top of his desk and buried his face in his right hand while using his left to reach into his pocket for a stick of gum.

"Here we go," he whispered under his breath.

"Is Lumbergh in his office?" Sean asked loudly, more in the form of a statement than a question.

With his chest bloated, Sean didn't intend on stopping at the lobby. He kept walking, making a beeline for Lumbergh's door.

"Not so fast!" Jefferson ordered in a much-practiced tone that was impressive in its authoritativeness. He held his arm up like a tollgate, blocking Sean's path.

Sean stopped and glared at him in subtle surprise before lowering his eyebrows. "Jefferson, get out of my way!"

With Sean momentarily distracted, Coltraine made a move to quickly try and shuffle around his large body in hopes of getting to Lumbergh's office first. Without taking his eyes off Jefferson, however, Sean grabbed the back of Coltraine's flannel shirt collar and held him in place. Coltraine let out a gagging noise as his top button pressed right up against his Adam's apple.

"There's a policy in this office, Sean," stated Jefferson. "Complaints come to me. They don't go straight to the chief. He's a busy man."

So far, Lumbergh liked what he was hearing. He continued to listen from his chair, leaning forward with his fingers forming a temple across the top of his desk. His mouth grounded a wad of Trident. He expected his men to deal with adversity, and there wasn't a better test of adversity than Sean Coleman.

"Busy doing what?" Sean ranted. "Signing autographs? This is important, dammit! If I needed someone to get me out of a parking ticket, *then* I'd come to you! This is *big time*, Jeffrey!"

Jefferson held his ground, taking exception to being referred to as "Jeffrey." He hated the nickname that Sean had given him, and Sean knew it.

"*Big time*? Oh really?" sneered Jefferson. "Just like when Emma at the laundromat was a *big time* drug dealer, or when you thought that kid down at the gas station was a *big time* international terrorist!"

Lumbergh held his fist in the air, and then retracted his elbow with an excited whisper. "Yes!" Jefferson was earning his pay that day.

Sean's right lower eyelid began to twitch as he glared right through Jefferson. His face turned red with anger, and his teeth sunk into his lower lip.

"Ya thought that young fella at the gas station was a dang terrorist?" Milo asked with enlightened eyes and some pep to his voice. His cheeks turned red and a half-second later he howled out in piercing laughter. "I hadn't heard that one! A terrorist of all things! Can ya imagine?"

Sean paid no attention to Milo. His pupils shrank and all he saw was fire. Jefferson had grown nearly eight inches taller since his high school days, but in Sean's eyes he was still the same mope, the same timid and awkward kid who Sean used to terrorize in gym class. Who was *he* to be telling Sean off?

The longer Sean's intense glare lasted, the tighter Jefferson's stomach cramped; Sean could see it on the officer's face. Jefferson paled, and Sean knew he was thinking of those distant memories of being on the receiving end of wedgies and pink-bellies—at Sean's hands. If the two men were anywhere else but the police station, Sean figured Jefferson might have immediately run in the opposite direction, also much like the old days; it was an effective tactic he'd used to escape Sean Coleman's bullying back in high school.

Sean saw the resolve slip over Jefferson's face. Sean was on *his* turf now. Jefferson had the backup and the authority, and Sean knew that Jefferson's boss was likely listening. The officer needed to hang tough. It wasn't every day that someone had the opportunity to put Sean Coleman in his place.

Sean wondered if he'd try it.

Jefferson continued with a forced, wide, condescending smile. "So tell me, *big time*, what's today's beef? Did Moses Jones cheat in that game of eight-ball last night? I heard he whooped your ass!" His tongue slid sleekly across his lower lip in gratification.

A muffled laugh could be heard from someone down the hall, close to the fax machine.

Sean's right arm trembled, and he formed a concealed fist. He wanted to punch Jefferson right in the face—right above that cheesy handlebar mustache. He pictured flattening that fat, rounded nose, and he relished the image of blood squirting from it. It took him everything he had to remind himself where he was and what Jefferson's uniform meant as far as police charges went. Sean forced composure upon himself, slowly nodding his head up and down.

With a burdened grin, Sean said, "I wasn't with Moses Jones last night, Jefferson . . . I was with Becky!"

Jefferson's eyes widened, and his teeth were visible at the mention of his wife.

The same voice by the fax machine now let out a low, "Uh-oh."

Sean was fully aware that Jefferson and his wife had been separated for about a month, and he took great enjoyment in reminding him of it.

All the confidence that Jefferson had been displaying left in an instant, and his nerve dissolved. His lip quivered, and he glanced at the watching eyes of his coworkers, who he felt were about to judge him by his reaction. Before he could compose himself enough to retort, Sean opened his fist, spun, and grabbed Milo's velvet hat from the top of his head. He pivoted back around and shoved the hat firmly into the center of Jefferson's chest.

"Make yourself useful and hang this up!" he growled.

The force of Sean's strong arm caused Jefferson to stumble backward on the slick tile. The back of Jefferson's long legs met the armrest of a wooden bench that stood behind him. He lost his footing and fell like a ton of bricks—down to his butt on the unforgiving floor.

Sean hadn't intended for Jefferson to fall but didn't feel bad for causing it. *Who does he think he is, with that condescending dog and pony show?* he thought. *He deserves to be made a fool of in front of everyone.*

"Sean!" The name lingered in the air, drawn out as only Lumbergh could stretch it.

His voice erupted like a volcano, prompting everyone in the office to stare with wide eyes at the sight of the small, wiry man now standing outside his door. The chief's legs were spread, and both fists were clenched.

Breathing hard, Sean glared into Lumbergh's eyes before noticing the veins protruding at both sides of his reddened face. It wasn't the first time Sean had seen him this pissed; it wasn't the first time Sean had *made* him this pissed.

"Well, well, well, Hollywood. It looks like you're not too busy to talk to me after all," Sean said with a quick smirk.

Lumbergh despised the nickname Hollywood. Sean had given it to him because of the celebrity-like adoration the chief enjoyed from the rest of the town. Lumbergh slowly and intensely shifted his head from side to side. He looked about ready to blow a gasket.

"Coltraine!" Lumbergh screamed. "Jefferson will take down your complaint, and I *strongly* urge you to file charges!"

"Yes, sir," the hatless Coltraine timidly answered, taking a step forward and then back.

"Sean . . . in my office! Now!"

Lumbergh didn't wait for a reaction. He turned and stomped back inside through his doorway.

Grabbing the knob tightly in his fingers, he waited for Sean to enter before slamming the door shut behind them. The force caused the window shade hanging from the top of the door to lose its hold and fall sloppily to the floor. It unraveled as quickly as Lumbergh's patience.

Before Sean could open his mouth to state his case, Lumbergh gargled out a loud spontaneous, incoherent sound immediately followed by a raw cough. The chief's unhinged anger had caused his chewing gum to slip down his throat. His eyes bulged, and he immediately hacked it back up and out of his mouth. The wad would have fallen from his lips to the floor, but Lumbergh purposely used his own hand to angrily slap it in Sean's direction. It bounced off of Sean's chest, causing the big man to flinch.

"What the hell's the matter with you?" Sean yelled in outrage.

Lumbergh heard nothing but the fizzling between his own ears as his eyes traced Sean's body up and down.

"Jesus, Sean!" Lumbergh bellowed with his nose scrunched in disgust. "What did you do? Piss yourself?"

Sean looked down at his pants which were still wet from the river.

Lumbergh pointed at his lower pant leg. "And what's that? Puke? You're a goddamned mess!"

"Gary, just shut the hell up and listen!" Sean yelled impatiently with his nostrils wide. His outburst roared out like the call of a large animal.

Necks were craned, and eyes peered over the walls of cubicles. Outside Lumbergh's office, a moment of deafening silence allowed for the sound of a sheet of paper to be heard making contact with the floor. Above it, a secretary standing in front of a copy machine stared intently with her mouth hung open.

Lumbergh wasn't going to be intimidated. He wouldn't let Sean continue. This was *his* house. He had all of the authority here. "Who the hell do you think you are, walking in here and spouting off like a lunatic? Those are my subordinates out there!"

Before Sean could answer, Lumbergh raised his arm out straight, pointing toward the door. "You have no right to come in here and disrespect me and get physical with one of my men! This isn't flag football at the park! This is where I work! You come in here with beer on your breath and looking like you slept in a trash dumpster last night, and—"

"I wouldn't have *had* to disrespect you if your ape would have just listened to me!"

"Why *should* he? Why should any of them?" Lumbergh was livid. The pitch of his voice was higher than he intended it to be as he raised his shoulders and threw his arms up in the air. His wide eyes blinked erratically. "They've heard all the same bullshit stories that I have! I mean, look at it from their point of view, Sean! Do you have any idea how many hours my people have wasted on your hair-brained theories and childlike imagination? And today, I'm sure you're here with another one . . ."

"So?" Sean retorted with a taunting shoulder shrug. "It's not like they have anything better to do! They should be thanking me for getting them out of your boot camp for a few hours! Now listen to me . . ."

Lumbergh raised his finger at Sean to cut in.

". . . a man died today, Gary!" Sean yelled out, breaking the stalemate of wild banter.

Lumbergh's mouth refused to follow up and instead was left gaping open. His arm slowly lowered back to his side. His demeanor went from outrage to awestruck in the time it took Sean to relay one simple but chilling statement. His eyes blinked as they peered into Sean's.

"A man died today," Sean repeated.

Chapter 4

"That doesn't make sense!" stormed Lumbergh with his arms crossed and his slender body aligned against the front of his desk. "Why would someone kill himself by shooting himself in the *back* of his head?"

His eyes were filled with doubt, and the skepticism didn't go unnoticed by Sean. After noticing a large peculiar coffee stain on Lumbergh's shirt, Sean replied with a head shake. "I don't know." A moment of silence ensued and with a glance at the ceiling, he shrugged his shoulders and offered up: "I *can* tell you *one* thing; he wasn't Chinese."

"Chinese?" Lumbergh enquired, interested. He leaned forward, his eyebrows narrowing the gap between them. "What do you mean?"

Sean's eyes returned to the ceiling, and his tongue slid to the corner of his mouth. He momentarily pondered his own words while trying to recall the details of an old episode of *Hunter* that featured a disgraced immigrant taking his own life. He soon shook his head in digression. "Oh, never mind . . . I'm thinking of a dagger through the stomach."

Lumbergh deflated back to his desk. "That's *Japanese*," he muttered indignantly under his breath, frustrated with himself for giving Sean an inch. "And it's called *seppuku*."

An annoyed and unimpressed grunt escaped Sean's mouth. "Well, very good; someone just earned themselves a gold star by their name."

Lumbergh ignored him, not desiring to fuel another unproductive outburst. "I'm trying to make sense of your story, Sean. You don't have the best track record for credibility."

"Oh, Jesus, Gary, don't start this shit again! Do you think I'm just making this whole thing up?"

Lumbergh's eyes left Sean for a moment, taking a breath and searching for the right words. "I'm not saying that, Sean. But you have a way of letting your imagination run wild. You know you do."

Sean glared at him, shaking his head in disgust. "I'm not making this up, Gary. It happened, goddammit. Right in front of my eyes!"

Lumbergh took a breath. "Sean, you had a *lot* to drink last night. I think that's pretty safe to say—"

"Oh, give me a fucking break! I'm hungover. I'm not crazy." Sean's blood was beginning to simmer again. "Are you going to check this out or not?"

Lumbergh looked sympathetically into Sean's eyes—the same way a father would look at a son who just missed the game-winning field goal. "Sean . . . I've given you a *lot* of leeway for obvious reasons . . ."

Out of frustration, Sean's face twisted and he quickly lunged forward, slamming his fist hard across the top of the desk.

Lumbergh's body jolted, but he kept his cool, raising his eyebrows to direct a silent warning.

"I've never asked you for *anything*, Gary!" Sean shouted. "And I don't want you to start doing me any favors! I just want you to do your goddamned job! You run this place like a Chicago police department, but when someone reports a dead body, you blow him off? Are you kidding me?"

"Enough!" Lumbergh held up both palms in front of Sean's chest. With his eyes large in sincerity, he said, "I'm going to check it out, okay?"

"You are?" said a stunned Sean. He alertly stood up straight.

Lumbergh held his hand beside his mouth and yelled, "Jefferson!"

Three seconds later, Jefferson was heard racing down the hallway. He opened the office door and poked his head inside. He purposely didn't make eye contact with Sean.

Lumbergh didn't look at his officer. "Pull the cruiser around back. We're going to Meyers Bridge."

A sly smile formed on Sean's face, and he crossed his arms in front of his chest. "And make it snappy, Jefferson," he added in a gloating tone.

"Shut up, Sean," said Lumbergh.

Jefferson pretended not to hear the exchange and attempted to leave, but Lumbergh stopped him.

"But first," the chief said, "give Sean's uncle a call and have him pick him up."

At the same time, but in different tones, both Jefferson and Sean replied with, "What?"

Lumbergh held his hand up to Sean. "You heard me, Jefferson."

Even before the door closed behind the officer, Sean was up in arms. "What are you calling *him* for? I'm coming out with you guys!"

Lumbergh shook his head and discreetly rolled his eyes. "We can take it from here, Sean. I've got the location. I'll have Jefferson call you if we have any questions."

"This is unbelievable! This is un-fucking-believable! I witnessed the whole thing!"

"And I listened to your entire story," Lumbergh sharply added. "Now you have to let me do my job! If what you say is true, a crime wasn't even committed. This will be open and shut."

Sean's eye twitched as he glared back at Lumbergh.

The chief lowered his head and took a deep breath. He then pressed his thumb against his police chief's badge, which shined proudly on his dress-shirt pocket. "Sean, this badge means that I have a duty to the people of Winston. They elected me to serve them to the best of my abilities. I'm convinced that having you there would only hinder our investigation."

"What are you talking about?"

"Jefferson and I aren't going to have time to answer all of your questions and entertain all of your theories. And we *certainly* don't need your abrasive attitude at the scene."

Lumbergh meant every word he said. Sean was a liability—a dreamer with a wild imagination—which often led him to overstep an imagined level of authority he never had in the first place.

"Gary, come on! I know what I'm doing!"

Lumbergh took offense to his words. "No, you don't, Sean! No, you don't! Watching *Law and Order* every week doesn't make you a cop! That badge you wear isn't a *real* badge; you're a security guard!"

In Sean's eyes, Lumbergh had just crossed the line. Sean was proud of his job, and he didn't like it being disrespected. "Do you think *your* badge scares me, Gary?"

He leaned in close with his forehead almost touching Lumbergh's. He glared into the chief's eyes with frightening intensity, and his right index finger pressed imposingly into the officer's chest. "Just between you and me, I would have kicked your scrawny ass years ago if it wasn't for Diana!"

Lumbergh bit his lip and twisted his body away from Sean. Retreating to the back of his desk with a red face, he suddenly held his hand in the air. "Are you threatening me now, Sean? Is that what you're doing? How many times do you think you can hit rock-bottom before you won't be able to drag yourself up again?" At that point, Lumbergh should have stopped. He immediately regretted that he didn't. But Sean knew just how to push his buttons, and Lumbergh let his bitterness get the better of him. "And the fact that you don't think I've done you any favors is a joke! Do have any idea what sacrifices Diana and I have made for you?"

Sean took a step back, his jaw squared and his chest heaving in and out. It took a second for Lumbergh's words to settle in, but once they did, he found himself at a loss for words. Lumbergh's eyes lowered to the top of his desk in guilt, and neither man spoke for what seemed like an eternity.

Sean finally mustered up enough nerve to respond. "So that's what this is all about, Gary? Sean's too *incompetent* to care for his own mother, so *Hollywood* has to quit the *big time* and move out here with his new wife to Jerkwater USA? Diana said she was homesick, but that was a lie, wasn't it?"

Lumbergh had promised Diana that he'd never bring up the sensitive topic with Sean. It was to remain a secret—an unacknowledged burden. However, the heat of the moment finally let the truth slip out into the open. Diana loved her brother dearly, but she knew he didn't have the patience or the capacity to effectively care for their stroke-stricken mother. Lumbergh couldn't bring himself to respond to Sean's question. Instead he just kept his head lowered.

After several seconds, in a tone odd in its composure, Sean said, "Well, Gary . . . I'm sorry I fucked up your life."

He then immediately spun around and sidestepped the fallen blind. Without another word, he opened the office door and gently closed it behind him on his way out.

Chapter 5

"Come on, you wuss! Don't give up!" yelled a young red-haired boy through his own laughter, glancing down at his plastic wristwatch. "Fifteen more seconds!"

"Fifteen *more* seconds?" came the reply, laden with exhausted disbelief from the boy's heavy-set friend. He sat waist-deep in a shallow stream of water along the smooth sand. His eyes were wide and his voice shaky but excited. "Are you s-s-serious???"

Jogging by briskly along an isolated beach, Lisa Kimble couldn't help but form a smile upon eavesdropping in on the boys' conversation. They were the same two kids she had seen the day before searching through the nearby woods for Indian arrowheads. Now they were in their swimming trunks, contesting who could sit in freezing-cold spring water the longest.

Lisa loved Traverse City, Michigan. It was a place she held close to her heart since the day her husband had first brought her there. The rain had stopped after two days of showers, and she took advantage of the calmer weather for a quick run.

The sun shone down unhindered above the clear blue sky and onto her bright blonde hair, which was tied back in a ponytail. It was so much easier to breathe in upstate Michigan. The air was crisp and clean—much unlike what she was used to.

The distant sound of a boat horn prompted Lisa to glance out along the calm and crystal-clear water of Little Traverse Bay. About a hundred yards out, a proud sailboat skimmed along like it floated on air. The lake looked just like the ocean—outlying buoys, swooping gulls, and water as far as the eye could see. The view was something she never grew tired of. The sand below her feet was bright and clean, as if it had been completely filtered of all impurities.

She saw the boy with the wristwatch wave to her, a large, toothy grin on his face, and she waved back. He reminded her of one of her students.

She sometimes ventured a glance into the future with her mind picturing children of her own playing along that very beach. Sandcastles, bodysurfing, picnics . . . It was a fabulous dream, but it seemed increasingly unlikely.

At thirty-three years of age, Lisa looked no older than twenty—a testimonial to a healthy diet and staying active. Her friends often joked with her about her youthful appearance. Most people might have taken such remarks as a compliment. However, Lisa felt that her youthful appearance often led others into not taking her seriously. Whether the perception was real or something merely in her head, it got under her skin when she felt people were talking down to her.

Her athletic frame and pretty face caught the eye of a couple of middle-aged men with overly tanned skin wearing almost matching white polo shirts with raised collars. They had been looking out along the water with their arms crossed in front of them—probably discussing their businesses or a golf game. One of them winked at Lisa. She pretended she didn't see him.

She turned to head up a narrow, angled dirt path that was almost hidden by a line of thick brush at the back edge of the beach. Keeping up her pace, she disappeared into a dense forest of tall cottonwood trees, which blocked out the sunlight like a blanket.

She liked to turn up the intensity at the tail end of her jogs, digging the tips of her running shoes into the steep incline and pumping her legs hard to make it to the top of the hill. With perspiration gliding down along her neck, she reached the top of the path, which intersected into her paved blacktop driveway. Emerging from the darkened woods, she decided not to slow down there, instead keeping her speed and continuing up toward the top of the driveway, which bent sharply to the right. She was pretending to race her husband, as they'd sometimes do, though they hadn't in a while.

Ahead, she thought she heard what sounded like the slam of a car door. A sense of wishful thinking pulsed along with her heartbeat as she rounded the bend. With bright blue eyes, she leaned her head at an angle in hopes of catching a glimpse of the sight she crossed her fingers would be there. He wasn't. Her momentum came to an exhausted halt once the front of the cottage's side garage came into clear sight. Only her car sat by itself outside. Her shoulders deflated like a punctured balloon. He still hadn't arrived.

Chapter 6

Lumbergh gazed expressionlessly outside the passenger side window of the new police cruiser. It still had that new car smell, which he liked. The vast mountain range alongside County Road 2 glowed under the bright, unhindered sun. Its decor of thick pine and low-lying aspen was always a captivating sight. He saw it as one of the few perks that Winston offered that he could never find in Chicago. It was a wonder the land managed to escape being converted into winter ski resorts for all these years—the direction several of the surrounding regions had succumbed to. Winston and the land around it were like secret hideaways, untouched by major civilization. Still, the scenery was a blurry haze through eyes of remorse. The pit of Lumbergh's stomach laid submerged deep in his body.

He asked himself why he even cared whether or not Sean knew the truth. His brother-in-law had been nothing but a thorn in his side and a pain in his ass since the day they met. *Maybe learning the truth would finally earn some respect out of that ungrateful jerk.*

Lumbergh often wondered how Sean and Diana could belong to the same gene pool. They were polar opposites. One was sweet, compassionate, and caring, while the other one was just . . . Sean. They didn't even *look* anything alike. Regardless, there was no way around it. Sean Coleman would always be a part of Lumbergh's life, like a persistent wart that can be repeatedly shaved down flat, yet keeps growing back.

Lumbergh's daze was abruptly broken by the unpleasant sound of Jefferson's thick lips smacking as the officer devoured the last half of a large jelly donut as he drove. The pastry left a thin layer of powdered sugar across the big man's freckled hand. Lumbergh's nose crinkled in nausea as he then observed Jefferson meticulously lick his hand before dipping it into his front uniformed pocket to retrieve an undersized plastic comb. His officer used the comb to shamelessly brush the crumbs from his thick and curvy mustache onto his lap.

"You ever think about trimming that off?" Lumbergh asked openly.

Jefferson's eyes widened, and he lifted his gaze from the road to glance at Lumbergh. The subordinate was noticeably concerned by the comment.

"Why? Do you think I should?"

"It might help your career."

"It might? Really?"

Lumbergh chuckled and relaxed back in his seat. "No. I'm just giving you a hard time."

Jefferson nodded his head and turned his focus back to his driving before saying, "Coltraine told me Sean's story. That brother-in-law of yours really can't hold his liquor, can he? You don't think there's really anything to it, do you?"

"Well, Jefferson, as we both know, he doesn't have the best of track records."

Jefferson chuckled.

Lumbergh's eyes traced the path of a small brown hawk that he noticed flying above. "To answer your question though . . . No. I'm thinking this is just another Sean Coleman goose hunt."

He couldn't help but shake his head. He had never used the term *goose hunt* before coming to Winston. The day before, he had joked with his wife that he was losing his social graces with each passing day.

"However," he added, "I wouldn't be doing my job if I didn't look into it."

Jefferson nodded his head and cleared his throat.

Squinting a bit, and glancing back out his window, Lumbergh reached into his front pocket for a stick of chewing gum. "There's only one thing that's got me thinking, though."

Jefferson glanced back over at him—always an attentive listener of his boss's insights.

"The level of detail in his story. *So* many odd details. It wasn't the regular paranoia . . . An injured hand. The way the guy shot himself." Lumbergh folded his thin piece of gum in half and pushed it into his mouth.

"Injured hand?"

"Milo didn't tell you about that?"

"No."

"Bloodstained bandages wrapped around one of his hands. Sean doesn't strike me as someone creative enough to come up with that."

Chapter 7

Sean felt like hell. He was dehydrated with a pounding head. The shouting match with his brother-in-law certainly hadn't helped. Sean's drying pants still clung to his legs, and his underarms smelled terribly rank.

Sitting on a green wooden bench outside the police department, Sean's body was doubled forward with his elbows resting on his knees and his hands covering his unshaven face. His fingertips tugged at his lower eyelids to play out an odd urge to air out his own eyeballs. Lumbergh's words replayed in his mind, leaving behind a wrenching knot in Sean's gut. His eyes lay transfixed on a long, yellow blade of grass that crept up from cracks in the uneven concrete sidewalk beneath his feet. Moving his fingers and letting his eyes tighten, he cleared his throat and moved a hand to the back of his head to scratch that same pesky itch.

An image of his mother, with her face twisted into a permanent scowl, flashed under his eyelids. That agonizing voice of hers, struggling for unfound clarity, echoed in his ears. He rarely visited her, even now that her health had disintegrated. Maybe he knew all along why Diana had come back. Maybe the convenience of it all prevented him from questioning the motive. Maybe he had convinced himself that her return was an advantageous out for him—a way of freeing himself from an obligation he should have been man enough to accept on his own. *Lumbergh may have been right; what good was Sean Coleman?*

Just when Sean felt the day had no other direction left to go but up, the familiar sharp and high-pitched dual ring of a bell drained the remaining energy out of his body. He shook his head slowly in annoyance.

"Hey there, Sean!" a child's voice exuberantly greeted.

"Toby," Sean muttered in subtle acknowledgment, without turning his head.

"Boy, it sure sounds like you had one heck of a night last night. Don't worry, though. Moses Jones may have gotten lucky, but he would be best not to make the mistake of underestimating you the next time you two square off."

The boy's words struck a final nerve, causing Sean to clench his fists and bite his lip. He kept his head lowered but couldn't keep silent. His hand slid from his face to his hairline, where he clawed his fingers into his very short bangs.

"How the hell does everyone in this goddamned town know about Moses Jones?" he snapped. "Was it in the morning paper or something?"

"Yes. Page three. There's even an interview with Moses. He said that alcohol wasn't a factor in his win, and that he'd be more than happy to offer a rematch."

The Winston Beacon claimed to be a legit newspaper, but the local news that graced its pages was often mere town gossip. Needless to say, Sean's antics had made print on numerous occasions. He even had a couple of front page headlines under his belt.

Sean was too tired and annoyed to display an appropriate reaction. He looked like a rotting, overturned tree.

"Hey, Sean?"

"What, Toby?"

"Do you know what I learned the other day?"

Sean scratched the back of his head more rapidly, offering no confirmation that he'd heard the boy.

Toby continued anyway. "Dachshunds were originally bred to hunt badgers in their dens. Do you think Rocco has ever tangled with a badger? I hope not, because I'm afraid Rocco wouldn't fare too well with his bad eyes. How is Rocco anyway? Has he lost any weight? I've been on a diet myself. Those carbohydrates are tough to stay away from."

Toby was only thirteen years old, but he often sounded more like a chatty grandmother that one might be trapped next to on a long airplane trip. Always inquisitive and often repetitive, it wasn't hard to mistake Toby's demeanor for that of any other high-strung and intelligent child. However, Toby was different—he had a mild form of the mental disorder autism known as Asperger syndrome.

While demonstrating many of the classic traits of most autists, he also displayed some atypical ones. Rather than exuding socially deficient behavior, he was quite accomplished in the arena of conversation; often too accomplished for Sean's liking.

Sean took a breath and reluctantly raised his head to meet the friendly smile of the portly freckle-faced boy who sat proudly along the banana seat of his bright-red Stingray bicycle. Toby's large, pale-blue eyes, beneath long lashes, were filled with clear adoration . . . a feat in itself that Sean had been told to take with the highest regard.

Commonly, those with autism avoid direct eye contact with others. Toby was no different, always keeping his gaze trained in a slightly different direction when socializing with people. However, there were two clear exceptions—people who he was comfortable enough with to draw into his sight: his mother . . . and Sean Coleman. Like most of the townsfolk, Toby's mother couldn't understand what her son saw in Sean. Sean was a bitter drunk and a bully; a bad seed no matter how one looked at it. He'd always been that way. But for whatever reason, Toby Parker saw something in the large bear of a man—something that the others didn't see. Sean was an unwilling role model. He himself didn't understand the boy's interest. In fact, he often went out of his way to discourage it.

Toby was heavyset, with a protruding belly and large eyes. His brown hair was formed in a crew cut, quite similar to Sean's, although Toby clearly needed a trim. Sean suspected the boy's choice of hairstyles wasn't a matter of coincidence. Toby's wardrobe seemed to consist primarily of multicolored, horizontally striped t-shirts. He had one on every time Sean saw him. Today's combination was white, red, and brown.

"Hey, Sean!"

"What?"

"I painted a new picture of that big oak tree in my backyard. You know . . . the one with the tire swing. Thanks again for those painting supplies. The brushes keep up well if you wash them right after using them."

Despite the drain on his body and in his head, Sean couldn't help but crack a feeble grin. As much as he tried to hide his smile—and he tried very hard—it found its way out anyway. The corners of his mouth raised, and a discreet chuckle crept out.

About six months earlier, Toby's mother had invited Sean to her son's birthday party. Actually, Toby had pleaded with his mother to invite his friend, and wouldn't let up on his insistence. She obviously had concerns. It wasn't exactly the brightest idea to invite the town's black sheep, and a drunk to boot, to a child's birthday party. Still, she knew it would mean the world to her son. It wasn't an easy feat, however. Sean made it painfully clear that he had no desire to attend. To him, it sounded like a total drag. A kiddie party wasn't exactly the place he wanted to spend any of the hours of his weekend. No beer. No eight-ball. No fun.

The persistent mother tried several times to change his mind. All attempts were unsuccessful. Guilt tactics didn't work, even when Diana was asked to help encourage her brother to come. The resolution finally arrived with a suggestion that Chief Lumbergh made. It was actually meant as a joke, and was met with rolled eyes by Diana . . . but it worked.

Bribery.

Toby's mother ended up paying Sean twenty dollars with an

additional ten dollars for Sean to spend on the gift of his choice for her son. The deal was sealed with the mention of the free food at the party.

Sean's choice of gifts wasn't difficult to make. He had repeatedly heard the townsfolk mention that young Toby was artistic. In fact, he couldn't for the life of him figure out why people made such a fuss over it. Sean had fancied himself a pretty good sketcher back in high school, but no one ever made a big deal out of *his* talents. It wasn't until later at the party that it was explained to Sean that Toby was autistic, not artistic. He remembered how much like a fool he felt.

"Bill Kenny wasn't too happy with me today," remarked Toby.

The boy seemed to change topics with each breath.

"Do you want to know what happened?"

Sean glanced over the boy's shoulder to look for his uncle. *What was taking him so long?*

"Sure," said Sean out of nothing more than morbid curiosity and a need to pass the time.

"Mr. Kenny was coming out of French's Pharmacy and walked right onto the sidewalk without looking both ways," the boy relayed. "I couldn't stop my bike in time and my forward progress was just too much to prevent a head-on collision. I've needed new brakes for some time now, you know. His mailbag of letters dropped all over the sidewalk. I tried to help him pick them up, but he wouldn't let me. He had a few colorful words for me, though—none of which my mom would want me repeating. I told him he should have looked both ways, because he really should have. I also asked him if he had updated his glasses prescription within the last year. People should have their eyes checked on an annual basis, you know. Do you know what he told me?"

"What?"

"To mind my own business."

As awkward and as bothersome as Toby often was to Sean, the boy every once in a while found a way to unintentionally amuse him.

"You're a wild man, Toby," Sean said with a slight smirk.

Toby smiled, his eyes aligned directly with Sean's.

The tap of a car horn caused both of their heads to turn.

"There's my man!" greeted a friendly, elderly male voice over the roar of a loud truck engine. "How's it going, Toby?"

"Hi, Mr. Hansen!" replied the boy, retaining his smile and gazing out along the hood of the light-blue Ford pickup as it pulled up to the street corner perpendicular to the parking lot.

An older but distinguished-looking gentleman proudly wearing a tall, straw cowboy hat flashed a charming smile at the boy through the open window. Well-kept, long silver sideburns trailed down both sides of his face. A matching goatee added a certain dignified element to his appearance—like a redneck Sean Connery. His license plate, surrounded by a shiny chrome frame below the grill, read *MR-GUARD*—a cheap plug for Sean's uncle's security service.

With a long toothpick angled out of the side of his mouth and a cunning shift of his eyes, he warned, "Don't let that bum borrow your bike, Toby! He looks a bit cagey!"

Toby's high-pitched laughter resembled more of a cackle as the boy's cheeks turned red and he glanced at Sean for a reaction. Sean displayed none.

Sean lifted himself upright with a loud grunt and slapped dust from his pant legs. Without so much as a farewell to the young boy, he scurried out along the front of the truck, tracing his hand along the hood, and made his way around to the passenger door.

"Let's get the hell out of here," he muttered to his uncle as the right side of the truck lowered from his weight as he got in.

The car door slammed shut.

Toby stood up on his tiptoes, straddling his bike and grasping the handlebars in front of him. "Goodbye, Sean!" he yelled.

Sean's only acknowledgment was the raise of a brow. It wasn't visible through the glaze of the dusty windshield.

Toby's hand waved feverishly and enthusiastically. Zed rolled up his window and returned the gesture with a wink. He then turned to Sean with a disapproving scowl.

"What?" Sean said in reply before turning his head away from the judging pair of eyes.

As the large truck left the curb with a roar, Toby Parker's bell rang out diligently through the air, as if it was signaling that dinner was ready. Zed watched him through his rearview mirror, observing the boy continuing to excitedly wave and ring. Toby kept up the salute all the way until the truck turned the corner and he had drifted from sight.

"You know, it wouldn't kill you to be a little friendlier to that boy," Zed suggested, arching a brow. "He idolizes you."

"No one asked him to."

After a quick glance at his uncle, Sean leaned forward and twisted a brass knob on the dashboard's A.M. radio. Sean was no fan of twangy country music, but he hoped doubling the volume would serve as a hint to his uncle to change the subject.

"You know that his daddy . . ." Zed began, before taking a second to sigh and lean forward to drop the volume back down. "You know that his daddy left him and his mother when he was a youngun'. I'd think you could relate to that a bit."

A scoffing gasp slid from Sean's mouth. "That kid should stay away from me."

"Come on," the old man snarled with a rejecting wince and a shake of his head. "Why do you always have to shit all over yourself like that?"

"Because it's true!" Sean snapped. "What does that kid want out of me?"

"Probably just a friend."

"A friend? What? Like someone to throw a football around with or someone to take him to the movies?"

"Maybe just someone to listen to him. To talk to."

"Well that ain't me. I ain't that guy. I'm the guy who gets smashed at bars and gets kicked out of his home because he pisses away his rent money on pool and poker." Sean's shoulders slumped, and he took a breath. A few moments later, he somberly continued. "I'm a joke in this town. No one takes me seriously. Not Gary, not even you."

With a discouraged grunt, Zed shook his head again and said, "Well, that's one hell of a thing for you to say to *me*, boy." His face turned to Sean, and his eyes burned right through his nephew. "I'm on *your* side, Sean. You're not a joke to me. You're my kin, and I'm proud of it. You wouldn't be working for me otherwise."

Sean's eyes lowered as his uncle's words sank in. He raised his head and glanced out his window. Mom-and-pop shops at the edge of town floated by. None of them had changed in years. Same look. Same owners. Same names. He could feel his uncle's glare from behind.

Turning his eyes back on the road, Zed asked without expression, "You're being evicted?"

Sean closed his eyes and rested the side of his weary head against the warm window beside him. He knew his uncle would gladly bail him out. He had done it many times in the past. But Sean had always hated asking for anyone's help, and with how he had lost the rent money this time, he wasn't about to let his uncle get involved.

"It's fine. There's no problem." He cleared his throat and dropped his head to take inventory of his appearance, gazing down at his muddied and stained clothing. What a sight he was. Zed hadn't remarked about the disarray of his uniform. Not one word. Sean found that odd considering the uniform actually belonged to his uncle's company.

Leaning back in the sheepskin-covered seat, Sean formulated how he would sneak down to the washing machine at the back of his apartment duplex without his landlord seeing him. Mr. Bailey lived on that very same side. A pawn shop that Sean frequented was closed on the weekends, but he knew that if he could hold off Bailey for another day, he could sell some items before work on Monday morning. Maybe . . . just maybe . . . he could make back enough to cover the rent.

An odd sensation of nakedness suddenly overcame Sean. The staple weight that normally caused his front pocket to slightly sag . . . it was gone. His hand quickly rose to his chest where he fumbled unsuccessfully for the item that always resided there on his uniform.

"Ah, shit!" he roared, before leaning forward and intensely scanning the floor and seat of the truck while distraughtly patting his hand across the other barren pocket.

"What's the problem?" asked Zed.

Sean felt too humiliated to say, instead punishing himself over losing his badge. Despite his fuzzy head, he clearly remembered reattaching it to his shirt after waking up at the bottom of the trench by Meyers Bridge. After the morning he'd been through, it could have fallen off just about anywhere in between.

He glanced up at his uncle's eyes. Zed's expression revealed that he had already gathered what was up.

"Lose your badge?"

Before Sean could say a word, his uncle attempted to put his mind to rest.

"It's no big deal, Sean. I have others." Zed read defeat in his nephew's eyes, and the look on his face showed that it pained his heart.

"Hey!" he said with a wink and a smile, understanding all too well the pride that Sean took in his job. With a friendly backhand to his nephew's shoulder, he added, "It's not the badge . . . it's the man behind it."

Sean had never questioned Zed's loyalty or sincerity. His uncle cared about him. He had no doubts about that. But after the morning he was having, Zed's words unintentionally prompted a sense of disesteem in Sean's gut; a challenge to the faith his uncle had invested in him.

"What did Jefferson tell you on the phone?" Sean muttered, watching for a reaction in his uncle's eyes, but finding none. Zed's silence indicated that he had indeed been briefed. "You believe me? That I saw a man kill himself?"

Zed's upper lip disappeared and his square chin extended. His lack of response generated an odd smugness from Sean, whose own need to self-deprecate had just been validated. Keeping his eyes trained forward on the road, Zed's throat tightened and his toothpick swept to the opposite side of his mouth.

After what seemed like an eternity, without removing his eyes from the road, Zed stated, "I don't think you made it up, Sean."

With a disdainful sneer, Sean shook his head. "It was a yes or no question, Uncle Zed, but at least you're being honest. It's just that drunken Sean Coleman and his silly imagination. Right?"

"Sean . . ."

"Save it!" Sean snapped. "You and everyone else can go ahead and think I'm crazy. I know what I saw."

Zed didn't respond at first, but he felt it time to get something off his chest. "Why do you think Lumbergh doesn't believe you, Sean?"

Sean sneered. "Don't need another lecture."

"Sean . . . Gary's a good man. He's a good husband to your sister. Now, I know the two of you don't see eye to eye, but—"

Sean interrupted. "You know, I am so sick and tired of everyone telling me how good of a guy Gary is. I get it! Okay?" He shook his head. "The man spent twelve years down in Illinois, kissing more ass than he kicked. Did you know he's never even fired a gun?"

Zed sighed and said, "Never fired a gun *in the line of duty*, Sean. Of course he's fired a gun before. He's a trained police officer."

"Trained at kissing ass, maybe!" Sean barked. "Diana always talks about all the promotions he got. If he's never even fired a gun before, how else do you think he got them? He comes into this town like a goddamned celebrity and they throw a police chief's badge right on him without even asking him a single question!"

"Sean . . ."

"Did you know that he voted for Al Gore?" He glared soberly at his uncle.

Zed winced at Sean's words, as if he had just stepped on jagged glass. He shook his head. "I did hear that. And I ain't making any excuses for that. But, Sean, we both know that this isn't about Gary's past or his politics . . ."

Breathing hard, Sean awaited his uncle's explanation while already articulating a rebuttal in his mind.

Taking his eyes off of the road to meet his nephew's glower, Zed said, "Sean . . . I've known you all of your life. You've wanted to be the police chief of Winston since you were a little boy."

Sean wasn't expecting those words to drop from his uncle's mouth. He didn't know what to say.

"Now, maybe that was a pipe dream," Zed continued. "Maybe it's something you outgrew. I can't say for sure. But something tells me that you feel he's got what should be yours. I think that's the reason you're always conning the police into looking into possible crimes. You think you're the one who should be calling the shots over there—not Gary."

Sean felt his temper simmer, but repressed the urge to unload on his uncle. Instead, he sunk his teeth down into his lower lip. He wasn't going to lie; he did have aspirations of one day being the big man in Winston. But too much time had passed. He never had the drive. He had no credibility left in the eyes of the town folk. He had tested too many people and burned too many bridges.

Zed was more perceptive than Sean had thought. *Was he, Sean Coleman, really that open of a book? Did others see through him as well as his uncle did?*

An uncomfortable minute went by with no conversation between the two.

"Your car's at O'Rafferty's, right?"

"Yeah. How did you know?"

"I read about it in the paper."

"Christ," Sean said in annoyance. "That Hughes kid stays up all night to get his stupid tabloid column to print. He should work for the *National Enquirer*. He needs a life." With his eyelids tightened, he leaned forward and began massaging his temples with his hands.

"There's some aspirin in the glove compartment, Sean."

Sean didn't waste a second, leaning forward and letting the steel drawer drop open. A white plastic bottle of medicine rested clearly in view, but it might as well have been invisible. Sean's gaze had been intercepted by the visual feast of a shiny and black holstered handgun that was now caressed in the glow of the small illuminating bulb beside it.

"Holy shit!" Sean rumbled with his lips slowly forming into an uncharacteristic grin. With wide eyes, he quickly turned to his uncle who was now displaying a smug smirk of his own. Zed winked an eye at him and turned his attention back to the road. His smile widened.

"Is this what I think it is?" an impassioned Sean asked.

Zed was grinning from ear to ear now. "Give it a look!"

For the better part of a year, Zed, who had a well-known passion for gun collecting, had been looking for a Heckler & Koch P9S Sport Mark III in a .45 caliber. It was an extremely difficult weapon to find, not to mention very expensive.

Sean's hand trembled as it carefully glided inside the glove box. Goosebumps rose along the back of his neck once his fingers brushed along the glossy wooden handgrip of the thirty-year-old German masterpiece of weaponry. He let out a long whistle of praise. His cautious handling and clear admiration of the gun prompted a giddy snicker from Zed.

He knew Sean would be one of the few to appreciate it. "Don't be shy! Take it out of its holster!"

With his eyes outlining each groove and curve, Sean said, "Tell me you're not keeping this baby in your glove box, Uncle Zed. This should be hanging from a rack above the fireplace." He knew his uncle normally only carried a standard revolver on him and left his hobby at home.

"Of course not. I just brought it along to show you."

"She's a real beauty."

The tip of Sean's tongue slid to the corner of his mouth as he popped out the gun's clip and snapped it back in place. The crisp sound of metal on metal prompted an approving nod from him.

"We should go to the range on Monday and turn her loose," suggested Zed. "There's hardly any recoil at all. It's as slick as snot."

"You've fired it?" Sean asked in surprise.

"Sure. What good is a lady if you can't take her for a dance?"

Sean had heard his uncle use that phrase several times before. He still didn't get it.

"Wait a minute," he said, confusion in his eyes after spinning his head toward his uncle. "I'm working on Monday."

"Eh . . . I tried to call you last night. They ended up going with Bodie's outfit. He put in a lower bid."

"Shit. You don't have anything else for me?"

"No. Not until Thursday. A museum over in Branston needs someone to work some exhibit they'll be hosting throughout next weekend. It will be a four-day job."

"Branston?" Sean said with a scowl. "That's almost an hour's drive. And over the weekend?"

With an agitated grunt, Zed eyeballed Sean. "What's the matter? You afraid of missing another lucrative game of pool?" After a brief pause, he continued. "It's good money, Sean, and don't tell me you don't need it."

Sean hesitantly nodded his head. "Fine."

Gravel crackled beneath the oversized tires of Zed's truck as the two men pulled off of the road and into the parking lot of O'Rafferty's. Sean's pale-blue '78 Chevy Nova sat by its lonesome along the east corner of the building.

Zed looked at the faded paint of the building. "When's old Ted gonna break down and give his shack a new paint job? I can barely even tell that the wood is red anymore."

Sean grinned, peering at the rotted and twisted planking that decorated the front of the small building just below the slanted crest and tilting tin entrance sign. "He better have left my keys on the dashboard."

"He always does." Zed came to a halt behind Sean's car.

With a deep breath, Sean carefully placed the gun back into his uncle's glove compartment.

"Well . . . thanks for the ride."

Zed nodded. A hint of a smile formed on his lips before his face contorted in thought.

"What?" asked Sean.

After a few seconds of reluctance, Zed asked, "How's your mother?"

The delivery of the question was clearly uncomfortable—for both men. Sean's face turned pale, which Zed hadn't expected.

"Sad, ain't it? I don't even know," Sean said. "I haven't been over there in a month. I guess she's fine. Diana hasn't said anything."

Zed recognized the look of despair in Sean's eyes. He'd seen it many times. It was the same look that Sean used to display when he'd asked about his father so many years ago. He was but a child back then, but those droopy eyes and those low shoulders sent Zed back in time. "Well, you've got me beat at least."

Sean dropped a sneer and let out a chuckle. "Yeah, but at least you have an excuse."

Zed slowly nodded his head and lifted his eyes. "Maybe I used to. But I'm not so sure I have one these days."

"Uncle Zed, we both know that her problem with you has always been her problem. You didn't do anything wrong. It didn't make sense then, and it doesn't make sense now."

"Well, no one ever said that guilt by association was fair. But I've got no bad feelings for her. I guess that when you hate someone that much, it's hard to see the face of his brother who looks a lot like him every time you go into town." Zed pulled his toothpick from his mouth and held it vertically before his eyes. It was well chewed and bent at the top. After tossing it out his open window, he said, "For her, I'm a photograph that doesn't fade. A constant reminder."

"You're not *him*. You're just related to him. Like me. Bad genes."

Zed reached into his front pocket and pulled out a couple of folded twenty-dollar bills. He reached across the cab and shoved them into Sean's front pocket—the pocket where his missing badge normally hung. Sean opened his mouth to protest, but Zed cut him off.

"It's an advance, on the Branston job." Zed's warm eyes glowed at Sean.

Sean's mouth curled at the edges. His eyes expressed gratitude. "Thanks, Uncle Zed."

Chapter 8

The constant peck-peck finally got to her. With her eyes narrowed and her soft lips forming a smirk, Lisa raised her head from behind her large glass of ice-cold lemonade and the hardback novel she was reading. Her nose, with its slightly raised tip, crinkled. After ten annoyed minutes, she thought that the woodpecker had finally moved on to another tree. No such luck.

Peck, peck, peck! She didn't know what puzzled her more—the woodpecker's persistence and decision to stick to a single tree or the fact that the subtle sound was bothering her so much. It wasn't the bird's fault that she was in a bad mood.

Sitting back on an old wicker chair with her shapely legs crossed and her feet propped up on a short wooden stool, Lisa could only shake her head in aggravation. The redwood deck sprawled out beneath her groaned from the subtle movement.

When would he show up? In an hour? A couple more days, maybe?

Her husband had a secret mistress—his career. It kept him away for days at a time and often bound him from even revealing to her where he was. She knew and understood this prior to the marriage, but living with it for the past couple of years had brought loneliness with little consolation. Once again, his job had even interfered with vacation plans despite his promises that *this* time would be different. *Would it ever end?* She had little faith left in her husband's ability to do his part—his part in holding together what was left of their marriage.

Wearing an aged and faded UNLV sweatshirt with matching shorts, she stood up straight and stretched her arms to the sky. Despite an afternoon nip in the air, the sun felt good against her face.

She walked to the backdoor at the edge of the porch. Upon opening it, she smiled at the sound of the attached doggy-door that flapped loosely from her action. Good old Cletus. God, she missed him. No one could have asked for a better dog. The German shepherd had kept her company and made her feel safe through so many lonely nights, whether it was there at the cottage or back in the city. He was a loyal friend up until he was hit by a car late last year. His companionship was difficult to forget, and it sometimes felt as if he had never left. Just that morning, she had routinely unlatched his door, fully expecting to hear his brisk clatter of nails echo up from the kitchen floor, as they had last summer when he would brush past her to play outside.

With her eyes glazed over in reminiscence, she thought about how odd of a paradox the human memory could be. Six months had passed, and she still remembered the sounds that Cletus made. It was like it was just yesterday. Yet, she couldn't remember the last time she and her husband had kissed—really kissed.

Something her father once told her just then drifted through her mind. *"Honey, you're smart in everything but men."*

At the time, the comment had infuriated her even though she knew deep down that he was probably right. Growing up, she'd always found herself attracted to the wrong boys; the ones who played by their own rules and didn't respect authority. Ironically, her husband was perhaps the only man she'd brought home who her father actually liked. He respected her husband's career, especially with the obstacles his disability forced him to overcome in order to achieve it. Even with her father's approval, she feared his original assessment of her might have still held true.

Her back slumped against the bottom cushions of a brown leather couch at the edge of the living room. It creaked with age. She interlaced her fingers behind her head, kicked off her running shoes, and found herself glaring straight up at the high ceiling. The silence was deafening, other than the sound of her own breathing and the occasional settling of the foundation.

Two years ago, the cottage was a place that promised a future of fond memories, like when her husband lay in the same position as she was now in, on that very couch, with his eyes closed and faint snoring drifting up from his mouth. He had, for once, seemed relaxed. From the open bedroom loft directly above, she'd sprinkled rose petals down across his body until he awoke with his hair disheveled and that bright smile she hadn't seen in so long. She remembered the spontaneous giggle that leapt from between her lips as he playfully ran up the spiral staircase, skipping every other step, to join her.

She yearned for those pleasant times to return. She had hoped that coming back to the cottage might rekindle some of those old feelings. Instead, with him being gone again, it served as a torture chamber of false assurances.

Chapter 9

The imposing howl of the Nova's shot muffler wreaked pandemonium across the otherwise tranquil forest. The smell of exhaust clouded out the usual scent of pine and mountain water.

With the sole of his boot clamped to the brake pedal at the center of Meyers Bridge, Sean's neck swung from window to window looking for the police cruiser or any sign of Lumbergh or Jefferson. Nothing. He couldn't believe they had already come and left, but that *had* to be the case. They had left the station for the bridge long before Zed arrived to pick him up.

With his ample back pressed into the deteriorating vinyl car seat, he found himself gazing out through the open passenger window and along the fast-moving water that roared steadily below. The river's path disappeared around a distant barrage of trees.

A suffocating feeling of insignificance overcame the small town security guard, and he coughed on his own breath. He popped the transmission into park, stepped out of the car, and crossed to the railing where the stranger had let himself fall. He dropped to his hands and knees, and extended his head over the guardrail, scanning for a splatter of blood along the metal and wood planking. He spent several minutes doing this, occasionally using his knees to work himself to the side. Nothing.

Sean's jaw squared, and he shook his head in disgust. He felt his blood boil, and he raised his head to the sky, aiming a scary glare at God. Sean was a Christian and never questioned his faith, but he couldn't for the life of him figure out why his Maker seemed to take such delight in hanging him out to dry. It was as if he was a prop for the Big Man's amusement.

He thought back to the sight of the stranger that sat on the edge of the bridge mere hours earlier. The hopelessness he must have felt, deciding that there was no other solution than to rid the world of his existence. At what point had enough become enough? At what point was the battle no longer worth fighting?

Sean knew hopelessness.

He had promised himself countless times before last night that he would never let it get that bad again.

The drinking.

No more blacking out, he'd sometimes tell his reflection in the mirror. Memories of old friends and family, who had long written him off, drifted through his mind as they often had. He understood their discouragement with his inability to come to odds with his problem. He knew they were right, but he always had an excuse for why they were wrong. He could understand what might put that man on the bridge.

A sudden, cool breeze whipped against his face as he climbed back to his feet. His right eye started to water up. He quickly used the back of his hand to sweep away all moisture. *Crying is for sissies. Sean Coleman doesn't cry.*

A moment later he was back in the car. His foot left the brake pedal and he pumped the gas, sending gravel and dust in his wake as he sped across the bridge. A quarter of a mile up the road, he passed the hunched-over frame of Ruth Golding who was clad in a white knit sweater and retrieving a handful of envelopes from her mailbox. She waved to Sean as he flew by, like she always did with any car that happened to be driving by while she was outside. He ignored her as usual, but then suddenly slammed on the brakes when a thought arose. He quickly backed up and popped his head out his window.

"Ruth!" he yelled.

The elderly woman was frail and slow, and had probably spent the last ten minutes crossing her property to reach the road. She was bent forward at the waist, retrieving a small American flag from the ground. Years ago, she'd started using the old classroom flag with its pencil mast as an outgoing mail alert after the plastic red one on her mailbox had broken off. The position of her body revealed more than Sean was ready for with the horizon of her pale blue underwear poking up from her skirt.

He looked away in disgust and again called out her name. Once upright and favoring her hip, she turned to greet him from under her frazzled white hair and large, dark-framed bifocals.

"Did you see some guy walking around here this morning?" he asked.

"Who?" she replied in a dainty voice.

"Some guy. I don't know his name. He was dressed in black. Did you see him out on the road this morning?"

She took a moment and squinted at him. "Who?" she repeated.

"Jesus," Sean said in annoyance. He raised his voice. "Anybody! Did you see anybody at all down here by the road this morning?"

Her wrinkled face twisted in befuddlement. She arched her back and her eyes rose to the air as if she was straining to recollect a memory from her youth.

Sean tapped the side of his door impatiently with the broad palm of his hand.

"Well . . . I can't say as I did."

Without another second wasted, the rear tires of the Nova spun circles and Ruth Golding was left behind in a cloud of dust as Sean advanced hurriedly back down the road.

———

Sean didn't answer his phone once that evening. He let his machine bear the torture. There had already been one scathing message left from his landlord. It had been awaiting attention since early that morning. A similar one came through around six p.m. *That fat bastard*, Sean thought to himself. Bailey lived right downstairs. He was either too lazy or too scared to come up and speak to him like a man. Sean took some gratification in believing it to be the latter, although he was fine with skipping the confrontation for one more day.

He spent the next hour searching through cluttered drawers and disheveled closets for possessions to sell off. It wasn't an uncommon practice, but each sale left him feeling like he had less of an identity. When he had moved out of his mother's house, she gave him what was left of his father's stuff. For years, she had kept the belongings around for some unknown reason. Sean speculated that as much as she hated him, it was her way of keeping up hope for her husband returning someday. Finally letting them go was her way of forgetting.

The mementos were Sean's only attachments to the man who had left his life so abruptly without as much as a goodbye. But like with his mother, each abandonment relieved his mind of another memory, whether it was an old pair of steel-tipped boots or a small HAM radio with rainbow-colored, entangled wires stemming from the back.

Pickings were now slim. Almost every keepsake that would bring in more than just spare change was now gone—all but one . . . the one that Sean once promised himself he would not part with. It lay nestled away safely in his locked, top right desk drawer.

He sat back on his large, overworked, brown leather recliner for hours in the dimmed living room that was growing darker with the sky. Time moved by slowly, like it often did. He found himself barrenly watching flashes of light from his nineteen-inch television set dance across the surrounding walls. The volume was turned down low. Now dressed only in checkered boxer shorts and a frayed t-shirt that had once been white, he repeatedly twisted his raised ankle in a clockwise motion to loosen up the aching and stiffness. One of his hands was wrapped around a warm bottle of beer while the other one massaged the ears of the old overweight dachshund who lay contentedly bundled up in a ball across his lap.

Rocco. The thirteen-year-old pooch had belonged to Diana before she left for college years earlier. She could have left him with their mother, but she felt the crotchety canine was a better companion for Sean. Both were rambunctious and ill-tempered—a perfect match. He had initially protested the gift, fearing that the responsibility would cramp his style. But as a favor to his pleading sister, he eventually gave in. He never regretted it. The two were kindred spirits—standoffish, territorial, and set in their ways. Rocco had gone completely blind from old age within the last year, but he was still tough. He didn't let the disability get to him. Through every fall and collision, he always managed to pick himself right back up. No whining. Sean admired that.

He moved a finger under Rocco's coarse, gray beard that years ago had shone with a reddish brown, smooth coat. Rocco always liked having his chin rubbed. It was the one thing that turned the grumpy dog into putty. His tail flopped from side to side against Sean's chest, and his nose pointed to the ceiling.

Around nine p.m. came that dreaded call. Lumbergh. Sean sneered at the somber tone in the chief's voice that emitted dismally out through the speaker. Lumbergh asked twice for his brother-in-law to pick up, but Sean answered only with a swig of beer. After a sigh, Lumbergh detailed out his findings. No surprises. There was no blood or shells on the bridge, or any other proof of what Sean had seen. A dead end.

Sean nodded his head, a sour scowl forming on his lips. He slowly cocked his arm back before snapping it forward and sending his half-full bottle of beer sailing at the wall above the kitchen counter where the answering machine resided. The thunderous crash sent glass and liquid spraying in multiple directions, and prompted Rocco to perch up on his front legs with risen ears. The aging dog twisted his head to face his master with eyes as cloudy as Sean's composure.

The clear image of the stranger's body dropping from the bridge *before* the shot was ever fired reverberated like a scratched record through Sean's mind. Gravity explained the absence of both blood and the shell.

Lumbergh offered up some additional, meaningless details before he concluded with, "I don't know what else to say, Sean." Click.

Consciously slowing down his breathing, Sean slid his fingers familiarly to the back of his head, and he found himself once again glancing aimlessly across the room. Rocco rolled back into a ball.

"Why would he do that?" he abruptly said out loud, with his face twisted in thought. "Why would that guy jump *and then* shoot?"

Fighting off exhaustion and humiliation, the gears in Sean's head began turning. Since that morning, the peculiarity behind what had happened at the river had taken a backseat to the importance of its believability to others. He was the one person who didn't need convincing. He knew what he saw.

One thing was undeniably certain: what he'd witnessed was no ordinary suicide. There was a story left to be told. There had to be.

The deterrent of the others' skepticism had kept hold of Sean's spirit like a pair of tight handcuffs, but now those binds were bending. Perhaps all he had needed was Lumbergh's withdrawal—in a sense, an admission of defeat. Now, it was Sean's turn.

No longer distracted with having to defend his claims, he made himself clear his mind and start from the beginning. If no one was going to believe him, it was time to take the matter into his own hands, if only in a defense of his own sanity.

With a straining grunt, he lowered his arm under the top of the end table to grab a thin spiral notebook from the middle shelf. He normally jotted down grocery lists in it, but he was about to put the pages to much better use.

He pulled a whittled-down, chewed-up pencil from the center of the metal binding and began tracing back through the timeline, feverishly writing down each image that came to mind. He included everything from the oddest of details to the seemingly most insignificant.

Sean's tired eyes steadily moved from item to item. They stopped on *Why the bridge?* Without even taking into account the man's preparations as he sat at the edge, on its own it was strange that he would bother jumping into a roaring river if he was going to shoot himself. Sean understood doing one or the other, but both?

Perhaps the stranger didn't have confidence that a gunshot was failsafe. Maybe he was afraid of only critically wounding himself and ending up as a vegetable in a hospital bed for the rest of his life. Maybe drowning was a backup plan. Put himself out of his misery, if needed.

Yet, if he was so worried about surviving the gun blast, why did he twist his arms into such an awkward position in order to shoot himself? Why not just stick the barrel in his mouth?

The clues were contradicting each other. Sean shook his head. The mental investigation reminded him of a brainteaser exercise his junior high class had once worked through. It was of a made-up story about a man who had been found dead, hanging by a noose around his neck in an empty room. Without any furniture in the room for the man to drop himself off of, it was up to the students to figure out how he had killed himself. The only clue was a large wet spot in the carpet, directly underneath him.

Most of the students suggested that the man hadn't committed suicide at all, but was murdered. Sean remembered receiving thunderous laughter from the other students when he suggested that the man had pissed himself after he died, which explained the wet carpet. The comment won Sean a quick trip to the principal's office. As he was escorted from the room by a teacher's aid, however, he had heard the correct answer given by the brainy girl with braces who sat in front of him: The man had stood on a block of ice to tie the noose around his neck. The ice had melted before the body was found. All that was left was the wet spot on the carpet.

It was a silly exercise, but reflecting back on it kept Sean motivated that there was a logical answer for every mystery. Solving it just required some focus and a little open-mindedness.

From outside, a slow, fluctuating patter of raindrops began to dance along the roof.

The silencer. What possible reason could the man have had for using a silencer to shoot himself? Why would he care if anyone heard the shot? It would have been too late for someone to talk him out of doing it. Could there have been a symbolic meaning behind it?

Sean flashed back to his initial interpretation that morning. Maybe the stranger had shot someone else earlier. Maybe it was done with a bullet through the back of the head. Could the killer have suddenly felt so much guilt that he couldn't live with himself? A murder-suicide, with an eye-for-an-eye twist. It would answer a few questions. Perhaps the man initially intended only to dispose of the gun off the bridge. Maybe the plan was simply to toss it on over, but then the shame hit him like a ton of bricks.

The theory seemed to make a reasonable amount of sense. Sean wasn't totally confident in it, but it seemed to pair answers with at least a few questions. What was left?

No car.

The absence of an automobile somewhat put a damper on the idea that the man didn't aspire to kill himself all along. If he had originally intended on dumping the gun and leaving, how was he supposed to leave? Walk? Standing at the edge of that bridge, the stranger was clearly paranoid about someone seeing him. It was highly doubtful that he would just take off on foot afterwards in broad daylight, where anyone would obviously notice a guy who was dressed the way he was.

Another question: Without an automobile, how did he even

get there in the first place? At this point, Sean thought back to the muddied shoes. The stranger had to have walked to the bridge and not along the road, which was fairly dry. Only one possible explanation: he came from the forest.

But Sean knew all too well that there was nothing in the immediate area. No buildings. No other roads. There was nothing for a few miles in any direction. Town was about a mile and a half away, even by a bird's eye. He came through the forest, but how did he get there in the first place?

Sean wrote down that very question at the bottom of the page. *Where did he come from?* He stared at that scribbled text for several minutes while roughly scratching at the base of his skull. He stopped when his skin began to burn.

The rain was picking up, sounding like popcorn popping above Sean's head. Its damp smell drifted inside through the narrowly cracked, darkened window at the front of his apartment.

Everything he had come up with was pure speculation, and he knew it. None of it was provable, and he had little desire to present his case to Lumbergh who would likely, once again, disregard it.

Sean's concentration was momentarily disrupted when the peppy, opening theme song of the evening news proved far too intrusive. Mute. *Ten o'clock already?* Where had the time gone? Sean had worked right through an episode of *Walker, Texas Ranger*. His finger nervously tapped the top of his remote as he listened to the rain fall outside.

Even in half-assed mode, Sean was sure Lumbergh would have searched around the bridge and possibly the road. *But did he go into the forest? Doubtful.*

As far as Sean was concerned, the forest was where it all began. If there were any answers, he would find them there. Only tomorrow wouldn't be soon enough. The rain was picking up. The uncertainty was grueling, and maybe it was all a waste of time, but if there was any kind of evidence waiting to be found, Sean wasn't about to let Mother Nature wash it away from him like she did the body.

Chapter 10

C hicken Parmesan. The tasty aroma lifted the police chief's low spirits as he wiped his boots carefully along a thin welcome mat and entered the house through the side door, leaving the evening chill behind him.

God bless her, he thought to himself, his empty stomach grumbling for attention.

Hearing some shuffling and the clank of a pot or pan coming from the kitchen, Lumbergh rested his back along the edge of the door frame as he removed his Italian Berluti boots. They resembled dress shoes, but the soles were thick and the tread was deep—perfect for working the mountainous area of Winston, and they looked slick in the process.

"Honey?" prompted a female voice from around the corner of the dimly lit, narrow hallway.

"It's me," he responded, twisting the knob of the closet door beside him.

He hung up his coat, positioned his Berlutis on the prongs of a custom-made oak shoe rack, and loosened his tie.

Heat originating from a quaint stone fireplace brushed the side of his face as he left the hallway and entered the cozy living area. Wood crackled, and mild flames cast dancing shadows along the wall.

"I've got a surprise for you," said the female voice in playful provocation.

Lumbergh entered the open kitchen area, lit up bright from a curved row of track lights along the ceiling, each bulb aimed in a different direction.

There he found Diana, her back to him, standing at the edge of a silver stove top. A billow of steam drifted from a large, metal pot in front of her. Her tall, slender frame was clad in a sleek long-sleeved, burgundy blouse and snug blue jeans. Shoulder-length auburn hair rested in waves along her collar.

"I smelled it from the door. You're an angel."

A playful giggle was her response as she turned her head to meet his tired eyes, which gleamed a little upon receiving her attention. Her bright smile was a welcome sight at the end of a long, bizarre day.

"And the best part about it . . ." she began as her body twisted to face him, hands on her hips, " . . . is that my mother's already been fed, so you get me all to yourself."

Lumbergh chuckled. "I'm sorry I'm late, but . . ."

He was about to elaborate, but a sense of apprehension cut him short. His wife had gone to a lot of trouble preparing his favorite dish. Beyond that, she was in a perky mood, which although not uncharacteristic, wasn't as frequent of an occurrence as it used to be. He didn't want to ruin the moment.

He quickly dismissed his internal debate and took a few steps forward with a gratified smirk.

"Come here," he whispered as he pulled her in close, his hand cupping her thin waist. His eyes remained on hers as he tilted his head and guided her into a kiss. Her arms found their way behind his back and she pulled him even closer.

She stood a little over an inch taller than him, a fact Lumbergh would never admit distressed his ego. Her knees were bent to accommodate the discrepancy.

After a moment, she craned her head back. "You're welcome," she whispered. Her bright, brown eyes gleamed with affection. "What's this?" she asked, her eyes lowered to the dry coffee spot on his shirt.

"A stain," he answered, thinking of Sean Coleman.

She pulled away to attend to the sound of boiling water dribbling over the edge of the spaghetti pot and fizzling along the burner.

Lumbergh leaned back, his elbows finding the countertop behind him. A smug grin formed on his face as he gazed approvingly upon Diana's lean physique. He sometimes jokingly referred to her as his "trophy wife," but it wasn't entirely a joke. He really did view her as a prize—not so much as a possession, but rather an escape. She was the only one in his life who could ever draw his attention away, even momentarily, from his one true passion—law enforcement. That distraction, he had come to realize, made him far more than a name or a reputation . . . it made him whole.

With that prize, however, came sacrifice—the sacrifice that brought him to where he was now—the proverbial *big fish in a small pond* that he had never set out to be nor ever wanted to be. But while the shadow of regret did sometimes creep out from the darkness to torment him, it was moments like this that chased that intruder back into the night.

His head shifted to glance at the small kitchen window above the large-basined sink. It had just started to sprinkle outside as he was walking in the door, but now the rain was coming down harder.

As the sound of raindrops intensified along the shingled roof above, Lumbergh's teeth instinctively gnawed at the small, expired wad of gum that had endured in his mouth from the moment he and Jefferson stepped foot on Meyers Bridge. He deliberated how he should break the news of her brother's latest farce. A fresh stick of gum often marked the commencement of a new train of thought for Gary Lumbergh—like the beginning of a new chapter in a novel.

"Gum. Trash," ordered Diana, who didn't turn around.

She didn't like to hear her husband chewing gum. It meant he was thinking about work.

He smirked and quickly disposed of it in the tall, narrow trash can beside him.

"Dinner's almost ready," she said. "Why don't you pour us some wine and relax?"

He snagged a bottle of merlot from a steel wine rack caddy on top of the fridge and popped off the cork. He disappeared into the adjoining dining room with the bottle in one hand and the stems of two wine glasses pinned between the fingers of the other.

The décor inside Gary and Diana's home represented a clash of cultures—small town charm meets big city elegance. Walls with aged, natural wood paneling were decorated with brushed metal sconces and abstract artwork within jet-black frames. Diana had deliberately transformed their quaint, indigenous house into Gary's metropolitan home away from home, or at least she did her best to. It was one of many endeavors to pacify her husband's former lifestyle.

Gary appreciated his wife's efforts. He truly did. But the mismatch of arrangements often left him with the same uncomfortable feeling he got when he strolled along the sidewalks of the town square on summer nights. Back in Chicago, cool, worldly jazz music could often be heard trickling out from behind nightclub walls. Chatter at outdoor restaurants was warm and intellectual. In Winston, it was blaring country music and classic rock from open bar doors, queue balls cracking, and drunken expletives echoing off the moon.

They had both made concessions.

Diana joined her husband in the dining room where he was finishing filling her glass about half full. With a bowl of salad in one hand and a bowl of spaghetti in the other, she glanced down at his wide grin for a second before placing both bowls on the glass tabletop. Thick, hot steam rose from the spaghetti as she returned to the kitchen to retrieve the rest of the meal.

Gary's mind wandered back to the bridge. He and Jefferson had searched it thoroughly, from end to end, and even underneath. There were no traces of the man Sean had described, even along the shore. The only piece of evidence that collaborated Sean's account was the discovery of his security badge on the ground. And all that did was affirm that Sean had been there, which Gary never had any reason to doubt.

In the past, Sean's suspicions of criminal activity at least had a foundation and some plausibility. A misunderstanding brought on by twisted speculation was one thing, but this time Gary could form no other conclusion than being outright lied to.

Prior to that day, his tolerance for Sean Coleman had already reached its limit, but a clear line had now been crossed. He was the police chief of Winston, and he was being willfully lied to by one of its citizens.

When Diana returned, her hands full once again, she found her husband's eyes dazed and transfixed on the dense steam that continued to billow from the pasta. He hadn't served himself any yet.

"Honey, what's wrong?" she asked, her lips forming a slight pout.

His eyes reluctantly lifted to meet hers. After a moment he answered bluntly. "Sean."

"Sean? What about Sean?"

An audible sigh escaped his lips before his gaze lowered back down from his wife's attentive face. He slumped back in his chair, causing the floorboard below him to creak. His attention rested upon the open wine bottle for a moment. He reached forward for it, extending his arm and opening his hand like he was searching for a lifeline. He robotically filled his own glass, not stopping until the rim was met.

"Sit down. I'll tell you about it."

Chapter 11

The boisterous chirping of worn wiper blades and the battering of steel cylinders ceased with the turn of a key. The only sound left was that of a steady and hollow drumbeat of thick raindrops bouncing off of metal. Dull headlights illuminated the outer edges of tall pine trees along with the sloped gravel road that lay between them. A small, orange guardrail reflector directed a shimmer of light back through the windshield of Sean's car.

Concealed inside the dark interior of his automobile, he switched off the headlights and quickly zipped up the olive-green rain poncho that snugly gripped his body. At one time, the garment fit. He raised both hands behind his shoulders to clasp the base of the attached, matted hood. He brought it over his head with the front seam resting at eye level. From under his seat, he retrieved a twelve-inch-long black Mag flashlight and flipped it on. Its batteries weren't strong, but the beam was bright enough to serve its purpose.

The car door opened with a shriek of rusted hinges. Cold night air flooded in while the sound of rumbling water bellowed about twenty yards ahead. It echoed off the surrounding forest as if flowing through a concrete tunnel.

That morning, Sean had awoken at the southwest corner of the bridge. He knew that the stranger, who had met his demise just yards ahead, couldn't have come from that direction because the man would have seen him or vice versa. That left three other directions. *Which corner to start from?*

The car door slammed shut, and Sean's neck twisted in a semicircle. He aimed his flashlight across the road. Its ray cut through the night and rain to expose thick foliage that prevented a long range of visibility. The area on that southeast corner was heavily wooded. There was little space between each tree, and branches interlaced together like the metal strands of a sewer grid.

While the stranger's shoes had displayed a good amount of wear, the rest of the man's clothes had appeared fairly clean and free of wrinkles and tears. If the man had come from the southeast, his outfit might have well looked like it had been run along a cheese grater.

North was the direction. The only question was which side of the river to check first.

With urging rain slapping his back and beads of water dropping from the top of his hood, Sean made his way down to the bridge. The wooden planks beneath his feet groaned as he walked to the center. The eery sound added anxiety to the ominous night air. He faced upstream, shining his flashlight into oncoming, churning water. Its intimidating, cool spray drifted up from the rapids and brushed against his chin. Panning the beam of light from side to side to expose hovering trees, he attempted to formulate which course would make the most sense, but there was no clear answer.

He went to Old Reliable to find that answer. He raised his shoulders and dug a hand down deep into his desolate, front jeans pocket. He retrieved a quarter and held the coin in front of his face.

"Heads is left. Tails is right."

He flicked the quarter into the air and moved to catch it with his opposite hand. Forgetting those fingers were already wrapped around a flashlight, however, he gasped and quickly lunged forward to use his free hand. The quarter bounced off the side of his wrist and dropped down into the misty darkness below.

"Son of a bitch."

He searched his pocket for another coin. Empty. He shook his head in annoyance.

Just then, déjà vu from a years-old memory unearthed itself from his conscience. He remembered committing a similar act at that very same spot as a child.

Diana and he used to spend hours playing in the woods around Meyers Bridge. Sometimes it was hide-and-seek, but it was usually Old West. Sean liked being the sheriff with his sister the loyal deputy. Tree-branch-rifles and twig-pistols. Fun, simpler times.

On one day, Diana wanted to switch roles. After some brotherly stubbornness, he said she could be the sheriff if she won a coin toss. As she eagerly watched, he flicked a penny into the air only to purposely let the spinning coin bounce off of his hand and into the river.

"Well, I guess you can't be sheriff," he said with a smug look on his mug.

His obvious stunt was received with an unexpected punch to the chest. Diana was never afraid to mix it up with her older brother. It was the same day that she had twisted her ankle and sliced up her knee after losing her balance along a knoll on the western slope. She had been providing backup for her brother during a fierce imaginary shootout.

Sean had carried her in his arms over a mile—all the way back home. She had cried the entire way.

Sean now smirked at the recollection. Back then, he was his sister's hero.

Upon arriving home that night in their childhood, Sean had promptly received the full brunt of blame from their mother. Anytime her angel got hurt, it was always her older brother's fault. Bed without dinner.

But as always, little Diana hadn't forgotten about her big brother. She smuggled him two oatmeal cookies once their mother had fallen asleep in front of the television.

"We always played on the west side," Sean whispered now, his words inaudible over the howling wind.

As children, they had always stuck to the western slope because it took in more light and was void of flat areas and trenches that maintained rainwater for days on end. The western slope was only muddy after a rain.

Prior to that night, it had barely rained in a week. If the stranger had mud on his shoes, he most likely came from the east.

The increasing wind forced Sean to tug his hood down lower as he climbed up off the road and onto a small embankment on the right side of the bridge. His flashlight traced the landscape, searching for disturbances in the moist earth. With fresh rain already eroding the dirt away with miniature streams, he knew he wouldn't find anything right there. With his shoulders raised, he disappeared between two thick pines, the branches of which smacked stiffly against the sides of his body like a warning to stay away.

While the cover of sheltering trees partially protected him from the rain, the assortment of dead branches, intertwining roots, and plant life effectively covered the ground like a large fishing net, leaving only patches of naked dirt where footprints would be noticed. Sean lit up each patch he saw, carefully searching for any outlines or imprints.

Fifteen minutes of intense scouring went by without a sign of human misplacement. Sean was thorough, but also understood that there was a large area to cover. He lumbered deeper into the forest, occasionally changing direction and making sure he swept exposed areas from side to side. He kept aware of the sound of the river in the background, knowing it would provide him a direction back to the bridge. In the sunlight, losing one's way wouldn't have been as much of an issue. At night, however, in the middle of a rainstorm, one had to be a little more careful. The fairly level ground and limited visibility didn't offer up any helpful landmarks.

Strong gusts of wind came in intervals from the north. Each time, he could hear the clamor of whistling and the disruption of tree branches about five seconds before the cold air would blast against his body.

The ache in his ankle, while simply a nuisance at first, increasingly protested as he continued to negotiate his body between trees and along shallow trenches. He persevered on.

Other than a few paw-prints and animal droppings, no signs of recent inhabitants were unveiled. Maybe he *had* chosen the wrong side of the river. Or, maybe his entire theory couldn't hold enough water to measure up with what moisture was trapped in his soggy shoes.

The further he ventured, the stronger a sense of failure began to burrow at the pit of his stomach. Was there really anything to be found out in these woods, or was he simply the armchair detective that Lumbergh believed him to be?

Several more minutes went by. Nothing. Another cold gust, this one stronger than the others, slapped up under Sean's hood and sent it flying backwards. With fat raindrops now smacking directly against the top of his head, he decided it was time to head back in defeat. Perhaps nothing was found because there was nothing left *to be* found. He began making his way back toward the sound of the river.

He'd nearly reached it when the wind died down, and the dull thump of what sounded like an object dropping to the ground prompted Sean's body to spin around like an unlatched gate on freshly greased hinges. The flashlight beam snapped from side to side as his wide eyes searched for movement. With only his wrist swaying, he listened intently for a good half-minute. Nothing but the constant fall of water from the sky. Perhaps he was growing paranoid, or maybe he was simply exhausted.

He took a breath and turned his foot in the mud to start his way back. It was then that he heard what sounded like the quick, coarse scrape of dirt being shoveled from the ground. It seemed to come from the same direction as the first noise.

"Who's there?" he shouted.

Without waiting for a response, he immediately galloped forward, leaping over a patch of low shrubs that sprawled out before him. Using his free hand to swing himself around the base of a large aspen, his flashlight dropped down low where it caught the quick glimmer of two marble-like eyes staring back at him.

Sean quickly choked up on the flashlight, ready to use it as a club, but its need as a weapon quickly diminished upon his assessment of what stood before him. Those glazed eyes were attached to nothing other than a small brown-haired creature whose appearance dropped Sean's jaw. A long-eared jackrabbit, just like the one that had paid him a visit earlier that morning. In fact, it could have very well been the same one. Its thick fur had been matted from the rain, causing its lanky body to look smaller, but the color and markings were dead-on. Once again, a sense that he was being judged relentlessly tapped Sean's body the same way the weather was buffeting him. However, the events that had taken place since their first meeting had placed Sean into a state that was anything but humbling.

"Get out of here!" he snarled before launching his body forward and kicking a large granite stone from the ground.

The rock slammed into the broadside of a thick, nearby aspen, sailing just a few inches above the rabbit's head. The frightened creature quickly high-tailed it into the darkness, leaving behind a recognizable thumping sound with each stride.

Sean had nearly knocked his shoe from his foot when he kicked the stone. With his shoulders low and the ache in his ankle now worse, he swore beneath his breath and lowered down to one knee. After setting his flashlight down on the ground, he latched onto his shoestrings, but his fingers quickly came to a halt, as did all movement from his body.

Just inches ahead on the ground, a flat white object lay directly in the Mag's light path. Its contrast with the earthy tones below, it was standing out like a burning bush.

He snatched the flashlight as he scrambled forward on his knees. He aimed it downward and lit up the small patch of ground that had been previously covered by the large stone he had sent flying with his foot.

His temper had unearthed the torn-off front page of a newspaper. He immediately recognized the title up top—*The Lakeland Tribune*.

The town of Lakeland sat about seven miles north of Winston. Years ago, the towns mirrored each other in population, culture, and seclusion. But today, Lakeland and Winston were polar opposites. Copper mining had put Lakeland on the map back in the late 1800s, but the town hadn't enjoyed any form of prosperity in decades. Its historical significance wasn't enough to keep a twentieth century economy sustainable. Thus, in the late 1990s, Lakeland found itself, with a handful of other small Colorado towns, on a petition to the state that requested the self-preservation measure of legalized gambling. Voters statewide eagerly made that request a reality, despite much opposition from many of the resident townsfolk—a handful of whom had actually ended up moving to Winston because of the decision.

Considering the trademark strong winds that routinely visited the region, it wasn't odd to find such an item in the woods outside of Winston: merely a piece of light trash carried through the air and eventually coming to rest. Only, it hadn't simply come to a rest. It had been lying directly underneath that rock, among freshly disheveled dirt. When Sean flattened out the paper, he noticed that the printed date was from only two days ago. He knew the find had some significance. With raindrops snapping against the newsprint and round water imprints forming, he quickly shoved the page into the front pocket of his parka for protection.

Lowering his gaze back to the loose, disordered earth in front of him, a tight knot formed in his stomach. There had to be something buried there. As his knees sank deeper into the cold, drenched mud beneath him, his hopes rose.

As if a starter pistol had just been fired off, he found his hands quickly sifting through the soil, probing for anything that could bolster the basis for him being in the middle of the forest by himself, in the midst of a frigid, late night rainstorm. If the trees had eyes, they'd witness a man desperately searching for his own vindication.

It didn't take long to find something. Sean's fingers hooked an object that felt at first to be a thick, smooth cord. He used his opposite hand to train the flashlight on what was quickly revealed to be a leather strap, each end still buried.

Like a pirate hoisting up buried treasure from below, he uprooted the attached object with a stern tug. It was some sort of rectangular satchel, about a foot and a half wide and three inches thick. The clearing of the filth and grime that clung to it revealed first a handle and then a strap with notches and a thin metal buckle that secured it shut. It didn't look all that different from the document brief bags that TV lawyers carried into court with them.

Sean found himself short of breath as he held the bag up in the air and illuminated it for a closer look. Inside it, there had to be some answers to his questions. He nearly yanked it open right then and there but paused for a moment to weigh the consequences of doing so. He worried about the concept of tainted evidence and feared that breaking open the bag would somehow diminish its legitimacy if he offered it up as proof to Lumbergh of what he'd seen transpire at the bridge.

He didn't ponder the dilemma for very long. He believed that going back to Lumbergh would only complicate things, and he didn't feel like being accused by the chief of planting the bag to further prolong a story that wasn't believed in the first place.

"Fuck it," he muttered before swallowing some bile and reaching for the buckle.

Chapter 12

Diana crawled into bed at 11:34 p.m. The small room was dark, but she could tell her husband was still awake by the sound of his breathing. Lying flat on his back, shirtless and with a forearm behind his head, he lifted the covers for his wife as she slid in next to him. Strong rain pounded the rooftop mercilessly. Water gushing through a drainpipe outside sounded like a waterfall.

"Is she back down?" he asked, not sounding at all tired.

"She went right back to sleep. Probably a bad dream," she said. "I tried calling Sean again. Still a busy signal. He must have taken the phone off the hook."

"In no mood for talking, I'd imagine," he added.

She placed her arm over his chest and rested her head along his shoulder. Clad in one of the oversized, button-down shirts she preferred to sleep in, she could feel the beat of her husband's heart against her shoulder. Minutes went by as they silently stared at the ceiling; the sound of the storm was almost inaudible against the thoughts racing through their minds. A loud roar of thunder suddenly sent a tremble through the house. When it ended, she spoke.

"Is it possible he's telling the truth?"

It was the same question Gary had been asking himself throughout the day. "Anything's possible, but I scoured that bridge. Believe me, for the sake of your brother's own sanity, I was hoping to find some blood . . . or *anything*."

"Did you check the forest?"

"Around the bridge, we did. We found nothing."

"Why would he make it up, Gary? It doesn't make sense."

He turned to her, cupping her shoulder with his free hand. "I stopped trying to figure out Sean Coleman a long time ago."

She turned more to him, studying him in the flashes of lightning for several moments. She kissed his lips. "I'm so sorry, honey. You shouldn't have to deal with stuff like this."

She ran the inside of her bare thigh against his and placed her hand behind his head, pulling him into a deeper kiss. He smiled in the darkness and pulled his wife on top of him. His hands slid down to her hips.

Pulsed flashes of lightning lit up the room from a side window. Diana let out a surprised gasp as she caught the reflection of a hunched-over figure in the wide mirror above her dresser. She quickly spun up off of Gary and to her knees, her head whipping toward the bedroom door. As another battering of thunder punished the sky above, his wife's sudden movement led Gary to instinctively reach for his nightstand drawer where he kept a pistol. Instead, his knuckles sent a small half-filled glass of water to the floor where it shattered loudly.

"Mom?" Diane called out.

Gary twisted his body away from the doorway and quickly felt for the small lamp beside him. When the bulb clicked on, he turned back to see Diana lunging toward her now-awake mother.

Catherine stood just inside the doorway, bent at the hip with her forearm resting along the top of a nearby dresser for support. Her pale blue pajama bottoms were clearly wet. She had had an accident. Diana held her mother's free hand and placed an arm around her waist, concerned that the elderly, stroke-stricken woman might fall.

"Broom!" Catherine groaned, which both Diana and Gary knew to mean *bathroom*.

Catherine's tired eyes lifted to meet her daughter's, as a stream of drool slid down the left side of her permanently twisted mouth—a result of the stroke she suffered two years ago.

Diana's eyes told Gary that she would take care of the problem. As she led her mother away, Gary sat up in bed and studied the mess of broken glass and water steaming its way along a floorboard. Down the hallway, he heard his wife offering instructions of what she was doing in a voice loud enough for her mother to hear. He turned to a seated position on the side of the bed and let his legs dangle. His feet almost touched the floor. His shoulders dropped, and his elbows rested on top of his knees.

"Damn you, Sean."

Chapter 13

G reen. Everything was as bright as day, and green—the sofa, the television set, Rocco . . . The old dachshund's lifeless eyes looked like a pair of illuminant buttons on a control panel. The goggles Sean had found *were* night-vision goggles.

Sean had thought they might be when he had reached inside the bag in the middle of the storm. His Uncle Zed used to have a similar pair of goggles a couple of years ago. He'd picked them up at a flea market in Frisco, Colorado, and later traded them in town for some ammo. But these were different—much more serious and expensive-looking. Possibly military issue or some mock variety that could be ordered out of a cheesy survivalist magazine. They were made of an imposing black metal, fastened to an elaborate head mount of canvas straps to keep the rubber eyecups suctioned to the wearer's head, leaving the wearer's hands free. They looked almost brand new.

Sean lowered the complex gadget from his exhausted, stinging eyes and laid it back down carefully across the small wooden kitchen table in front of him. The table's bad leg caused it to wobble. His hand found the back of his head and scratched at the persistent itch. A few more hours and the sun would be up and with it a new day, but he feared little light would be shed in the form of answers. In fact, his late night finding prompted more questions than anything.

Other than the goggles, the most notable item in the brief bag was a woven stocking cap, deep purple in color. The fluffy trim along the rim suggested that it was designed for women. There was no suicide note to be found and no forms of identification, just a well-used red ballpoint pen, an empty book of mailing stamps, and a handful of paperclips and binding clips. Not exactly the enlightening evidence he had hoped for.

But Sean was confident that the bag definitely belonged to that stranger on the bridge. Those wide red marks he saw under the dead man's eyes were the tip-off. They were large and clear enough for a hungover drunk to see from forty yards away. They weren't caused by large eyeglasses as Sean had initially thought. They were caused by the night-visions, and judging by their prominence, they had been worn by the stranger for quite some time prior to him sending a bullet through the back of his head.

The stranger had to have been the one who buried the bag in the forest, but Sean hadn't a clue why. However, he did have a clue where the man had come from—Lakeland. It was the only explanation for that page of the newspaper that led Sean to discovering the bag. He had worked all throughout the area and had never seen it sold anywhere other than in the town itself. Judging by the way the stranger was dressed, he probably didn't live there, but he had certainly come through that way.

Still, there was nothing concrete and certainly nothing that would convince Lumbergh. Sean pictured the condescending expression the chief would have on his face if he marched back into his office and dumped out the contents of the bag on his fancy desk—*"Which five 'n dime store did you buy this stuff from, Sean?"* Sean needed more.

Rubbing some sand from his eyes, he picked up the pen and studied it—the third time he had done so since opening the bag. He half expected it to have some convenient information inscribed on its side, like the name of a company. Stuff like that happened often enough on television. This was real life, however, and there was no inscription.

Still, Sean glanced along its side again. He leaned back in his chair to stretch out his back, rapidly clicking the pen open and shut with his thumb.

Curled up on a shaggy, brown rug on the tile floor inside the kitchen, Rocco's ears raised and his head tilted at the sound of the pen. This caused Sean to smirk.

His eyes narrowed, and he soon found his fingers twisting the pen open, pulling out the deep red ink cartridge and holding each end up to the light, taking turns staring through the cylinders as if they were telescopes.

"Stupid," he muttered to himself, knowing before he even began that dismantling it was a lame idea—as if some rolled-up treasure map would spill out to the table top.

He dropped the pen parts to the table and held the brief bag itself upside down, above his head, shaking it wildly—for the second time. Nothing.

The book of stamps looked like they could have been bought anywhere. Liberty Bells. First class.

The stocking cap was pretty standard. Most of it was deep purple in color, but the shaggy trim along the bottom sported a lighter shade of purple. Sean held it to his face and breathed in deeply, searching for a scent. He found one: it seemed to him to be perfume. An interesting peculiarity in his mind, as the person on the bridge was undoubtedly a man. He dumped it back on the table with a sigh.

He eyed the page of the newspaper again, lying in a crinkled up wad by itself at the corner of the table. He leaned forward, grabbed it, and began spreading it out as flat as he could along the table top. It was still a little damp, but he was careful not to let it fall apart. The torn edge was fairly smooth, as if someone had placed the full newspaper down on a flat surface, held it down with one hand, and used the other to yank the front page off quickly.

Latching onto the sweating bottle of cold Coors beer beside him, Sean scanned the headlines. There were stories about a new casino opening, a group of lynx that had been spotted in nearby Summit County, a proposal to increase local builder fees, a children's fishing contest, and a few other typical mountain town items highly unlikely to drive a man to kill himself. He took a swig of beer and flipped the page. His eyes shifted from left to right, like a typewriter, before dropping to the bottom of the page.

It was then that he felt a large lump swell in his throat and his eyes widen. Along the bottom of the edge were a couple short, pen-written sentences, the ink red. He didn't understand how he had missed it earlier, and wondered if his own fat fingers had gotten in the way. Written in a style that seemed to be partially cursive and partially in manuscript, he read the notes; *Holdings entered into Amendment No. 2.* A briskly drawn arrow pointed to the abbreviated sentence, *Orig. agreement.* Beside the writings, along the margin of the paper, was a single, standard-looking math problem. Long division, with more digits in the numbers than Sean used to struggle with back in school.

Sean's lips mouthed the cryptic verbiage as he read it. Maybe it was written by the dead man. Maybe it wasn't. But the ink was red, which matched the pen.

Slivers of sunlight gleamed through the narrow openings of dusty, half-drawn blinds at the top of Sean's kitchen window. Abrasive snoring sent steady quivers through the small room as if there were a multicar locomotive engine roaring down a track only ten feet away.

Without warning, a fierce eruption of pounding bounced off the walls of the small home, causing Sean's groggy body to snap forward in his recliner. With his eyes still closed tightly and his head pleading for coherence, a half-full bottle of beer nearly dropped from his grasp, but he managed to catch it by the neck.

"Coleman!" shouted a sharp, familiar voice from outside the front door. "Coleman! I know you're in there! Open up!"

"Bailey," Sean cursed under his breath, still wearing the ripe gray undershirt and dirty jeans from the night before. He had racked his brain until about three a.m., when he slipped away, unsuccessful in his painstaking attempts to make sense of the day before. The dead man's motivations were still a mystery, as were the clues Sean had unearthed from the mud.

Rocco's nose went to the ceiling and the tips of his long ears drooped to the floor. Delayed in his reaction to the landlord's commotion, he ejected a loud, sickly howl into the air—the sound of which echoed that of water jetting through rusty pipes.

Sean trudged out of his chair with an artless stumble, a palm fastened to the side of his head. He yanked open the front door just as his landlord was about to subject it to another rapid beating. Bailey's fist nearly swiped Sean's chin.

"Jesus, Bailey! What do you want?" Sean asked, already knowing the answer.

Hank Bailey was a short, stocky man with a round face, round nose, and a reddened, bald head that shone like a bulb under the morning light. He looked half-dressed with his torso clad in a snug, white, tank-style undershirt with frayed armholes. His hairy, thick arms and shoulders were decorated with ancient tattoos from his days as a Marine. They were so faded and stretched that they looked like large splotches of bread mold. His short, stumpy legs were attired in gray, creased trousers with a waistline concealed by his protruding gut.

Sean found Bailey's scornful, baggy eyes honed in on him like torpedoes.

"Need the rent! Now!" he barked like a drill sergeant. "Now!" Bailey always spoke loudly and in short bursts.

"Just . . . calm down," Sean replied, wincing and raising his hands in the air as if he was trying to avoid touching something. "Just a minute."

He retreated into his bedroom and grabbed the forty bucks his uncle had given him from the pocket of his damp work shirt that was crumpled up in a corner on the floor. He scrounged together another eighteen from his wallet and dresser.

Bailey was left standing outside on the steps, and Sean knew the man had his arms crossed in front of him. It was his signature pose, and he could hear him breathing heavily the entire time.

"What is this? What is this?" Bailey snorted turbulently as Sean returned and padded his palm with the disorganized bills.

Sean nodded to the money.

Bailey shuffled the wad in his hands. A light breeze ruffled the gray, wiry hairs sprouting from his ears, but it did nothing to cool his temper. "This ain't even sixty bucks. You owe me two-fifty!"

"Two hundred fifty?" Sean feigned confusion.

"Wipe that *stupid* off your face, boy. You know what you owe me. Where's the rest of it?"

"Listen . . . I've got some stuff I'm going to take over to Bernard's first thing Monday. I'm going to get the rest of your money—"

Before Sean could continue, Bailey snarled and slammed his fist hard against the doorframe. Rocco yelped.

"Monday? Monday? I gave you 'til today! Two month's rent! Right now!"

"You're not listening! I'll have it on Monday!" Sean shouted grudgingly over the yap of the fiery ex-soldier. "I just need a day! Just gotta make it to the pawn shop. It ain't open 'til then."

Sean knew he couldn't come up with the rest of the money by Monday. He had nothing left to pawn but cheap junk. Still, the disingenuous words kept flowing naturally from his mouth. He had become a five-star bull-shitter when it came to buying himself time. He had plenty of practice, but it wasn't working this time.

Bailey was at his wits' end. "Whatcha got to pawn, Sean? Empty beer bottles?"

He slid his head in through the doorway, looking at the musty disaster of a living space inside. Broken glass on the floor. Clutter everywhere. Sean navigated his body to block Bailey's view.

"You've got money to fork over to Moses Jones, but none for the Big Boy!" Bailey sometimes referred to himself as *the Big Boy.*

Sean clenched his fist at the reference to Friday night's pool game. He pictured his hands clasping the neck of Roy Hughes at *The Winston Beacon* and not letting go. The kid had made Sean's life an open book of folly for the entire town. The fact that Bailey knew about the money he lost to Jones was particularly infuriating.

Bailey launched his body inside the apartment, his stout frame firing past Sean like a cannon ball. Sean was surprised by the landlord's quickness and angered by the imposition.

"Whatcha got? Whatcha got?" Bailey repeated, his head flipping from side to side like a tetherball. "I wanna see what you're gonna sell. If you've got it all figured out, I wanna see what you're gonna sell."

The tenacious landlord clearly wasn't buying Sean's story. His bluff had been called. Sean's mouth opened, but the words didn't flow. He looked like a fish snagged by a hook.

Bailey threw up his hands in the air, waiting impatiently for a response with arched eyebrows and wild eyes.

Ding-ding!

Sean's body almost collapsed to the floor. The loud chirp of Toby Parker's bike bell from outside the open front door pierced Sean's skull like a bullet. As always, the kid's timing was impeccable. Sean clenched his fists, and his eyes lost their focus. He felt himself off-balance, the room spinning.

"What the hell is that?" Bailey asked, his own attention seemingly redirected.

Sean's shoulders hung low, like a wire clothes hanger supporting a heavy coat. "The Parker kid," he muttered in a glazed tone, shaking his head a little.

"No. *That!*"

Clearing some cobwebs, Sean's eyes went to Bailey's hand, which was now pointing to the distinctive, black goggles resting on the kitchen table.

"Um. Goggles."

With an intrigued elevation in his voice, Bailey asked, "Night-visions?"

"Yeah."

The sound of footsteps could be heard creeping carefully up on Sean's short front porch. Neither man paid the noise any attention.

Bailey's tongue slid along his lower lip. His hands rose to his hips and his anger seemed to turn to curiosity before Sean's very eyes. A glimmer of light flicked on in Sean's head.

"Bernard wants those," asserted Sean, gauging Bailey's reaction.

A creak of a floorboard at the front door caused Bailey to crane his neck over Sean's tall shoulder. There stood the buoy-shaped silhouette of Toby Parker, silently standing at the doorway, waiting to be noticed. He was wearing a tight, yellow t-shirt with black horizontal stripes along with black sweats and his trademark black high-top sneakers. He somewhat resembled a portly bumblebee.

Sean didn't turn around. Bailey gazed back at the goggles.

Sean continued. "He offered me a hundred, but I think he's trying to lowball me. We'll get it straightened out tomorrow."

"A hundred?" The wrinkles along Bailey's forehead deepened. "And he's already seen 'em?"

"Yeah," replied Sean, trying hard to sound convincing. "But you know Bernard—always trying to get something for nothing. I walked away."

Bailey *did* know Bernard, and he knew the pawnshop owner to be as shrewd as a snake. If he was offering a hundred for an item, it was certainly worth more. Bailey's left hand went to his chin, and his right snatched the goggles up off the table. He held them up to the beam of light that was shining in through the doorway, turning the contraption in his hand and studying it.

Sean could hear the gears turning in his landlord's head. He was buying the story, and Sean knew it. Sean bit the inside of his cheek to conceal the curls that were forming at the end of his lips.

"Hey, Sean . . ." Toby whispered from behind.

Sean turned his head to the boy, angling his eyebrows and waving him off with his hand. He was reeling in Bailey and he feared Toby would find a way to cut the line. When he turned back to his landlord, he was struck by the awkward sight of two thick, black, long-scoped eyes glaring straight up at him. Bailey was now wearing the goggles. A large, thirsty grin of uneven teeth decorated his round face, making him look like a villain from a Mad Max movie. Bailey snapped his head to the side and stomped over to the open door of Sean's bathroom, where it was dark with no windows.

"What's he wearing on his face, Sean?" Toby asked, now standing beside Sean. The boy's wide eyes glowed in awe of Bailey's creepy appearance and erratic movements.

Sean didn't answer the boy's question but shared in the bemusement of the spectacle. He had only hoped to convince Bailey that he had the means to make a rent payment. He wasn't expecting a personal interest in the item. But it suddenly made sense to him; Bailey had often bragged about technological advances in the Marine Corps that either weren't around or weren't standard issue when he served. Now, he had one of those advances laced around his head like a turban, and he was acting like a kid in a candy store.

Bailey let out an enthusiastic whistle and howled, "This is high-quality shit! Slick as you know what!"

He raised the goggles to his forehead and looked out the doorway. "Where'd you get these babies? They're not hot, are they?"

Sean shook off the assertion and claimed that he won them from a Super Bowl bet with a friend up in Lakeland. Bailey asked if the friend was in the Corps. Sean claimed that his friend knew someone who was.

"I'll take a hundred off your rent for these," stated Bailey after slipping the headgear up off his shiny head as he marched back to Sean. "That matches Bernard's offer, and it saves you a trip." His eye twitched as he stared up at his tenant.

Sean's mind raced. The goggles were evidence of what he had seen on Meyers Bridge the previous morning, but they weren't enough to prove anything to anybody. He also knew Bailey didn't intend on reselling them right away, so they'd be right downstairs if they needed to be acquired later.

"Two hundred," Sean said with a straight face.

"Two hundred?" Bailey crowed. "Yah kidding me? That's double what you could get from Bernard!" His teeth were showing, nostrils wide in indignation.

"A hundred was his *first* offer. We both know he'd go higher than that."

Bailey knew Bernard all too well. "One-twenty!" he barked.

"One-seventy!" Toby shouted excitedly.

Sean grunted and turned to Toby, displaying an annoyed glare. "Don't," he snarled, before twisting his head back to Bailey and saying, "One-seventy-five, and I get 'til Wednesday to get you the rest of the rent."

Bailey folded his arms in front of him, breathing heavily. "One-thirty," he said in a tone that felt final.

"One-fifty!" Toby shouted.

"Toby!" Sean snapped angrily after his head flipped back to the child's smiling face. "Do you *have* a hundred and fifty dollars?"

"No."

"Then shut up!"

Toby's eyes went to the floor.

"Yeah, shut up," added Bailey.

The two men haggled for another minute before reaching a deal at a hundred and fifty dollars, plus a three-day grace period for the rest of the rent. Bailey triumphantly strutted his way out the front door with the goggles still suctioned to his forehead, sure of himself that he had gotten a bargain. Before he even made it outside, Sean noticed that Bailey had left the original fifty-eight dollars behind on the table, having placed the crumpled up bills there when reaching for the goggles. The landlord had forgotten about it in all of the excitement. Sean quickly snatched up the wad and jammed it deep into his pants pocket. If Bailey came back later to retrieve the money, Sean would insist he'd left with it.

"I heard about the dead fella," said Toby with wide, shiny eyes, looking up at Sean.

The child's words were spoken loudly enough to prompt Sean to hurry to shut his door, not wanting Bailey to catch any of the conversation.

"Who told you about that? Milo?" he quickly asked.

"No. It was in the paper this morning. Mom read it to me while I was eating Lucky Charms. I like that cereal, but I am a far bigger fan of the marshmallows than the oats. The oats just don't have much of a taste. I suppose you need the oats though, or else it wouldn't be cereal. At least with Count Chocula, you get the chocolate corn bits along with the marshmallows, so—"

"Stop!" Sean interrupted. "It was in the paper?"

"Yeah. I know you're telling the truth, Sean. Mom thinks you're making it up, but I told her you wouldn't do that."

"Jesus," Sean whispered.

"Did he really have bright blonde hair, Sean?"

Sean guessed it had to be either Milo or Jefferson who squealed to Roy Hughes of the *Beacon*. Lumbergh wouldn't have done it. It probably would have violated some policy, and the chief followed policy like it was gospel. Not that it mattered. The news was out, and soon the whole town would start giving him strange looks again. Bailey must not have read the morning's paper; otherwise, he'd have said something for sure.

Sean lifted an eyebrow. "Why are you here, Toby?"

"I want to help you find that dead guy."

At least someone believes me, Sean thought. *Too bad that someone was a mixed-up kid.* "We aren't gonna find him, kid. His body could be halfway to Santa Fe for all I know."

"Guess what, Sean?"

"What?"

"The river doesn't flow all the way to New Mexico."

"I know. It's a figure of . . . Oh, forget it." Sean crossed the room and collapsed back down into the recliner. He leaned back, placed his hand to his head, and gazed up at the ceiling.

"What are you doing, Sean?" asked Toby.

"Thinking."

"About what?"

Sean turned his head to the boy, uncertain where to begin. Toby was now leaning back on a wooden kitchen chair with his own hand pressed to his own head, emulating Sean. A soft thunk could be heard from Rocco conking his head up against the kitchen pantry.

"I'm thinking that Rocco needs breakfast," Sean said with a sigh. "Want to give him some?"

"Sure!" The boy rose from his seat in excitement. "What do you feed him?"

Sean motioned to the same pantry that Rocco had just bumped up against.

"Bottom shelf."

Toby went to work while Sean glanced out a window. It was a beautiful day; the sun was strong and encouraging.

"We should look for that dead guy," Toby stated after returning the bag of dog food to the pantry.

"We'd never find him, Toby."

"We should still look. You never know. He might turn up—maybe get hung up on a branch or something. If he has bright blonde hair, he might stick out."

Sean shook his head.

"Did you already throw away the comic section?" Toby asked, picking up the scrap of newspaper from the kitchen table.

"No. That ain't even our paper," Sean answered, marveling at how spontaneously the boy's attention pivoted.

The boy's eyes darted along the scrap's wording like the print head of an old dot matrix. Toby then said, "Who do you know in Traverse City, Michigan?"

Sean's face displayed puzzlement. "No one. What are you talking about?"

Toby looked up at the big man with a mischievous grin draped across his full face. "You sent a big letter to someone in Traverse City, Michigan. I saw it."

Sean leapt up from his chair and pressed Toby to clarify. Toby pointed to the written notes in red ink on the newspaper and slyly boasted that he recognized Sean's handwriting. Sean quickly snatched the paper from Toby and re-read it.

"I didn't write this, dumb-ass! Someone else did!"

Toby's shoulders lowered and his expression turned to one of puzzlement. "So then . . ." he started. "You know someone who knows someone in Traverse City, Michigan."

"Toby, you're starting to piss me off. What are you saying?"

Toby retold the story he had told Sean the previous day, about running into the town's postal carrier with his bike, resulting in a bag of letters spilling out over the sidewalk. While helping the angry mailman pick up his letters, Toby's eye had taken notice of a large envelope with the address labeled in red ink.

"One-fourteen Bluff Walk Road," Toby added.

The boy explained that the handwriting on the envelope was the same as on the newspaper before him. Typically, Sean would have disregarded such a claim as nonsense or a child's imagination, but Toby's statement triggered a not-so-distant memory. At Toby's birthday party months earlier, Sean had watched in awe as the boy successfully identified the giver of each gift by matching the handwriting on the outside of each card with his memory of the returned RSVP cards. Though he knew that Toby's autism came with mental gifts that he couldn't understand, Sean was initially convinced the display was some sort of trick. However, some of the other boys and a couple adults continued testing him by each writing a few words on scrap paper. Toby had then rattled the correct names off without hesitation.

"Look at me, Toby!" Sean said soberly.

The boy rarely looked anyone in the eyes, but for Sean he did so reliably.

"Are you sure the handwriting's the same? It's really important."

"Yes, I'm sure."

"How sure?"

"I'm positive. It looks like it was written with the same pen, too."

Sean read honesty and certainty in the boy's eyes. He knew that Toby had no reason to deceive him, and he wasn't sure he was even capable of deception.

"Are you going to tell me who wrote this?" the boy pressed before lowering his eyes back to the newspaper.

Sean watched the boy's attention turn to the map for the fishing contest. Toby began carefully tracing the roads with his finger.

Several emotions filtered down through Sean's head: unspoken gratitude to the child for his help connecting missing pieces to the puzzle, some guilt for how he typically treated Toby, and a strong sense of relief, as if a release valve had been opened in the corridors of his mind. After a few moments, he answered the boy's question.

"Toby, once I find out, you'll be the first to know."

He placed the palm of his large hand gently along the top of Toby's head. A dash of familiarity quickly flirted with Sean's memory. It was the image of Sean's father doing the same to him the night before he had left for good.

Toby repeated the address again at Sean's request. Sean wrote it down on a notepad. It made sense why Toby originally thought the handwriting was Sean's. Sean hadn't RSVP'd to his party, nor given him a birthday card. Toby had never seen Sean's handwriting and naturally assumed that the writing on the newspaper belonged to him.

"What was the name?" Sean asked, his eyes glaring at the address.

"What name?"

"The name on the envelope. You know, above the address."

"L."

"Elle? As in Elle Macpherson?"

"Who's Elle Macpherson?"

Sean glared at Toby in apparent disgust. "You seriously don't know who Elle Macpherson is? Please tell me you're joking. You like girls, don't you?"

Toby's cheeks turned red, and his gaze dropped to the floor. "It wasn't someone's name," he said in embarrassment. "Just the letter L."

Sean asked the boy if he had seen another address in the top, left corner—a return address. Toby answered that there was none.

Sean glanced back at the address in his notepad and then re-read the mysterious, pen-written notes from the newspaper. A lightbulb turned on in his head and he scooped up the empty book of postage stamps that he'd found in the dead man's brief bag.

"There were a bunch of stamps on the envelope, weren't there?"

Toby nodded, his eyes not leaving the map.

"And the stamps were Liberty Bells."

The boy nodded again.

Sean's thoughts leapt back to Lumbergh. He could hand over the address to the chief who could possibly use a computer in the office to find out what was there. Sean sure as hell didn't know how to get the information on his own. He had no access to the Internet, and the local library was closed on Sundays. He wasn't convinced either could have helped him anyway. There were few people more computer-illiterate than Sean Coleman.

The police station computers would have surely been the best resource, but after thinking it over for a minute, Sean was convinced that Lumbergh wouldn't go for it. He recalled one of the events Lumbergh had rubbed in his face the previous day at the police station—Sean's suspicions that a teenager who was working at the local gas station was a terrorist.

Tariq was his name. He was a young man probably close to twenty—a hitchhiker making his way west. Arabic, with thick black hair and a matching beard, he stuck out like a sore thumb in Winston. Sean was driving through town the day he was dropped off by an old van with out-of-state license plates, heading south. Wearing sun-faded clothes, worn-down shoes, and a large army-green backpack over his scrawny shoulders, he walked into the only gas station in town—Perry's Pump-It.

What Sean didn't know as he drove out of town was that Perry, an elderly and overweight man in his seventies, was laid out on the floor behind his cash register at the time, suffering a heart attack. Tariq found the immobile station owner and quickly phoned the police. Perry lived and felt so much gratitude toward the young outsider that he offered him a paying job and the back room of his station, where a cot and washroom were turned into a makeshift home.

The town largely accepted Tariq, but Sean had always been suspicious of him. Having recently watched a Denzel Washington thriller titled *The Siege*, the small-town security guard had formed a heightened sensitivity toward what he deemed as odd behavior coming from the Middle Easterner. He had noticed Tariq making several late night calls from the phone booth outside the station and had overheard from others that the outsider spent a lot of time up by the Cedar Canyon Dam north of town. When in town, Sean found himself keeping a close eye on Tariq.

His suspicions were amplified after he saw Tariq stroll out of Bernard's Pawn Shop one day with a bag that looked to be quite heavy, judging by the way he was walking. Being that Sean was a regular customer, Bernard had no problems addressing his inquiry about the purchase. Tariq had bought a metal ammo can and a handheld stun gun.

Twenty minutes later, Sean barged into the police station,

demanding action. With the chief out of town, Jefferson was successfully bullied into starting a computer background check on Tariq. When the chief returned and caught wind of the situation, he was absolutely furious. Jefferson took an epic verbal beating and was ordered never to use any of the office's technology for anything relating to Sean Coleman, short of it being used to book him.

Days later, Tariq was gone. Back hitching along the road, having given Perry the ammo box as a parting gift and carrying the stun gun for protection during his journey.

The chances of Lumbergh having a change of heart on tracking down a lead from Sean: slim to none. However, Sean was exceedingly coming to terms with the fact that his interest in the dead man and the puzzlement surrounding his death was a venture he was pursuing alone. It was almost better that way.

Lumbergh had written him off. He didn't believe Sean's story. No one in Winston would either.

Sean had something to prove: he wasn't the immaterial blow-hard and useless town drunk they pegged him for. A man had died right in front of him. The reason behind the death was a significant riddle that deserved an answer. For Sean, it needed an answer. Regardless if it was for the benefit of the man's family, the benefit of the truth, or the benefit of himself, Sean would find that answer.

Then he would find some respect.

Sean leered at Toby and asked, "Toby, how would you like to look after Rocco for a few days?"

Chapter 14

On his way out of town that morning, Sean made a quick stop outside Roy Hughes's house. He felt *The Winston Beacon* reporter's car had far too much air in the tires, so he remedied the problem with the blade of a four-inch buck knife. All four tires.

Sean was at ease leaving Rocco in Toby's care. The boy asked if the grouchy dachshund could stay at his place, but Sean knew the boy's mom wouldn't be too keen on that. Besides, the blind dog would spend the next few days cracking his skull on every piece of furniture over there. At home, the placement of the room was familiar. Sean left instructions for two check-ins a day and didn't tell the boy where he was headed—just that he was going out of town. Most people would have asked where, but Toby didn't. He was too focused on his new job as caretaker. Sean didn't want anyone to know anyway.

It was still early when he made it onto I-70. He hit some thick Sunday traffic, mostly weekenders returning from Copper Mountain, Breckenridge, and Vail to head back to work the next day. Once out of the mountains, he headed north, advancing along the foothills.

He found a gas station that accepted a personal check shortly before he crossed the state line. He signed the check with a garbled signature that couldn't possibly be confused with his natural one. Above it, he wrote his driver's license number with a few digits out of place, laying the groundwork for a fraud claim once the check inevitably bounced. He gambled on the droopy-eyed, gum-smacking teenager at the cash register not noticing the discrepancy, and he won that bet. He hoped to use the same technique to finance more of the trip if he needed to. Within minutes, he was cruising through the farm lands of Nebraska.

The old Nova was dependable—one of the few things in Sean's life that was. Other than a shot muffler, it ran smooth. Zed helped him maintain it over the years, and he seemed to take pride in doing so. It had been years since Sean had driven out of state, and he had forgotten the sense of freedom that came with it.

Outside of Winston, he was a stranger. There was no monkey riding his back out on the open road—just fellow travelers adjoined only by their shared anonymity. When a couple of bikers on Harleys passed him on the left, he perused them with mild envy. Most people may have looked at guys like them as hoodlums who'd voided their lives of any real responsibility. Sean, however, found himself admiring them and the way they embraced independence. They lived with the wind in their face, exploring new places and meeting new people. *What was so wrong with that?*

Sean had a long drive ahead of him, but with each new stretch of pavement and every slope and bend came a heightened sense of conviction that had eluded him most of his life.

Chapter 15

"Stifle it!" Edith Bunker shouted at her husband Archie, much to the delight of the studio audience who roared with laughter and broke into applause.

A thin strand of drool dropped from Delores Coleman's slanted lower lip when she opened her mouth to unleash an abrupt chuckle. Diana leaned forward over her mother who was seated stiffly in a firm, tightly cushioned chair stationed across from a twenty-five-inch television in the corner of the living room. With a dash of sadness tainting her faint smile, Diana reached for a napkin held to Delores's chest by two alligator clips strung around the elderly woman's neck like a piece of jewelry. A few dabs did the trick.

She planted a quick kiss on her mother's cheek, taking a moment to search for a hint of reaction in her mother's eyes. There was none. The sitcom had her full attention. Diana returned to the side window where a half empty bottle of Windex and a roll of paper towels rested on the narrow ledge below. She felt the inviting warmth from outside taunt her hands and face while she continued wiping the single-paned glass in a circular motion.

This wasn't quite where she saw her college degree taking her—working as a full-time caregiver for her mother in the small Colorado town that she'd grown up in. Like her husband, she missed the city—the museums, the dining, and even the shopping, though she never considered herself a girlie-girl. But Illinois never felt like home. The small town of Winston—the place she'd spent years daydreaming of leaving—tugged at her heart while she was away. For her, the return didn't stem solely from the sense of responsibility she had to her mother. Life was simple in Winston. Easy. Safe. The folks, most of whom she'd grown up around, were usually friendly and always genuine. Here, she knew the hand she was dealt. The Chicago area was a wildcard.

Three months before her mother's stroke, Diana had received an unexpected, late night call from her husband—one that chilled her to the core. She hadn't a clue what her sober-sounding but out-of-breath husband was talking about when he kept repeating, "I'm okay," over and over again.

She'd turned off the television early that night to curl up with a new book in their small but cozy townhouse, else she would have seen the grainy video of flashing emergency lights as a lead-in to a breaking news report. Gary had been involved in a shootout.

He was accompanying a gang unit officer whose regular partner was at a nearby hospital witnessing the birth of his first child. The officer was working a lead in a homicide investigation in the downtown area. There'd been some miscommunication on the address of a possible witness. Moments after knocking on the wrong apartment door and identifying themselves, the unsuspecting policemen were greeted with a round from a shotgun through a rusty mail slot just inches from them. Directly through his knee, Officer Jose Torrez took a mixture of shrapnel from the slug and a metal plate blown loose from the wall. Gary, luckily, wasn't hit.

While Gary pulled the fallen policeman around a hallway corner to safety, the man inside the apartment tried to flee through the aged fire escape that dangled outside his rear window. In his haste, he lost his footing and fell three stories into a life of permanent paralysis below the hips.

It turned out that the shooter had been running a small meth lab out of his kitchen. An avid user of his own product, his chemically induced paranoia led to the end of one man's career and another one's legs. It also served as a weighty wake-up call to the lieutenant's wife.

Diana knew that a career in law enforcement was laced with a heightened degree of danger. Gary had been very honest with her about that fact as far back as when they started dating. But it wasn't until that night that the romanticism of being married to a highly respected officer was trumped by the grim reality that the job was one of life or death. What if Gary had been standing to the left side of that dimly lit apartment door instead of the right? What if the gunman had aimed a couple feet higher? What if her husband had been alone that night working that lead?

Those questions conducted a provocative dance in her mind for months. The city of Chicago had lost its esteem, and her husband's responsibility to it no longer felt rewarding. Dark alleys that used to go unnoticed were now precarious to Diana. Incidental eye contact with strangers on the street now brought uneasiness. Perhaps most disturbing was her husband's stoic demeanor following the incident. He was all business, as if it never happened. *My God*, she found herself thinking, *was the cloak of the city strapped so tight that it couldn't let out what it pulled in?* She never admitted it to Gary, but she felt her mother's stroke may have opened a window to a better life.

So there she was, back home and taking care of the woman who'd taken care of her for most of her life. Delores wouldn't have taken to a nursing home, and leaving Sean in charge of her well-being wasn't even a consideration. Too much bad blood between the two, and a lack of reliability, maturity, and patience on her brother's part. Unlike Sean, Diana had always had a tight bond with her mother. Their relationship had once resembled that of two sisters, acting as each other's best friend and support systems through good times and bad. Throughout the years, Diana was often forced into a parental position, portraying the role of mediator in her mother and brother's loud and animated squabbles. It was an unnerving and tedious job, but she did the best she could.

She thanked God often for a husband whose loyalty to her let them uproot their lives, despite the passion Gary felt for his job, but that afternoon as she washed the windows it was her brother who occupied her thoughts. She'd left four voice messages for him over the past eighteen hours. None had been returned.

Looking outside through streaks of bubbling foam, she noticed a faint trail of dust rising up from the gravely switchback that led up to her driveway. Someone was about to stop by for a visit. She hoped it would be Sean, but it wasn't. Gary's Jeep Cherokee crested the hill and rounded the thick blue spruce that shaded the front porch of the house. He waved to her from behind the windshield. He parked at the edge of the short cobblestone walkway, killed the engine, and climbed out. Even from the distance, she could see his mouth work a wad of gum mercilessly.

"Slow day," Gary remarked with a dash of disappointment in his tone after he pushed open the screen door and wiped sweat from his forehead with the back of his hand.

"Hot day," Diana countered.

He tossed his car keys across the corner of an end table.

"Thought I'd come home for lunch." The door smacked shut behind him.

She used her free hand to lift up a small wastebasket from the patch of carpet beside her. A cagey smile directed her husband to spit his gum in it, which he did.

"Well, this is a nice surprise. We've got leftovers in the fridge."

She warmed up a plate of spaghetti as he gave her a nod and made a quick trip to the bathroom. Upon returning, he snagged the TV remote from the living room coffee table and turned down the volume on Delores's sitcom. The move was met by his mother-in-law's agitated moan of dispute.

"Now, Mom," Diana reasoned. "It was up too loud." She quickly set him a place at the kitchen table and within moments was watching her husband twirl spaghetti along a silver fork.

"You know, Sean still hasn't called me back," she said.

Gary's eyebrows rose as if he had something relevant to say. He held up a finger and wolfed down a mouthful of pasta. He then swabbed the corner of his mouth with a cloth napkin. "He's gone."

She watched him gather another bite. "What do you mean?"

"I took a drive out there about an hour ago. You know, to check up on him because he wasn't answering his phone. When I got to Meyers Bridge, I saw Toby Parker messing around down by the river, right by where Sean said he saw the guy fall. I asked him what he was up to and he told me that he was looking for the body."

She responded with a sigh. "Oh, dear."

"Yeah, unfortunately it's the talk of the town after it wound up in the paper. But get this . . . he said that Sean left town for a few days and that *he's* taking care of Rocco."

"Toby is?" she questioned. "Is Sean doing a job for Uncle Zed?"

Gary nodded. "I assumed so. I probably should have asked, but I was having trouble hearing him over the water. Plus I couldn't keep the kid's attention. He was literally turning rocks over down there. A man on a mission."

"Why wouldn't Sean just call me to take Rocco? He usually works so hard to avoid Toby."

He drained a gulp of cold lemonade down his throat. "Probably too embarrassed to talk to you, I'd imagine. You know how he gets. Whenever there's a Sean Coleman public snafu, he hides under a rock for a few days. He probably chose Toby because he's the only person in Winston not laughing at him right now."

Her shoulders shrunk. With a frown, she said, "*I'm* not laughing at him."

He lowered his drink to the table and leaned back in his chair. "I'm not laughing either, honey," he said with some empathy. "I'm just telling you the perception."

She pulled out a chair and sat across the table from her husband, windows forgotten. She planted her elbows along the tabletop and rested her chin along the top of her clasped fingers. She turned her head to the kitchen window where she gazed out at a row of three short pine shrubs she and her husband had planted last year. A hummingbird buzzed on up to a red sweet-water feeder hanging from the overhang of the roof.

"Give him a few days, honey," comforted Gary. "He'll be fine. Getting out of Winston for a little while is probably good for him."

Her husband's words were easing. Diana nodded her head, letting her eyes drift from the window to him. A smirk formed across her lips. "Thanks for checking on him. That was very sweet of you."

He grinned. "It was no problem, ma'am," he replied playfully.

One of her fingers began to toy with her hair before her soft smile shifted to an enticing, wider one. "Well, Chief," she said. "I wish there was some way I could repay you for your thoughtfulness."

Her eyes motioned toward the open bedroom door behind her husband.

His eyebrows suddenly formed sharp arches. He sat up in his chair, quickly directing his eyes to Delores in the living room, then back to his wife.

She snickered. "She'll be fine," she insisted. "*Andy Griffith* is on next."

Chapter 16

The sun felt warm against Sean's shoulders, gleaming through the rear window as if it were urging him forward like the flame behind a rocket. When it set behind a flat horizon—unlike in his hometown, a sight he wasn't used to—it was the rising moon that drew him forward. Hours passed and the oncoming headlights grew more and more infrequent.

He made it past some moonlit fields on the outskirts of Des Moines, Iowa, before he found himself nodding off at the wheel. The lack of sleep he'd been managing through over the past 48 hours had finally caught up with him. He spotted a small business district along an upcoming exit. There wasn't much there other than a couple of 24-hour gas stations, a closed restaurant, and a short strip mall. The mall, however, had a decent-sized, dimly lit parking lot where he noticed a couple of semis resting. That told him that he probably wouldn't catch any hassle for parking there overnight. He had a bit of money in his pocket, but he wasn't going to spend it on the luxury of a motel, even a shoddy one. He had to make that cash last a few days. He flipped the blinker.

Spending the night in the back of that Nova used to be a fairly regular practice when he was younger. Sometimes it was because his mother had kicked him out of the house. Other times, it was to sleep off a stupor. It had been years though. His body wasn't what it used to be—now aged and heavier. Multiple attempts to contort his large frame along the bench seat in different positions didn't prove fruitful. Whether it was an aching neck, too much blood rushing to his head, or not enough blood flowing to his legs to keep them both awake, he found himself snarling in aggravation. After twenty minutes or so, he was sitting up straight and rotating his neck to alleviate some stiffness. He watched the headlights of sparse traffic glide back and forth along the interstate while the odor of spilled oil along the cracked pavement beneath the car urged him to breathe through his mouth.

When he swallowed, his mouth felt dry. Like he'd just been granted a wish by a genie, he turned his head to meet a small, lit-up establishment sign over at the far end of the strip mall. He remembered seeing it from the road but was too groggy to focus on the content of the sign itself.

The Cuckoo's Nest Pub.

Other than the gas stations, it was the only business in sight that showed a hint of activity. Only three cars were parked out front, but it was definitely open.

Minutes later, he found himself sitting in a dark corner inside with a hand wrapped around the throat of a cold bottle of beer. He'd chosen a booth in the back and kept his head low, sending off a vibe that he was just there to drink and not socialize. He savored the beverage unlike he normally did, appreciating its amplified value after a long day of travel. With each swig, the tension seemed to drain out of his body as the drink drained down his throat.

The bartender was a haggard-looking woman with a tightly curled mane of hair and a complexion and physique that suggested she'd given up on her appearance long ago. She occasionally glanced over at him with judging eyes, probably wondering if her chances at a tip were better than 50/50. Had she known him better, she'd never have given him such favorable odds.

A long day on the road had gotten him farther along than he'd hoped for, but the fatigue he felt was making him pay the price. Having been wedged in a near permanent position for the past twelve hours, his rear end felt like he'd bounced down ten flights of stairs on it. His eyes were red and they stung like hell, but they still managed to continually wander over to a young couple at the other end of the room who were both wearing what appeared to be serving uniforms.

He guessed that they probably worked at the closed restaurant across the parking lot and had stopped in before heading home. They didn't look twenty-one and probably shouldn't have even been inside a bar, but no one seemed to care. He watched them gaze into each other's eyes that were ripe with excitement and untamed youth—not the kind of demeanor one would expect to find after midnight in some hole-in-the-wall place in No-Name, Iowa. Seated next to each other instead of across from one another at a small table, they couldn't keep their hands to themselves. Sean half expected them to go at it right there.

He was surprised to see there was actually a bouncer on duty. It seemed pointless, given how few patrons there were, but maybe with truckers stepping in for a nightcap before settling down in their rigs, there was the occasional dust-up between blowhards. The bouncer was Hispanic with short, slicked-back hair and a mild goatee. He wore a tight-fitting, yellow t-shirt tucked into black slacks and shoes that made him look like an event staff worker at a rock concert. He wasn't close to Sean's size in bulk, but it was easy to tell he'd spent some time in the gym. The guy seemed to take his job seriously, alert and drinking coffee out of a cup that the bartender would refill from time to time.

Sean had grown mildly irritated with the screechy street-slang spewing out of a skinny loudmouth that had stepped in with a much quieter friend shortly after Sean had sat down. The loudmouth, probably in his early twenties, was clad in an aqua and orange University of Miami velour jogging suit—probably the only such jogging suit that existed within a two-hundred-mile radius. He wore what had the appearance of sunglasses, but because the lenses were the identical shade of aqua as the jogging suit, it wasn't clear if they actually provided protection from the sun or if they were just for fashion. He wore the top zipped two-thirds down, exposing his concave, hairless chest, which he seemed to take great pride in showing off. He had a white baseball cap that he wore at an angle. His buddy was much less flashy, in a black rock concert t-shirt and jeans with short, blonde hair. He looked the same age.

"It's like this . . . it's like this . . ." Practically every sentence that left the loudmouth's flap began with the words, before transcending into some tale of a sexual escapade with some chick that probably didn't even exist.

His buddy would just nod his head and sip his drink, never bothering to crack a smile, even when the loudmouth would leap into a high-pitched cackle that resembled that of the main character from the old sitcom, *What's Happening?* He'd probably heard it all a million times.

After a while, Sean managed to largely tune out the rhetoric, and his thoughts turned to the remainder of the long trip that he'd complete the next day. At one of the rest areas he'd stopped at earlier in the day, he'd thumbed through a road atlas with a dusty cover that hadn't left the floorboard of his car in years. He calculated the mileage and estimated that he'd end up in Traverse City some time in the late evening. He'd given up guessing what he might find once he got there. It was all that had occupied his mind from the moment he'd left Winston. Instead, his fluctuating conscious drifted to a memory of when he was seven years old.

It was only a few months after his father had left. After watching a PBS special on Bigfoot, the ape-like creature of folklore, young Sean decided he was going to search for the animal in the woods outside Winston. He'd been determined to find and capture it. Over and over again on the projector of his mind, he'd replayed the famous footage of the tall, hairy beast lumbering through the forest with those long arms, turning back to take notice of the cameraman for just a moment before vanishing into the forest.

Sean had told a couple of older boys who lived down the road about his plan. They laughed and teased him for it, but Sean wasn't deterred, relishing the imagined looks on their faces when he returned triumphant. What a find it would have been. The long, national mystery solved. Everyone would finally know the truth. His name and face in the paper. Maybe his dad would even read about him.

The next afternoon, his mother called the police after he'd been missing for hours. A search party was formed. They canvassed the mountainside after the two neighbor boys came forward with what Sean had told them. He was found around ten o'clock that night, much deeper into the forest than anyone would have guessed. It was his Uncle Zed that tracked him down.

A sudden chill swept along Sean's spine as he sat in the dark corner of the bar, recalling how his uncle had found him shivering from the bitter cold, clinging to the base of a rotted pine with a toy bow hanging over his shoulder while water poured from the night sky. The whole town soon knew of Sean's naiveté and failure. It was a painful lesson learned.

He wasn't sure what exactly had dredged up that memory, years later as he sat in a lonely bar in the middle of nowhere, but he thought it might have something to do with the fear of setting himself up once again for a crushing defeat.

The loud, abrupt collision of pool balls from a sharp break echoed across the small room and commanded Sean's attention like a dog who'd just heard his name called. His head spun in its direction.

"That's right bitches!" the loudmouth yelled in triumph.

His curly haired friend, standing beside his buddy at the table, expressed an apologetic glance to the bouncer who seemed a bit torqued by the profanity. Curly shrugged his shoulders and shook his head in assurance that the term *bitches* was directed at him alone and not anyone else in the establishment. The loudmouth couldn't have cared less and was oblivious to the exchange of body language as a cigarette dangled from his mouth.

Sean had noticed the table when he'd first come in, as he did anytime a pool table was in his vicinity, but it had been vacant. He watched the two play with some interest as he finished his beer. If the loudmouth was half as good at pool as he was at trash-talking, he could have gone pro. Though he was pretty average, he was still better than Curly and sunk the eight-ball after ten minutes to win the game.

"Slap it down there, bitch!" he howled with a cackle.

Curly jammed a hand into his pocket and retrieved a ten-dollar bill that he then laid across the edge of the table. Sean's eyebrow rose along with his pulse. The loudmouth snatched up the bill and shoved it in his own pocket.

Sean watched them play another game with the same outcome. Ten down. The loudmouth's cockiness and intrusive laughter stirred Sean's competitive juices. He knew he needed to make his money last for the trip, but an opportunity had been dropped right in his lap to thicken that wallet. The loudmouth was no Moses Jones. It was a sure bet.

He felt his body fending off fatigue with adrenaline as he rose from his chair and crossed the room. Curly noticed him first and met him with a curious gander. The loudmouth noticed him, too, but pretended not to.

"Let a new player in?" Sean asked politely.

The loudmouth grinned widely and flashed a wink through his shades to his buddy that went unnoticed by Sean. After scissoring his cigarette with his fingers and prying it from between his lips, he turned to greet the much larger man.

Smoke escaped his mouth as he spoke. "Well, that depends. Will you give me a better game than this jackass?" He motioned to his friend whose eyes rose to the ceiling.

"Oh, I think so. Twenty bucks? Eight-ball?"

The loudmouth twisted his eyes and mouth into an expression of feigned bedazzlement that hinted to Sean that he was being mocked. It made him want to wrap his hand around the twerp's throat and squeeze some seriousness back into his face. He kept his cool though.

He opened his mouth to speak, but the loudmouth cut him off. "Okay, man. Twenty it is." He placed his finger on Sean's chest and added, "You rack 'em."

Sean didn't like being touched, but he just smirked and went to work. After laying a twenty and his beer along the top of a small, round cocktail table beside them, he snagged a wooden triangle rack from a coat hook on the nearby paneled wall. He formed the balls tightly along the well-worn burgundy felt that lined the table.

The loudmouth chalked his stick, broke, and immediately sunk a solid, which incited a toothy grin in the direction of his comrade. He missed the follow-up shot, which opened the door for Sean to sink three stripes in a row. Despite his tiredness, his game was clean and he made short work of his opponent, dropping the eight while three solids still rested on the table. The loudmouth had quieted down a bit, but to Sean's surprise, he didn't let the loss deflate his spirit.

"How about double or nothing?" he asked with a chortle. He glanced at his friend as if he were confirming that his ride could stay a bit longer. Curly didn't seem to be in a hurry and just shrugged his shoulders.

Sean was eager to increase his winnings and motioned to his competitor to rack up. The loudmouth seemed a bit sharper on the second game, and Sean grew nervous after his streak of four sunken balls in a row. The game had commanded the attention of the others inside. The young couple leaned forward in their seats, occasionally offering words of encouragement to both players, and the bartender even crept out from behind her perch a few times to follow the action. The bouncer showed little interest, watching from afar while he sipped from his warm mug and greeted a couple of truckers who arrived separately.

The loudmouth's cigarette smoke played games with Sean's weary eyes, but he wasn't going to complain about it. Someone had punched in some Ted Nugent on the retro jukebox near the entrance and the rhythm of the song "Stranglehold" accompanied the smooth, crisp flow of Sean's ownership of the table. When he sunk the game-ender in a corner pocket, he earned a smatter of applause from one of the young couples. He wasn't sure which.

"Son of a bitch!" the loudmouth shouted.

The smirk and the stylin' were dwindling. The Miami Hurricane had dissipated, and Sean chuckled as two crisp twenties were added to his coffer. The only thing that would have made the moment better was if Roy Hughes from *The Winston Beacon* was there and forced to document the victory. Forty bucks wasn't anything to do an end zone dance over, but at that very moment in Sean's life, it was a small fortune—enough for the last gas fill-up he'd need to get him the rest of the way to his destination.

The loudmouth pulled his partner aside and seemed to be consulting with him in the corner of the room. The reflective material of his jacket danced under the dim rays of a couple of dome lights above as he angrily pleaded with Curly about something. Sean figured he was trying to borrow more money from his quiet friend to continue on. His instincts told him to walk away, urging him not to ruin a good thing, but he was caught up in the moment of an impressed group of peers and the sensation of rare success. He held a chalk block up to the tip of his cue stick and ground it loudly, signaling that he was game if his adversary was. The bartender brought him a fresh beer. He nodded to her in acknowledgment but forked over no money, opting to settle up later. He could sense annoyance in her conduct, but he didn't care.

When her boyfriend retreated to the restroom, Sean caught the young girl from the table flash him an approving smile. She was trim with long, blonde hair and blue eyes, and she was a real beauty. She was in a different league than her boyfriend and the town itself, in Sean's opinion. Her brief gaze reminded him of the looks he used to get when he played football back in high school. Back then, it wasn't so much that he was handsome, because he wasn't, but there was a brand that came with being a winner that got people to take notice, and more importantly take him seriously.

"One hundred dollars!" he heard the loudmouth shout from across the room, as if he were placing a bid on an auction item.

The sharp proposal yanked Sean from his haze of nostalgic daydreaming and dragged him back into the realm of current day reality. He felt the hair on the back of his neck stand at attention. Those words were not at all what he was expecting to hear. He'd even doubted there'd be another game, but the loudmouth had somehow convinced his reluctant cohort to pool their money together for one last hurrah. He felt every eye in the bar bearing down on him. The reasoned approach would have been to walk away forty ahead and not risk losing the remainder of his cash. He knew this and he thought of the devastating loss to Moses Jones that, though still fresh in his mind from two days ago, seemed like ancient history.

His gaze wandered to the cute blonde whose eyes looked electric and seemed to be urging him to accept. He dug into his back pocket and pulled out his wallet, thumbing through the bills and adding the amount to his earlier winnings. His thumb rubbed the irritated spot on the back of his head.

"I only got ninety-eight dollars," he dryly replied to the loudmouth and his friend.

"Yo, my man's only got ninety-eight dollars!" he sung out like a court jester trying to create a spectacle for a royal audience, raising his arms and tilting his head to the side with a grin.

Scorn could be read in Sean's eyes as he glared at the obnoxious sideshow being put on by the jive-talking clown, sure he was ridiculing him.

"Don't you worry, brah," he added as he self-assuredly stepped up close to Sean. He patted the palm of his lanky hand on Sean's bloated chest and continued in softer, more precise tone. "We'll make that work."

The guy's cigarette was dangling dangerously close to Sean's face and the potency of the smoke and the condescending pat drew his blood to a boil.

Sean grabbed the loudmouth's insulting hand and twisted his wrist at a sharp angle. An intense, almost sadistic grin forged across his mouth as he took delight in watching the loudmouth's face contort in pain and his cigarette drop to the floor from his open jaw.

Across the room, the bouncer's eyebrow arched and he was on his feet in no time.

Sean wasn't deterred. He pulled the loudmouth in even closer to where their foreheads were nearly locked together like combating bighorn sheep. The room was silent other than a twangy country song now blaring from the jukebox.

With his concentrated glare burning a cauterized hole right through his challenger, Sean said, "Rack 'em."

When he released the loudmouth's wrist, the bouncer's composure returned. His hawkish eye remained on Sean, but he lowered himself back down to his stool.

"Okay, okay, brah. There's no need for none of that," the loudmouth backpedaled as he shook his wrist and straightened his body. "We're all playahs here." He traded glances with his friend before retrieving the triangle from the wall.

Across the room, the kid returning to his chair from the restroom whistled at the drama of the night's unfolding entertainment and the promise of a new contest. His girlfriend's exuberant smile eclipsed her face, brandishing an appetite for the rise in stakes. One of the truckers, wearing a straight-billed baseball cap and filthy windbreaker that might have been gray, watched curiously from his barstool with his thin arms crossed in front of his chest.

Despite the pressure, Sean felt good. The loudmouth's games hadn't impressed. He was a mediocre player at best. After insisting that Curly lay the bills on the cocktail table alongside his, Sean was feeling even better.

He chalked the edges of his cue, giving it a few extra turns, which left a plume of fine blue powder hovering in the light of the three-bulb billiard lamp that hung from above. The coated wood of the base of the stick felt like a natural extension of his hand. He gripped it tightly and paced over to the far end of the table. He kept an eye on the loudmouth's placement of the balls in the triangle, making sure the front ball was on the table dot and the formation was at a straight angle. It looked clean. He felt the warmth of the bulbs above as he leaned over the table and worked on his cue ball placement. He rarely centered the ball. He liked to come at it a bit from the left. His eyes narrowed as he lined up a shot with the ball out about a foot from the edge nearest him.

If he hadn't been completely focused on preparing to break, Sean might have noticed the fleeting exchange of mischievous, smug glances between his opponent and his quiet, curly-haired investor. It was the kind of transaction that suggested that this wasn't the first time the two had conned some bar-room stranger into an innocent wager contested along the top of a pool table. It was the kind that suggested that they all too well understood the psychology of luring a hapless victim into a false sense of confidence by throwing the first two games before raising the stakes and schooling the poor casualty. It was the kind that suggested they understood how a little trash talk could provoke a competitive spirit and dull better judgment.

With his fingers guiding his aim dead center at the cue ball, Sean bobbed his stick in and out a few times before holding his breath and unloading with a wicked release.

A split-second was all it took for him to realize that something hadn't quite gone right. As if some unseen force had nudged his shoulder at the exact moment of contact, he didn't hit the cue ball square. Still, the sharp crack of the break sounded like a string of firecrackers igniting. Balls bounced fiercely off every edge, colliding and spreading out along the table.

He watched intently with his eyes blitzing the trajectory of every movement on the table. His pulse accelerated when he spotted the eight-ball crisscross the cue ball at a speed far too brisk for comfort. As if he were watching his own heart being yanked from his chest, the eight-ball dropped into a corner pocket with a dull thud while the cue ball proceeded at a more gradual pace toward the opposite corner of the table. The hole there suddenly appeared much larger than it was—a gaping abyss affirming its dominance by drawing in the ball with magnetic pull.

A gasp could be heard from somewhere behind Sean, and nearly every occupant of the room found themselves steadily drawn into a loose huddle around the table to witness the epilogue of the shot. The ball was slowing, as was the world around Sean, who felt paralyzed and powerless. Its fate let it dangle on the edge of the pocket for a moment before it disappeared, the sight of which commanded complete silence from every stunned witness.

"Holy fuck!" the loudmouth screamed exuberantly with bulging eyes behind his aqua-visors and his spread-open hands holding an imaginary sphere in front of his face. He exploded into high-pitched, hideous laughter.

He was the only one speaking or making any noise, jumping sloppily up and down as if he was attached to a large spring that had just been freed from a giant, tin box. The rest of the onlookers had trained their attention on the face of the man who'd defied astonishing odds to actually lose a game of eight-ball on the opening break.

Sean's legs wobbled under him as if the floor beneath him was opening up. He placed a hand on the edge of the table to stabilize himself. His stomach turned, and he feared he was about to puke up the beers he'd just downed. Pondering the meaning behind whatever kind of sick, divine intervention had just repaid him for a past act or thought, he found himself hostage to his own lifeless gaze that panned the room. The expressions on the faces of the young couple nearly mirrored each other. Both displayed a mixture of awe and sympathy. The trucker with the hat was shaking his head in disbelief, probably just thankful that it wasn't him for whom the bad luck had befallen. Curly almost looked frightened, taking a few steps back with his head lowered submissively as if he were half expecting Sean to implode into a nervous breakdown. The bartender was visibly agitated, most likely due to a hunch that the adrift loner hadn't bothered to factor in his bar tab before placing the lost wager.

"I've never seen nothin' like that, brah!" the loudmouth chortled as he delivered a firm, jovial slap to the back of Sean's shoulder. "I mean . . . I mean . . . I don't even think I've *heard* of something like that! I've seen a cue ball go in on the break. I've seen the eight go in on the break. But both?! Holy fuck!"

Curly placed a hand on the loudmouth's shoulder like a parent redirecting their child in a less dangerous path, but he was swatted away.

"You know what? You know what?" the loudmouth badgered. "I've gotta call my bro. He ain't gonna believe this shit!"

While he dug into his pocket to retrieve a cellphone, Sean stewed, barely able to see straight. He'd already made it clear to the gleeful punk that he didn't like being touched. He liked losing even less. But beyond personal space issues and his competitive nature, he had just lost every cent in his pocket, in the middle of nowhere, nearly 700 miles from where he needed to be. And the worst thing about it was that he'd done it to himself . . . again.

A few more seconds went by before Sean heard the music of the jukebox again; he homed in on his surroundings. He turned to the small cocktail table beside him where his bottle of beer sat. He wanted to crawl down as deep into its throat as he could and let the demons erase his thoughts and worries. But beside the bottle, he also saw the pot of well-worn tens and twenties curled up tightly, and newfound clarity spared him from collapsing over into the abyss.

He stole a glimpse at the bouncer whose face played host to half a smirk and half a grimace, unifying the collage of post-game attitudes that composed the bar's patronage. Sean's eyes went back to the money, then to the door. The loudmouth was preoccupied with his phone, but he could sense Curly beside him, waiting for Sean's large body to move aside so he could collect the winnings.

No one in the bar knew who Sean was. The bartender hadn't ID'd him. He never laid down a credit card or wrote a check. No one would have passed his car on the way in. It was still at the other end of the lot, parked in the dark. To them he was a belch in the wind. He stood his ground, keeping his body between Curly and the table while pretending he wasn't aware of his presence. He looked for security cameras along the walls and ceiling. He saw none. He looked at the money again, then the bouncer, then the door. He could hear the loudmouth still behind him, jiving away on his phone in homie street-slang. He felt Curly step in closer.

Sean positioned his pool stick so he could hold it with both hands, horizontally in front of him. When he saw the bouncer hold his mug of coffee to his lips, it was then or never. In a flash, he spun around to face Curly and lunged forward, using both arms to drive the stick against his chest and shove him violently backwards.

Sean didn't look at his casualty's face, but he could only imagine the pain wrenched across it as the swell of his back was driven into the edge of the pool table. Sean released the stick with his right hand and launched a colossal round-house punch square into the unsuspecting loudmouth's face, nearly impaling his own cellphone through his glasses. When he spun again, he barely noticed Curly's writhing body on the floor as he quickly grabbed the wad of cash and shoved it deep into his pocket on his way to the door.

The coffee mug had fallen from the bouncer's hand and spilled its brown warmth across the bar. His stool overturned and crashed to the floor as he leapt to his feet.

Sean heard a snarling, incoherent scream from the bartender as the bouncer charged at him. He wasn't going to make it out the door without a confrontation, and he'd known this before he'd even dropped Curly. As the bouncer rounded the corner of the bar, Sean held the pool stick in both hands and choked down on it like a baseball bat. The bouncer saw it coming and raised his forearms in front of his face. Sean went lower, sending a devastating swing across the exposed upper chest of the stocky man. A sickening crack could be heard as the stick snapped in half. Sean knew he had gotten him good and watched him drop to the floor, but the guy still had some fight left in him. Sean suddenly felt the bouncer's thick forearms clamped around his ankle like the teeth of a bear trap. An anchor, weighing Sean down and keeping him from escaping.

"Get off!" Sean roared before grabbing a wooden barstool and smashing it across the bouncer's back and shoulder.

The stool splintered at its base, and Sean felt the bouncer's grip loosen. He yanked his leg free and was halfway out the front door before he turned to the cute blonde girl inside whose mouth had dropped open wide. He flashed her a parting wink.

He then fled into the darkness with his legs moving as quickly as his overweight frame would allow. He wheezed in the cool, night air, not looking back until he had practically made it to his car. Even from his distance, he could see the outside bar door propped open by someone whose head appeared to be swinging in multiple directions.

He knew they'd spot him once the dome-light in his car came on, but he was far enough away for it not to matter. He jammed his hand deep in his pocket to grab his keys, and seconds later, one of them was turning in his ignition. The engine cranked, and the obnoxious sputtering of the shot muffler ripped through the night. He popped the car it into drive, keeping the headlights off so as not to illuminate his license plate. The old Nova flew across the parking lot as the engine roared with exuberance. In the rearview mirror, he thought he saw someone running across the parking lot. Seconds later, he noticed faint brake lights facing away from the entrance of the bar.

Fearing that someone might be trying to follow him now that streetlamps had given away his position, Sean turned on his headlights and took the on-ramp heading west back on to the interstate. Once he was convinced he could no longer be seen from the exit, he slowed down to a near stop before crossing through the high grass in the median and onto the east-bound lane. This was easy with such sparse traffic headed in either direction. He sped up and crossed the off-ramp bridge of the town he'd just left, wondering if any of the cars headed in the other direction were looking for him. He paid attention to his speedometer, making sure he wasn't over the limit. Someone back at the Cuckoo's Nest would surely call the cops or the highway patrol, and he wasn't going to get pulled over long enough for them to put two and two together.

He straightened his legs and pried the wad of cash out of his tight pocket. He held it up to the dashboard lights and counted it while his thighs hugged the steering wheel. Nearly two hundred dollars. He howled at his rare victory, as anarchistic as it was.

Fifteen miles down the road, he spotted a low-lying motel sign along an off-ramp. With the neon-pink vacancy light flickering on and off under the promise of a $25 room, he decided to invest some of his new cash in a decent night's sleep before another long day of travel. The place looked like a dump from the outside, but the unlit parking lot located in the back away from the interstate and frontage road was an asset. It was highly unlikely that anyone from the bar could have identified his car in the first place, but there was nothing wrong with a little extra caution.

Once inside his musty room, Sean took a long shower that drifted between hot and cold water on its own terms. By 12:30 a.m., he was sacked out in his boxers between a springy, queen-sized mattress and a multicolored bedspread that reeked of a smell he couldn't identify.

As he lay there alone feeling a little too warm, listening to outside traffic and watching passing headlights glide across the dingy wall opposite the window, he briefly drifted back to that memory of when he was seven and got lost in the forest while looking for Bigfoot. The memory had somehow fluctuated into something different, however. It no longer ended with Sean's uncle finding him freezing and alone in the forest. It ended with Sean finding Bigfoot and kicking his hairy ass.

Chapter 17

The pulsating screech of a small, digital alarm clock coated with the grimy smudges of fingerprints from past occupants tore Sean from a lumbering sleep. He hadn't set the alarm, but he was relieved that the guest from the previous night presumably had. Eight-thirty in the morning. He stared at an egg-shaped, reddish-brown water stain on the ceiling for a minute or so before he heard the slamming of two car doors just outside his window. He lurched over to the drawn blinds to make sure the police hadn't come for him, but before he even reached the glass, the loud voices of two Spanish-speaking men squelched the worry. They seemed to be arguing. Their conversation was soon muffled out by a loud car engine that torqued to a start.

Cursing his own grogginess, Sean stumbled around in the dark. With the window facing the opposite side of the building from the rising sun, his body was convinced it was earlier than it actually was. He got dressed in the previous day's clothes and thumbed through his road atlas.

On his way to his car, he tossed his room key with its orange, plastic key chain shaped like a diamond across the check-in counter in the motel office. The kid working the desk paid him no attention and instead doodled pictures of rock band insignias in a wide-ruled notebook with a dull pencil.

When Sean stopped later for gas at a station along the exit, he grabbed two overcooked hotdogs and a Coke from the connected convenience store. A wrinkly faced woman in her fifties with wiry hair and a peach-fuzz beard worked the register. She told Sean the dogs had been sweltering under a heat lamp all night and she was about to throw them out. That was fine by Sean, who got them for free.

With the hotdogs stacked in aluminum foil sleeves and cradled above his forearm as if he were holding a football, Sean's gut sank the moment he stepped outside of the station. A teenage girl with long, blonde hair was walking toward him on her way up to the entrance of the station. Her head was tilted down as she intently shuffled her hand through her denim purse, searching for something inside it. At first glance, he was sure it was the waitress who had sat next to her boyfriend in the bar last night. He swallowed before stepping aside to let her pass, worried she'd lift her eyes at any moment to recognize the man who'd run out of the bar in the midnight hour with a couple hundred dollars that wasn't his.

Her head did rise, but a sigh of relief rather than a gasp was the reaction that dropped from his mouth. It was a different girl. A woman, really, whose older age became apparent when her sunken eyes revealed themselves. It was merely her button nose that made her appear more youthful.

The side of his mouth curled before twisting into a full-fledged grin. This didn't go unnoticed by the woman, who brandished him a thoroughly annoyed glare in return, as if she thought she was being ogled by some creep who didn't deserve to be breathing the same air as her.

Back in the car and on the road again, the miles and miles of flat farmland that surrounded him on both sides as he roared down the highway were now entirely visible under the bright sun. They were spread out across the vast horizon and served as a testament to how far he had already come. He knew the landscape would change significantly as he swung up to the north.

His thoughts leapt back to his brief run-in with the woman at the gas station and the scowl she had flashed him. It was either her face or the expression on it that reminded him of someone from his past. After a few seconds, he realized who. Susan. She was a woman he had once gone on a date with a few years back. Similar build. The same button nose.

He had met her in the back office of a ranching equipment warehouse just east of Lakeland. She was a receptionist. Sean was there for a two-night job, watching over a couple of high-end tractors that were being stored for an expo in town. She'd been friendly with him during the stint and had engaged him a few times in some small talk that he didn't find irritating like he found it with most people. He noticed as she was signing the invoice check to Hansen Security on the last day that she wore no wedding ring. He built up enough nerve to ask her out, and he was pleasantly surprised when she accepted.

He had never felt comfortable dating. He found it to be a tedious, completely unnatural ritual of portraying something that he just wasn't: a charming, considerate person. Numerous times throughout his life he'd heard the standard advice, "Just be yourself." It's what his sister, Diana, would tell him. It's what the talking heads on daytime television talk shows would say. However, the phrase always struck him as cynical and simplistic, because it had to have been concocted by someone who had clearly never met a man like Sean Coleman.

Even back in high school it was difficult. He played football, a warrior's sport where female fans typically swooned over the combatants. They never swooned over him, though—at least not the ones from his own school. Most high school girls in Winston had grown up alongside him from an early age, sharing small classrooms where he often occupied a corner at the command of spent teachers. The local girls knew all there was to know about Sean Coleman, and if they ever forgot, their parents would remind them. He would get some attention from the groupies he'd meet at away games, but it would never take long for their interest to dry up as well.

He learned that wisdom didn't accompany age when it came to courting women. In fact, meeting people became a more grueling process as the years passed him by. He was well aware that he wasn't getting any younger. The scant, gray hairs that stemmed up from his scalp were gaining friends. The joints in his knees were growing tighter. The meter on his bathroom scale seemed to be laughing at him.

He fancied himself a rugged individualist, but he knew loneliness, and he didn't like that time sometimes felt like a persistent adversary intent on condemning him to a fate of solitude. Whenever his uncle would give him a hard time about women, Sean would insist that he was happy with the bachelor life and planned on avoiding marriage like the plague, but that was a lie. Sean suspected that all men who talked like that were lying. He had no interest in being terminally single.

It was that fear that made taking women out to a restaurant for dinner an exhausting routine. It wasn't about trying to have fun and getting to know someone. Instead, it felt like the heat of a self-imposed microscope was bearing down on him, intent on exposing his slightest misstep as a lethal contaminant in a time-sensitive experiment. The pressure would reliably lead to a self-fulfilling prophecy of failure, as it did with Susan.

By the end of their date, Sean had accidentally laughed at a sentimental story she had told him of her grandmother's funeral, got caught in a lie about being co-owner of his uncle's business, and spilt hot coffee across her lap during the loud and animated retelling of a memorable football play from his glory days.

It was possible that something could have still been salvaged from the night if he hadn't wrapped a headlock around a man in the restaurant parking lot after watching him back his car into the Nova's bumper.

The drive back to Susan's place was silent and overbearingly awkward, and when he walked her up to her front door and asked her if she'd like to go out again sometime, the appalled expression on her face burned itself into his memory. It was the same look he received from the woman at the gas station—the scorching condemnation of not only his gall but his mere existence.

As the sun bore down on his thick arm resting along the lower window frame of the driver's side door, he wondered if anyone back in Winston had even noticed he'd left. He rubbed a nagging soreness at the back of his head before twisting the tuner knob on his factory radio from country song to country song until he found a classic rock station that was winding down "Hot Blooded" by Foreigner.

The open road provided him with a lot of time to think about the stranger from the bridge and Lumbergh's flippant handling of his claims. The last sentence the chief had left on his answering machine the night before he'd left kept replaying in his mind: "I don't know what else to say, Sean."

He wanted to give the chief something to say, and that something would be, "I'm sorry, Sean. You were right and I was wrong."

But the longer he drove, the more he came to realize that it wasn't just about Lumbergh. It was also about himself and what he believed was a ripe opportunity to finally follow through with something in his life—to see something through until its end. And when he completed his journey and had answers to his questions, only then would he have proven his relevance not just to him, but everyone who knew him.

Chapter 18

A jubilant grin had been pinned to Toby Parker's round face from the moment he'd peeled a bag of dog treats off a dusty general store shelf that drizzly late morning. Beef flavored, in the shape of bones. Despite the dampness in the air and on the ground, he briskly rode his bike along the pebbly and intermittently steep back roads of Winston to Sean's place. He paid no mind to the splattered mud gathering on his shoes and pant legs. Instead, he pictured the gritty old dachshund's gray jowls flopping from side to side as he devoured the food from his open hand.

The boy wasn't really a dog lover, but he was fascinated with Rocco. Being Sean Coleman's companion certainly earned the dachshund points, but it was more than that. Rocco was also a lot like his master—tough, tenacious, and blind to the things around him.

Toby's mother often asked her son what he saw in Sean Coleman. "He's not nice to you," she'd say. "He's not nice to anyone."

One time, after pressing for an answer to her question, Toby reluctantly responded, "He treats me like he treats everyone."

His mother took the statement as a validation of her argument, but that wasn't what the boy meant. He was drawn to Sean Coleman for his *blindness*. The crass security guard never treated Toby like someone whose feelings required special consideration. He never viewed Toby through a window of sympathy. He treated the boy with the same annoyance and discontent as he treated the rest of the town of Winston. The boy's mother probably never considered that her son was well aware of the favorable discrimination he was subjected to, but he was. He certainly didn't begrudge those who treated him as someone who was different, but he felt unsolicited loyalty toward the one person who didn't.

The boy pinched the bell on his bike as he pulled up to Sean's front steps—a special greeting to let Rocco know he had arrived. Though he didn't feel that cold, he could see his own breath.

Large evergreens hovered above. Steady beads of water fell from their branches and tapped the ground cover below. The faint, more constant sound of slow-flowing water trickled up from the creek that wound its way along the opposite side of the building. There were no other buildings in sight. Sean's home was fairly secluded. Far enough away from others to avoid chit-chatty neighbors but close enough to town for him not to be mistaken for a hermit. Bailey lived in the walkout basement below. Neither he nor Sean liked company.

Toby leaped up the stairs, skipping the middle step and nearly wiping out when he got to the slick landing. He jammed his hand into the pocket of his beige cargo pants to retrieve the spare key Sean had left in his care. Because he always preferred to be underdressed for the weather, his mother had to plead with him that morning not to wear shorts. She also had to compromise on a windbreaker instead of a more suitable coat.

While fiddling with the door, he was curious why the dog hadn't responded with an aroused flurry of barking. The boy had never walked up Sean's front steps before without receiving the coarse greeting. Perhaps he was still asleep. Toby unlocked the door, entered, and closed the door quickly behind him, unsure whether or not the dog would try to bolt outside. He figured it was unlikely, but he didn't want to take the chance.

Particles of dust swam aimlessly in the faint glow of hampered daylight that streamed in around the edges of the closed living room curtains. He took notice that the well-worn curtains nearly matched his orange and white striped shirt that hung down from under his jacket. Still, nothing from the dog—not even the pitter-patter of paws.

"Rocco," the boy said slowly with a mischievous smile draped between his cheeks. "I've got something for you."

The loud creak of a floorboard sounded off from a dark corner of the room, prompting him to turn his head.

"Something tells me that you're not Sean Coleman," an unexpected statement plunged out from the gloom.

Toby gasped and felt his body hurl itself away from the haunting voice. His wobbly legs collapsed under the weight of his own indecision, and he toppled to the floor with a loud thud. His heart battered the inside of his chest while his breath eluded his lungs. The bottomless tone and calmness of the male voice left a deep chill in the already cold air. The boy rapidly scooted backwards on his butt, creating a rasping sound from his nylon jacket until he felt the corner of a kitchen cabinet press into the swell of his back. His eyes shifted feverishly back and forth from the darkened corner to the closed front door until he spotted some movement from the corner, accompanied by another groan from the floorboards. Entering into one of the narrow beams of light was a large hand clasping an even larger, black pistol. Toby's watering eyes adjusted to the dimness of the room and he could make out the silhouette of a large figure nearly six and a half feet tall with very broad shoulders.

"I know Mr. Coleman lives in this shit-hole. Who lives in the shit-hole downstairs?" asked the voice.

Toby couldn't speak. His head was light from adrenaline pumping through his body. His eyes bobbed back and forth in every direction. The intruder almost sounded as if he was speaking through some sort of low-pitched, voice manipulation device, but the clarity and steadiness of his query suggested otherwise. The voice waited for the boy to answer.

Trembling, Toby forced himself to talk. "Mr. Bailey, sir. Mr. Bailey lives downstairs. Did . . . did he let you in?"

The man ignored the boy's question. "Who are you, kid?"

Toby's lips felt numb. The trembling was getting worse, making his next attempt to speak even more difficult.

"Who are you?" the man pressed.

Toby tried has best to focus. "T . . . T–Toby. I'm Toby, sir," he said before flipping his eyes back to the door.

"Don't look over there. You keep your eyes on me."

Toby's eyes swept back to the man's hand, still partially illuminated. He glanced up toward the man's face for a second before looking back to the hand.

"So tell me, Toby . . . What brings you here today?"

Toby swallowed and replied, "I'm h-here to feed Rocco." He could hear the man's steady breathing, as if he was closer than he really was.

Seconds that seemed like minutes streamed by before the stranger spoke again. "Is Rocco the dog?"

Toby nodded quickly, then discreetly scanned the room with his eyes. He had still heard nothing from Rocco.

"Keep your eyes on me," the voice calmly commanded.

Toby homed back onto the gun. "I'm s-s-sorry. Yes, sir; he's the dog."

The intruder asked Toby how he knew Sean. The boy managed to keep himself from hyperventilating. Seconds later, a sporadic, largely incoherent account describing the time when Sean and he first met began dribbling from Toby's mouth. If someone would have asked him a minute later what he had just said, he wouldn't have remembered. He stopped the story short when he saw the man raise his gun toward him.

"You're friends. I get it," the intruder said. "Where can I find your friend?"

"I don't know where he is, sir. I know he's not in Winston, but he didn't tell me where he was going. I know he'll be back in a few days. Maybe you can come back then."

Toby attempted to form a smile, his eyes pleading with the man for some sense of kindness or at least some alleviation from the intensity of the situation. His eyes ticked up from the gun to the man's face again. He could see him better now. Short, wavy hair. Glasses that looked to have metal frames, possibly gold in color. His unshaven jaw was square, and his cheeks had noticeable pockmarks. He wore a lightweight jacket with small straps above the shoulders, jeans, and cowboy boots. Toby couldn't see beyond the lenses of his glasses. They weren't tinted, but the darkened room kept them opaque. Regardless, the boy could sense diabolism staring down on him.

"Kid, I don't know if you're stupid or if you're trying to be funny. For your sake, I hope you're just stupid. Listen to me carefully," the man said. "I'm going to ask you some questions, and you're going to answer them. If you don't, or you lie to me, I'm going to shove this gun down your throat, pull the trigger, and leave you here with a second asshole. Do we understand each other?"

Toby swallowed hard. The crater in his stomach opened wider. No one had ever spoken to him like that, not even Sean. Despite the volatile threat, the man's tone was still one of composure, as if he was unemotionally reading his words off of an affidavit.

"Y–y–yes, sir," he managed to respond before collecting a couple shallow breaths.

The man angled his gun toward the kitchen table under the window while running his knuckles along the underside of his grainy chin. "Where'd your friend get that briefcase?"

Toby's shoulders shook as he slowly panned his head from the man to the kitchen table where the dead man's satchel rested on its side. It was still caked with dried mud. He explained that he didn't know where Sean had gotten it. The man then reached into his jacket pocket with his free hand and pulled out the spiral notepad that Sean had written down unanswered questions in Saturday night regarding the man who'd shot himself on the bridge. He held it out in front of Toby with his large hand making it look close to the size of a Post-It notepad.

"Did your friend write this?"

Toby squinted and leaned forward with his eyes quickly tracing the text. "I actually don't know, sir," he said before managing a breath. "I . . . I was recently led to believe that handwriting that was not Sean's was his, but I was wrong. It belonged to someone Sean doesn't know. But he said that he would let me know once he found out who it belonged to."

Though Toby could not see the man's eyes, he could read a mixture of fog and irritation in his face. The boy pointed to the open notepad and continued. "*That* handwriting does not belong to the person who wrote on the newspaper and on the envelope, so it may indeed belong to Sean."

The man said nothing for a few seconds, seemingly digesting the unintelligible babble. He just stood there like a statue. Seconds later, his mouth slowly formed what appeared to Toby to be a smirk. Toby smiled in return.

The man suddenly took a step forward, startling Toby, causing him to conk the back of his head against the cabinet door behind him. With the gun still in his hand, the man walked to the center of the living room only a few feet from the boy and sat down on a dinged-up, wooden coffee table nested at the front of the recliner. He leaned forward toward the boy, keeping his gun trained. His face was well lit now. He had completely gray hair that looked nearly silver in the way it was illuminated, though he didn't look old enough for the color to be natural. His eyebrows were darker and thick. The shade of his skin suggested that he was either Hispanic or Arabic.

"How old are you, Toby?" he asked.

The boy's eyes lifted and he glanced through the lenses of the man's glasses before reacting with a crippling wince. The intruder's eyes were dark gray, like charcoal. Toby quickly looked away, as he did with most people, but those eyes stuck with him.

"How old are you?" the man pressed.

"Th–thirteen, sir."

The man nodded. The smirk slowly transformed into a large grin. His large teeth were divergent; some angled sharply in their outright crookedness. "It's a fun age, isn't it?"

Toby timidly nodded. A tear streamed down his cheek and he couldn't make himself take a second glance at those dead eyes.

The stranger continued. "Here's the problem I have, Toby. I'm used to having these little, uncomfortable chats with people who are, let's just say, a little spooked. So I know they're not necessarily going to react to me with the same dignity and composure they would when chatting with a friend or someone . . . let's say, in their comfort zone. I get that. It makes sense."

The boy's eyes were glazed, unfocused.

"But here I am with a gun in my hand, asking you over and over again to look at me, and you can't bring yourself to do it. That's something more than fear. That makes me think you're hiding something from me."

The man couldn't have known was that Toby was autistic. Asking him to look in his eyes would be like asking him to stop his body from shaking. For Toby, it was an instinctive response to avoid eye contact, especially under his current circumstances.

Toby's head shook back and forth like that of a bobble-head toy. He'd heard the man loud and clear, but he was so overwhelmed and out of breath that he knew, in his exhausted mind, that he couldn't deliver what was being asked of him. He thought of his mother, then of Sean. Random, insignificant memories of them both. He heard a gust of wind press against the outside of the building, then the clanking of a wind chime. Then he felt something moist along the outside of his right hand. It was a sensation that he'd felt a minute earlier but hadn't immediately processed. He lifted up his arm slowly and rotated his hand. Blood.

The man flicked his wrist to open up a page in the notebook that had been dog-ear marked.

"There's an address here . . . Traverse City, Michigan. Do you know who lives there?" He turned his sights back to the boy.

Toby was preoccupied with the blood smeared along his hand.

The man watched the boy, saying nothing and seemingly curious in the child's assessment of his discovery.

Toby skimmed the trail of blood up the side of his forearm to determine the source of the cut he assumed he'd given himself when he'd fallen to the floor. He didn't find it. His eyes lowered to the wooden floor beside him where he caught a shimmer of something reflective in the light. More blood. The boy's heart sank. An explanation of why he hadn't heard a thing from the dog suddenly hit him like a Mack truck. Toby let out a howling, tormented scream that brought the shocked intruder to his feet.

Toby's eyes bulged wide and his pupils jerked from side to side. "He's dead! He's dead!" In reaction to this realization, his body flopped along the floor like a fish out of water. "No!"

He sprang to his knees momentarily before falling to the floor again. His arms pounded the floor planks and his legs kicked wildly along the side of the wooden cabinet in a tantrum that the intruder clearly had not predicted.

"Shut up!" yelled the man in his first tone of unrestrained anger. He drove the bottom of his boot into Toby's chest, pinning the flailing boy's body between the floor and cabinet.

Toby's limbs continued to pummel everything around him in a manner so savage that the large man nearly lost his balance. The raw, terrorized screams of panic kept erupting from between the boy's lips as the man continued to yell at him to shut up. In the panic, the man's foot slid from the boy's chest.

He snarled, then shoved his pistol somewhere under his jacket, dropped to a knee beside Toby, and grabbed the front of the boy's shirt with both hands. He yanked him away from the cabinet in one vicious movement and pulled him across the floor before whipping a leg around the boy and straddling him. A trail of the dog's blood was painted along the wooden floor where Toby had been dragged. The man yanked both of Toby's hands together above his head before pinning his wrists together with one hand. He clamped a hand down hard over Toby's mouth. The boy's eyes were still ballooned and his sweaty face was the color of a tomato.

The man leaned forward and edged his face to just an inch above Toby's. "Calm down! Calm down right now!"

Suddenly, the distinct sound of a car door slamming was heard from outside. Keeping Toby pinned to the floor, the man's attention whipped to the front door.

Chapter 19

Zed Hansen couldn't believe his eyes that morning when he observed a portly brown figure stumble out of the dense, wet woods and onto the dirt road about eighty yards in front of him. He half wondered if he'd just discovered the famous creature his nephew had once attempted to hunt down over thirty years ago. He chuckled over the memory. But as he drove closer, it quickly became apparent that it was just Hank Bailey, Sean's landlord. Clad in brown camouflage garb, black military boots, and some sort of headgear, Bailey's curious appearance compelled Zed to stop for a little back and forth.

With a twelve gauge shotgun hanging from his shoulder and a canvas bag heavy with rabbit carcasses grasped in his gloved hand, Bailey explained that he'd gotten up before sunrise to try out some night-time hunting with his new goggles.

"Works like a charm!" he said. "Yah just gotta close your eyes before you shoot or you'll get a wicked flash in the peepers!"

Zed was curious when Bailey mentioned where he'd gotten the night-visions. Sean hadn't said a thing about them to his uncle, who wondered where his admittedly broke nephew would have found the money to buy them in the first place. Zed took the opportunity to probe Bailey and discovered out how much money Sean still owed him for rent. The always compassionate uncle traced his finger along the dangling chain to his aged, leather wallet in his back pocket. He retrieved some bills and shoved them into the damp front pocket of Bailey's coat.

"He'll work it off," Zed pledged to Bailey, who couldn't have cared less about the detail but was happy to get paid.

Zed offered him a ride, but Bailey turned it down. It was no secret the former Marine liked returning from missions on his own. Zed tipped his hat and let the smooth roar of the truck engine and the smell of wet dirt flutter their way in through the open windows as he wound his way on up the road. He dug into his front shirt pocket and pulled a fresh toothpick from an open, plastic prescription bottle nested there. He quickly slid it between two teeth along his upper jaw. The founding owner of Hansen Security had been addicted to toothpicks since giving up a decades-long smoking habit a few years earlier. It felt naked not to have something dangling from his mouth, and he liked the natural taste of wood.

Sean's car wasn't parked out front at his house, which surprised Zed as he pulled up to the front steps. His nephew wasn't known to be an early riser or even a mid-morning riser. He was equally surprised to see Toby Parker's bike out front. He killed the engine. It rumbled for a few extra seconds before winding down. Stepping out and shutting the door, he raised his arms above his head, clasped his fingers together, and arched his back. A muffled, satisfying pop could be heard from just above his hips. His joints often got tight from the weather.

He happened to glance farther up the road where the path dead-ended into the forest. There was a dark gray, late '90s Buick sedan parked just behind a cluster of trees. He nearly didn't notice it, but the reflective chrome on the front bumper stuck out a few inches. He didn't recognize the car. It wasn't the kind one would typically see in Winston. It was then that he noticed the out-of-state license plate. The car was too far away to tell from where, but the colors didn't match any of the Colorado state–sanctioned ones—of that he was sure.

He raised his hat just long enough to wipe some stray beads of rain off his forehead with the arm of his long-sleeved, collared shirt. He proceeded on up the porch steps.

No one answered after the first set of knocks, so Zed tried again. He was sure he could hear movement from inside. "Sean? Toby?"

He walked down off the steps and over to the living room window to try peeking in through the curtains. Before he got there, however, he heard the creak of the front door and the cry of dry hinges. His head snapped back and he saw the door slowly opening. It stopped about a foot open and Toby's large head popped through.

"Toby!" Zed shouted in greeting with a large grin on his face. "How the hell are you?"

"Good," the boy replied almost before Zed had even finished his question. "Sean isn't here."

The boy didn't look well. His face was red and wet with perspiration. When Zed walked up the front steps and back onto the small porch, he thought it odd that Toby didn't open the door any wider, as if he was concealing something. He also noticed that the boy was out of breath.

"What's that ornery nephew of mine up to this morning?"

Toby quietly explained that Sean had left town for a few days and that he'd been asked to look after Rocco. This was news to Zed.

"He didn't tell you where he went?" Zed asked with narrowed eyes.

"No, sir."

Zed crossed his arms in front of him and nodded. He couldn't imagine where his nephew would have headed. Sean didn't take trips and had few if any friends outside of Winston to visit. "Well, I've got a job for him in a couple of days," he said. "He knows about it. I suspect that he'll be back before then. He's going to need this."

He dug into the front pocket of his jeans and pulled out a silver badge—a brand new one that read "Hansen Security." He held it up for Toby, who surprisingly seemed to take no interest in it. The boy didn't even glance down. His eyes stayed on Zed's like a hawk, nearly staring right through them.

"Are you feeling all right, bud?" asked Zed, lifting a brow.

Toby nodded and forced an awkward smile.

"Well, can you leave this for Sean?" Zed asked, holding out the badge for the boy to take.

Toby nodded again, his eyes still glued in place. He opened his hand and took the badge, but didn't look at it.

Zed knew something was wrong. Toby had never acted like this. He was typically a fountain of cordiality who could spew out a conversation on practically any topic for minutes on end, all while wearing a smile on his face. With the boy's head craned through the doorway and his suspicious behavior, it crossed Zed's mind that the boy might have just broken something in Sean's apartment and was too embarrassed or scared to let him find out about it. A plausible scenario for a boy his age, but it seemed unlikely. He'd always known Toby to be a straight shooter, even when the truth he told was inappropriate in the given setting. If he'd broken something, he'd speak up about it.

The boy cracked another dry smile and said nothing. He had something shiny and new in his hand—his hero's badge of honor—and he wasn't even looking at it. Zed had been in security for years. He had a trained eye and a deep instinct for things that were out of place and didn't add up. A talent he hoped he had passed on to his nephew. Something was very wrong—he knew it.

The old floorboards inside Sean's living room often creaked. They probably should have been replaced years ago. Any movement or shift of weight typically generated an audible groan. When those sounds echoed out at a moment Zed was sure Toby hadn't moved a muscle, it grabbed his attention.

"What have you got planned for the day?" he asked calmly as his eyes traced the narrow gaps between the door's hinges, suspecting that Toby wasn't alone inside.

He saw nothing along the inner side of the door. Too dark. With Sean's car gone and the display of genuine fear in Toby's eyes, Zed was certain his nephew wasn't the puppet-master. He subtly glanced back at the Buick. It was too well concealed by the trees to tell if anyone was sitting inside it, but his instincts told him there wasn't.

Had Toby walked in on a burglary? he wondered. *Someone who Sean owed money to, now coming to collect? Where's Rocco? Why didn't he bark when I knocked on the door?*

He turned back to Toby when the boy didn't answer his question. There was now pure, unmistakable panic in the boy's face, as if his brain had already been overloaded and Zed's last query finally froze it. The lack of response would surely not go unnoticed by whoever was on the other side of that door. Zed couldn't recall a time when Toby had ever looked him straight in the eye, but he'd been doing just that from the moment he'd opened the door. Those eyes were pleading for help. No doubt about it now. There was someone standing on the other side of that door—someone dangerous. Zed sometimes carried a pistol in a holster along his hip, but not this day. He had the .45 caliber in his glove box, but at that moment it felt a mile away.

He almost mouthed the boy a message, but felt whoever was inside might see him through the darkened crack along the edge of the door. He kept his head level but his eyes dropped to the keyhole at the center of the doorknob. Scratch marks as if someone had jimmied it. Zed maintained a composed facial expression, even forming a grin as he nodded his head. One more glance back at the Buick before it was time to escalate things. His mouth formed a pucker before he shot the toothpick out of his mouth as if he was discharging a blowgun.

"Well, I'm going to take on off, Toby," he said in the friendliest valediction he could muster.

He didn't wait to observe the boy's reaction. Instead, he planted his feet as firmly as he could along the damp porch, left foot spread out in front of the right. He launched forward, latching onto the front of the boy's jacket along his chest line with clenched fists. In one fluid movement, he violently yanked the boy toward him while sending a sharp kick into the dead center of the wooden door. The door swung open to about a forty-five degree angle before it cracked into something solid, bringing its momentum to an abrupt halt. Zed twisted his hips and let Toby's off-balanced body fly passed him, crashing down along the porch steps before rolling to the ground in a heap.

"Run, Toby!" he yelled. "Don't turn back!"

He saw a large set of fingers latch onto the outside edge of the door, preparing to swing it open. The door whipped inside and so did Zed, driving forward and lowering his shoulder into the chest of the tall figure he'd barely gotten a glimpse of.

Toby scrambled along the ground, breathless to get to his feet. His head spun to the door. His wide eyes captured a brief view of two men wrestling violently along the floor inside. A stray boot swung into the door and it slammed shut. Loud, angry obscenities and the sound of raw, barbaric battle poured out from inside—breaking glass, splintering wood, and objects crashing down to the floor.

The sight of Zed's red face with a large vein protruding at the center of his forehead as he shouted commands was etched in Toby's vision like the lingering blast from a flashbulb. It transposed everything else. The moment Toby sprung to an upright position, the ear-splitting rage of a gunshot brought the calamity inside to an immediate end. His mouth hung open. He nearly fell back to the ground but heard Zed's last order echo through his skull a second time.

He could feel his heart pounding as he lumbered toward the side of the building. He looked back to see the intruder step out onto the porch and hurriedly scan the scene outside. His head pivoted toward Toby and their eyes met. The man's arm swung up, parallel to the ground with his hand firmly latched onto his firearm.

Toby's shins collided with a foot-high, rotted wooden planter. He cried in pain as he toppled over it, landing chin and chest first in an aggregation of wet, wild flowers and weeds stemming out from the other side of the planter.

"Hold it, fucker!" a sharp command echoed out from the opposite side of the building.

The voice didn't belong to the intruder, but Toby wasn't going to stick around to find out who issued it. He crawled to his feet and glanced back as he scurried down the short hill that led around toward the basement entrance of the building.

Toby noticed blood soaked along both of his pant legs in front of his shins. He was missing a shoe now, but he kept his legs moving.

The man who'd held the boy captive inside looked frozen except for his neck, which slowly rotated in the direction of the commanding voice.

"Drop that piece! Now, asshole!" Hank Bailey threatened thunderously with his twelve gauge shotgun pointed directly at the intruder from about fifteen feet away.

The moist sack of dead rabbits lay in a clump beside his boots as the out-of-breath landlord kept one eye closed and the other aimed through his sights. The night-visions were still suctioned to the top of his head with the lenses pointed up to the trees.

The intruder glared emotionlessly at the bald and stout old man dressed in camo holding him at gunpoint.

"I said drop it!" Bailey shouted again.

The intruder lowered his head and opened his hand. The pistol dropped over the porch railing and down to the dirt ground with a thud. An almost sadistic grin formed on Bailey's mouth under his flared nostrils as he ordered the stranger to raise both hands, turn around, and face him. The stranger complied as Toby's footsteps could still be heard in motion around the corner of the building, though they were becoming fainter.

"Where'd you get those goggles?" the stranger brazenly asked.

"*I'm* asking the questions, dickhead! What the fuck's going on here?" Bailey shouted. "Where's Zed?"

"Who?" said the intruder with dismissive, almost bored eyes.

"The man whose truck's parked right here beside me!" Bailey answered, his face beginning to turn red. "The Big Boy wants answers, and he wants 'em now!"

The intruder responded, "Oh, that guy. I killed him."

The man's words were laced with such callous apathy that Bailey wasn't sure he'd heard him right.

"Down off the porch and get down on your chest!" the anxious Bailey wailed. The former Marine's tongue slid across his upper lip as he kept a sober aim on the man. He wasn't sure he believed the man's previous statement but he wasn't taking any chances. "Zed?" he yelled toward the house.

The intruder smirked as he steadily walked down off the porch with his hands raised.

Once the man's feet were on the ground, Bailey noticed how truly large in size he was. He carefully dropped to his knees, his eyes and smirk still stuck to Bailey.

There was no answer from inside the house.

Small rocks and gravel lined the ground in front of the porch and they crackled under the man's knees as he lowered himself down to his chest. He left his neck arched and rested his chin on the ground so he could face the landlord. His arms were spread out to his sides, posing his body in the shape of a crucifix.

Keeping aim, Bailey carefully edged his way over to Zed's truck.

The stranger's eyes followed him.

Bailey knew Zed kept a CB on the dashboard.

When Bailey momentarily lowered his left hand off the gun stock to grab the door handle, the intruder discreetly shifted the torso of his body at a slight angle.

Toby scurried across some of the large protruding rocks that rested at the bottom of the shallow creek. With no traction under his right foot, he lost his footing and fell knee-deep into the water. The water was ice-cold, but he quickly maintained his balance and sloshed over to the other side. The forest was thick with pine beyond the creek. Small bubbles squished their way out through the boy's saturated, frigid shoe with each step he took up the hillside before him. His other foot felt practically numb. In seconds he had tree cover, but he climbed higher, brushing away needled branches and avoiding stepping on dead wood so as not to generate any loud sounds.

A sudden, piercing array of sirens and horns honking in succession erupted through the valley. The sound was immediately recognizable to Toby as that of a car alarm. The boy's gaze shot up from the sight of his bloodstained legs to a sliver of space between two large pine branches. He winced at the clamor of gunshots that immediately accompanied the racket. They sounded more like popping firecrackers from the distance. His face shriveled and the tears returned while he bit down on his lower lip. The sirens and honks continued for nearly twenty seconds before they halted.

A sharp chirp emitted somewhere from under the hood of the Buick, and its driving lights flickered on and off one last time. The stranger's distraction had worked. He returned his remote car key to his side pocket and looked down in annoyance at the mud now caked on the front of his jacket. Just a few yards in front of him lay Bailey, motionless. Three shots through his chest, which looked like a roadmap of blood that drained off along different side streets. The intruder's hand gripped what looked like a small toy gun, similar to a fancy, pistol-shaped, metallic cigarette lighter from a scene in a retro movie. He rolled up his jacket sleeve, revealing a leather cast wrapped around his thick forearm. It was bound together at the ends by two buckle straps. At its center, a metal sliding rail was attached to it. Out from it extended a metal rod that was attached to the small pistol. The man tried to push the gun back toward the opposite end of the sliding rail, but it only slid back an inch before the sound of a spring popping preceded a complete loss of pressure along the rail. With an agitated sneer, he quickly unbuckled the cast and yanked it off his arm, tossing it to the ground. He briskly walked across the front of the house, retrieved his pistol, and hustled over to where he'd seen the boy scamper down the hill.

Before him, about fifty yards away, stood hundreds of pine trees blanketing the side of the hill, beginning at the foot of a narrow creek that meandered its way slowly down a decline that ran parallel with the dirt road. Starting at about thirty or forty feet above the ground line, a layer of fog or mist began, concealing the top portion of the hill. His eyes slowly panned the landscape, searching for the child.

The man continued his scan for another minute while listening for sounds along the hill. He heard nothing other than wind, flowing water, and a couple of birds. He then walked back toward Bailey, picking his sleeve-gun up off the ground on the way.

Toby had been able to see the man, not well, but clearly enough from his momentary hiding spot behind a group of large rocks that jetted up skyward like a natural defense barrier. Thick trees that spawned out from under the formation lay crisscrossed in front of him, concealing him well. He watched the dangerous man as his gaze methodically swept from side to side. Toby sat completely still and silent.

Once he saw the man disappear back behind the house, he breathed again. He was sure Zed had been killed and feared that he would surely be next if he gave the strange man time to catch up with him. After taking one last glance back down the mountainside, he turned toward the face of the mountain and began climbing again.

He'd been told not to stop by the man that saved his life, a man that was probably dead, and he was going to honor that command.

The man paused when he got to the dead Marine. Shaking his head in revulsion, he leaned forward and grabbed the goggle netting wrapped around Bailey's head, pulling the head up with it. He yanked the night-visions off of him. The landlord's head dropped back to the ground with a dank thud. With the goggles and sleeve-gun contraption dangling from his fist, the man re-entered the house to snag the briefcase. Moments later, he was back outside and walking up the road toward the Buick. Within seconds, the car was cruising down the dirt road, back the way Toby had ridden in from that morning.

Toby never heard the crank of a car starting up or the roar of an engine; all sound was blocked by the wind and his own labored breathing as he dashed up the hillside.

Chapter 20

Something was wrong. She was certain of it.

It was the heightened sense of a chronically tired, single mother whose entire life was invested in her son. With the challenges she faced on a daily basis, it was the strict adherence to rules and routine that kept her grounded and sane. Her son had learned to be compliant. It had taken years of trying patience to get there through sometimes unconventional practices, but the two now had a clear, mutually respectful understanding that he'd have his freedom within the limits of Winston as long as she knew his whereabouts at all times. It had been suggested in a book she'd read by one of the many experts in the field. At his age, it was time to "pull back, give him more independence," but keep a tight hold on the itinerary. That schedule always included him being home each evening by six o'clock for dinner, even during the summer. By 6:15, she was already in her car, looking for him.

Joan Parker slowed to a stop and studied each side street with an intense scrutiny. Her worried eyes from behind thick-framed glasses traced the shoulder of each road until it disappeared around a bend or up over a hill. The sun set early for those living between tall mountain ranges, and dusk had already arrived.

She'd worked her way backwards from where he was supposed to be last—Crowley's Books in town. Toby enjoyed spending time there. He rarely purchased anything, but the owner, Pat Crowley, never seemed to care. Though the boy would usually talk his ear off when he first got there, the boy would soon end up at a small, round table hidden near the back of the shop. There, under a bright brass lamp, his face would be buried in a picture book or atlas for roughly thirty minutes alongside a caffeine-free fountain drink from Perdey's, the local convenience store. Neither Crowley nor Perdey had seen him that day.

Before that, he was supposed to have let Sean Coleman's dog out and feed him dinner. But with the Arapahoe Café being right in town, Joan stopped in to make sure Toby had eaten lunch there earlier in the day. He hadn't. In fact, his favorite waitress had even prepped a French dip sandwich with fries for him, but it had gone cold and was tossed in a waste can at his absence. Something was indeed very wrong.

Despite the chill outside, Joan kept both side windows on her pale blue Ford Maverick rolled down, praying to hear the high-pitched sound of Toby's bike bell as she made her way to Meyers Bridge. At one point, she thought she'd heard it, prompting her to slam on the brakes and skid about ten feet. After stepping outside her car and calling his name several times, however, she was convinced she was wrong. That didn't stop her from staring intently through her rearview mirror as she left the area. Leaning forward in her seat, she couldn't help but notice how old and sunken her eyes looked. She was too young to have eyes like that. They told a story of hardship that she had never burdened others with the details of.

Once she reached the abutment, she parked and flung open the driver's side door, and before she knew it, she was down alongside the fast flowing river, navigating stones and saturated tree limbs. Her short, delicate frame would have made her look like a child to someone watching from a distance. The spray wetted her neck as she twisted her head under the bridge, looking for any signs of her son. The dampness in the air flattened her short, graying hair to her head. She knew her son wouldn't have gotten himself close enough to the rapids to be swept away. He'd grown up in the area. He knew better. But she also knew not to underestimate his misguided commitment to earn the unobtainable respect of the town idiot, Sean Coleman.

Her son was convinced that the obnoxious and self-centered security man was a friend despite all evidence to the contrary. She'd read in the paper of what she perceived to be the drunken delusions of an attention-starved worm who thought he'd seen a man kill himself. Ironically, her son seemed more motivated to clear Sean Coleman's name than Sean himself was. Otherwise, why would he have left town after making such a ridiculous assertion? Still, Toby believed he was telling the truth when everyone else didn't. And if there was anything that was going to knock her son off his schedule, it would be his determination to vindicate his hero by finding that body. But Toby wasn't at the bridge either, nor was his bike.

With Sean out of town, she simply hadn't seen the harm in letting her son take care of the aged wiener-dog that he often talked about and whose breed he had even researched. She believed now that it had been a mistake. Anything to do with Sean Coleman was poison, and a storm of regret punished her soul as she sped up the soggy dirt road that sprayed her car fenders brown.

When she reached the darkened house, her headlights first exposed Zed Hansen's truck parked out front, and soon after, her son's bicycle leaning along the railing beside the front door. A wave of relief warmed her chest. Despite the piece of rotted fruit on his family tree, Zed was a good, responsible man who would insulate her son from any half-cocked influence that Sean might apply to him. Her relief instantly turned to anger, however, once it became clear to her that her son had completely deviated from his schedule and let her worry so terribly. She was certain the explanation would somehow lead to Sean, and she prepared herself to lay out a verbal assault on him once her son was sitting safely out of earshot in the passenger seat of her car.

She got out and slammed the car door behind her, leaving the engine running and headlights on. She marched loudly up the handful of planked steps to the front door, intending for the angry stomps of her feet to be heard by all inside. She found it curious that the front door was partially open and there was no light coming from inside.

"Toby?" she said in a stern voice. "Toby!"

When no sound could be heard from inside, she slowly pushed the door open. Its dry hinges whined in dissent. She poked her head inside. "Toby?"

The headlights from her car had lit up the entranceway from a favorable angle but did practically nothing to shed clarity on whatever was inside. A chill in the air forced her to raise her shoulders to protect her neck under the thin collar of her jacket. She pushed the door open until it was wide and reached along the inside wall, fumbling for a light switch. She found it, and her howling scream quickly funneled its way up through the small canyon surrounding the house.

Cries of her son's name bounced off every corner of Sean's small apartment as Joan frantically searched through each room, flipping up more light switches and swinging open closet doors. She staggered back outside to the porch step and held onto the wooden railing to keep from collapsing. She raised her head and screamed her son's name again in utter desperation and helplessness, not knowing what fate had befallen him.

She carried no cellphone. They rarely worked in the mountains of Winston so few of the residents owned them. After overcoming the invisible barrier that was averting her from stepping over the wide-eyed, pale, and bloody body of Zed Hansen on the floor, she managed to steady her hands long enough to poke the number for the police station into a wall-mounted phone she'd spotted near the kitchen. When no sound came out of the receiver, she frantically pounded the hook switch, to no avail. Her mind leapt to Zed's truck parked outside and the large, trademark antenna stuck to its roof.

Joan was back out the door in seconds, running in and out of the beams of light cast by the Maverick's headlights. As she got to the truck she raised her hand toward where she believed the handle was, but suddenly felt her legs being swept out from under her by an unseen, large object lying across her path. She fell on top of it, nearly cracking her head against the partially open driver's side door. Her glasses had fallen from her face but she didn't need them to know that the weight and shape of the object below her was a body. Her heart stopped.

"No! No!" she tried to scream out, but the words left her mouth in more of a whimper.

Her hands feverishly followed the body up to its face as tears spewed down her own. Her fingertips searched for Toby's dimples but instead found a coat of coarse whiskers and a bald head that made her snort in alleviated relief in an otherwise horrific situation. Her head bent down to the man's chest as she nearly passed out from the frenzy of emotions that pumped rapidly through her body.

When the brights from Chief Lumbergh's Jeep lit up the teetering outline of Joan Parker's dainty frame, she resembled a zombie from a horror film with her drained, emotionless eyes and colorless skin. Her arm was raised to capture the attention of the oncoming vehicle. The chief's eye quickly detected a streak of what appeared to be blood along her chin. He began flicking brass switches that commanded the rack of lights mounted along the roof. They flashed on and illuminated the entire area. A spotlight above his side mirror came on too. His teeth were already pounding a stick of gum.

Out of breath from the moment he'd received Joan's distressed and disjointed broadcast from the dispatch speaker hooked under the dashboard of his Jeep, the chief turned to his wife in the seat and told her to stay put until he checked things out. He'd been halfway up the dirt driveway to his own home when the call began.

He'd planned to take Diana out to catch dinner in town. He'd even changed clothes before he left work. Never could he have imagined the night would have taken such a harrowing, life-altering turn.

Diana wasn't about to sit still. Her uncle was dead and only God knew where her brother was. With eye shadow and lipstick decorating her attractive face, she looked more like she was arriving at an awards banquet than a crime scene.

The Jeep skidded to a halt and when both doors flew open, the cold night air poured in. The dome light exposed Lumbergh was in civilian garb—plaid shirt and khakis with brown leather dress shoes. His Glock was drawn from the brown, leather side-holster he'd strapped below his ribcage on the drive over.

"Where is he?" Joan shouted as she quickly approached them. "What's that bastard done to my son?"

She sounded so exhausted that Diana could barely make out her words. When they neared, the chief's wife threw her arms around the distraught mother's shoulders and pulled her into a tight embrace. Joan's arms went straight down to her sides like a puppet that'd had its strings cut. Though showing indifference to the support offered by the sister of the man she blamed for her torment, she didn't adamantly reject it. Tears welled up in her eyes again.

Lumbergh was all business, directing both of them to the side of his Jeep. He told them that Jefferson would be there soon and to stay where they were until he got there. The area was not secure. With his eyes shifting back and forth from the front door to the corners of the house, he cautiously moved in, his gun out in front of him and his other hand clenching the upper neck of a Mag light in case he needed to club someone dashing out from the night. His instincts, however, told him that the action was long over.

As expected from the details of Joan's broadcast, he spotted Bailey first. A clump of brown camo with dried blood splattered thoroughly along his chest and some on the ground beside him. Lumbergh didn't bother to take a pulse. He'd seen enough dead bodies in his time to know not to bother. Bailey's shotgun was off to his side and next to it there was a spent shell. Gary wondered if the strong, stout Marine had gotten a clean round off at the assailant. Also beside the body was a large, brown burlap bag that also appeared to have blood on it. Against his professional crime scene judgment, Gary gave the bag a nudge with the outside of his foot. A couple of rabbit carcasses poured out through the opening, with the promise of others inside. *All of those rabbits' feet but no luck for Bailey*, Lumbergh thought with irony.

It was a challenge for him to keep his mind focused on the task at hand with the stakes so personal. *My God*, he thought, *what part did Sean play in this?* He knew his brother-in-law had serious problems. He'd even speculated, on occasion, that he might be mentally ill. But he couldn't fathom the notion that Sean Coleman would harm his own uncle, or shoot *anyone*, for that matter. He couldn't have been behind the morbid scene, but it had to come back to him somehow. Ideas flashed through his mind: Maybe Sean owed someone money and the person who did this was a lender. Maybe Zed showed up at the wrong time, a confrontation ensued, and all hell broke loose. Was that why Sean had skipped town? To avoid collection?

Joan's bellowing forced the investigation to the back of the chief's mind. First things first. With his gun at his side, he slid inside through the open door and into the lit room. There, he saw Zed's body among overturned furniture, a broken chair, and shattered glass—some brown, probably from beer bottles, and some clear chards that he couldn't place the source of. It had been one hell of a struggle. Scuff marks and scratches marked the wood floor. He was thankful that Diana was outside. Zed had been shot through the throat. The bullet looked to have exited out the back of his head and probably came to a stop somewhere in the wall or floor. His eyes, still exuding a sense of kindness, were left in a gaze aimed up at the ceiling. Lumbergh fought the urge to choke up. Zed was a good man. He was family.

A separate, thin trail of blood led Lumbergh around the edge of Sean's kitchen counter. There he found the crimson-laced carcass of Rocco. Gary's face twisted in puzzlement at the site. *What kind of sick person would do that? Why would he bother?*

He quickly checked out the rest of the house. He found nothing of note. The place wasn't ransacked, just messy by nature because of Sean's chosen lifestyle. A burglary didn't appear to be the motivation.

When he saw the flashing, colorful lights of Jefferson's cruiser beaming through the curtains, he stepped outside and yelled to the officer to call in the county medical examiner before bringing in the cameras.

Gary walked down around the corner of the house to Bailey's side. His door was locked, which wasn't a surprise. Bailey's clothes suggested that he'd been outside when the attack started. He sent an elbow through a glass pane on the door, then reached around and unlocked it from the inside. It didn't take him long to secure the living quarters.

As he began to make his way back up to the vehicles, a partially open steel telephone box on the side of the building stole his attention. He narrowed the beam of his flashlight through it and saw that the phone wires had been yanked.

"Jesus," he muttered before recording a mental note that fingerprints should be taken there first due to the smooth surface of the box.

When he got back to the vehicles, Gary pulled Diana aside after briefly eavesdropping on Jefferson's radio conversation to make sure correct requests were being made. With his lips close to his wife's ear, he spoke softly and calmly of the scene inside. He excluded the gory details but provided enough information to answer the questions she surely had. Her strong-scented perfume, which he normally found alluring, tickled his nose and provided a stark contrast between what the evening should have been and what it had become. He felt her body tense up when he spoke of Rocco.

While riding quietly over from her house alongside her husband, Diana had prepared herself for the impending specifics on her uncle, but a thought hadn't crossed her mind about the beloved pet she'd rescued from an animal shelter in Denver over a decade ago. The composure she'd admirably shown since their arrival suddenly dissipated like the warm, visible breaths that left her mouth. She buried her head in Gary's shoulder where her eyes soaked through his shirt. She felt the palm of her husband's thin hand along the back of her head.

She sensed a pair of eyes beaming down on her and she turned to meet Joan's lost, sunken gaze. The befuddled mother's mute demeanor was a disjointed blend of anger and helplessness. Diana knew she blamed Sean for the carnage and her son's disappearance. Joan had made that quite clear while Gary was checking out the house. There was nothing Diana could do to lessen her pain.

"We're going to find your son," Diana heard her husband say with a level of confidence that was so direly needed.

Joan's unchanged expression proved that she didn't believe him. Everyone knew her son was her life. Without him, she couldn't imagine a reason for continuing to live.

Regret for not pressing Toby for Sean's whereabouts the other day at the bridge left an uneasy feeling in Gary's gut. Sean didn't carry a cellphone and he wasn't one to check in with family or anyone else.

"I've got a shoe over here," Jefferson reported loudly from the far side of the house.

All heads spun in the direction of the officer's voice. None of them had noticed his meandering away from the police cruiser. With all attention now on him, his sneer dampened; this was no time to gloat in the knowledge that he'd found something important—something that would surely impress his boss. He kept his flashlight trained on a black high-top shoe that was largely concealed by tall grass and other groundcover. It looked too small to belong to an adult.

Once close enough, Joan excitedly identified it as Toby's.

"What does it mean?" asked Diana of her husband.

She peered down along his face as he gazed out at the dense hillside beyond the winding, slow-moving creek just outside the perimeters of Bailey's property. She could almost hear the turning of gears in his head under the hurried gnawing from his jaw. The chief slowly raised his flashlight out at the vast layer of evergreens. Taking his boss's queue, Jefferson did the same.

Chapter 21

"It sounds like it's working, Mrs. Kimble," a friendly male voice acknowledged through the speaker with a chuckle.

"Thanks, Marty," answered Lisa with a hint of embarrassment in her voice. "I'm sorry to bother you."

"It's no bother at all. Are you expecting Mr. Kimble tonight?"

Lisa's shoulders drooped. "Tonight and the two nights before that."

Silence on the other end.

"Mr. Kimble has a very imposing and unpredictable work schedule, Marty," she explained. "It's not uncommon for days to go by without us talking."

Her elbows lowered to the flat face of the marble bar counter resting in front of her. An audible sigh dropped from her lips. She glanced out the large kitchen window that overlooked the winding driveway which was dimly lit by staggered accent lamps. "We planned this trip some time ago. I was hoping that his job wouldn't interfere this time, but it did. He promised it wouldn't take more than a day or two, and then he'd meet me out here."

"You haven't heard from him at all?" asked Marty.

"No. No phone calls at all since I got here. That's why I thought I'd have someone call me back to make sure this thing is even working. Again, I appreciate you doing me the favor."

"Does he carry a cellphone with him? Or a work number you could reach him at?"

"No," she answered, eyeing the remnants of a salad she'd fixed for herself earlier in the night. "He's not in the office and he can't easily use a cellphone in the field."

"The field? What does he do?"

She didn't answer and kicked herself for offering up such information.

After a moment, Marty spoke. "I'm sorry, ma'am. That's none of my business."

"It's okay," she quickly interjected, recognizing that it wasn't fair to make him feel awkward for asking a common question. "He's an accountant."

There was no acknowledgment from him. She visualized the expression most likely draped across his face—one of puzzlement over why an accountant would work such odd hours when it wasn't tax season and why contacting him was so difficult. She leaned back against the backrest of her stool and crossed her legs in front of her. It would have been a good time to adjourn the conversation, but she felt drawn to continue. She hadn't chatted with anyone for days. She was lonely.

"Marty, are you married?" she heard herself ask.

Perhaps too personal and probing of a question for a resident to ask, but he didn't seem to mind.

"I'm divorced."

"Kids?"

"Yes. I have a daughter. Her name is Katy. She's four. The light of my life."

She smiled, absorbing the pride and sincerity in his voice. "How long have you been divorced?"

"About a year."

She nodded her head, took a moment, then asked, "Has it been tough?" She heard what sounded like a sigh on the other end. It was a question that most certainly had no short answer. She winced. *Definitely too personal.* "I'm sorry, Marty. Now that's none of my business."

He quickly replied, "Oh, don't worry about it, Mrs. Kimble."

"You can call me Lisa."

"Lisa. I don't mind talking about my marriage. It's just not the type of conversation I'm used to having with residents. Those are usually along the lines of *Do you think we'll get any rain today?* or *I'm expecting guests for dinner.*"

She giggled. "Yes, I suppose that's true."

Marty explained that the divorce had had its ups and downs. Child custody was an issue, but both sides eventually settled on an arrangement he could swallow. His ex-wife was already remarried, which made things difficult on him and created concerns with his daughter's living situation. As the call continued, the conversation became more comfortable. Lisa soon felt like she was talking to an old friend—one with some gentlemanly maturity. She reminisced about growing up outside of Billings, Montana, and complained of the brutal summers in Nevada. She'd lived there since college, choosing UNLV after her high school boyfriend had earned a football scholarship there. They broke up before graduation. She didn't bring up her own marriage, however. She wasn't ready for that.

"Thanks for lending me your ear tonight, Marty. I really appreciate it. I know it's not in your job description to help pass the time for bored residents in the middle of the night."

"Believe me, anything away from the normal routine is a good thing. Things down here have been slow, and I've enjoyed the company. Only a half hour to go and I'm done until the morning."

She could feel him grinning through the receiver. She glanced up at a wooden clock that lined the dining room wall. Since her arrival, its intrusive ticking had worn on her nerves. She'd even considered stopping the pendulum the day before. But for the past hour, she hadn't noticed it once.

"Oh my. It's eleven thirty," she said.

"Yes ma'am. I mean, Lisa."

She didn't want to hang up the phone, but knew she'd long outworn her welcome. Still, she felt wide awake. "One last thing. A couple years ago, I checked out a movie at your station down there. Do you guys still do that?"

He answered yes, but quickly apologized for the weak selection of video tapes. He began reading off titles, none of which was newer than four years old. She stood and stretched her free arm up toward the open bedroom loft, then walked into the living room where the flush carpet felt good under her bare feet.

"*Last of the Mohicans*," she decided. "I love a good romance."

She crossed in front of a wall mirror and stopped to take inventory of herself. The slow moving ceiling fan high above dabbled with her hair. She reached back behind her head and unhinged her ponytail, letting her blonde locks float down to just above her shoulders.

"Sounds good, Lisa. I'll watch for your headlights."

"Marty," she responded, "why don't you bring it up in thirty minutes once you're off . . .? And why don't you stay and watch it with me?"

Chapter 22

The circular outlines of the traffic lights were hazy and nearly conjoined as best Sean's weary eyes could decipher. He used the palm of his hand to tug at his lower eyelid in an effort to keep his right eye open enough to read the street signs. It was very late by the time he'd finally arrived in Traverse City. Despite the darkness and the humidity that his windshield defroster battled, he could tell that upstate Michigan was lush with heavy trees and occasional wide open areas nestled in between them. Boats sitting on trailers were a common sight. Street lamps were few and far between, which left his car's headlights the only warning signal for the frequent roadkill that littered the roads. There was a constant dampness in the air though he had encountered little rain on his way in.

Most things in town were closed but he wasn't concerned with the business district. He was determined to reach his final destination, the location that appeared to be taking him to the outskirts. He'd picked up a city map at a gas station after conservatively electing to fill his tank a quarter full. There, he grabbed some individual slices of pepperoni pizza—the second heating lamp delicacy he'd enjoyed in less than twenty-four hours. They were easy to eat while he drove. The last fifteen minutes had been spent flicking the dome light on and off to verify on the map that he was heading in the right direction.

After he crossed a three-way intersection, a new subdivision crept up on the left. Its perimeter was surrounded by an eight-foot-high, unlit brick wall with overhanging foliage and thick tree limbs sprouting out from behind it. It was clear to Sean that he had just entered an upscale area. A break in the wall up ahead suggested an entrance. He didn't notice the discreet black and white street sign labeled Bluff Walk Road until he had practically passed it. Bearing down on the brake pedal, he prepared for a sharp left turn, but an imposing black, steel gate stood in opposition. He caught a glimpse of a small brick building in front of it with a single light turned on inside its side window. Yanking the steering wheel to the right to turn off onto an adjacent side street, he grimaced at the honk from an annoyed late-night driver behind him as he screeched off the main drag. Sean flipped a U-turn along the narrow street and parked under a row of fruit trees where he could see the gate from about forty yards away. He turned off the headlights and engine.

Sitting inside the small building, which he recognized as a guard station, was a uniformed man. He appeared to be on the phone, engaged in a cordial conversation. Though Sean could only see him from the waist up, he seemed to have a thin but athletic build and was probably in his early forties. With blonde, short feathered hair and clad in his neatly pressed light-blue uniform, he reminded Sean of a toy soldier.

With his nagging fatigue dividing what should have been a moment in triumph over arriving at his long-awaited destination, his mind chose to allocate what little energy it had left to wondering what kind of wages the guard was pulling in. Sean was certain it was more than he, just based on the geography alone.

He pressed the palms of his hands into the steering wheel, straightened his arms, and flattened his damp back into his seat. The crackling of his joints brought some marginal relief after a hard day's drive. His eyes were fluttering and he was convinced whatever was on the other side of that gate would have to remain a mystery until the morning. He incautiously crawled back over the driver's seat and his large body crumbled down into the back. He remembered little else before he drifted off to sleep, other than the faint smell of nectar and soothing, crisp night air.

Chapter 23

"Toby!" His name was shouted throughout the darkened forest for nearly thirty minutes, echoing under the spitting sleet that dropped from the sky.

Their cries had prompted no response and the men from the Winston police department lost track of the boy's trail. They knew he'd made it at least to the other side of the creek, but couldn't find much sign of him beyond where his footprints had disappeared into the underbrush. The only crumb of comfort came from the fact that the unusually large footprints, which were assumed to belong to the killer, could not be found in pursuit of the boy. They instead led to an area behind some trees where tire tracks revealed that a car had been parked. Lumbergh called on Ron Oldhorse.

It was fair to say that Oldhorse was an eccentric, a term that could have easily been applied to many who lived in the secluded, mountainous region that surrounded Winston. Adopted and raised by a small restaurant owner and his wife in the Denver metro area, his legal name from years ago was Ronald Wilson. Oldhorse's childhood was pretty typical of most kids brought up in the city: public schooling, intramural sports, a part-time job working for his parents. Yet, he never sensed that he quite fit in with those he lived among, even in a region somewhat known for its racial diversity and multiple ethnic backgrounds.

In his teens, Oldhorse had formed a deep fascination with the history of the Lakota Indian tribe that he'd discovered his biological parents were descendants of. His mother and father had died in a house fire when he was an infant. His interest in the tribe became an obsession once he returned to Colorado after a few years in the US Army infantry, much of which he'd spent overseas. Despite the bonds he'd formed in the military, he returned to the state as a loner after his adoptive parents retired and moved to Florida. Over the next couple of years, he'd tracked down and sought wisdom among Lakota tribe elders, even traveling throughout the Dakota states and learning to live off the land while he worked as a ranch hand outside of Rosebud, South Dakota.

No one knew what eventually brought Oldhorse to the hills outside of Winston. Some suspected that he'd gotten in some sort of legal trouble up north, but it was nothing more than pure speculation among a rural citizenry that loved its gossip. He was rarely seen in town, infrequently turning up in a local store, picking up supplies or selling well-crafted wood carvings. His home for the past several years had been a bare-bones cabin without a phone or electricity, wedged along a slope near Red Cliff about three miles from Bailey's house.

Lumbergh had once been told by the previous police chief that Oldhorse "seemed like a man who was on an endless journey to find what he was looking for, but had long ago lost track of what that was." He'd also been told by the former chief that Oldhorse was the best hunter and tracker he'd ever met. When out in the woods, no blemish escaped his notice and no prey escaped his crosshairs.

Lumbergh watched Jefferson pull up the driveway behind his Jeep and join multiple county squad cars already on the scene. The area was a flurry of officers and activity. The perimeter was being taped off, photographs were being snapped, and multiple work-lights on tripods lit up the range.

Oldhorse was riding shotgun alongside Jefferson, and in his officer's eyes Lumbergh read a tale of considerable stress. Jefferson's face was pale, and he looked like he'd been sweating. The men stepped out of the car. Oldhorse seemed emotionless. His salt and pepper, long hair that had been jet-black in his youth was uncharacteristically void of a ponytail. Looking a little heavier than the last time Lumbergh had seen him, he wore an oversized denim shirt under a half-dozen beaded necklaces with stone pendants and jeans with tall moccasin boots that came up to just under his knees. A sparse mustache decorated his upper lip.

The men approached the chief, and before Lumbergh could thank Oldhorse for coming, the rugged Native American quickly spoke in his eerily monotone voice: "Tell me that the lost boy isn't Sean Coleman."

Lumbergh was taken aback by the statement. He looked at Jefferson, who shook his head and rolled his eyes.

Oldhorse continued. "Tell me that I'm not being asked to find the yuhektob who once called me Tonto and asked if there was gambling on my reservation."

Lumbergh's shoulders sank. "No. It's Toby Parker who's lost," he clarified. "Didn't Jefferson explain that?"

Jefferson loudly jumped in to defend himself. "It's a little tough to talk when a knife is being held to your throat!"

An annoyed and dismissive grunt left Oldhorse's gullet before he turned toward the officer with irritated, narrow eyes. "As I said; I didn't know it was you that was floundering up my hill like a wounded rhino."

Jefferson puffed out his chest. "Well if you had a driveway like a normal person, you'd have seen my squad lights and—"

Lumbergh grabbed Jefferson's shoulder and commanded his silence with a parental glare. He quickly explained the situation to Oldhorse, who sponged up the details without expression. In fact, the quirky recluse displayed such little acknowledgment that Lumbergh half-wondered if anything he'd said had been heard. He looked to be in a hypnotic trance, as if he'd been driving through the desert for hours. Only when his small, precise eyes began shifting from side to side did Lumbergh recognize a hint of comprehension.

Just as the chief turned to point toward the creek where they had lost Toby's trail, Oldhorse jetted off in an adjacent direction, walking purposefully toward Lumbergh's Jeep where the boy's mother was sitting inside the open passenger door.

A sheriff's department coat was draped over Joan Parker's low-hanging shoulders, and her short legs hung outside of the vehicle. Her face was wooden and her spirit dead. Lumbergh watched Oldhorse approach her. She didn't react to him until he was standing directly in front of her. As her eyes rose to meet his, his hand went tenderly to the side of her face and he leaned in close to her ear to speak.

The two lawmen watched from afar in wonderment.

Lumbergh sensed Jefferson turn toward him in search of some sort of insight, but he had none to offer to his officer. He hadn't a clue what Oldhorse could be saying to the mother. Whatever it was, the chief noticed an expression of cautious reassurance develop in her demeanor, and that was a good thing.

"Do you smell that?" asked Jefferson.

Lumbergh raised an eyebrow. "Smell what?"

Jefferson tilted his head back and let his nostrils flare.

"You don't smell that? It's kind of like perfume."

The chief shook his head and answered, "That's my cologne, Jefferson. I had plans with my wife tonight, remember?"

"Oh yeah. Okay," Jefferson said discreetly. "It smells good."

"Thanks."

Seconds later, Oldhorse was on his way back to the lawmen. He passed them both without missing a stride but muttered the words, "I'll find the boy."

The chief felt a hand on his shoulder and he turned to catch the supportive gaze of his wife, who flashed him a look that let him know she knew that they would find Toby. She offered to stay behind with Joan and he thanked her, understanding the unsaid maternal instincts in force. He gave her instructions to radio him if the boy made it back on his own.

The county sheriff had yet to arrive on the scene, but Lumbergh hadn't enough patience to wait. Within minutes, the small convoy of men had made their way across the creek with beams of flashlights pointed out in front of Ron Oldhorse, who took the lead.

Oldhorse seemed to pay little attention to the men behind him, as if they were just along for the ride. Two of the county deputies took up the rear, carrying canvas backpacks with blankets and water. Radio equipment dangled around their waists. Jurisdiction etiquette and respect for the police chief kept them in a subordinate role. Lumbergh and Jefferson had slipped on coats and hiking boots while Oldhorse was content with his denim.

Conducting a search at night was outside standard procedure; typically a search would begin in the morning. But what had happened that night was personal, and Lumbergh couldn't bear the thought of sitting still while a boy with Toby's challenges was missing in the dark and frigid temperatures.

Without hesitation, Oldhorse surpassed the area where the others had lost track of Toby's trail and began climbing up the steep embankment beyond it, forcing the others to hustle to keep up. Within minutes, they reached an area where large, coarse rocks jutted out from the side of the hill. Oldhorse paused there only for a moment, squatting down with his flashlight and placing his hand on a small carpet of moss that covered the underside of one of the trees that grew out from the formation at an angle. He soon took off again, digging the toes of his moccasins into the mountainside with large strides as he climbed higher.

Lumbergh felt the bite of the cold, even through his well-lined jacket. He couldn't imagine how Toby was faring with lighter wear and missing a shoe. He placed his hands to his mouth and called out the boy's name loudly, prompting others in the pack to do the same. Oldhorse remained silent.

When the group reached an area where the incline leveled out a bit, Jefferson bore down on his pace, huffing and puffing to catch up to the chief, whom he'd fallen behind.

"What do you make of all this, Chief?" he asked in an out-of-breath voice. "Who'd come through Winston, kill two men, and chase a kid off into the woods?"

"The boy wasn't chased," Ron Oldhorse intervened from far enough ahead of the two that they were surprised he'd heard them. "It's just him out here."

"We already know that, Oldhorse!" Jefferson shouted back in annoyance. "This is a private conversation between me and the chief, so just mind your own business!"

Lumbergh screeched to a halt and latched his hand firmly around Jefferson's arm.

He stepped up to his officer's chest and spoke in a calm but direct tone. "Jefferson, I know I've been telling you to be more assertive, and I'm guessing your pride's still a little on the mend since Sean dressed you down the other day, but Oldhorse is doing us a favor here. He's the best chance we have of finding the boy quickly and finding him alive. You need to show him the proper respect."

Even in the dark, Lumbergh could visualize Jefferson's lowered head and the humbled slump of his frame. Jefferson quietly apologized and Lumbergh gave him a motivational slap on the shoulder before following after Oldhorse.

Each time Toby's name was cried out by a member of the group, the others would join in, like a pack of wolves howling at the moon.

"I wish I knew . . ." spoke Lumbergh out of the blue after lunging forward to step over some downed limbs.

Jefferson, uncertain if his boss was speaking to him or himself, said, "Knew what?"

"The answer to your question, from before. About what kind of person would do this."

When Jefferson didn't respond back to him, Lumbergh asked him if he had something to say. After thinking it over, Jefferson decided he did, and built up a breath of nerve.

"Listen, I don't want you to take this the wrong way, like I'm saying this because of a beef with your brother-in-law or something like that . . ."

"Just spit it out."

"Well, I've been thinking . . . The story that Sean told us, about the guy who shot himself on Meyers Bridge . . . Do you think this has something to do with that?"

Lumbergh raised an eyebrow. "If you've got a theory, I'd love to hear it."

Jefferson took a few seconds to catch his breath before continuing. "Well . . . It's just that . . . What if there really was a dead body?"

"I'm listening."

"Okay, let me just throw something out there. I've known Sean for a long time. Longer than you. We both know he's got a temper. We both know he's not afraid to mix things up."

Lumbergh's face twisted in confusion behind the cloak of night. He couldn't imagine where his officer was taking his theory, but he felt compelled to humor him by letting him continue.

"What if he ran into that guy after he left O'Rafferty's?"

"The dead guy?"

"Yes, on Friday night. Maybe out in the parking lot or on the way home. Maybe he got into a fight with the guy over something and something bad happened. Maybe . . ."

"Maybe Sean killed him?" Lumbergh interrupted.

Jefferson said nothing.

Lumbergh continued. "That's what you were going to say, isn't it? What if Sean killed some guy, then made up a ridiculous story about the guy killing himself, right?"

Jefferson remained silent as the men continued along the mountainside, navigating around trees, rocks, and an endless barrage of nature's obstacles.

After a choir of voices shouted out Toby's name again, the chief added, "Finish your thought; I want to hear it all."

"First off, I'm not saying that it happened on purpose. Maybe they were tussling and the guy fell wrong or something. Anyway, let's say that a buddy of the dead guy figured out what happened to him and found out that Sean was behind it. Maybe he saw them together or read about Sean's story in the paper, so he came looking for Sean. You know, looking for answers. Maybe Sean knew this person was coming for him and that's why he left town."

"And instead, Zed, Bailey, and Toby were the ones home when the bad guy showed up?"

"Yes, exactly!" Jefferson's excitement broke through. He clapped his hands together, grinning from ear to ear. He was ecstatic that the chief had followed his involved logic.

Lumbergh let the idea settle in his mind. The fact that the killer had taken out Sean's dog suggested that there may have indeed been a personal grudge at play. And Lumbergh had already deducted that Zed and Bailey had most likely been victims of poor luck rather than targets. It all went down in Sean's apartment, after all. Yet, there were more holes in the officer's theory than there were scurrying nightcritters in the forest through which the five men were trouncing. If Sean had really killed someone, why would he report anything about the man to the authorities? His story alone would establish a link between the two, and if the guy came up in a missing person's report, or if his body was found, Sean would be the prime suspect.

Logic would have led the chief to entirely disregard the notion of the dead man in the river, but there was a particle of history that suddenly wedged its way into his mind: Tariq—the drifter that Sean believed was an Islamic terrorist.

When that went down, Sean had absolutely convinced himself

that he was acting as the frontline investigator in a terrorist case and was going to take down a very bad man to win the long desired admiration of an entire community who largely thought of him as a nuisance. When that didn't happen and he became the butt of new jokes, his pride was dealt a devastating blow.

Lumbergh's mind twisted in acrobatics that he hadn't exercised since his days in Chicago.

Could it be possible that there was a dead man, and he had died at Sean's hand?

And could it be possible, that after Sean had tossed him in the river, he began developing grandiose thoughts about concocting a mystery—a mystery that he would publicize by bringing it to the law? Maybe he knew the police would never take him seriously, and when they didn't, he'd prove the naysayers and his brother-in-law wrong by finding the body himself and looking like a hero. Was that where he was? Downstream somewhere searching for the body?

If that was the plan, though, it would mean that the man's death was no accident. Sean was adamant about the man shooting himself in the back of the head, so if he existed and his body was found, it would have to have a bullet hole there. And, because no one accidentally shoots someone in the back of the head, the whole suicide notion would be Sean's only out unless he was willing to implicate a third party. The thought was ice-cold, like the sleet that continued to drift down from the night sky.

The scenario was nearly unfathomable, and if Lumbergh had heard it offered by anyone else, it would have probably made him laugh. A sense of guilt taunted him for even considering it. He shook his head, weighed the absurdity of it all, and reminded himself that there wasn't a shred of evidence to suggest that the mystery person who Sean described to them even existed. Trying to link a hypothetical dead body to the carnage at the bottom of the hill was completely unfounded.

Oldhorse came to a sudden stop when they reached a crest in the hill before it rose up another fifty or so yards. The trail of men behind him halted in response. A couple of them leaned forward with their hands on their knees to catch their breath. The Indian didn't speak. He stood motionless with his flashlight pointed to the ground before him. Half a minute passed and he remained statuesque. Lumbergh left the others behind to walk up beside him.

"What is it?" He spoke softly, getting no answer. "Ron?"

Just as he was about to place his hand on the Indian's shoulder, Oldhorse raised his flashlight and switched direction, climbing along the shoulder of the hill the group had just crested.

Lumbergh watched the woodsman's beam move quickly and deliberately like a bloodhound on the heels of a convict. The others picked up their pace and concentrated their beams on the same targets as Oldhorse did.

Ahead lay a rocky area where a short row of weather-rotted fence posts, surely several decades old, were planked vertically in what seemed to serve more as a marker than a property boundary. Oldhorse's light beam traced the ground around a couple of boulders before it rose up and caught the reflection of a small pool of water sitting in a shallow crevice on top of a large rock with a flattened top. The other beams followed suit, illuminating the water hole, much of which was rust in color and home to clumps of bird droppings.

"Did he stop here?" Lumbergh directed at Oldhorse.

Before Oldhorse could reply, an audible moan rose up from the other side of the rock. One of the lawmen reached for his gun in case it was an animal. Oldhorse quickly waved him off before disappearing around the side of the rock. The lights followed him to the ground and the first thing one of the beams homed in on was a pair of feet. Resting above a black, high-top shoe was a foot covered only in a densely muddied, white, damp sock.

"Here!" a voice sounded out as all men scrambled to spotlight the body of the boy who was curled up in the fetal position.

He was shivering furiously, lying on his side with his arms crossed in front of him to fight the cold. Directions were shouted back and forth and a pair of blankets poured out of one the backpacks the men were carrying. They were quickly wrapped around the child.

Lumbergh felt the dampness of Toby's pants and wrapped his hand around the boy's exposed foot to find it ice-cold and brittle. Toby's eyes were closed and his mouth seemed to be uttering out a muted conversation with someone who wasn't there.

"Toby?" Lumbergh spoke in an attempt to gain the boy's focus. "Toby!"

The child was lost in a different world. His head was lifted by one of the searchers and a folded-up coat was placed beneath it. His windbreaker had some moisture on it and it was quickly removed by the men. Before it could be replaced with a thicker coat, Oldhorse scanned the boy's body for injuries. He found none other than scrapes and bruises. When his pants were removed, the men found a couple of gashes across the front of his legs that had stopped bleeding but were still quite tender. They wrapped him up in a cocoon of blankets. All along, the boy continued his one-sided, cryptic, and muttered conversation.

"Radio my wife!" the chief requested of one of the men. "Channel thirteen! Let the mom know we've found her boy!"

Chapter 24

T he illuminating projection from the large television screen in the corner pulsed along the darkened room's long walls. At the center of the screen, Daniel Day-Lewis brushed his long black hair from his face and took off in a sprint through a forest. So low was the volume of the film's soundtrack that it was nearly inaudible under the dueling sounds of impassioned breathing.

Two wine glasses, one empty and one half full of White Zin, lined the wide top of a thick coffee table near an open bottle. A centerpiece with two tall, lit candles sat beside the wine glasses. An unseen wall clock's pendulum glided back and forth. It almost sounded like a faint, comforting heartbeat under thin, metallic hands that read a quarter 'til one.

Lisa had never noticed it before, but Marty bore a notable resemblance to her husband, especially right then as she twisted her fingers in his short, silky blonde hair. She guided his head in again to press her glossy, carmine-shaded lips to his ear. It had been so long since she'd felt the warm breath of a man along her neck. Though it felt wrong, it also felt good.

When Marty had arrived at her doorstep with a VHS cassette in tote and clad in his light-blue, neatly pressed guard uniform, he was noticeably nervous. Lisa figured that thoughts of losing his job had occupied his mind the entire drive up. He was charming though— not in an overconfident or cocky way, but almost boyish. Maybe he knew why he had been invited up, but his cautious demeanor signaled that he was ready to interpret the slightest hesitation from her as a stern indication to leave. Now wearing tight-fitting jeans and a low-cut, black silk top, Lisa was certain she wasn't giving off any rejection vibes.

She quickly and methodically unbuttoned his shirt as they kissed. A gratified sigh left her lips as his hands went to her slim waist. She hugged his hips with her thighs. Both expressed a hunger that hadn't been satisfied in some time. She saw her husband in the guard, not just in his hair, but in the shape of his chiseled face that was detailed by the glow of the flames. His touch didn't feel distant or uneasy, but familiar.

"God, you're beautiful," she heard him say between breaths and before he lowered his lips to her neck, just above where the edge of her shirt rested.

Her mind wandered to a memory from a trip she and her husband had taken a year and a half ago. A ski trip over a long weekend at the Copper Mountain resort in Colorado. Their room overlooked the white evergreen landscape that had just enjoyed a fresh dusting of snow. She'd told her husband that she loved him when their eyes met above the thick, burgundy carpet where they had laid a white, feather comforter underneath them. When he didn't hear her, she placed her warm hands along the sides of his face, held his gaze, and mouthed it clearly. She recalled the wide grin that formed on his face, illuminated by flames of a similar ambiance to what she was lost in now. She thought she had forgotten what it felt like when she and her husband kissed, but she hadn't after all.

When Marty's face rose to meet hers and their eyes connected, it was no longer her husband she was with; it was the nice man she'd sometimes greet in passing on her way to and from town. A good man, she was sure of by now, but not Kyle.

A swooning feeling of indiscretion arrived unannounced. Her body went motionless and removed. He quickly noticed.

"Hey . . . Are you okay?"

She smiled apologetically and cupped his shoulder with her hand. "I'm sorry."

His head lowered, not in complete disappointment but in acceptance of a half-expected outcome. His mouth revealed a smirk to let her know that he understood. "Mr. Kimble's a lucky man," he said a bit louder than a whisper.

His words drew out an appreciative smile from the lonely woman beneath him. He slid to the carpet and rose up to his feet where he began buttoning his shirt back up. His body eclipsed the flickering light from the fireplace and Lisa lost track of the contour of his face in the dark, but he seemed to her to be having trouble with his shirt.

"What's wrong?" she asked.

After assessing himself for a moment, he chuckled and explained that she had yanked off one of his buttons, right at the center of his shirt. She giggled and apologized, and he told her not to worry.

She grinned when he extended his hand to her. A gentleman until the end. She took it and let him pull her to her feet.

He picked up his things and was out the door in less than a minute's time.

She watched the red taillights of his car vanish, and she thought of how awkward it would be the next time their paths would assuredly cross. She wondered if she'd find the strength to look him in the eye and speak to him, even in casual conversation.

It wasn't until she picked up the television remote to flip off the picture that she realized Marty had left the movie behind. She'd make sure that it found its way back into the guard station at the front gate, but she would probably return it during a different guard's shift.

She blew out the two candles on the table, and she was suddenly left alone in the dark with her thoughts. The room felt warm so she shuffled along furniture in the dimness until she found a side window that she cracked open with the twist of her wrist. A light breeze poured in and she took a deep breath that relieved some of the tension in her chest.

She switched on some track lighting near the staircase. It wasn't terribly bright but it shed enough of a glaze across the evidence of her late-night visitor that she scowled at the scene. She snatched her wine glass from the coffee table and downed it quickly, which left an unpleasant burn in her throat. Her glare then swung to the telephone that sat along her kitchen counter and she crossed the room to it in no time. Her fingers began to press a combination of buttons but she stopped herself before the call was completed. She slammed the receiver down on the base in frustration.

Her eyes tightened and she flipped on the power button of a small radio that sat next to the phone. The dual speakers emitted a familiar melody amidst accompanying static that dissipated when she toyed with the tuner. Her eyes closed and the fine features of her face soothed to the slow tune of an old Ray Charles song titled "You Don't Know Me." It was a personal song to her, and its random timeliness was nothing short of eerie. It was the song she and her husband had danced to on their second date when they ended up in a nightclub inside the Golden Nugget casino in the wee hours of the morning. She'd loved the song ever since watching Bill Murray and Andie MacDowell dance to it in the movie *Groundhog Day*. She enthusiastically tried her best to reenact the scene with her husband-to-be that night, guiding him through the steps as best she could as an uneasy grin resided on his face, signaling he hadn't a clue what was going on.

She later set the same song as a digital ringtone on his cellphone so it would play aloud when she called his number. Though she never expected him to pick up, she hoped that those he worked with would hear the tune and know that he was loved, and perhaps ask him questions about her. She added it to her own phone as well.

When the song ended and the calm voice of a late-night deejay took over the air, her eyes opened to absorb the stillness of the dark, barren cottage, and her husband was still not there.

"Damn you, Kyle!" she screamed at the empty room.

Chapter 25

His eyes stretched to determine if he was really seeing what he thought he was. It can't be. *How could I have missed this?*

The chirping of morning birds and the clamor of sporadic road construction down the street poured in through the driver's side window that had been left open a crack overnight. The temperature was comfortable, possibly in the high sixties already.

Sean's large shoulders dangled over the edge of the vinyl bench seat with the top corner of his head resting along the floorboard. His eyes were transfixed on the narrow opening below the passenger seat and they pulsated as they adjusted to the morning light. He sluggishly turned his body at a sharper angle to shove an arm up underneath. His lips curled in satisfaction when he felt an aluminum cylinder in his hand. Out came an unopened can of beer that had dwelled there unnoticed for months. Sean pulled himself to a seated position and straightened his stiff neck before punching open the tab. Warm but wet, the contents felt good sliding down his parched throat. It would have gone better with the pizza he'd devoured last night, but a dry belch of layered cheese and pepperoni did make for a more complete breakfast.

After crawling back into the front seat, he was stunned to see that the same guard as before was still out by the front gate. He even looked fresh, suggesting that he had either left during the night and came back for another shift, or that he was super-human. Sean very much doubted the latter. The guard was now outside his station doing some tidying up.

"Pussy," Sean muttered to himself with a smirk as he watched the guard clean the outside window of his station with a bottle of Windex and a fistful of paper towels.

It was Tuesday morning. It didn't seem right to Sean that it had only been three days since he'd watched that desperate stranger blow a hole through the back of his head, but after recounting the pivotal events in his mind, he realized it was indeed true.

He leaned forward in his seat and glared into the rearview mirror. His eyes looked as tired as he felt. Patches of his short hair were flowing in multiple directions, and the overgrowth of his thick whiskers made him look like a lumberjack. He couldn't remember when he had last brushed his teeth. His hand glided to the back of his head where he scratched the constant itch.

The slowing speed of a car along the main drag caught his attention as he lowered himself back down into his seat. It was a shiny, dark gray BMW with its signal on, preparing to turn onto Bluff Walk Road. He watched the security guard take notice of the incoming car and lower the spray bottle to his belt loop. The driver pulled into the small entrance in front of the gate. From Sean's vantage point, he saw the driver exchange quick pleasantries with the guard who then reached his hand inside the station's doorway. The gate slowly opened by electronic motor. The car coasted in and disappeared around the edge of the wall that obscured Sean's view. The gate closed and the guard returned to the window.

Sean was confident he didn't have the credentials to just pull up to the front gate and be let in. He wasn't sure if one had to be a resident or be on a guest list, but his ability to charm—or bullshit, in lay terms—wouldn't trump his scanty appearance. Unshaven, wearing a weathered gray sweatshirt with dirty jeans and black work-boots, and driving a late '70s clunker—it would have taken one hell of a story.

Sean started the Nova up and pulled back onto the main street, hanging a left and crossing in front of the entrance. He turned right when he got to the end of the brick wall and rounded the corner. The road only went down about fifty yards before it dead-ended into another wall, this one a couple feet taller with a darker color of brick that looked newer than what surrounded the gated community. A couple of multicolored newspaper vending machines stood in front. There was a bit of a shoulder to the road just before it met brick. He parked there.

Through his open window, he heard the distant sound of water splashing somewhere on the other side of the larger wall along with faint cries of what had to be seagulls. He figured there was probably a lake nearby. He leaned across the bench seat and peered up from the passenger side window. *Getting over that eight-foot wall shouldn't be that hard.* There were no security cameras that he could see. He'd just have to wait for the traffic to clear from the main street for a few seconds so as not to be seen. He opened his window and began to climb out before hesitating. His eyes shifted to his glove box. He had no idea what he could expect to find at 114 Bluff Walk Road, and that concerned him. All he knew was that the location was somehow tied to that stranger on the bridge whose last possessions included a gun with a silencer, a bloody bandage, and a pair of night-vision goggles.

"Yep," he grumbled before letting the glove box drop open and pulling out a Magnum revolver.

It was a six-inch barreled Colt Python with a nickel finish that shone from the sun above. The seasoned wooden grip was comfortable in his hand. It had belonged to his father, and it was the only inherited item he was never able to bring himself to pawn, even during the toughest of times. This was partially due to Sean's fondness for guns, but it was more than that. One of his last memories of his father was the two of them out in the forest, shooting at beer cans and paper targets with that gun. His father rarely spent any one-on-one time with him. He was largely a stranger to Sean as a young boy—working all day and coming home late at night, and consumed with his own interests on the weekends. But that day had been different. His dad was different. He *wanted* to be there with his son, even packing lunch for them to eat.

That day, Sean's father had taught him to shoot. He taught him how to load, align the sights, take a deep breath, and squeeze that trigger. Sitting in the car alone now, with that gun in his hand in an unfamiliar place, Sean drifted back to that day long ago. He felt his father's large arms around him, helping him to steady his aim; his father's chin draped over his shoulder; the smell of chewing tobacco from his father's shirt pocket. *Take a breath, steady yourself, and squeeze.*

It occurred to him years later, that on that day, his father already knew he'd be leaving. Perhaps his dad wanted to be a father to his son once before he was gone. Or maybe it was his way of teaching Sean to replace him as the man of the house, to take care of his mother and Diana. The new protector. Whatever the motivation, it was a memory that Sean held close to his heart.

He slid the barrel of the gun down the back of his jeans, letting his clumpy sweatshirt conceal the grip. He locked his car, waited for traffic to subside, and leapt up the wall. His arms hooked the top of the wall and he pulled himself up with a grunt. He quickly dropped down to the ground on the other side where shade engulfed him.

He suddenly found himself in another world—almost as if in a story book. He stood at the edge of a thick forest that served as home to trees of all sizes and varieties. Most were tall, with dark trunks and limbs and shiny leaves. Mixed in were smaller aspen whose white and black bark reminded him of Winston. A few pine trees also found their way among the vegetation. The soil was dark and damp beneath his feet. Sporadic, light-colored wildflowers accented the landscape, which angled its way up a hill of moderate steepness that Sean hadn't been able to see from outside the wall. From a distance, he could make out the paved road—Bluff Walk. It led from the entrance into a curved path up the hill. The pavement was very well kept, looking almost new.

As long as he stayed a distance from the road, he was sure he wouldn't be noticed as he made his way up the hill toward where the homes presumably resided. The trees and brush were dense—easy enough to duck behind if needed. His clothes were dark, which was helpful. Keeping an eye on the road, he began tromping his way up the hill, weaving in and out of trees and putting a little distance between himself and the brick wall that also flowed upward, increasingly away from the road. Before long, he noticed a row of black mailboxes resting on individual posts along Bluff Walk. There looked to be nearly twenty of them. One for each house, he assumed.

There was a lot of movement in the forest. Branches and leaves shifted from small birds darting in and out of treetops. Squirrels, with fur a little darker in color than the ones Sean was used to, scampered through limbs, over rocks, and along the ground. A light breeze made the walk comfortable. Had it not been for the reason that brought him to where he was now, it would have felt like he was on a restful vacation.

Through a small clearing in the trees about sixty yards in front of him, he spotted the side of a brick building. Breathing heavily, he picked up the pace, keeping an eye on the road for traffic. A curved, cobblestone driveway with a carefully trimmed two-foot-high hedge led up to the building from the road. His shoulders sank lower as he approached the raised edge of the driveway.

An abrupt, sharp cry of metal rubbing on metal ripped through the tranquil setting, sending him down to his hands and knees. He scrambled quickly along the ground, positioning himself for cover between the hedges and thick shrub. Forcing open a small crevice in the hedges with his hand, he now had a full view of the building: a two-story, stately house with a mostly brick exterior, light-red in color. Glaring white wood trim and large latticed windows hung proudly along the front of the home. An arched entrance that hugged and partially concealed the front door stood about ten feet tall under the sharply angled roof. It seemed higher from Sean's low vantage point.

The front lawn was small, but trim; the grass less green than the forest that circled it. Colorful flowers stemmed from broad ceramic pots along the porch.

The two-door garage was open and the light from the ceiling above suggested that the noise he had heard came from the garage door. Brake lights from a cherry-red car inside flashed on. He watched as the driver backed his Lexus convertible onto the driveway, coming to a stop only a few feet from where he knelt. Sean could only see the back of the man's head—salt and pepper hair under what Sean had occasionally described to others as a rich asshole hat, more commonly known as a driving cap.

The screeching noise returned as the garage door lowered, and he tasted exhaust as the car briskly disappeared down the cobblestone driveway. No other cars were parked in the garage. *Probably no one else home*, he decided.

He stayed put for about a minute, looking for any movement through the windows of the house, before checking behind him through the forest. Staying behind the hedge, he circled around toward the entrance. Underneath a large copper wall lantern, to the side of the front door, hung the number 103. He was looking for 114. An annoyed grunt left his mouth at the thought of how long it would take him to find the right house, meandering through the forest on foot in such a broad area.

"Are you here to fix the sprinkler?" a voice spoke from behind him.

Sean spun around. His eyes bulged and his stomach clenched. Before him stood two boys, probably twelve or thirteen in age. Both were dressed in t-shirts, shorts, and flip-flops. One was thin with red hair, bangs dangling down to his eyebrows. The other had shorter brown hair and was quite a bit heavier.

Sean answered quickly, "Yes."

It was a tactic he had learned years ago from an episode of *Simon & Simon*. When confronted in a precarious situation, simply answer yes to the first question you're probed with. It immediately reduced suspicion and provided an angle to exploit. The same tactic had served him well two days earlier with Bailey and the night-vision goggles.

He inflated his chest, attempting to compose himself. Though the boys had been standing behind him, he was certain they hadn't seen the gun in the back of his pants. His sweatshirt hung too low, and there was no fear in their eyes.

The redhead grinned through his freckled face and spoke: "My dad thought you were coming this afternoon. He just left."

"Shoot," Sean answered, placing his hands on his hips. "I'll just come back later."

"Oh no. You don't have to do that. I can show you where it is."

Sean bit his lip and nodded. After a moment, he answered. "Okay, you show me."

He followed the boys toward the back side of the house, tracing their footsteps around a small flower garden in the side yard. The backyard wasn't much bigger than the front. It was spread out about thirty feet before edging up to a retaining wall that looked out over a small ravine in the forest. The vast majority of the property was taken up by the house.

The boys led him to a rectangular, light green fiberglass cover imbedded in some dirt at the corner of the yard.

"There you go!" said the redhead, pointing to the ground.

"Thanks, guys," Sean replied with his hands on his hips again, his eyes aimed down.

Both boys stood there, looking at him. They weren't leaving.

"Did you guys need something?" he asked, not looking up.

"Can we watch?"

It was what Sean was afraid of. He took a breath and lowered himself down to his knees. "Sure."

He lifted the cover and saw an intersection of multiple valves and piping between the partially submerged encasing. He placed his hand to his chin. He had never worked on a sprinkling system in his life and he knew nothing about plumbing.

Feeling the boys' eyes peering down on him from above, he leaned forward and began turning one of the valve handles, first to the right and then to the left. He then moved onto the next.

For the first time, the brown-haired boy spoke. "How did you get in here, mister?"

"What do you mean?" Sean asked, continuing to work the valves.

"If Tommy's dad didn't think you were coming until later, who let you in through the gate?"

Sean's face turned pale, but he kept his hands busy, now massaging the piping and pretending to look for flaws. "The guard."

Both boys chuckled.

"I know," the larger boy pressed. "I mean . . . Who told the guard to let you in?"

Your mom, Sean fought back the urge to respond, but he understood how important it was to keep the charade going. He'd driven halfway across the country to find out what was at 114 Bluff Walk Road and he wasn't about to screw it up by arousing suspicions that he shouldn't be on the north side of that gate.

He took a moment to find an answer to the boy's question. One soon came to him. "I did some work at another home in here this morning. You guys are my second stop of the day. They let me in."

". . . Oh," replied the redhead.

"What's wrong with your head, mister?" Sean heard the brunette ask.

"What do you mean?"

Sean knew what he meant. Out of the corner of his eye, he noticed the redhead jabbing his rude friend in the side with his elbow.

"It looks like a spider or something bit the back of your head. Is that a bite mark?"

"Nope." Sean felt as though he was being talked down to and it was pissing him off. He bit his lip and clenched onto his composure.

Regardless of which valve he turned, there was no sound or tremble of water pressure. His assumption was that if someone had been called to fix a problem with the system, there was a leak somewhere in the line. That didn't appear to be the case. The only pipes close to eruption were the ones forming on his forehead as he became increasingly frustrated with the situation and the inquisitiveness of the fat kid.

"Where are your tools, mister?"

Sean snapped his back upright. The sudden jolt of movement caused both boys to leap backwards in surprise. His head spun and his narrowed, agitated eyes met those of the interrogator. Both kids' faces deflated with angst. Sean imagined hammering a fist right into the fat boy's chest, sending him toppling ten feet backwards and onto his back.

Seconds of fierce tension dragged by. No one moved.

Sean's hands felt around to the side belt loops of his pants. He accentuated the action to get the boys' attention.

"You're right," he muttered. "I don't have my tools. I must have left them at the last house."

As he stood up, both boys cautiously took a few steps back.

"I'm going to need to go get them and come back," he added.

He sensed the boys breathing again and forced a smile across his rigid chops. An idea had come to mind. "You know, I've got a third house to do after this." He wiped his brow with his arm. "One-Fourteen Bluff Walk Road. You guys know which one that is?"

The boys looked at each other.

"Well . . ." the redhead began. "We don't really know many people in here. Most of us just live here in the summer. But the numbers get higher as you get higher up the road. The last one is one-fifteen, so it's probably near the top."

Sean smiled and thanked the two boys, promising to return later. He sensed some remaining discomfort from them, but not enough for him to worry about them calling security. As he walked down the cobblestone driveway toward the road, he was sure he heard the redhead say to his friend, "I thought he was going to kick your ass."

He turned back and waved to the two of them still standing in the backyard. Only the redhead waved back. Once Sean had crossed a knoll and was out of sight of the two, he hustled off the driveway and back into the heart of the forest, following the path of the road from a distance.

Chapter 26

He'd have rather been in South Padre along with his buddy who'd flown out two days ago. He'd never been there, and MTV's spring break coverage from a few months ago made it look too good to pass up. Chicks in bikinis, ninety-degree weather, swim-up bars, and loud music. What fun his friend from the university must be having right now. *Oh, to have rich parents*, he thought to himself.

Instead of the arid sun sautéing his sprawled-out body and the indiscriminate spray from the ocean occupying his raw senses, he found himself crumpled up in a fetal position. He hoped it would counter the biting morning frost that neither his dome tent nor his mummy sleeping bag seemed to give him any protection from. About five miles from his hometown, he supposed it could have been worse. At least he had another couple of months before it was back to the stress of exams and projects.

He'd hoped he'd be able to fall back asleep, but the deceiving sunlight and the abhorrent snoring coming from the tent next to his rattled him awake. There wasn't going to be any refuge that morning until he got a fire started. It was the argument that eventually won the debate he'd carried out in his own mind. He summoned the nerve to unzip his bag and quickly crawled over to his hiking boots that lay in a clump near the tent's nylon door. Somehow, he managed to keep his gnashed teeth from rattling as he absorbed the full brunt of the thin, crisp mountain air that heckled his clumsy attempts to pry the tongue of one of his boots from its wedged position above the bridge of his foot as he pulled on the footwear. The more practical answer would have been to remove the boot that he'd never untied in the first place and start over. It was his frigid toes that poured out through the holes in his well-worn sock, however, that won the appeal.

Clad in an asparagus-colored canvas jacket with a plush, gray collar that he had buttoned up to his chin, the nineteen-year-old exited the tent, and in his haste to keep moving, didn't bother to zip the hatch back up behind him. His dark, muddled hair from the restless night would have made him a natural fit in a Seattle grunge band, but his personal appearance was the furthest thing from his mind at that moment.

The surrounding area was lit up pretty well, despite the sun having not yet topped the mountain range that stood proudly above Beggar's Basin.

Beggar's Basin was a popular recreational area with the locals, mostly for picnics, fishing, and some canoeing. A couple outlets off the Blue River, a tributary of the Colorado River, rejoined there in a partially manmade reservoir before winding back to the Colorado several miles downstream. The reservoir resided about four miles south of Winston.

Just a few days ago, the area had been overflowing with activity. An annual fishing contest produced a record number of participants. Raised rods and tackle-laced hats decorated every nook and cranny along the shore. But this morning, the boys had the entire valley to themselves. Three campers, two tents, and unbridled nature.

He hustled over to the stone fire pit where his comrades had spent half the night dousing thick, flaming logs with gratuitous portions of apparently dispensable lighter fluid. Now, there was nothing but piles of gray and black ash and the sparse remnants of burnt timber. In a fluster, he searched for the large box of matches that he distinctly remembered leaving on top of his red and white cooler before turning in for the night. It was nowhere to be found. *What have those idiots done with it?* He soon answered his own question when he spotted the charred corner of the cardboard box resting along a large round stone on the inside perimeter of the pit. They'd torched it.

He knew he was the only one of them who'd had the foresight to bring something with which to light the fire. He'd chastised his buddies about it when they'd first arrived the previous evening.

Dueling chipmunks taunted each other from opposite ends of the campsite, chirping loudly before one took off after the other and they disappeared behind a group of small boulders.

He glared in agitation at the classic A-frame tent that stood beside his own, where one buddy was still snoring loudly and the other was seemingly unaffected by the clamor. Both had been sucking on the ends of two-liters of Purple Passion the last time he'd seen them. It must have been the recipe for a solid night's sleep, even in an ice cooler. He contemplated just crawling into the front seat of his parked Mustang and letting the car's heater warm his body, but a warm engine wasn't going to cook him the crispy strips of bacon and scrambled eggs he'd been craving for breakfast since about 2:30 a.m.

He paced over to his pals' tent and dropped to a knee. In a single motion, he latched onto the bottom of an exposed steel pole and yanked it free of its propped-up position before guiding it outside of the tent. The triangular-shaped canvas slowly deflated behind him as he made his way back to the fire pit. He turned over a thick, sawed log and took a seat on the flat end. After collapsing the top portion of the pole inside the bottom, he held one end to his mouth and guided the other down, just above the ash at the center of the pit. A couple strong breaths exposed some residual ember that still had a little life left in it. He gathered some reasonably dry twigs and formed them in the shape of pyramid above the ember. After ten minutes or so of repetitious puffs through the pole, he had a small flame going.

A sense of pride triggered a grin below his hunched shoulders and he glanced over at his friends' tent, wishing they were awake to marvel at his achievement. Despite having half of their tent sunken flat around their bodies, neither had budged and the blustering snoring had continued on unaltered.

After adding sticks and dry leaves to feed the fire and absorbing its welcome warmth for a few minutes, he grabbed a large frying pan from an Army-green duffle bag inside his tent. It hadn't been used in a while and hadn't been cleaned all that well since its last use, so he took it down to the water with a half-depleted roll of paper towels. He squatted along the edge of the shore where a narrow inlet formed a lazy whirlpool of motion and submerged the face of the pan. When he lifted it back out of the water, his peripheral vision caught what he assumed was a trapped log bobbing horizontally against the rocks. He turned his head to take a closer look and his eyes expanded to their brinks.

The pan fell from his hand, causing a splash he didn't hear.

He was back up on his feet in a flash and screaming his friends' names so loudly and alarmingly that they thought he was being attacked by a bear. Still half-plastered with throbbing headaches, they joined him at the shore moments later.

All three gazed at the mangled, bloated human body before them, covered almost entirely in black.

Chapter 27

S ean stood at the base of a short embankment blanketed with dead, matted leaves from the previous fall. New, thick blades of grass stemmed out from under them like green whiskers. He wished he had brought binoculars, but in his rush to leave Winston, he had not thought to. He was sure though that the digits along the face of the building read "114." Like the last house he'd perused, the garage faced away from the road. The style of the home, however, looked much different.

It was a multilevel building that sprouted up from a sloped landscape that had no real yard. Instead, the terrain was composed of large, decorative rock that accentuated staggered bushes and trees, similar to the raw forest that surrounded the residence. A curved row of concrete steps began parallel to the driveway and led up to a secondary row of wooden steps attached to a railed front porch. The edge of a larger sun-porch could be seen wrapped around the backside of the home. The building itself was constructed of dull, gray brick with sections of sprawling windows, and the roof had a mild angle to it. It wasn't as flashy or homey as the house he'd just left. It was probably a bit older. Still, it was just as large and conveyed a wealthy aura that was unmistakable.

The driveway was paved but sported a similar route to the long, cobblestone one he had walked down after leaving the two boys. It led to a closed garage door whose color matched the brick.

His eyes had traced numerous windows multiple times over the past few minutes. There had been no movement from inside. He was unsure of how to approach the situation. A cop would just walk right up and knock, ask some direct questions, but he knew that an out-of-uniform rent-a-cop wouldn't command the same respect. Sean looked down and evaluated his appearance. A slept-in sweatshirt and dirty jeans. He doubted the sprinkler guy gimmick would work on anyone other than a couple of kids.

A dull, pounding sound caught his ear. Footsteps . . . coming fast from down the hill behind him. After a few seconds, he was sure they were only getting louder. Most of the forest was lush with trees, but he had little cover between where he stood and whoever was coming his way—nowhere to hide in time without causing a commotion. He dropped to one knee in an attempt to make himself less visible, careful not to make a sound.

A figure in navy blue apparel emerged from the crest of a small hill to his right. It was a woman jogging. Her eyes hadn't met his. Thin, white earphones hugged her head above a blonde ponytail. It flipped from side to side with each stride. She was concentrating on pushing her way up the hill along a worn dirt path that Sean hadn't noticed until just then. He stayed perfectly still and was careful not to make any movements that would catch her attention. Her snug tank top accentuated her athletic frame, and he took notice of her shapely legs that stemmed up from a pair of white Nikes. She passed maybe twenty feet from him, so close that he could hear the music from the little speakers in her ears. She looked young. He guessed somewhere in her twenties. After she disappeared behind some aspens, he directed his gaze back up at the house. A few seconds went by before he heard footsteps again. This time, they came from the driveway. It was the same woman, now nearly sprinting as she made her way up toward the house.

"*She* lives there?" he whispered under his breath. *Was this who received the dead man's letter?*

When she reached the garage, her shoulders collapsed and her hands went to her knees.

He could hear her heavy breathing. He watched her glance at her watch, then press some buttons on a keypad beside the garage door. The door rose steadily without much noise. As it began to lift, she dropped to a squatting position, seemingly impatient and eager to look inside where a single car resided in the two-car garage. It was a black Audi. The sight seemed to anger her, as he was sure he heard her drop of an f-bomb. He found it a bit amusing. She walked inside and disappeared from view as the garage door steadily lowered back down.

Sean's fingers scratched the back of his head.

"Well, what the hell was I expecting?" Lisa asked herself out loud before reaching a hand back behind her head and setting her hair free from the ponytail in her kitchen. Her legs felt tight from her run.

She peered over at the answering machine resting on the counter. The digital display read "0." She took a breath and made her way through the kitchen, snagging a bottled water from the fridge before strolling into the living room. Still breathing hard, she found herself gazing at a framed picture of her and her husband set on a two-inch thick redwood mantel in front of her, propped up at a slight angle. The photo had been taken at a friend's anniversary party a year and a half ago. Him in a black suit and her in a dynamic red dress. Both smiling. She pulled it face-down along the mantel.

An unexpected knock at the door brought a jolt of excitement that shook awake her fatigued body. In one quick motion, she positioned the picture back in place. With a wide grin that lit up her face, she raced to the front door, taking a moment to stop beside a large horizontal mirror on the wall to check her hair. *Not ideal*, but she didn't care. Her heart flapped briskly like a wild bird that had just been freed from captivity. She swung open the door, ready to wrap her arms tightly around her husband, but the reunion was not to be.

Before her stood not her spouse but a tall, imposing figure—the sight of which instantly erased her joyous smile and the gleam in her eye. The man's broad shoulders nearly eclipsed the sunlight that had made its way through the arms of a towering tree above. He looked rough to Lisa, with his unshaven, weathered face and grimy clothes. He was completely out of place in the upscale, spread-out community that surrounded her. Even for someone who worked the grounds or maybe maintained equipment, he didn't look right. She was certain she had never seen him before. She never forgot a face.

"Hi," she heard herself timidly say.

"Hey," answered the man, whose lumbering hand went quickly to the back of his head where he appeared to scratch an itch.

A large black bird balancing on a tree limb high above them cackled loudly.

Lisa waited for the strange man to state his business. He was clearly uncomfortable and seemed almost confused. In a way, it reminded her of the behavior she'd seen from boys back in high school who were building up the nerve to ask her out on a date. But this wasn't high school, and the prolonged awkwardness was beginning to send a chill up her spine. She felt like a fool for opening the door before looking outside, and even had an impulse to quickly slam it shut and turn the deadbolt before any possible harm could come to her.

Sean read fear in her eyes as he stood there facing her and understood the obvious tension she felt from his presence. *Just say something*, he said to himself.

There were several ways that he could have eased into a conversation with the woman to try and pry information out of her—information that would have helped explain the hard-sought identity of the man from the bridge. However, there was something in his gut that told him that the answers didn't need to be extracted through one of his bullshit stories. He'd come so far, and the woman standing before him didn't appear the slightest bit threatening. It was time to be bold and direct, and hope that he was making the right call.

"I'm sorry to bother you," he began. "But I think someone you know is dead."

"What?" she yelped. She clearly thought she hadn't heard him correctly. "What do you mean? Who are you?"

He shook his head at his own poor phrasing. He then forced himself to breathe and looked her straight in the eyes.

"My name is Sean. Sean Coleman. Three days ago, I was in Winston, Colorado. That's where I live. I saw a man kill himself." He noticed the confusion and fear spreading in her. He kept talking. "That same man sent something to this address before he died." He could only imagine what thoughts had to be sprinting through this young lady's mind.

She said nothing and appeared almost paralyzed by his words.

"Listen, I know I sound crazy here," he said with a forced chuckle. "But I'm telling you the truth. I'm here because his body fell from a bridge and into a river . . . and it's gone. I don't know his name, and no one even believes me, that I saw what I saw. I just know that he sent something to this house, so you must know him." He realized he was rambling, but the required words were coming out.

"And if you *don't* know him, maybe I *have* gone crazy," he concluded with a tremble in his voice.

Sean watched her body begin to shake and her eyes begin to well up. Her hand latched onto the doorframe as she turned faint, trying to steady herself. Her eyes left his and went blankly up over his shoulder. He didn't read doubt in her reaction but rather morbid realization.

She barely managed to ask, "What did he look like?" It came out in a quick gasp before she looked as if she swallowed some bile.

"He had really blonde hair and . . ."

Before he could continue, she let out a piercing howl that echoed off the surrounding trees, making birds there quickly flee. She collapsed down to her knees in a heap before Sean could catch her by the arm.

Her hands went to her face and her eyes bulged in terror. "Oh, God!" she screamed. "Oh, God!"

Chapter 28

"That's him," he answered somberly.

Lisa closed her moist eyes and lowered her head. The framed photo she'd taken from the mantel dropped from her trembling hands and cartwheeled across the lush, carpeted floor. It ended face-up.

Sean experienced a guilty sense of vindication. After all, he had proven them all wrong—Lumbergh, Jefferson, Coltraine . . . even Uncle Zed. And Sean wasn't one to let them forget it. He thought of the exuberant grin that would surely be pinned across Toby Parker's loyal face once he learned of the news—the news that son of a bitch Roy Hughes would have to write about in the paper for the whole town of Winston to read. Sean fought back the urge to smirk.

The end zone dance would come later, though. Right now he was audience to a world of pain. He had leveled a wrecking ball against the young, broken lady who stood adrift before him. Her face, twisted with emotional pain, told a story of helplessness and disarray.

Sean understood loss. He understood the pain and the tears of this woman who had abruptly been left by someone vitally important to her. Someone irreplaceable.

"You should sit down," he suggested, nudging his head toward an armchair just beside them.

Lisa found herself seated at the center of the surrounding room. The living area now felt completely foreign and unwelcome to her, as if she was in someone else's home. The walls seemed taller than before, the ceiling so high above that she couldn't tell where it met the walls. The large, rugged man beside her who had altered her world in a snapshot of time felt like part of the room rather than a person. She observed him as if he were a painting—a brash canvas covered with abstract meanings and untold origins.

Sean examined the sprawling interior of the affluence that encircled him. Large leather couches, framed art and lacquer vases everywhere, an imposing fireplace built with enameled river rock, and the largest coffee table he'd ever seen. Its glossy, oak top was about the dimensions of the pool tables with which he was all too familiar. Lights were everywhere—dome lights, track lights, tall lamps, a large chandelier above. At the edge of the living room stood a wide open kitchen with a glistening hardwood floor, stone countertops, stainless steel appliances, and a towering, ceiling-mounted rack that hosted a hodgepodge of metal pots and pans.

His gaze traced a spiral, steel staircase that led up to an upstairs area. He assumed it led to the lofted room above that looked out over the living room. This woman and her late husband had money.

He glanced back at her and found her watching him.

"Nice place," he said, feeling like an idiot the moment the casual words left his mouth.

To his surprise, the distraught lady who sat before him burst into a chuckle, finding some instinctive amusement at the absurdity of the remark. It quickly changed back to sobbing.

"Is there someone you can call?" he asked uncomfortably. "You know . . . a friend or something? Your parents?"

Consolation had never been Sean's strong suit. Yet, even for a man who was well-known in his hometown for demonstrating a sharp deficit in the area of compassion, it didn't sit right in his gut to just walk out the door after dropping a grenade on someone. And at that moment, he felt that it didn't make sense for him to be anywhere else. He was broke. He didn't have enough gas money to make it back out of the state, let alone back to Winston. Over two days of traveling, practically every scenario imaginable of what he'd find at 114 Bluff Walk Road had danced through his mind. He hadn't pondered once, however, what he'd do once he finally found his answer.

Achieving some momentary composure, Lisa lowered her hands from her face and asked, "Why are you here?"

"What?"

"You drove all the way from Colorado to tell me my husband's dead? Couldn't you have just called or notified the local authorities and had *them* contact me?"

Before he could respond, she continued, raising her voice and clenching her fists. She quickly rose to her feet, prompting him to take a step back.

"My husband's been dead for how many days now?" she asked curtly.

"Three," he answered under his breath.

"Three days! And I'm just *now* finding out!"

Her exasperated voice echoed along the walls of the house. Her face was a wet mess that she repeatedly used the palms of her hands to dab at. He cringed as she tore into him.

"My God! How do I even know you're telling me the truth? Who are you? I don't even know who you are!"

He raised his hands out in front of him and it was all he could to do not to shove her. She was inching closer and closer, and he wanted to plant her back down into the chair behind her. He chose a different tactic.

"Knock if off!" he roared with such ferocity that Lisa was nearly taken off of her feet. "Everything I'm telling you is true! I didn't call you because I didn't have a name or number! Just an address! I *did* tell the authorities, back in Winston! They thought I was full of shit because there was no body!"

Her shoulders lowered. She took a careful step back.

"I watched your husband shoot himself and fall into a river!

Those are the facts! What was in the letter he sent you? Didn't he say what he was gonna do? "

Her eyes welled up again. She slowly sank back into her chair as if being lowered steadily by a pulley. "I never got any letter," she muttered before weeping again.

He exhaled and let his chest deflate. "Listen," he said. "Is there someone you want me to call?"

Her glazed eyes didn't react.

"Your mom? Are there people in Colorado who might be looking for him? Friends? His family?"

Her eyes narrowed upon mention of his family. She bit her bottom lip and began shaking her head in disgust.

"Oh, I'm sure *his family* is looking for him."

She raised her gaze back upon Sean. This time it was fueled with such an unexpected and unsettling presence of pure rage that he was taken aback. Her eyes seemed to burn right through the straggling tears that remained above her cheeks. He wasn't sure what he could have said to cause such a stark change in her demeanor, but a nerve had somehow been struck.

She soberly asked, "What's your name again?"

"Sean. Sean Coleman."

"Mr. Coleman, I appreciate what you've done . . . Bringing me this news. I didn't mean to blow up at you."

To Sean, it was as if he was suddenly talking to an entirely different person. He began wondering if she had snapped.

"Don't worry about it," he answered calmly.

"I hope you don't find this rude, but would you mind leaving?"

"Leaving?"

"Yes."

"I'm not sure if I should . . ."

"I'll be fine, Mr. Coleman. I need to be alone right now."

He was speechless. Was he really being asked to leave? Just like that? He'd driven 1,500 miles in two days, gotten hardly any sleep, his wallet and stomach were empty, and now it was time to leave? He never envisioned a reward for his persistence, but he had hoped to experience some grand sense of closure that didn't seem to be materializing.

"We're gonna need to call the police chief in Winston," he said. "We need to let him know that the guy I saw was your husband—that he was for real. It's the only way they're going to look for the body."

She nodded. "There's a notepad on the kitchen counter. Leave his number and I'll call him."

"Just let me use your phone and I'll call him right now," said Sean as he made a beeline for the kitchen.

"No!" she snapped, stopping him in his tracks. "I need you to leave, Mr. Coleman. Please! I promise I'll call him. I need to be alone right now."

Sean cocked his head at an angle, looking like an alert canine who heard a whistle from a distance. His mind strained to puzzle together her request. He thought about how he'd react if the situations were reversed. He supposed that wanting to be left alone made sense, but he couldn't grasp the passiveness toward recovering her husband's remains. He accepted what he deemed irrationality. He'd leave and find a pay-phone in town to call Lumbergh. He at least had enough money for that. Maybe he could even get the Winston P.D. to spring for a little compensation for doing their job for them. Of course, that was all reliant on Lumbergh even believing him without the dead man's wife on the line to vouch for him.

"Fine," he said as he walked toward the counter. "Can you give me the number here? So I can reach you?"

She hesitated but complied, rattling off the digits that he took down on the notepad. He wrote the number for the Winston police station on a separate sheet and left it attached to the pad.

He eyed the phone again, a little annoyed that the woman was making things complicated for him. He noticed a small machine resting along the counter in front of it. It had a keyboard on its face but was smaller than an old fashioned typewriter, and didn't appear to be a laptop computer. Sean had seen one before but it took him a few moments to place where. He recalled the image of a heavy person describing one to a dark-haired man when it suddenly came to him; an episode of *Jake and the Fat Man*.

A lightbulb lit up in Sean's skull and his head whipped back to Lisa. "Was your husband deaf?"

Her eyes peered up at him in a demeanor that looked to Sean to be one of annoyance.

"Yeah. So?" Before he could respond, she spoke again. "How did you know that?"

"I just noticed your phone. Isn't that a . . . ?" His mouth was left hanging open when he couldn't recall the term for the contraption.

"A TDD. A telecommunications device for the deaf. It's how we talk . . . talked." Her gaze dropped to the floor again and she swallowed to compose herself from another weeping spell.

Sean took the queue to concede that he'd worn out his welcome. "All right then," he concluded.

He made his way toward the front door, feeling a little as though his tail was between his legs. He didn't like the sensation of leaving the business unfinished one bit. He opened the door and was halfway out before he stopped, hesitated for a moment, and craned his head back inside.

"I'm sorry this happened to you."

She offered an acknowledging nod through dreary eyes.

He closed the door softly behind him.

Standing on the front porch, it occurred to Sean that another lingering question had just been answered by his discovery of the TDD. When he had raced along the dirt road toward that bridge on Saturday morning in the futile effort to stop her husband from killing himself, he'd yelled his head off and never received even a hint of recognition from the man. It puzzled him at the time that the man didn't appear to hear him, even with the clamor of the roaring river and the sheer focus written across his face. The real reason was that he physically could not hear Sean's cries.

He scanned the perimeter, trying to judge how to best get back to his car. As he did, he heard a chain lock rattle from inside the door—another less-than-subtle indication that he'd overstayed his welcome.

He knew his car was parked somewhere southwest of his location. He was certain about that. But something nagged him the same way that the itch at the back of his head often did, which he took a moment to rub. It was another unanswered question that he felt he'd earned the right to have resolved. He'd come too far not to. After making his way down the driveway, he headed southeast, back toward the road.

Lisa watched the tall stranger disappear around the corner through a parting of open curtain. The sunlight glistened along her wet, sunken face. She palmed her eye and marched for the phone resting on the countertop, brushing the notepad aside in her haste. Her index finger pounded eleven digits with memorized accuracy. After a single ring, there was a hesitation, then a woman's voice.

"You have reached the Federal Bureau of Investigation, Las Vegas Division. If you know your extension, please enter it now. Otherwise, please select an option from the following menu . . ."

Chapter 29

"What in the hell is going on?" Lisa screamed in frustration at the phone receiver gripped tightly in her hand.

Her arms trembled in anger and a new weeping spell ensued over the obstructionist voice menu that once again looped her back to the opening options without letting her speak to an actual person at the Bureau. It was as if the entire office was out to lunch, which couldn't possibly be the case. Ten minutes of redirects were enough to push her over the edge, if she hadn't already crossed it.

She slammed down the phone in defeat, but quickly picked it back up after biting her lip to dial 411. A sentient voice on the other end let her breathe a sigh of relief.

"I need the number for the FBI office in Las Vegas, Nevada," she sputtered out.

When the number was read back to her automatically, she compared it with the one she'd always used in the past and found that it was slightly different. Two digits off. She found the discrepancy odd, but quickly marginalized it by considering that the number she'd routinely used to reach her husband's office might have been reserved solely for digital communication.

The front door was suddenly rattled by a loud knock. Her balmy lips twisted in aggravation and she laid the receiver back down on its base.

"Please, Mr. Coleman, I just need some time," she pleaded loudly as she approached the front door, wiping a tear from her cheek.

She twisted the knob and pulled open the door. It only opened two inches before coming to a snapping halt. She had forgotten she'd chained it.

Poking her head around the opening while fiddling with the chain, she continued. "Listen, I know you've come a long way, but—"

Her words stopped short and her eyes widened when she realized that the man standing at her front steps was not Sean Coleman. What she had expected to be the coarse mug of the man from Colorado was replaced by the kind smile of an older gentleman, perhaps in his late sixties. It took her by surprise.

Dressed in a full-rimmed canvas hat, yellow polo shirt, and khaki shorts, the tall, wrinkly-faced man with basset-hound jowls lowered his head down to her eye level.

"I'm sorry to disturb you ma'am," spoke the voice of a polite, articulate, and seemingly well-educated gentleman. "I was hoping this was the right house, but it seems I'm mistaken."

Lisa was a disheveled, nervous wreck and her frame of mind wouldn't allow her to react. Her appearance didn't go unnoticed.

She could see the concern in his eyes through his thin, circular-framed spectacles. He squinted, hesitating as he then asked, "Ma'am, are you okay?"

"Yes," Lisa instinctively answered as she shook her head and rubbed a hand to her swollen eyelid. "I . . . I'm sorry. I . . . I thought you were someone else." Her muddled mind struggled to find clarity.

The man chuckled and smiled. "Well, I've got the opposite problem. Some friends of ours are expecting us for brunch and we can't seem to find their cottage."

"Brunch?" she asked with resigned confusion.

"Yes. Ronnie Wilson and his wife Mary. My wife and Mary went to school together. We've never been over to their summer home before, and, well . . . Ronnie assured us that it would be a cinch once we drove in through the front gate, but apparently my ability to read directions isn't what it used to be." He chuckled again, holding up a half-sheet of notebook paper with sloppily handwritten notes.

Her eyes went from the piece of paper to the beige Volvo coupe whose tail end she saw sticking out from her driveway.

Lisa was in no mood for talking, and she felt she could get rid of him quickly by just pointing him in the right direction and sending him on his way.

"Oh . . . yes. Of course, the Wilsons," she said through a raspy voice. "Ronnie and Mary are at lot one-twelve. This is lot one-fourteen."

The older gentleman's eyebrows raised, and he removed his hat to wipe a bead of sweat from his forehead. His bald scalp was red from sunburn, but it was the quarter-sized, darkened bruise partially covered by a butterfly bandage that was more noticeable.

"Honey!" he yelled in the direction of his car. "It's lot one-twelve, not one-fourteen!" He turned back to Lisa. "I'm so sorry, ma'am. I appreciate your help."

"It's not a problem."

"Now, do I want to go left when we get to the bottom of your driveway?" he asked while scratching the top of his freckled head.

She tried to keep her diminishing patience concealed. "No, you need to go right, and then turn . . ." She shook her head. "Just a second . . ." She closed the door to unchain it and then stepped out onto the short wooden patio alongside the lost stranger. "It's kind of complicated. Their place is even more secluded than ours."

She turned and pointed toward the bottom of the winding driveway. "At the bottom of the hill, take a right. You want to go down to the second road and turn left. Don't turn at the first left. That's just another driveway. From there, I believe it's the third or fourth lot. The driveway is clearly marked out front, so you shouldn't have any problems."

Standing behind her, the man said. "Great. Thanks. You've been a big help."

Her eyes narrowed as a memory from the day before suddenly skipped across her mind. While running along the beach, she had heard a couple of resident blowhards joking about how Ronnie Wilson's wife wanted to go to the Hamptons that month, so the couple wouldn't be making it to Traverse City until later in the season.

Lisa's face turned pale, but it wasn't from the conflicting recollection of the previous day's conversation. It was from the full view she now had of the Volvo parked in her driveway. From inside the house, she could only see the back end. Now she could clearly see the entire automobile, more specifically, the driver and passenger seats. Both empty. No wife to be seen.

She quickly spun around to face the stranger who had asked her so innocently for directions. What she saw wasn't his face, but a bare-knuckled fist headed straight below her mouth.

Then nothing.

———————

The metallic taste of her own blood forced her to spit up the soggy, claret-colored liquid pooled behind her throbbing mouth. A couple of teeth seemed loose and her jaw didn't feel right. It was either a bit off center or maybe just swollen. A dizzy spell flattened her back to the floor when she tried to climb up from her hands and knees. She felt a depressed weight on the floor beside her. The rasp of a floorboard signaled that he was standing right next to her.

"Why, Mrs. Kimble," greeted the man whose voice was eerily calm. He spoke almost cordially, as if he was still standing on her front step.

Lisa forced herself to crawl toward an extra dining chair that stood against the wall beside her. Her rapid breathing caused her to gag on some remaining blood that had trickled down the backside of her throat. She latched onto the seat of the chair with her arms and pulled herself up to her knees. That's when she felt the large sole of a shoe pressing against her shoulder. With a single shove of his leg, her body spun sharply and she toppled onto her back.

From the floor, she could see him now. Looking every bit as

harmless as he did when she'd opened the door, the man even formed a kind grin when their eyes met. He removed the hat from his head and leisurely tossed it onto the top of a small end table beside him. That's when she saw another object resting along the table that drew a startled gasp that sprayed up from her chest. It was a black pistol. She assumed he must have set it there while she had faded in and out of consciousness. She dug her heels into the carpet and briskly scooted against the wall behind her.

He grabbed onto the back of the chair beside her and dragged it a few inches away from her before sitting down in it, crossing his legs.

A drop of blood diluted a strand of drool that webbed along the side of her chin as she sat up on the carpet.

"What do you want?" her shaken voice inquired.

"Your chin," he expressed with the nod of his head before reaching into his front pants pocket to retrieve a cream-colored handkerchief.

He tapped the side of his own cheek like a mother indicating to her child that she'd missed a smudge of jelly after lunch. He tossed the handkerchief underhand, down to the floor beside her. Her eyes followed the piece of cloth but they quickly returned to him.

"You know, I saw your picture once," he said. "You and your worse half, smiling with glee. Backpacks across your shoulders. A fun, desert hike on a sunny day. A precious memory, I'd imagine."

Lisa fought to wrap her mind around the situation she was in. She knew immediately which photo the man was describing. It was taken by a young couple she and her husband had met on a hiking trip over two years ago, near Lake Tahoe. Kyle had kept the photo in his wallet. *Who is this man? How did he know my husband?*

He continued. "I must say that you're far more stunning in person. It makes me wonder what hidden talent the man must have had to be such a killer with the ladies. What? Was he hung like a horse?"

She said nothing. Her eyes nervously danced around the room

looking for a means of escape or at least a weapon she could use to defend herself against him.

A boyish smirk rippled along his mouth before he spoke again. "Listen, I just heard you talk. I know I didn't whack you hard enough to mess up your speech. I just want to chat for a moment."

After some formulation, she envisioned herself quickly climbing to her feet, sidestepping the intruder, and dashing toward the front door. However, those hopes were dampened when she realized that the man had secured the multiple locks that lined that door.

"Just tell me what you want," she asked with a quiver in her words, immediately fearing how he might react. "How do you know my husband?"

"Well, I don't think that's all that relevant of a question," he quickly replied before sitting straighter in the chair and placing his open hands across his knees. "I've got a better one. What brings you to the great state of Michigan today? Why did you come out here?"

She struggled with how to answer, confused with the unknown context of the man's question. Was it possible he was someone her husband had investigated? His presence had to be tied to the timing of her husband's death, but she hadn't a clue how.

"Oh, come on! You can tell me!" he persisted before throwing his hands up in the air excitedly. He glared into her confused, sunken eyes. The subtle curve of his eyebrows seemed to almost express a sense of enlightenment. "Maybe I'm asking the wrong question," he speculated before leaning back in his seat. "Let's try this one, Lisa. What did your husband do for a living?"

She hesitated to answer, unsure if releasing the truth would escalate eminent harm upon her.

"A traveling salesman?" he said with the shrug of his shoulders. "Nah, too easy. Oh, how about a bus driver? A Greyhound bus driver! Now *that* would have been a good one. It would explain all those lonely nights. Wait, wait, I got it! A circus mime! He'd have been *made* for that job!"

She just stared. This man clearly knew her husband well, including his schedule and disability. She conjured up the most conservative job title she could think of and answered. "An accountant! He's an accountant."

"Oh, come on!" An almost devilish grin draped above his chin. "That's no fun! Although I suppose keeping it real made it easier to bullshit you."

Staying seated, he straightened out a leg and jammed a hand into his shorts pocket where he retrieved a small white, plastic tube. It had a cone-shaped cap that he quickly unscrewed to reveal a nozzle.

Lisa's heart seemed to stop as the thought that it might be some sort of syringe overcame her. She breathed in relief once he raised the tube up and implanted the nozzle inside one of his nostrils. He squeezed the tube and inhaled deeply to greet the rush of saline that jetted up his nasal cavity. He did the same with the other nostril. The process ended with a satisfying sigh.

As he returned the container to his pocket, he nonchalantly shrugged his shoulders and explained: "Allergies."

"Listen, my husband's not here right now. I don't know what kind of business you have with him, but I haven't heard from him in days. Tell me what you want and . . ."

"I know you haven't heard from him in days, Lisa. Can I call you Lisa?"

She offered a timid nod.

"I know you haven't heard from him because he's been dead since Saturday."

Her eyes widened and she swallowed hard, unsure of how to respond.

"But you already knew that, didn't you? You see, I suspected it when you answered the door with those sad, puffy, red eyes." He mockingly put his hands on his hips and folded his lower lip. "But what clinched it was the fact that I've been talking about Kyle in the past tense this entire time, and you haven't asked why."

He snickered, causing his loose jowls to waver like a curtain behind an open window. He seemed to enjoy reading the fear and confusion in her eyes, as if he were getting off on preemptively narrowing any wiggle room she had in telling him anything other than the truth. "That raises yet another question, of course . . . How did you know he's dead when no one else knows he is?"

He leaned back again, this time recoiling his elbow along the top of the end table beside him and using the tip of his index finger to tap the grip of the pistol he'd left there.

Lisa squirmed along the carpet and wondered if the man who sat before her could hear the pounding of her heart. She hadn't enough ammunition in her arsenal of knowledge to predict the answers that would ensure her safety. She decided that a web of deceit would be obvious and counterproductive. Careful emissions of information were a safer gamble.

"A man . . . someone I'd never met before. He came to my door this morning and told me."

The intruder's face turned dead serious. He stood up from his chair and her heart stopped. *A bad gamble*, she instantly thought.

"What man? What was his name?"

She swallowed and answered, "Coleman. Sean Coleman."

The intruder's mouth gaped open and he snatched his pistol from the coffee table.

"Oh, God, no!" she screamed. Her hands flailed in front of her and she hid her face behind her shoulder.

"How long ago was he here?" he yelled.

"Just now!" she cried. "He left right before you got here! Please, don't!"

The intruder's free hand clogged the pocket along his shorts. His breaths were short as he pulled out a small, gray cellphone and punched in some numbers with his thumb. He held the phone to his ear with his teeth gnashed together, cursing the delay of waiting for the other party to pick up.

"Come on, come on!" he grunted impatiently.

With his attention directed at the phone, Lisa eyed a stout, glass candleholder that rested on top of the same end table where the intruder had previously laid his gun. She knew it was heavy and thick and that its size would make it a perfect fit for the grip of her hand. Her gaze then flipped back to the diversion in his eyes, waiting for an opening, perhaps once he was engaged in whatever conversation he was about to have.

Chapter 30

The lengthened stride of Sean's legs winded down as he rounded the long driveway on his way back up to Lisa's house. His mind was wandering and he nearly overlooked the brand new Volvo V70 parked in front of the garage. It hadn't been there the first time he'd showed up at the cottage, but its color resembled that of a car he'd seen from a distance through a curtain of trees as it skimmed its way up Bluff Walk Road. Sean had been headed in the opposite direction, making his way down the slope of the forest floor.

He clasped a thin manila envelope in his hand, having played the hunch that it had arrived from Colorado, and sure enough, it was sitting in Lisa's mailbox at the bottom of the hill. It may have arrived as recently as that morning. The envelope looked small in his large hand. Across the top of it was the slightly smeared ink postmark from the main post office in Lakeland, Colorado. The postmark had cancelled out a row of first class stamps that looked to have been hastily sealed to the envelope, judging by their uneven placement to the edge. The destination address was written in red ink and the envelope itself displayed a fair amount of wear from travel.

The Volvo had Michigan plates. Sean assumed it belonged to a friend of Lisa Kimble's: possibly a neighbor, though the car had a rental decal on it. It made sense to him that she would want a familiar shoulder to cry on in the wake of the terrible news he'd delivered to her a mere thirty minutes earlier.

He deduced that he'd be far from a welcome sight to the grieving widow who'd essentially kicked him out of her house, but it mattered little. What mattered was what he had to tell her.

He lurched up the steps, still breathing heavily from the jog up, and let the stately door have a set of sharp knocks from the back of his knuckles. Almost immediately, he heard an abrupt crash as if something had fallen to the floor close inside. The sound's peculiarity was instantaneously replaced by the harrowing scream of a woman that heightened his pulse in an instant. His eyes broadened, and he reached for the doorknob.

His stomach was clenched into a ball at what could have made the sound from inside. The doorknob wouldn't budge as he twisted it, and he continued to hear sharp movements from the other side of the door. Another wail of distress from the person he was now certain was Lisa filtered out from behind the walls.

He reached for the back of his pants to retrieve his gun and dropped the envelope to cup his other hand beside his mouth.

"Mrs. Kimble!" he yelled into the air. "What's going on?"

His mind was fluttering with possible explanations of the calamity inside—other than the one that seemed almost an afterthought in the letter he'd just read. Could *they* have found her?

With his heart racing and his adrenaline bubbling over, he erred on the side of disaster. He took two steps back across the front deck. He couldn't say for sure what he was about to get himself in the middle of, but his combative nature was about to get him there.

With a clenched fist, he readied himself to launch a fierce kick into the door to bust it wide open, but his eye caught movement in the front paned window to his left. He quickly twisted his head, and despite some glare from the sun, could make out the figure of a man who stumbled backward and into the glass with a thud. His back shattered a section of one of the panes, sending broken glass crashing down along the inside sill.

The intruder turned to face Sean and the two men's eyes met for a chilling, mutually confused moment. With blood noticeably dripping from the side of the man's head, Sean froze. He quickly snapped out of it when his eyes found a black pistol rising along with the man's arm. The sunlight highlighted the weapon for Sean with such clarity that there was no mistaking what it was.

Eyes widening, Sean gasped and threw himself over the railing on the opposite side of the deck. As his body awkwardly hit the ground below shoulder-first with an echoing thud, he heard the clamor of more glass shattering behind him. Despite there being no sounds of a weapon discharging, he knew he was being shot at. With his elbows, he quickly pulled himself along the dense ivy and moist earth, keeping low to the ground.

It was *them*. They had come for her.

Inside, Lisa heard the intruder stagger back to his feet among the thick glass shrapnel that littered the floor. His gun remained in his firm grip despite his momentary disorientation. His arm swung toward her as she retreated, but she had already disappeared around the corner of the living room hallway.

Lisa recognized Sean's voice calling from outside, but upon hearing the wicked sound of crashing glass coming from the living room she feared he could very well be dead. Her life may again be in her own hands. She raced down a hallway toward the backdoor where she came to an abrupt halt. A heavy oak bookcase blocking the exit made her heart stop. She and her husband had placed the bookcase there at the end of the previous summer to make room for a new desk in the office. She had forgotten about it. Filled full of large hardback novels, she knew she couldn't move it aside in the amount of time that meant life or death. She glanced over her shoulder as she heard running footsteps quickly approaching. Her stomach clenched in a large knot as she realized that she had no direction to go but up. Beside her was the spiral stairs that led to the lofted bedrooms above.

Sean got to his feet and flattened his back against the closed metal garage door at the front of the house. It rattled from his weight, which he dreaded might give away his position to whoever was inside. He raised his gun up by his chest. Seeing no windows above the garage, he was confident that he was concealed from all lines of fire from the house. Still, he feared the shooter could run out that front door at any second, and Sean couldn't afford to wait and hope for the best.

He held his father's Colt tightly in his hand, pointing it in front of him as he cautiously circled around to the opposite end of the house. He felt it too risky to go up to the front door again. Too exposed. His boots slid on damp soil as he crept along the frame of the cottage, careful to keep his head low when passing under the windows.

He found a small set of wooden steps leading up to a backdoor. It was locked, too. Holding the gun at his chest, he counted to three and lunged forward, slamming the bottom of his boot solidly beside the doorknob.

Lisa held her breath while crouched down on all fours beside the king-sized bed in the master bedroom. Concealed on the opposite side of the bedroom's entranceway, she feverishly searched under the bed and behind the end table for anything she could use as a weapon. A pair of slippers and dust bunnies was all she found. When she heard the rattle of the staircase, she knew her attacker was close. Her teeth chattered and she bit down hard to suppress the noise. Tears flowed from her red eyes and down the sides of her cheeks. Her body trembled as she lowered herself as flat as she could to her stomach. She lifted the dust ruffle and searched farther underneath her bed. While the ruffle draped down along the opposite side as well, there was a raised area of about an inch that provided a fabric-encased peephole to the entrance to the bedroom. An internal debate ensued as to whether or not to slide her body completely under the bed; it was a tight fit and she didn't want to immobilize herself.

The creak of a nearby floorboard sent chills up her spine. She stayed on her stomach, digging her fingernails and toes into the carpet—positioning herself to be able to spring to her feet at a moment's notice. Her eyes remained focused on the little section of open cloth. Her heart stopped when the point of a brown loafer came to rest mere inches from the edge of the bed.

She gazed in terror. He was right there . . . no more than six feet away. She knew she was trapped, and she closed her eyes.

A loud thud echoed up from main level, and she realized the man from Colorado was still alive. Silencing her breathing, she could hear her assailant's feet shuffle back into the hallway in reaction to the noise.

Sean's force cracked the door from its frame, but the opening was no wider than an inch. He slammed his fist down across some of the splintered wood along the frame and drove his shoulder hard into the door. Something blocked it from opening any further. He threw his shoulder into it again, this time using more of his body.

He heard a row of thick books fall from the bookcase on the other side of the door, landing like a ton of bricks. He was left with a little more of an opening, but it was still too narrow to squeeze through.

A portion of the frame suddenly exploded into splinters from a gun blast close to Sean's face. He raced away from the door, certain the assailant had about as good of a view as he did. Desperately looking for another way in, he spotted another door—a white one at the side of the house along the back deck.

Another creak of floorboards told Lisa that her attacker hadn't gone far. It sounded like he was standing just outside the doorway of the bedroom, waiting for Sean to enter the house.

From the floor, she peered forward at the open terrace at the edge of the loft. There was a four-foot-tall safety barrier and then nothing but open air and light fixtures. The living room was somewhere between twelve and fifteen feet below. In her mind, she struggled to remember how the furniture below was positioned. The sofa had to be right below the edge of the loft. Lying flat on the floor, she was like a sitting duck. Holding her breath, she counted to three and launched forward, driving her knees at a sharp angle and sending herself toward the opening.

Out of the corner of her eye, she saw her attacker swinging his body in front of the doorway, but she didn't turn to face him. She jetted off her feet and dove over the barrier. As she did, her right hand clasped onto the horizontal edge of the wall in an instinctive attempt to prevent her body from overshooting the couch. Hooking herself along the edge, she quickly let go and dropped straight down. As she did, she could hear the sound of drywall being punctured by bullets and crumbling above her. She fell horizontally for what seemed like an eternity before her shoulder slammed into the armrest of the sofa. Her body buckled and she bounced to the floor with a thud.

Pain surged through her back, but she hadn't a second to spare. She scrambled to her knees and dove out of the line of fire underneath the loft just as she heard fabric slice beside her and saw foam spread out into the air from a cushion on the sofa. She howled in panic, recalling her attacker had secured every lock on the front door. With thundering footsteps pounding from above, she knew she couldn't make it through the door in time. The backdoor was blocked by the bookcase; her only chance was the side kitchen door. She darted to it.

The steel spiral staircase rattled with ferocity, and Lisa knew her pursuer would be right behind her in a matter of seconds. Her burning shoulder slammed into the hallway wall as she got to the kitchen. There would be only one lock to contend with and she prayed she'd be able to quickly get it open. Linoleum screeched below her feet as she made it there. The door was just ahead, visible only a few feet away. Her legs felt like they were in quicksand in some horrible nightmare as she desperately held her hand out, preparing to work the lock. But with just a few feet left, her eyes widened in shock. At the flap of the dog-door in the backdoor, a large fist thrust through, grasping a larger gun than the intruder's. Sliding through behind it was a large arm.

She braked herself, feet slipping out from under her, making her drop straight to her butt. Her arms instinctively raised in a defensive position in front of her body. "No!"

Sean's arm and the right side of his face were as much as he could force of his body through the narrow doggy-door. With a loud snarl and instinctive focus, he trained his sight just above the panicked woman sitting directly in front of him.

"Move!" he commanded in a voice loud enough to make a drill-sergeant jump.

Lisa quickly spun flat to her stomach and wrapped her arms over the back of her head. She shut her eyes, lips moving in prayer.

Sean took a breath, steadied, and squeezed the trigger.

Ear-piercing shots thundered wickedly into the air above Lisa's body.

A hideous, agonizing shriek from the attacker echoed off the walls of the kitchen, followed by the sound of a metal object crashing to the floor.

Sean found himself virtually paralyzed in awe as he watched the tall, lanky figure stumble backwards into the hallway, the man's hand glued to the side of his throat. As he spun off balance, his wide eyes helplessly glimpsed his own blood splattered across the wall beside him. More blood ran through his fingers like water streaming through the cracks of a fractured dam.

Lisa, shaking uncontrollably from the thunder of bullets and bloodcurdling cry, managed to lift her head in time to see the assailant drop to a knee and then flat to his chest with an imposing thud. Above the ringing in her ears, she heard a gurgling noise coming from his mouth. His legs twitched for a few seconds and were then still.

Her face was white as snow as she turned to meet Sean's own blank stare.

Grimly compliant in each other's silence, their equally frail eyes asked a hundred questions of each other.

Chapter 31

Lisa's body twitched sporadically, like she was experiencing the aftereffects of being tased.

"Please!" she snapped. "Please . . . I just need a second."

She was intensely frightened, confused, and didn't want anyone's hand on her shoulder—even if that person had just saved her life. Sean hadn't placed his hand there to comfort her. He was just trying to get her to stop shaking. She had barely found enough composure to lift herself up off the floor and let him inside.

His state of mind wasn't much better. He was practically hyperventilating, chest heaving in and out with a hand pressed to his stomach to contain the nausea. He had never shot a man before, and never dreamed he'd have to. It wasn't like on television—cut and dry, even glorified. The reality was one of absolute sickness. The imposing stench of lingering gunfire still hung in the air, the blasts rang in his ears, and the feeling that his heart was going to pound a hole through his chest heightened the nausea. But the worst part was the instantaneous guilt and remorse of taking a man's life. Sean knew he had done the right thing, but his transient conscience was far from content.

The assailant's gun lay on the center of the tile floor, not far from the corner where Lisa sat, still trembling, with her knees pulled into her chest. She had remained there since letting Sean in.

He slowly walked toward the lifeless body, craning his neck to peer over the fallen man's shoulder. The sight of those large, wide-open eyes came into view along with the blood that surrounded the man's head like an abstract halo. Sean's knees went wobbly and he placed his hand on the wall to keep upright. There it found a warm splotch of fresh blood, which caused his labored stomach to turn.

"What the hell is going on?"

He heard Lisa's shaky voice from behind him. He spun his head to meet her eyes. The way she looked, with her distressed scowl, pale face, and quivering lower lip, looked strangely familiar. After a moment, he realized that the sight reminded him of his sister Diana—the way she had looked years ago, when their parents would scream and fight in the next room.

He swallowed some bile, then cleared his throat. Coughing the shakiness from his voice, he answered, "Listen, you're in danger."

A spasm of spontaneous, awkward laughter erupted from deep within her. It was the second time Sean had prompted such a reaction from her that day. She couldn't help it. Again, it disappeared as quickly as it came. She placed a hand to her face, her fingertips pressing against her forehead while she stared at her knees.

He could see the obviousness of the situation pass over her face. She had just been brutalized by a man now lying in a pool of blood in her hallway and the man who now stood before her was announcing that she was in danger, like that wasn't apparent.

"Well, Mr. Coleman," she began without looking up. "It would appear you're right." She dwindled into tears and shook her head.

He was at a loss. He wasn't built with compassion or the capacity to comfort others. He let her cry and turned his head back to the man on the floor. He carefully stepped over the body's outstretched leg, avoiding a puddle of blood that aggregated there. Sean had gotten him in the leg as well. Squatting down beside him, he shook his head and guided his index finger and thumb into one of the man's back pockets.

"Jesus! What are you doing?" Lisa inquired through narrow, puffy eyes. "Just call the police!"

He glared at her blankly, as if he was carefully deciphering her words, then he dug his hand into the other pocket. A confounded expression resided on his face when he then stood back up.

"No wallet," he muttered.

The loud, unexpected pulse of the doorbell commanded quick silence from both of them. Sean jolted before snapping a look toward Lisa who quickly scrambled to her feet and gazed numbly back. He yanked his gun from behind his waistband and held it at attention.

"Were you expecting anyone?" he whispered sharply.

She shook her head.

He squared his jaw and motioned for her to stay put. He carefully stepped over the dead body and blood, staying close to the wall as he made his way down the hallway toward the front door.

Unsure whether to abide Sean's wishes, Lisa crept her way up to the dead man but went no farther. She watched Sean from there.

He reached the end of the corridor and poked his head around the corner. She saw him steal a glance through the small shattered window along the front door. He turned to her just as the bell rang a second time. This time, it was followed quickly with hard banging.

"Hello?" a male voice shouted. "I'm with security! Is everything okay?"

"It's some guy with a uniform!" Sean hissed.

She scurried down the hallway to his side. She peered around the corner, along his shoulder. Even amongst the chaos, he found himself taking note of how pleasant her hair smelled. The man at the door's face was only partially visible from their vantage point, but his uniform was unmistakably that of the gated community's security team.

"It's okay," she declared as she whisked by Sean and toward the front door.

"Wait!" he said, still assessing the situation.

Before he knew it, she was working feverishly to unlock the door.

Her rapid breathing muffled the sound of broken glass crackling beneath her shoes.

He grunted and quickly slid his pistol down the back of his pants.

"Mrs. Kimble?" came the man's voice.

She nodded. "Yes!"

"I thought I heard what sounded like a gunshot from the road. Was there . . . an accident?"

"Someone attacked me!" she exclaimed as she swung open the door, causing a sheet of shattered glass to crumble to the floor.

She lunged forward to embrace the man, but quickly realized that it wasn't Marty. In fact the guard who stood before her looked more like a teenager—wide-eyed with an oily complexion and short, brown hair that was spiked along his bangs. He was a bit on the short side, thin and unable to fill out his uniform that looked a size too large. He looked to be in his early twenties and smelled of cigarette smoke.

"You were at–attacked, ma'am?" He spoke in a shaky, nervous voice. He swallowed hard with his eyes fixated on Lisa's beat-up mouth. He quickly fumbled for the handgun in a black, leather holster at his side and drew it out in front of him. "Is the p–p–perpetrator still here?" he quickly asked as he used his free hand to hook Lisa's shoulder, pulling her to shelter behind him. His trigger hand shook noticeably.

"No. No, no," she quickly clarified. "He's dead!"

"What?" the guard yelped in confusion.

"He's dead!" Sean stated loudly from the hallway.

"Jesus!" the guard cried as he dropped to a knee and briskly swung his gun in the direction of the new voice.

Sean's eyes widened, and he quickly raised his open hands out in front of him to expose that he wasn't a threat.

"No!" Lisa yelled to the guard.

"Calm down, kid!" shouted Sean. "The bad guy's dead! He's in the hallway!"

"Just . . . Everybody shut up for a second! Please!" pleaded the newly out-of-breath guard who struggled to cling to some semblance of professionalism.

He rose back up to his rubbery legs and asked Sean if he was Mr. Kimble. Before the big man could answer, Lisa explained Sean to be a friend and that her husband wasn't there. She continued on, excitedly relaying a vague version of the series of events that had just taken place from the moment the gunman appeared at her door. She said nothing of the death of her husband, which Sean found interesting. The three walked down the hallway to the body with the guard reluctantly in the lead and Sean hovering closely behind him.

Sean studied the young guard as he leaned over the body in curiosity with his gun aimed down cautiously at the corpse.

He glanced back at Sean and Lisa with a sick look on his face. "You sure he's dead?"

"Oh yeah," Sean answered confidently with a raised eyebrow, observing the kid's reaction. "What's your name?"

"Josh. Josh Jones," he answered with his eyes now directed back on the body.

Sean leered at the kid like a hawk, evaluating his movements and mannerisms.

"Have either of you already called the police?" asked Josh.

"No," replied Lisa. "We were about to."

"I'll do it," he said with a nod back toward the entrance of the house.

The three made their way back toward the front room. Lisa led the way and Sean motioned the guard in front of him.

As they left the hallway, Sean's forearm slammed into the side of Josh's neck like it was discharged from a mortar. He hammered the smaller man up against the wall behind him, yanking on his wrist and sending the guard's firearm to the floor where Sean quickly kicked it down the hallway. Framed pictures crashed to the floor, knocked loose from their mounted positions as he smashed the overwhelmed kid's head into the drywall.

Sean could hear Lisa's pleading screams at the violent beating that she turned around to witness. Shocked and confused, she demanded for Sean to stop. The guard looked like a rag-doll in the hands of the much larger Sean who repeatedly slammed his thigh into his gut. Josh crumbled to the floor with bulging eyes, mouth gaping for air.

"What are you doing?" Lisa screamed. "Stop it!"

She could hear desperate, gasping sounds wheezing out from the kid's mouth. She lunged toward Sean and fiercely grabbed onto his short hair with one hand while she sunk her fingernails into his flesh just above his eye. He winced and unloaded an open hand to her sternum that sent her stumbling backwards onto her butt.

"He's full of shit!" he snarled defensively before planting the sole of his boot into Josh's neck and pinning him to the floor along the baseboard of the wall.

He retrieved his pistol from his pants and swung the weapon up before his body, pointing it directly toward Josh's horrified, pain-stricken face. The kid's eyes were crossed as they homed in on the silver barrel just inches away.

"Stop it!" Lisa screamed again, this time from her knees. Tears streamed down her bruised face

Sean turned to her. "He's no goddamned security guard!" he shouted. "This asshole stumbles in here, sees breaking and entering, assault and battery, and a *dead* guy on the floor, for God's sake! And he hasn't touched his radio once!" He aimed his pistol toward the black, compact walkie-talkie opposite the guard's gun holster to direct her attention to it. "It ain't even turned on!"

Her face twisted in confusion. "Tell me you're joking!" she cried out. "You're beating the shit out of him because he didn't call anyone on his radio?"

Sean's head shook in disgust.

"If you've got back-up, you use it!" he snarled while keeping his boot on the kid and glaring angrily into his eyes. It was a line he remembered Jimmy Smits delivering on an episode of *NYPD Blue*.

"Where's your name tag, asshole?" he interrogated. "The guy down front had a shiny gold pin right there on his shirt pocket! Where's yours?"

He pried his foot from under Josh's neck and shoved it into his chest to keep him pinned. Josh let out a sick breath before several hoarse coughs erupted from his gaping mouth.

"I just started!" the kid unnervingly answered. Speaking must have been painful because his hand went right to his throat. "I'm getting it next week!"

Sean shook his head, sneering skeptically in response. He turned back to Lisa. "The guard down front at the gate . . . Do you know him? Don't say his name, but do you know him?"

She nodded, and Sean's head spun back to Josh.

"The guy down front, the pretty boy with the blonde hair . . . Tell me his name!"

"Martin! His name is Martin!"

"He's right!" Lisa injected. "That's his name. Call him! Call him right now and we'll straighten this all out! This kid's just trying to help us!"

The gears in Sean's brain spun rapidly as he glared down at the sight before him—a helpless, beaten kid pinned to the floor and looking up at him in anguish. Seconds went by. He thought of what had happened with Tariq back in Winston, but he also sensed that Jones's story was being adlibbed the same way as the one Sean himself had fed to the two children down the hill.

"Nah," he said. "I ain't buying it!"

"Oh my God!" shouted Lisa, throwing her hands up in the air. "Why not?!"

"I came back to your house for a reason. That letter . . . The envelope I told you about, that your husband sent . . . It was in your mailbox."

Her demeanor sobered, eyes narrowing in befuddlement. "You opened it?"

"Hell, yeah, I opened it! I didn't drive halfway across the country just to hand you your mail!" Sean quipped. "The guy I shot . . . He's not on his own. Not by a longshot!"

Josh's face was blank when Lisa's attention turned to him.

"Your husband was in some deep shit," said Sean. He steadied his gun hand and guided his pistol closer to Josh's face. "But you already know that, don't you, dickhead?"

"Please, mister! I swear to God I work here! I just started!"

Sean yelled at him to shut up. He bit down on his lip and shoved his gun to the back of his pants before lunging forward and pressing his knee down on Jones's chest to keep him floored. Jones squirmed wildly as Sean's hands reached under his body. When he felt Sean's spread fingers cradle each cheek of his buttocks, his eyes bulged from the aggravated violation.

"What are you doing, man?" he cried in utter appall that matched the expression on Lisa's face.

Sean leapt back to his feet and retrieved his gun, directing it back on Josh Jones. "Yeah, that's what I thought! He doesn't have a wallet either!"

"So?" Lisa asked.

"So . . . Neither one of these guys are carrying a wallet! The only reason a man doesn't carry a wallet is if he doesn't want to be identified!" Sean couldn't place which television show he'd acquired the theory from, but he felt the logic to be sound.

Jones shook his head fiercely. "It's in my locker, back at the station!"

"Bullshit!" yelled Sean.

"What was in the letter?" asked Lisa in a constrained tone that grabbed his attention. Her concern for the kid on the floor had seemingly drifted to the back burner for a moment.

"A lot of shit, but I ain't gonna tell you any more in front of *Josh Jones* here." He placed some sarcastic stank on the pronunciation of his name.

Her eyes fluttered back to the man on the floor. They soon honed in on his chest.

"Oh my God!" Lisa suddenly shouted.

"What?"

When she quickly crawled over to Josh, Sean warned her not to get too close. Her narrowed eyes quickly traced up and down the guard's body before they widened in confirmation of the button that was missing from the center of his shirt.

"He's wearing Marty's shirt! That's Marty's shirt!"

"Son of a bitch!" yelled Sean before planting a hard kick into Josh's gut.

"Where's Marty?" Lisa screamed.

Sean leaned forward and grabbed the radio from the kid's belt and yanked it loose. The second he flipped the "ON" switch, a loud, angry voice erupted from the speaker in mid-sentence: ". . . aren't you at your post, Marty? One of the residents just told me that the front gate is wide open!"

Sean snarled and glared at the wide-eyed Josh who raised his hands defensively but not quickly enough to blunt the heel of Sean's boot that came crashing down along his skull. Josh was out cold with a stream of blood quickly creeping out from under his gelled hair along the side of his head.

"Josh Jones my ass," Sean mumbled as he surveyed the sight before him. "Fake-ass name. Might as well have been John Doe."

Lisa's shaking hand covered her mouth as she winced at the view of the beaten stranger and the realization that he had done something to the nice man she had spent time with the night before. She looked to Sean for some sort of direction, acknowledging that his suspicions had validity to them after all.

"What was my husband into, Mr. Coleman?" she asked in a single breath. "The guy you shot . . . He asked me all kinds of questions about him. None of them made any sense."

"Later. We need to leave. Right now!"

She shook her head. "Leave?"

"Yes."

"Why don't we call the police?"

"No time. There may be more of them outside somewhere. He was planning on using your phone, remember?" he said. "Probably to call his friends."

He grabbed onto her wrist and pulled her close. She resisted only for a second, out of impulse. She hardly knew this man whose firm grip was cutting off the circulation to her hand, but she understood that if he wanted to hurt her, he would have done it already. He'd saved her life, probably twice, and there was no one else around to trust.

She was whisked out the front door beside him, following his lead. When they got to the front steps, he quickly climbed over the railing that he had unceremoniously been forced to tumble over when the chaos first erupted. From under a pine shrub, he grabbed the manila envelope he had retrieved from the mailbox down the road. It was now decorated with dirt and chips of mulch.

He held his gun in front of him as his eyes carefully scanned the area. He saw and heard no one.

"My car!" she yelled as the two trounced down the steps toward the driveway. "His car has me blocked in."

"We're not taking your car; we're taking mine."

He led her down a slope into the thick foliage at the edge of the curved driveway, glancing back at it as they disappeared behind a row of trees. He thought in the moment that he caught a glimpse of a small, gray car parked where the drive met the road, but he wasn't about to stick around for a closer look. The large, flush trees felt like a protective shield as he did his best to estimate how far west he had parked his car. He slid his gun back into his pants as he kept the envelope clutched to his side.

For Lisa, she felt that her last glance back at the cottage was like watching a door close on her life as she had come to know it.

They made their way through the forest and before long Sean heard the sound of crashing water—the same sound he had heard on the other side of the large wall in front of the cul-de-sac he had parked by. They approached an opening in the woods where sunlight divided the trees like a hot knife through butter.

"Your car is down here?" she asked, breathing heavily.

The sun's reflection across a body of water glimmered brightly, almost blindingly in contrast to the cover of the forest. The steepness of the hill turned abruptly sharp, causing both of them to pick up speed as they flailed down the slope across elevated roots and through low-lying limbs.

Something on the ground hooked Sean's foot. He lost his balance and stumbled wildly forward. His arms flung before him to break his fall as he crashed chest first into what looked for a second like snow under the radiant sun. But it wasn't snow. It was sand—soft, white sand like one would see in the trenches at a golf course. Lisa leapt down to his side where she saw him scrambling to climb to his feet after grabbing the envelope that he had dropped.

As he rose and adjusted his eyes, it was as if he had entered a portal into a different world. Sleek, crystal-blue waves stemming out from an endless horizon of water that crashed when they reached the shore. A large schooner could be seen far from land, skimming smoothly across the water. Seagulls hovered in the air, crying out into a light breeze as they dropped in unison to greet an elderly man with glasses and a brown leisure hat. A young child beside him held scraps of bread above his head. The child's laughter sounded as foreign as French to Sean at that moment.

"I don't get it! Did you come in a boat?" he heard Lisa ask.

Geography had admittedly never been Sean's strong suit, and he hadn't a clue until just then that Lake Michigan resembled a coastal ocean. It was radiant and beautiful, like a painting, crushing the preconceived notion of a large pool of glorified sewer water that he had long pictured in his head.

"What?" he asked, realizing that she'd spoken.

"Where's your car?"

Their attention immediately turned to the sharp sound of wood snapping somewhere up along the hillside they had just repelled down. He peered to his left where he saw the large, imposing wall at the far end of the beach about a hundred yards away where sand flowed out from under slabs of concrete and large rocks.

"Come on!"

He grabbed her wrist again.

She complied but glanced back at the old man and apparently his grandkid as they ran, wondering if she should have pled for their help or asked them to call the police.

Sean continually snapped his head back to check for anyone coming after them as they sprinted through the sand that hindered their forward motion. No one.

When they reached the wall, the out-of-breath duo climbed up a short hill of gravel and jagged chunks of broken cement to an adjacent retaining wall. Sean bent and deftly hoisted her up by her ankle with surprising grace, glaring back down the beach as he did. He gasped as he made out a male figure jogging out from the forest and onto the beach. He reached for his gun, drawing it out in front of him in one fluent motion. When a female figure joined the male in an affectionate embrace, however, Sean took a breath.

Lisa had hooked her arms across the top of the wall and pulled herself up. Sean did the same, but it took two tries. They straddled the top and crawled their way along, prying some imposing tree branches aside in the process. The sound of traffic trickled in through the leaves before they crossed an intersection where the two walls met. One last stolen glance from Sean detected no one. They dropped down to the other side of the wall where they were no longer visible from the beach.

Moments later, the bald tires from the old Nova whined as Sean rounded a corner quickly. Lisa's small body was pumping with adrenaline. She hadn't bothered with a seatbelt and she paid the price for that oversight when the sharp turn sent her sliding along the front seat's slick vinyl and into Sean's shoulder. She felt the sweat of his sleeve along her face for only a moment before scrambling back to her side.

She spun around to face the rear window, straddling the seat and draping her arms over the backboard to check for pursuers.

"You see anyone?" he asked, finding it difficult to share his attention between the curves of the road and the rearview mirror.

She shook her head, chest heaving in and out. She swallowed and turned toward him with questioning eyes.

"Please pull over," she asked in a tone that echoed her glazed and reddened eyes.

"What?"

"Just . . . I need a minute. We need to figure this out."

He checked the mirror again while a couple strands of sweat traced the outline of his jaw before disappearing into the scruff of his shallow beard. Once content that they weren't being followed, he took a left turn at the next intersection and quickly whipped down the first side street.

The two found themselves at the inlet of a residential dead end where he was sure they couldn't be seen from the main road. The unfinished homes that surrounded them were skeletons of natural wood and plastic tarps. Only a couple of them looked anywhere close to being finished.

Lisa began to speak, but he stopped her with a finger. He turned his head to glare out the back for a good ten seconds to verify they didn't have any company. He then turned his attention to her.

"We need to call the police. Do you have a cellphone?"

He shook his head and held out his hand in an attempt to calm her though his heart wasn't beating any slower than hers. "You need to know some things before we do anything else."

She looked at him as if he were crazy. "We *have* to call the police!" she shouted like a mother scolding her child. "Are you kidding me? I was attacked! People are trying to kill me!"

"I know that!" he snapped back. "I was there, remember? What you don't know is the whole story! There's more going on here than . . ." He wasn't sure where to begin. "There's a lot of stuff you don't know about!"

He reached between his legs and pulled the large envelope out from under his thigh. "Your husband wrote you a letter," he said gravely. "Read it before we call anyone."

The Previous Friday

Chapter 32

An uneven row of green and brown beer bottles implode at their centers as speeding lead slashes through them like they were decapitated by the single swipe of a samurai sword. Fine, glass shrapnel floats in the light breeze behind them, appearing as dust before dissipating into nothingness.

The rest of the men look to be cackling like crows around me, and they are slapping their hands together in applause. I join in when Alvar twists his head in our direction. The glare from the diminishing, early evening sunlight bounces off his glasses and his mane of silver hair, sparing me from the fountain of pride that is most certainly emitting from his dark eyes judging from the way that those crooked, yellow teeth of his show in a smile. The small shadows cast inside the deep pockmarks along both sides of his cheeks make his face look like one of the numerous weathered rocks that line the forest floor. In his large hands, he's holding a weapon Frank described to me as a "scoped thirty-thirty rifle." I have no idea what the number means but it looks shorter in length than most rifles I've seen. It has a wooden stock behind black metal and it doesn't really seem to fit Alvar, who's a city guy like the rest of us. Neither do his new cowboy boots that he bought in town yesterday. But when in Rome, I suppose . . .

The scenery here is beautiful. It really is. Standing among the tall, needled trees and struck with the surrounding smell of pine, it's an aura I'd nearly forgotten.

From his post about forty yards away beside the remnants of the bottles, Tony excitedly yells something into his walkie-talkie, which prompts everyone else to laugh. It's absurd that he's even using the radio. It's not as if the others couldn't hear him if he just raised his voice. He's not all that far away. Alvar likes his toys though, and he likes them even more when he has a playmate. The transmitters are fancy, with more buttons than you'd find on a phone. I'm sure each feature has its own useful purpose, but right now they're as pointless as two paper cups with a long string fastened between them.

Frank is squeezing a rush of saline solution up his nose again. It's the third time I've seen him shove the tip of that white tube up his nostrils today. His allergies don't like the climate. I'm surprised he even came along on this trip. He's getting up there in age, and if there's any muscle work needed, it shouldn't be anything that Alvar can't handle. Clad in a burgundy polo shirt and slacks, he's cleaned up a little more than usual.

"Your head's getting a little color," I tell him after eying the redness along his bald, freckled head.

Without bothering to turn around to face me, he raises his middle finger in response. He's not enjoying himself at all out here in the wilderness.

I glance over at Moretti and Arianna. He's decked out in a charcoal Italian suit that was probably tailor-made for him years ago. It still looks sleek and in fine shape, but its buttons are pulled so tight that it seems they could burst at any second. Every shoe-polished, black, glistening hair is in place along his broad scalp. Arianna is dressed to kill in a short, black cocktail dress far more suitable for a night out on the Vegas strip than in the mountains of Colorado. Moretti never misses an opportunity to show her off to business partners though, and tonight will be no different. She's clearly feeling the chill from the stirring wind, even with a fur stole draped over her bronze-colored shoulders. Her toned arms are crossed in front of her, and her glossy, thick lips are puckered in annoyance.

Moretti notices my attention turned to them and he nudges his stout elbow into Arianna's side, misinterpreting my gaze as an appeal for someone to relay to me whatever joke Tony just made. Visibly irritated by his touch, her yellowish eyes greet mine and she signs to me what Moretti is certain to believe is an interpretation.

"Have you ever fucked in the forest?" is the message she articulates with her hands.

Moretti laughs under his thick mustache when my eyes widen, thinking I'm reacting to Tony's words. He hasn't a clue what she just told me. Arianna's lips twist into a seductive smirk, and I'm forced to look away to avoid turning red.

Alvar raises the partnering walkie-talkie to his mouth, with the muzzle of the rifle in his other hand lowered toward the dirt. He broadcasts a message back to Tony, turning his back to us first so I'm not sure what he's saying. From across the narrow, open alley in front of us, Tony, with a cigarette dangling from his mouth, disappears behind a bordering tree. He retrieves what looks to be a long, broken-off tree branch. It doesn't look completely dead like the hundred other ones that litter the ground around us. It's got some green on it and is rather flexible, bent into the shape of a cane. Tied to the tip of the cane is a short piece of rope or twine that is attached at its bottom to a dangling object that has some weight to it—weight that is the cause of the bend in the branch. At first glance, it looks to me like a child's stuffed animal. When it begins wildly flapping around in the air, I realize it's no toy. It's a wild rabbit, scared out of its mind.

"Oh, you gotta be kidding me," I see Moretti mouth with a half-smile draped across his face. "Who are you now? Elmer fucking Fudd?" He snorts in captivation.

Arianna's not amused, but Tony sure is. He's dancing around like an idiot teenager while holding the branch up in the air as a trophy, like a fisherman who's just caught the big one. He then wedges the base of the branch between two of the relatively flat rocks that played table to the beer bottles. The branch holds firm and vertically in place as the rabbit squirms and kicks, to no avail. Tony skips out of the line of fire.

Alvar gets off on this stuff—tormenting the helpless. At least it's just a rabbit today. Lord only knows how he managed to trap it alive in the first place.

He's hunched forward now, sizing up his new target. From behind, his pearly hair above his broad, tall shoulders makes him look like a silverback gorilla who's envisioning himself devouring a banana. To everyone's surprise, he lets the rifle drop from his hand to the ground. We all exchange glances, wondering what theatrics are in store for us. He twists his shoulders parallel to the direction of the struggling animal. He then slowly raises his arm closest to his prey. He holds it there, outstretched to its extent, and he looks like a magician ready to will something to appear in front of him. He holds perfectly still in the position and seconds that seem like minutes go by. Arianna doesn't bother to watch, completely agnostic to the display. But she jumps when Alvar's elbow snaps and gray mist appears in front of him. I can tell by the others' reactions as well that a sharp noise just discharged.

I poke my head up over Alvar's shoulder and see Tony again bouncing around like an imbecile, now pointing to the bloodied, lifeless corpse of the rabbit. When Alvar turns back to us to take a bow for his performance, I spot a small, toy-like gun poking its muzzle out from under his jacket sleeve. Frank snickers at the sight of it and asks to take a closer look at the weapon, but Alvar shakes his head in rejection. The magician's not revealing how his trick was pulled off. This irritates Frank, who swats his own hand in the air and starts walking back toward the house in protest, much to Alvar's toothy delight.

Tony comes sprinting in from his stage with his cigarette pinched between two of his fingers, trying to latch onto Alvar's glory like a pilot fish swimming under the belly of a shark, eager for scraps. No one pays him any mind, even with his trademark dopey, attention-begging grin plastered on his face. With his dark hair spiked out in front of him and his oily complexion, he looks more like he could be

Moretti's teenage son than one of his paid flunkies. He's wearing a dark gray, short-sleeved dress shirt with his bolo tie in an apparent attempt to fit in among the other Colorado ranch hands in town. He probably bought it wherever Alvar bought his boots.

Moretti slaps Alvar on the shoulder, thanking him for the entertainment, and tells him something about an "appetizer for tonight." He holds Alvar's stare, then the two men exchange mischievous grins as if an inside joke had just been recollected.

Moretti then turns to me and says with a laugh, "You're not gonna get scared and lonely by yourself tonight, are you Kimble? I hear there are bears up here!"

"No, sir, I think I'll be just fine," I answer quickly before lending him the assured grin he's expecting.

"Good. I'll try not to feel too guilty eating steak and drinking wine in town while you've got your head stuck in the contracts."

The counterfeit grin remains on my face. "Have a good time tonight," I reply, fighting back the urge to tell him to go fuck himself.

Moretti raises his hand and drags his index finger toward the house, motioning us to follow.

"I'm going to take a little walk around, if you don't mind," I say. "Catch a few more minutes of that mountain air before I bury my head in paper."

He nods his head and leads the rest of the group back, jubilantly shouting something up toward the sky like a war cry. His lackeys laugh like hyenas in response. As they walk away, I leer at Arianna's legs. Her chiseled calves, preserved from her early years as a trained gymnast and countless hours on the StairMaster, stand above her black, stiletto heels. They're never easy to ignore. I imagine them wrapped around me like they were three days ago. She steals a glance back to me and flashes a wink in my direction. It's amazing that she can walk through the forest in those shoes, but I'm always in amazement of the things she can do with her body.

I take a gander out at the thick forest to the west. The large, imposing army of pine trees with peeling bark on their trunks seems to go on forever among their dead and rotted ancestors lying along the battlefield.

It's good to be outside for a change. I was beginning to think that the closest I'd get to the mountains on this trip was the scenic views I'd grab from inside the car or behind the windows of buildings. With my hands in my pockets, I meander along a little aimlessly and can't resist the temptation to step on pinecones and feel them crunch beneath the soles of my shoes like I used to do often as a child. The forests in Kentucky never had such a wide assortment of pines, though. What used to be a form of amusement is right now more of a stress reliever than anything else.

Tomorrow, maybe Sunday if there's another holdup, there'll be white sand beneath my feet as I walk alongside the lake with Lisa and uncomfortably sputter out the words I've been working on for weeks. Most would think it's one hell of a sick plan to tell your wife "it's over" in the midst of a presumed romantic vacation. They'd be right. Still, I feel like I at least owe her one last trip up to the cottage before I end it. She loves it there. Besides, I need Moretti and this life out of my mind for a few days. No distractions.

This trip's already taken a day longer than expected due to a last-minute renegotiation over the Colorado deal. It's just about done now. I'll get the contract reviewed tonight and everything will be signed first thing in the morning. *The Timberland Hotel and Casino*—it's got a nice ring to it.

A couple of scurrying brown critters weave in and out of a family of large, rounded rocks as I make my way up a modest slope. Either squirrels or chipmunks. I'm not sure which. I think I used to be able to tell the difference.

I'm sure I look a bit ridiculous, hiking out here along the rugged terrain in a pair of Oxfords and pleated pants, but besides the crew, no one's around for miles. I need a little bit of this to clear my head. I won't be out here long.

The sun's already beginning to dip below the treetops. I find myself longing to hold onto its brilliance for just a few more minutes, so I climb to the top of a boulder and stand on my toes to embrace its fading warmth on my face. When I can no longer see it but only its influence on the bright, crisp outlines of churning clouds hovering above, I hop down. The dimness reads as another closing chapter in a series of novels, with the promise of a new book beginning sometime in the near future.

I've never been much of a history buff, but the solitude that surrounds me in the forest makes me think of the journeys of the pioneers that once traveled through here, unsure of what they'd find in these mountains but fearlessly carving their way toward a better life nonetheless. I wish I had their courage, like I did the first time I started anew in a world unaware of my past. This time will be different. This time, I'll have to go to great lengths to assure my past won't come looking for me.

The shape of a heart carved with a knife into the side of one of the larger trees reminds me that I'm no pioneer. The wording spelled out inside it reads *Leslie and Jaime*. I wonder which one is the guy and which one is the girl, and if either is related to Moretti's new business partner.

If you're going to have hundreds of acres in your name, it might as well be out here. In addition to the casino, Moretti's partner owns a couple of residential properties in the area and was generous enough to let us stay at one. Three cheers for the man with the comb-over worse than Donald Trump's. After one of the meetings, he mentioned something to Frank about a river marking the western boundary of this property. It looked like he called it the Blue River, but I might have been mistaken. I'll just assume that if I come upon water, I've reached the end of the line. I probably won't even get that far. It's getting dark.

After a few minutes of trouncing along rocks, occasional animal droppings, and splotches of wild grass that snag my socks with burry-stickers, I come upon what looks like the bottom portion of an old chimney sticking less than six inches up from the ground. There are four walls of gray, stone bricks formed in the shape of a square. Their color and texture nearly let them blend in with the natural surroundings. Each wall is somewhere between four and five feet in width. It looks to have been constructed a long time ago, as attested by the crotchety wooden planks that cover the opening at the center.

Despite its resemblance, I'm certain it was never part of a chimney. When I put the weight of my foot down on one of the planks, I sense some depth below it. My curiosity gets the better of me and I find myself on my knees, leaning forward with my inverted head acting as a periscope while I peer down through an open divot where a knot in one of the planks used to reside. I smell water, and I'm sure I see a sliver of reflection from what little light is creeping over the sloped horizon to the west. No sooner do I realize that I'm kneeling above an old water well does the plank I'm resting my arms across crack in half. I only fall about shoulder deep before the other planks fork my body and halt my momentum, but that doesn't stop me from nearly having a heart attack from the short drop. I pull my arm out and check it for cuts but find only minor scrapes.

The well is deep enough that I can't find the bottom. The reflection I'd seen was from some rainwater trapped in a small pocket of concrete along the wall. Long, thick mazes of spider webs line the shaft that I sense was abandoned and boarded up decades ago. I take the evening's drama as a sign to head back and get to work, but not before I toss a couple of large limbs over the lair of the well. I doubt the area gets any hikers, being that it's on private property, but maybe I'll spare a mountain lion or something from falling to its death.

The others have already left by the time I reach the house. Both cars are gone from in front of the cobblestone garage that serves as a walkout basement below the main floor. I muse over the celebratory havoc Moretti and his entourage will wreak tonight among the locals and tourists. Bottles emptied into bottomless glasses. Live up the good life while you can, Moretti. Once your prize possession is gone, you might learn a long-deserved lesson in humility.

It surprises me that Alvar went along. He doesn't do well in social situations, and it's not like Moretti to bring him along unless his expertise is needed.

I smell some moisture in the air and I wonder if I might be in for a bit of a storm as I marvel again at the unique style of the custom home. It looks like a rustic lodge with dark-stained wood and three large gables in the formation of a pyramid across its face. Under the sloped roofs of the bottom two are sprawling windows and a walkout porch that joins at the top of the short flight of steps leading to the front door. I guess it's around 4,000 square feet of modern luxury, and probably worth somewhere around two or three million. Not bad at all.

I'm relieved when I find that the side door to the garage was left unlocked. I didn't even think to ask Moretti for a key before he left and my pulse skipped a beat when the knob along the front door wouldn't budge. I peel off my shoes once I enter onto the brilliantly lit hardwood floor of the kitchen and pull seed barbs from my socks. I retreat to the office at the back of the house where I've been doing most of my work. It's largely bare, other than a good-sized oak desk with a curved metal lamp on top and a couple of tall bookcases lined with more bookends and figurines than actual books. The room doesn't seem to get a lot of use. I pore through the papers stacked on the desk.

An hour later, I'm rubbing my strained eyes and notice beads of water crawling along the window beside me. When I tilt forward in my chair in the dim room and twist open the shutters, I see that the sky has gone dark and it's beginning to sprinkle outside. I'm taken aghast by the sudden, streaking flashes of light from above that accompanies the shower. I've heard about how quickly Colorado weather can change and now I'm experiencing it firsthand. Minutes go by and the rain doesn't pick up all that much, but the lightning is a different story. It dresses up the night sky like a lattice of Christmas lights blinking randomly but in continuous succession. I find myself mesmerized by its brilliance.

When I scoot myself back to the front of the desk, I steal a departing glance out through the window and notice a reflection in the glass beyond the glare from the lamp. It's in the shape of a large man, standing in the hallway behind me and remaining perfectly still.

Chapter 33

"Jesus, Alvar!" I yelp after spinning in my chair.

My heart pummels inside my chest while I glare at him in abashment. There's no grin on his face, which isn't typical for him just having spooked me. That kind of thing usually gives him a rise. His shoulders are damp from the splatter of rain and his hair's flat to his head. He's breathing harder than usual and he looks almost strung out, like he's just returned from a late night out on The Strip. He's saying something but the hall light behind him leaves me with little more visibility than a silhouette. Unable to read his lips, I motion for him to turn on the overhead light. He does. Though it's a single bulb and my view of him hasn't been significantly enhanced, I make out what he says.

"I'm going to be downstairs for a while. I don't want to be bothered."

I shrug my shoulders and say, "Okay," letting him know that I couldn't care less. I had no plans of even leaving the room until I finished the paperwork. I ask him if everyone else is already back as well and he tells me, expressionless, that it's just him. He stands there an extra few seconds after I turn my head back to the books. I sense him glaring at me and the awkwardness of it gives me a chill. It's as if he's assessing my reaction to his request, for which the paranoia is lost on me. He disappears behind the doorframe, but I can see his shadow cast along the floor in the hallway and I know he hasn't left.

My body stiffens with uneasiness that nags me with the feeling that something is very wrong. I extraneously shuffle through the pile of papers on the desk in an attempt to diffuse any lingering sense of his unusual behavior. A moment later, the shadow disappears and I let myself breathe. I shake my head and get back to work, wondering if he's headed down there to snort some coke.

The lightning is rising in intensity outside, as is the wind that I feel pressing against the back of the house. When the floor beneath me rattles, I can only imagine the wicked crack of thunder that just whipped down from the angry sky. After fifteen minutes or so, there's a flash that gleams in through the slits in the wooden shutters so brightly that the entire room is aglow. Seconds later, all lights go out and I'm left in the dark. I wait for them to flicker back on but they don't. I collapse back in my chair, frustrated by the distraction. Visibility only comes in spurts when dazzle from the spectacle outside imposes itself. Time rolls by slowly and out of boredom, I eventually feel my way along the walls of hallways until I reach the living room where a large arched window overlooks the Continental Divide. With my thumbs hooked in the pockets of my pants, I observe Mother Nature's extravaganza perform its way through the valley below, illuminating the forest range and humbling the vast line of mountains that towers above it.

I'm surprised by a pair of headlights that is hastily revealed along the stone driveway below. It's Alvar's Buick, already rolling quickly in reverse. He reaches the private dirt road where he flips the car at a wicked angle, sending light gravel into the air before he winds up facing the opposite direction. His wheels spin and in no time, he's tearing down through the valley like a Roman chariot pulled by wildly whipped horses.

"What in the hell is he doing?" I say out loud, just moments before his taillights disappear around a bend.

I find a deep, comfortable couch and I settle into it to watch more of the lightning show. No more than ten minutes drag by before I feel a pulse of life through the walls of the room. Decorative lamps and some overheads flare up. The ceiling fan above begins to rotate. I unravel my interlaced fingers from behind my head and begrudgingly rise to my feet. I return to the office to find that the dim light hung from the ceiling is now on but the desk lamp is not. I flick its switch at the base a few times and determine that it didn't survive the surge. Great. My work is laid out in purposeful piles along the desk so I don't want to relocate, but I definitely need more light.

I check a couple of hall closets and some cupboards in the kitchen—places one would expect to find a replacement bulb, but I find none. I do find a cold bottle of ginger ale in the fridge though, and I remove the cap and take a swig before I head down the staircase and into the basement. It's the first time I've been down here, and I'm surprised to find that the area is small and unfinished—a stark contrast from the luxurious furnishings in the rooms above. It makes me wonder what Alvar was doing down here before he took off like a dinner bell had been rung. I check the furnace room and find nothing but dusty paint cans, extra sheets of drywall leaning up against the walls, and cobwebs. Whatever he was doing, it wasn't cleaning.

At the end of the short hallway, there's a thick door with a silver security lock above the knob. I suspect it might be a storage room so I twist the knob and give the door a push, but it doesn't budge. I assume that if Comb-Over uses the house for guests, there's probably certain stuff he doesn't want visitors messing with and keeps it in locked storage. I take another taste of my drink and walk back toward the stairs. Before I reach the bottom step, though, it occurs to me to turn back and check the top of the doorframe for a key, in hopes that I'm lucky. I am. I feel the thin metal under my fingertips and I pull it down. It fits in the keyhole, and I feel the door give when I push on it this time.

The room inside is completely dark and the light in the hallway is of little help. It smells musty. I feel around along the wall for a light switch and soon find one. I flick it and the room lights up.

There's a row of aluminum shelves right beside me lined with boxes and some landscaping equipment. I hold up the rim of my drink to my lips and turn to face the rest of the room. When I do, I flinch wickedly at the sight of a man, terribly bloodied and beaten, laying on his side along the cement floor just a few yards in front of me.

My heart stops and my body goes numb. I feel the bottle of ginger ale shatter beside my leg when it crashes to the floor. My mouth is gaping open as I absorb the horror my eyes are struggling to accept. The man is strapped to an overturned steel folding chair. His wrists are bound behind him and his ankles are sealed to the front legs of the chair with duct tape. Beneath him on the floor is a large, doubled-over sheet of clear plastic like what would be used as a drop cloth when painting a room.

The man's eyes are shut tightly, and he twists his blood-soaked head to the floor to escape the glare of the light from above. His face is contorted in pain, which offers more evidence that he's alive. A few feet away from him is a large chain with thick steel links coiled along the floor. The man's blood decorates it.

My gut tells me to turn around, shut the door, and leave. I wasn't supposed to see this. It's not what I'm paid for. It's what Alvar is paid for. Whatever this poor sap has done to incur Moretti's wrath, it's not my concern. I'm very aware of the stone cold brutality my boss is capable of, but I'm purposely sheltered from that side of the business. To Moretti, having a deaf bookkeeper isn't a liability; it's an asset. I don't hear the kind of things I'm not supposed to hear. I've never eavesdropped on an incriminating conversation because I can't. I'm a prosecuting attorney's worst nightmare of a witness.

God, Alvar really beat the shit out of him. On his head, there's a welt the size of a golf ball and a deep gash along his cheek under his sickly swollen eye. What looks to be a tooth is coated in a splatter of blood in front of him on the plastic sheet. I don't think he's making it out of this basement alive.

I wonder what the unfortunate bastard did. We aren't in Vegas anymore. The guy can't be some smalltime dealer stepping on the boss's turf. It can't be related to the Colorado deal, either. It's on the up and up—at least for now. No one was getting their skull bashed in over a casino that Moretti hasn't even taken ownership of yet. I speculate that Moretti may have caught some yahoo in town staring too long at Arianna's ass and he went ballistic. It wouldn't be the first time, but those beatings were always quick and to the point, ending on a sidewalk or in the back of an alley. He didn't bring that shit home with him. If he only knew who was *really* getting a taste of Arianna.

The man's not gagged, which means he must have been screaming his ass off while that maniac, Alvar, worked him over. I'm sure the racket could be heard throughout the entire house, blaring up from the registers while I was right upstairs reviewing contracts and crunching numbers. All the pleading and crying . . . fallen literally on deaf ears.

Resting on a two-by-four that's part of an unfinished wall is a pair of black, polished goggles with a canvas strap weaved in and out of hooks beside the eyecups. I've seen them before. They're night-visions that Alvar picked up somewhere in Vegas. Alvar has never spotted an overpriced, eccentric combat tool that he didn't purchase.

The poor guy on the floor probably didn't even see a lot of those shots coming. Once the power went out, Alvar probably took the opportunity to grab his goggles from the car to continue the beating from the pitch dark. Knowing Alvar, he got off on it, the same way he gets off on making derogatory comments about me from just a few feet away when my back is turned so I can't read his lips. He doesn't do it when Moretti's around, but he likes to get a rise out of the boys. Having the edge on someone is like porn to that lunatic.

Now adjusted to the light, the man on the floor opens his eyes and glares at me. I gaze down to avoid a connection. Instead, I scrutinize the thick streaks of blood painted across his flannel shirt and the dried caking of mud along his denim jeans. I glance back up and I find him staring right through me. His face is a mixture of desperation and something else I don't quite recognize. He opens his mouth and a web of blood drips from his lips and onto the plastic. I begin backing my way out of the room when I feel something crack under my feet. Glass from the ginger ale bottle. Alvar and Moretti will know I was down here and saw their punching bag. I better clean up the mess.

I turn back to the shelves and wade through boxes and rubber containers as if I'm engaged in a weekend project, pretending for just a few moments that I'm in another world. Below a mounted pegboard with a handful of dangling tools, I find a ball of plastic grocery bags and a wad of cloth rags.

I keep my focus on the floor beneath me, carefully picking up shards of glass and placing them in one of the bags. I envision an empty room settled behind me rather than the crimson clump of a person withering along the floor. *He's not my problem*, I tell myself again. Once I'm convinced there are no more bits of glass twinkling along the floor, I use the rags to dab up the liquid. My breathing fluctuates when I notice that enough has been absorbed into the pores of the concrete to keep it looking wet. It's going to have to dry on its own but I worry how long that will take. Alvar could return at any time. I toss the rags into the trash bag with the glass and make sure that the items on the shelves are in the same positions as they were before I entered the room.

To survey the rest of the room for blemishes, I'm forced to glance back down at the man on the floor. Again I see his eyes. So intent are they on me that it's tough to look away. He raises his head an inch up off the floor and he says something to me. It's not *help*. I'm certain of that. He swallows and tries again. It's something that starts with a C or a K. It looks like *kill*. My adrenaline is pumping hard and I continue to have trouble catching my breath. I force the thought that he's begging me to end his misery out of my mind.

I begin to back up toward the door, feeling like the walls are closing in on me, yet I find myself peering again into his pleading eyes. Like before, I read something more than desperation in them. I turn and exit the room, flipping off the light switch on my way.

I close the door and am about to turn the key clockwise when an icy chill funnels down along my spine. I realize what I saw in his eyes: recognition.

He wasn't saying kill. He was saying "Kyle." My name.

Chapter 34

I swing back open the door and flip on the light. As I quickly pace toward him, I read his stained lips.

"It's me, Valentino Greco," he says.

I'm bulldozed to the floor. Valentino Greco. I prayed I'd never hear that name again. He's barely recognizable beneath the grime and swelling. Short hair now and no sideburns. He's gained weight. His face is fuller, but some of that might be from the swelling. The fact that Valentino is lying right here, right now, means that an atomic bomb has been released from high above and it's dropping fast. Its shadow's looming over me and is growing larger. Impact is imminent.

I fall to my knees as the room seems to spin. I grab Valentino by the chest of his shirt, feeling his blood ooze between my fingers and shout at him to explain why he's here. I can tell by his eyes that he doesn't understand exactly what I say. He always had trouble with that. He's no idiot though. He knows the gist of my query. I hone in on his soggy lips to read his response.

"Moretti fucking found me, man," he slurs.

"How?" I scream.

He shakes his head and says he doesn't know. He explains that he owns a shop in town now, and that Alvar was waiting for him when he stepped out back to empty the trash at closing time. I miss some of what he's saying behind his frothing, but it sounds as though he was stuffed in the back of Alvar's car and brought to the house.

I wouldn't have guessed in a million years that Valentino would have ended up in Colorado. When I told him that he needed to take his money and crawl under a rock, it seems he chose the Rocky

Mountains. I figured he'd end up blowing it all in strip joints, maybe
south of the border. At least, that was his style when I knew him.
Instead it appears he opened a reputable business. Even so, it seems
he couldn't bring himself to stray too far from slots and blackjack
tables.

He pleads with me to untie him, but charity isn't on my mind.
My ass is.

"What did you tell him?" I ask as clearly as I can muster, leaving
no room for misinterpretation.

He looks confused and again begs me to set him free.

I'm in no mood for his bullshit. I place my thumb in the open
gash along his cheek and press in. His mouth broadens as he screams,
and I can see every tooth left inside it.

"What did you tell him about *me*?" I shout. "Does he know I got
you the money? Does he know about me and Arianna?"

I watch his eyes look past me, and I can't tell if he's debating the
truth or if he's trying to figure out which answer I want to hear so I'll
let him go. His lower lip trembles, and I watch as a thick tear streams
down the side of his nose, pulling blood with it before falling to the
plastic in a blob.

"What did you tell him?" I scream at a volume that makes him
wince.

"I didn't tell him a fucking thing!" he screams before lowering
his head to the floor.

I fall back to my ass. Air escapes my lungs. I know Valentino's
lying. It's written all over his mangled face. He squealed everything.
It all becomes stunningly clear.

Alvar had stood in the hallway upstairs earlier to make sure I didn't
poke my head out and see him drag Valentino into the basement. I
doubt that moose knew a thing of my involvement before then. But
when Alvar sped out of here, it had to be because Valentino had
given it all up after taking the beating. The maniac was probably

salivating to tear me limb from limb by the time he reached the top of the stairs, but he wouldn't put a hand on me without Moretti's blessing, or else there'd be hell to pay.

It takes me a moment to figure out why Alvar didn't just call Moretti at dinner for instructions. He couldn't have. Cellphones don't work up here and the power outage took out the LAN lines because the house's phones, like most these days, need an electrical outlet. Right now, he's on his way to tell Moretti. He never counted on me coming downstairs and finding Valentino before they returned.

Arianna needs to be warned, but even if I knew how, it's surely too late. It only takes fifteen minutes to drive into town and Alvar has been gone for twenty. By now, Moretti knows it all.

The affair. The money. Everything.

It's almost a year to the date since the last time I'd seen Valentino Greco. He was Moretti's prize stooge back then, who held a master's degree in ass-kissing. I think the boss saw a younger version of himself in the kid, from the pompousness and that big, slicked-back hair to the over-the-top, cocky swagger whenever he walked into a room.

When Moretti was recovering from gallbladder surgery across town, Arianna and I were certain we had the place to ourselves. Greco showed us how wrong we were when he found her naked, sweaty body on top of mine in the boss's own walk-in closet. I was sure my life was over; if I hadn't convinced Greco to take the money and run instead of ratting me out, it would have been.

Nearly a million and a half . . . That was the price of my life that day. A large shipment of methamphetamines was due two days later from Mexico, and the Mexicans only dealt in cash. We had the bills wrapped up tight in cellophane blocks in the bottom of Moretti's wall safe outside his study.

I'm the only one Moretti trusted with the combo. He thinks of me as family, and he knows that I know what he'd do to me if I ever stole from him. I usually only access the safe to retrieve and return his financials, contracts, and other private paperwork that he's too skeptical to store digitally.

I knew Valentino was an opportunist; it exuded from every crooked smile and fake laugh. I prayed he'd see the big picture—a one-time opportunity to make more in five minutes than he could in thirty years as Moretti's chump. I also knew that he had no family. His parents were dead, no wife, and no kids—no one for Moretti to punish in his absence.

Still, it was a breathless gamble on my part, and one hell of a sell job. It could have easily gone the other way, with Valentino's eagerness to please the boss outweighing his personal greed. I made the case that if he ratted me out, he'd suffer the same death sentence that I would. Moretti's a big man in Vegas. He has an image to protect as someone who's always in control—three steps ahead of anyone who would dare cross him. I explained to Valentino that the boss wouldn't risk the secret getting out that his wife had been fucking his personal accountant behind his back. He wouldn't trust that secret to a bigmouth wiseass like him. I don't know if Valentino ever bought that part of the story. Dollar signs may have been enough to sway him.

Of course, the scheme wouldn't work unless I could prove to Moretti that the combination was hammered out of me like candy from a piñata. I let Valentino whale on me for a good five minutes. It was one hell of a beating, nearly rivaling some of the ones my old man used to give me. Like my father, Valentino enjoyed giving it, too, bruised knuckles and all. It was the final wing of his former life, and I suppose he was going out with a bang.

I still remember the appalled look on Lisa's face when I got home that night. One of Moretti's doctor friends cleaned and bandaged me up, but I still looked like a monster. I told Lisa that it had happened during a field assignment, delivered by a suspect escaping from a hidden room in a house that the agency didn't know about. It was just another lie among a marriage of lies.

The irony was that the next week was the most real my marriage had ever felt. Lisa took good care of me. Real good care. She loved having me home and having my full attention. The guilt was tough to stomach. There she was, washing my face, changing my bandages, and signing that she loved me . . . and none of it would have ever come to be if I hadn't been screwing another woman. Between the undeserved affection and the constant fear that Moretti's guys would nab Valentino before he disappeared for good, it was a wonder I didn't have a stroke that week.

Ah, Lisa. There've been times when I've been caught in her captivating gaze and I'd swear those beautiful blue eyes of hers were peering deep down into my soul and unearthing my web of lies, but they weren't. I've gotten too good at pretending to be someone else. Still, I'd always figured that one day the ruse would unravel to the point where I could no longer snip a loose thread and save it. It was always my greatest challenge to preserve the lie, but right now, it's the least of my worries.

It's nearly unfathomable to believe that what started out as a mere pickup line turned into a two-year charade.

I noticed Lisa the moment she first set foot inside Moretti's casino. She was with a group of friends—fellow teachers out for a fun night on the town. She was a radiant jewel among dull stones with that perfect face, bright smile, and unrehearsed elegance that accompanied every movement. I'd always had an eye for beauty, and she personified beauty.

I followed her through the maze of slots and tables like a love-struck school kid, looking for an opportunity to be noticed. The problem was that people like her don't typically notice people like me. Sure, my work for Moretti has afforded me the luxuries of being able to dress nice and look professional, but life has routinely dealt me reminders that a man can't completely shed his skin. There's still a part of me that will always be a backwoods Kentucky hick who ran away from home at the age of fourteen to find a new life in an electrified desert in Nevada.

I learned soon after I arrived in Sin City that you can get just about any form of fake identification one can dream up. Not just licenses and passports, but also birth certificates, social security cards, and occupational credentials. For a couple years, I even worked for a guy who was an expert at making them. I learned the trade, inserting photos into cards and passport pages, emulating government stamps, laminating the finished products. When I wasn't doing that, I was managing my boss's finances for room and board.

Working the numbers has always been my real talent. Back in school, teachers used to stand in awe of my ability to breeze through math problems. They told me I had a future. It's a shame they didn't pay as close of attention to the bruises and broken bones I'd show up to class with. If they had, I might have been freed earlier from a man who cited religious beliefs for denying me antibiotics that would have kept a bout of scarlet fever from eventually decimating my ability to hear.

Along with a phony Diner's Club card, I was carrying an FBI badge in my wallet the night I met Lisa. I had made it mostly for grins, but had used it a few times to get laid. I didn't have quite the physical build at that time to put myself over as agent. Instead, after sharing a blackjack table with her for twenty minutes, I introduced myself, after some feigned reluctance, as a forensic accountant for the bureau—one of the guys who goes to arrested suspect's homes or offices and dissects paper trails and computer entries.

She wasn't the first woman I'd met who'd been impressed with the tale, but she was the first that I really cared about impressing. I could tell by her demeanor that she was completely comfortable with my disability, which is a rarity. Most people feel they have to speak with precision and slow down their dialogue in order for me to understand them, but that night, she spoke to me like she would speak to anyone else. She was smart, witty, and genuine. The beauty inside her mirrored the outside, which is unheard of in a town packed full of plastic women with bleach-blonde hair and abnormally large breasts, serving as walking canes for rich old farts.

I wanted badly to be with her, which meant perpetuating the lies to keep things going. Someone like her would have had enough self-respect to kick me to the curb if I had come clean and copped to my bullshit. There's no future for a woman like her with a shady casino man who works alongside thugs.

It was an impulsive deception that turned epic. The lengths I've gone to have been nothing short of astonishing—mostly motivated by the fear of losing her, but also by my wanting to be something I'm not.

Early on, I asked her a couple of times to drop me off in front of FBI headquarters three miles from the casino with the explanation that my car was in the shop. I'd enter through the front door of the tall, imposing building and walk right back out of the lobby to catch a cab the moment her car turned the corner. I never had to go as far as security screening. After that, I managed to avoid using that location as a meeting place all but once or twice. There were times when she expressed interest in wanting to see my office, but I always cited security clearance issues as an excuse or found a way to change the subject.

The handful of coworkers on my side of the aisle at our small wedding consisted of paid prostitutes and chauffeur drivers. I had one of them even record an automated FBI phone menu through a separate line to redirect to the TDD in my office at the casino or to my cellphone.

A rare advantage of being deaf is that you have a natural excuse for not being readily accessible. This became particularly helpful when I needed to go out of town for a few days at a time to serve as a numbers guy for the business. Whether it was on the other side of the state or in California or Arizona, it saved me the stress of having to lie to her for a while. I told Lisa long ago that when I'm in the field, she can't reach me. She bought it from the beginning.

Finances had been a bit of a hassle. It took a lot of work convincing Lisa that the public school system offered a better health plan than the FBI, but enough phony paperwork prodded her in the direction I wanted. My salary was directly deposited into our savings from a business account I set up under the name Freelance Business Incentives. I made certain that the acronym, FBI, was what showed up on our statements.

Whenever I got backed into a corner over contradictions or inconsistencies, I always managed to somehow weasel my way out of the mess.

However, I've never been put to the kind of test I face right now, standing in this dungeon of a basement in the mountains of Colorado with the fidgeting body of Valentino Greco dressing the floor.

Chapter 35

Trying to roll back what has already happened is as futile as attempting to scrape toothpaste back into a tube, but my mind explores the possibility anyway. It's the curse of being wired that way. I consider the fact that only Alvar heard Valentino's confession firsthand and weigh the approach of drawing a line of loyalty in the sand by trying to convince Moretti that Alvar is lying for some reason. That, however, would require Valentino's unhindered cooperation, and there's about as much chance of that happening as there is a meteor falling from the sky and landing on Moretti back in town. Valentino would throw me under the bus in a heartbeat if he felt there was any chance it could save his ass.

My only confidence at all comes from the fact that Arianna is an extremely gifted liar. She's as good at lying to her spouse as I am—and that's saying something. That skill alone will at least keep her safe until Moretti can sort out whether or not Valentino's story is true. What happens after that is hard to say.

As much as I try, I can't fathom a solution in which my presence in this house, when Moretti gets back, can possibly work in my favor. If I stick around while Valentino spills out more of the details from that night, I fear that no amount of bullshitting on my part will be able to save us.

My trembling hands form a lean-to against my forehead, and I force myself to breathe. My mind darts into the depths of dampened corridors and dead ends, struggling to devise a solution that will somehow let me see the light of tomorrow's sunrise. There aren't any weapons in the house. Alvar's a walking arsenal who keeps his toys close. I know he stores an extra gun in his car, but he and his car are gone. It wouldn't matter. There's no way in hell this pencil-pushing accountant who's never fired a gun in his life is going to pick off four men, especially when one of them is Alvar. If I'm here when they get back, they'll sink their talons into my flesh and I'll never break free.

I have nothing with which to bargain for my life. Or do I? Moretti's financial ledger is upstairs on the desk. Inside it is enough juice to do some damage to Moretti if it was handed over to the authorities. It's a desperate play, but it's the only thing I have. What I do know is that I can't negotiate in person or else I'm dead. Can I negotiate the books for Arianna and speed up our plans? God, I can't think straight.

The realization that I've got maybe ten minutes tops before Moretti and the gang are back zips through my mind. I glance at Valentino who's squirming around on the floor as much as the chair bound to his limbs will allow him. He's cursing me out, and I feel paralyzed despite knowing I can't afford to waste any more time. I can't take Valentino with me. I can't trust him and he'll slow me down.

I run out of the room and slam the door, locking it behind me. *Sorry, Valentino; you made a deal with the devil, and now you're on your own.* I find myself glaring at the key in my hand instead of placing it back up above the door frame. It occurs to me that if the crew can't find it, they'll spend time busting the door down to check on Valentino. That's time that they won't spend in pursuit of me. I shove it in my front pants pocket and race up the stairs, skipping every other step.

I stop in the kitchen and toss my bag of broken glass into the tall metal trashcan, just to get rid of it. Panting while I glare wide-eyed out the window above the sink, I see no headlights coming up the drive yet. I sprint down the hallway, nearly losing my footing across the hardwood floor as I lunge into the office. The ledger that holds the secrets behind all of Moretti's finances resides on top of the oak desk I'd been using to finalize the Colorado deal. I grab my brief-bag that's resting at the foot of the desk and slide the notebook and a slew of loose papers, envelopes, and everything else that my broad-armed swipe along the desktop takes. Any leverage that can save my ass is in that bag. I'll figure out how to best use it later. *Hold on, Arianna. I'll figure a way out of this for us.*

Back in the kitchen, I search through the cabinets, high and low, yearning for a flashlight. I know I'll be blind out in the forest without one, and I can't afford to be without another sense if I hope to make it back to civilization on foot. Unfortunately, there is no flashlight to be found. I dart out into the cold, empty garage. The closest thing I find is a hook lamp that requires an outlet. There's got to be a fucking flashlight somewhere in this house but there's no time. By the time I get to the front door, sweat is streaming down my forehead and it stings one of my eyes. I spin a fist in my eye socket as an epiphany arrives, Alvar's night-vision goggles.

They're better than a flashlight because Moretti's guys won't see a beam flickering through the forest. I jam my hand in my pocket and snag the key for the downstairs door. When my hand emerges, my haste leads to the teeth of the key catching the lip of my pocket and propelling it out of my grip and across the floor. It topples along the glossy wood finish toward the baseboard of the back wall and I watch in morbid helplessness as it drops between two grooves in a brass furnace register.

I shout out obscenities and lunge forward, sliding along the floor on my knees before coming to a stop at the register. I claw my fingertips at it, prying, noticing quickly that it's secured with two screws. I don't have time to waste scouring the house a second time for a screwdriver. With desperate savagery, I force the tips of my fingers under the excruciatingly narrow gap between the plate and the floor and place my feet against the wall, yanking it toward my chest, clenching my teeth with effort. Half of the plate snaps off and I fall to my back. Excruciating pain tears across the palm of my hand from the jagged metal that winds up embedded in it. I yank it out with my free hand, immediately witnessing a crevice of blood streaming from its center. It flows to the floor beside me and I grab my wrist to combat the throbbing laceration.

Stumbling into the kitchen, I grab a white hand towel from the drawer and wrap it three times around my hand and form a fist to keep it in place. Returning to the register I find I've created a large enough opening to reach my good hand in and retrieve the key. Once I do, I survey the disarray I've created between the bloody streaks along the floor and the demolished register.

For a fraction of a second, I find myself musing that the sight might make Moretti think that someone else had gotten to me first and had saved him the trouble. It's then that my body freezes with only my heartbeat and brain left in movement. My observation urges me to ponder how my desperate situation might be remedied in part if I leave Moretti with a different assumption—an assumption that I didn't find Valentino, but Valentino found me. If Valentino escapes, takes me as a hostage, and flees into the wilderness, it changes many things. At worst, they'll form a search plan based on where they think he would flee to and not me. After all, he knows the area and I don't. They'll waste time checking out his shop and wherever he lives in town. Most importantly, it will delay the substantiation of his story and buy Arianna and me some time. If I play my cards right, Moretti will view an assault on me from Valentino as a shadow of doubt cast across Valentino's entire claim.

I rush to the window and check again for headlights. I then unwrap the blood-soaked towel from my throbbing hand and imagine what kind of struggle would take place if I was suddenly attacked by a desperate man who'd just escaped from a torture chamber. I smear my hand repeatedly along the textured wall above the broken register, streaking blood across it as if I had been trapped against it. I yank a large picture frame from the wall, snapping its mounting wire and letting it crash down in a heap that cracks the sheet of glass encased in it. I kick over a nearby chair before clenching my fist and letting more blood drain from it onto the floor and the edge of a large, oval-shaped rug that leads into the dining room. After rewrapping my hand, I grab one of my shoes from in front of the door that leads to the garage and drag the heel of it through one of the small puddles of my blood. I streak it across the floor as if I was manhandled and dragged.

There's relief in Valentino's eyes when I fling the door back open. A grotesque smile shapes on his face as he struggles to lift his head back up off the floor. He's wearing a beard of his own blood, which makes him look like a feasting cannibal. Battling time, I skip filling him in on my plan until I finish business first. I close the door behind me and grab a short crowbar that I had noticed earlier hanging from a mounted pegboard above some shelves. I wedge its claw between the edge of the door and the doorframe, and grimace from exertion as I yank at the bar wildly for what seems like minutes but is probably no more than twenty seconds before wood splinters and the door gives. I drop the crowbar on the floor, making certain the others will see it first when they return. My blood's on it, but they'll assume it belongs to Valentino. I use the key and secure the lock on the doorknob, then wipe it on the chest of my shirt to make sure there's no visible blood before I return it to its original position above the outside door frame.

I stretch the headgear straps of the night-visions behind the back of my head and let the eyecups rest against my forehead. The entire time, Valentino looks at me as if I'm crazy. He hasn't a clue what I'm doing and I wouldn't expect him to. I stand before him and lean forward, speaking clearly and concisely so he'll understand me as I tell him that I'm setting him free but we have to leave together.

The gratitude in his eyes is accompanied by glistening tears. He says something that appears to be a question that I can't quite read so I use the back of my sleeve to wipe blood from his mouth. He tells me that he'll need help walking because he broke his ankle trying to get free. My heart stops and I gape at the sight of his twisted foot, which I hadn't noticed before, pinned underneath the steel chair leg, which was bent—probably from the collision when he fell to the floor.

My head goes light as the adrenaline rush that had been pumping through my veins is suddenly squelched. I drift back a step, feeling my sense of balance faltering. I realize immediately that this changes everything. Those guys will be here any minute. With Valentino anchoring me down, we won't get thirty yards from the house before they catch up to us. My entire plan is shot.

"Come on, man!" he yells. "Let me go! I'll do my best!"

He scrutinizes the glaze covering my eyes and he shouts again for me to set him free. My shoulders are sunk and I feel the helplessness of defeatism that I'm convinced God has dealt on me as punishment for the sins I've committed throughout my life.

I circle behind Valentino and hunch down before I begin peeling at the strands of duct tape constraining his wrists. I can see from the widening of his cheeks and movement of his head that he's talking to me. I assume he's lavishing gratitude upon me. While I steadily strip away at his bonds, I think about today's sunset that lowered behind the tranquil mountains out behind the house. I wonder if it's the last time I'll ever see the sun. I then remember nearly falling through the large hole in the earth, which I concede could have served as a metaphor for the events that have transpired tonight. The obscure cognizance calls on me to stop what I'm doing.

I peer down at the sight before me as if I'm outside my body, hovering above the room. I see the back of Valentino's head and his contorted body hunched forward in the shape of the overturned chair he's strapped to. In front of him is the clear, plastic sheet Alvar had laid underneath him to keep blood from seeping into the concrete.

My despairing thoughts convince my mind that my plan is too good to jeopardize, and my warped sense of reason offers little resistance. Valentino's inability to participate can't detour my only shot at my new life with Arianna. I tell myself that it's the only chance we have of breaking free and starting over. As if I've resigned control over my body to a darker force, I find myself leaning forward and stretching my arms along each side of Valentino's head. Before he can take notice of the evil brewing behind him, I grab a handful of the plastic sheet in each hand and savagely pull it back toward me. It covers his face and his body reacts in panic, jerking and buckling as much as his constraints allow him to. I step over the back of the chair and place my shoe into the back of his neck, forcing his head deeper into the plastic as I keep it taut.

I close my eyes and see only waves spreading along the Lake Michigan shoreline with Arianna lying in my arms in the white sand. I repress the thought that if I could hear Valentino right now, I'd be sickened to death by the sound of a man dying at my hands. A well of tears eclipses my eyes and they roll down my face as I relentlessly keep up the pressure.

God forgive me. It's all for you, Arianna. It's all for us.

Chapter 36

The last step is a brutal one, as were the twelve before it. With Valentino's heavy body draped across my shoulders, the act of reaching the top of the staircase feels for a moment like I've conquered Everest. He weighs more than he looks. I hope that I mashed in his chair enough to make it look like he twisted through the tape and broke free of his own accord. Catching a fresh perspective of the raw scene just outside the kitchen, I'm confident that the calamity appears authentic as if a massacre took place. I carefully slip my feet into my shoes, relieved they're monk straps so I don't have to deal with laces with Valentino's dead weight bearing down on me.

The temperature outside is surely much cooler than it was before the sun set and the storm came through. Coupled with the fact that my shirt is a bright cream color and might catch someone's eye in the dark, I reach for my trench coat that's hooked along a wooden knob beside the front door. The moment it touches my hand, however, I realize how suspicious it will look for me to take only my own coat when it's supposed to be Valentino who's in control. I grab both mine and a dark jacket that Tony left behind to collaborate the perception that two men left. I also snatch Arianna's stocking cap that she left behind. It will conceal my golden-haired homing beacon of a head.

I freeze when I see a flash of light dance off the wall beside me. It's coming through the front window. They're here. Shit.

I preserve as much composure as I can possibly muster as my eyes bounce from one side of the room to the other, taking inventory to ensure there's nothing I missed. My brief bag is strapped over my shoulder with the coat and jacket draped over it. I place my arm over everything like a paranoid man checking for the bulge of his wallet in his pants pocket.

When Moretti realizes that his books, along with all of his account numbers and proof of his ties to the cartel are missing and presumably in the hands of Valentino, it ought to send a piercing shock through his dark soul. I hope it gives the fat bastard a second heart attack.

My legs feel like they're weighted in cement as I hurriedly but carefully glide toward the side door that leads to the garage. I nearly lose my footing when Valentino's weight shifts the moment I drop down a step onto the pavement of the garage floor. I manage to stay upright and a second later I'm out the backdoor of the garage and diligently hurrying along the flat concrete of the back porch. It has a glimmer to it from the thin layer of moisture brought in by the lightning storm, so each step is carefully planted. The smell of rain is still in the air, and I worry that there's enough moisture on the ground to leave traceable footprints behind on the forest floor.

I reach up and pull the goggles down from my forehead to my eyes, exposing my vision to the surrounding landscape with clarity and a distinct shade of green. The goggles are loose from being sized to Alvar's larger head, but I'll adjust things later.

The cover of trees grows thicker the farther from the cabin I get and the bite of the brisk breeze that flows through it creeps in through my clothes.

I look behind me to examine what kind of trail I'm leaving in my wake. I see no legible tracks among the scrub and pine needles that line the soil, and I sigh in relief. My attention is drawn to the blazing light that ignites from behind a window at the back of the house. A second and a third one follow moments later. By now, they've seen the blood on the main floor and have probably split up, checking each room for me and Valentino.

The combination of fatigue and high altitude leaves me gasping for breath, but I push forward like my life depends on my steadfastness, which it does. Worry builds in me when I can't find the tree with the heart carved into its base, but it soon reveals itself under the green brilliance of the goggles.

I feel a sudden tug along my shoulders and my heart screams when I fear I've already been discovered by one of the boys. Valentino's body is ripped from my shoulders and I'm propelled forward to my hands and knees. I spin around with my arms out in front of me, prepared to absorb a bullet or the toe of a boot but find nothing but the body lying by itself in a heap. I quickly crawl back to it, feeling rocks and twigs under my knees, and discover a dead pine branch about four feet long with a couple of its top twigs hooked under Valentino's collar. The splintering along the thick end suggests that the body was snagged from the large tree I just crossed under. I worry that the loud sound of cracking wood just echoed through the encompassing area, but I stay focused.

In my good deed of covering the well earlier, I inadvertently camouflaged it among other fallen branches. I know it has to be close though. My legs feel like rubber when I rise up, even though the burden of Valentino's weight has been lifted. The thin mountain air wheezes in through my open mouth as I scramble along the ground cover. I fight the panicked urge to punt congregated limbs out of my way to expose their undersides, fearing the noise it'll create. When I spot the shallow lip of the well beneath a low teepee of branches, I quickly clear it.

With the wind intermittent in its powerful gusts, I wait for a strong rush and then pry each board up with my hands from its nailed position along the well's frame, hoping the cry of rusty nails isn't audible. The planks are rotted and light in weight, and they come up easier than I could have hoped for. Before I retrieve the body, I carefully pan the area to look for pursuers. Seeing no one, I grab Valentino by the back of his shirt collar and drag him along the dirt.

I don't even remember positioning him for his fall but his

body drops through nonetheless into the deep hole with nothing hindering its rapid descent. I'd find my indifference to his inelegant burial unnerving if it wasn't so damned crucial to me staying alive. They'll never find him down there—not tonight and not years from now. He's down so far that not even the night-visions pick up a trace of him. I lay the boards back across the opening and press the nails back through as best I can with the bottom of my shoe. I cover the planks again with the limbs and add several more for good measure, wary not to make the aggregation appear artificial. I'm sure that none of the guys have tracking expertise, but despite this I sweep the surrounding dirt with the needled end of a thick pine branch like I've occasionally seen in movies.

When I'm confident there's nothing left to be done, I lean forward with my hands on my thighs and breathe. I still feel Valentino's weight on my shoulders, and I dread that I always will.

I tighten the goggles to my head, shove my trench coat into the brief bag, and slide my arms into Tony's jacket. It fits me pretty well. I pull the stocking cap on over my head. It smells of Arianna's perfume.

The strength of the wind that's rushing along the mountain seems to be building. I hope its shriek has drowned out whatever clamor I've caused. A burning beam of a concentrated light flickers through the flush branches of a tribe of wavering pines, and I fear that my hope is squelched. Its source is a flashlight, and I make out two figures approaching quickly from behind the glare. One tall and the other short. They're advancing from the direction of the house. I halt to a dead stop and watch breathlessly as the imposing beam slices through a family of thin, bare aspens beside me. My eyes drop to the side of my jacket that the beam flashes along. It passes on by. Whichever one of Moretti's thugs is guiding it didn't notice me. I drop down to my hands and knees, cradling the brief bag in my arm so it doesn't scrape along the ground. To my relief, they take off in an adjacent direction away from me and away from where I dropped the body. The mountain and wind are most likely playing tricks with their senses.

Before they disappear, I recognize one of them as Tony. The shorty. The sight of his raised shoulders above bare arms prompts a smirk along my lips. I imagine the cold mountain gusts are a little much without his jacket, which is warmer than I would have guessed when I snatched it.

Their light disappears in the distance, and I lower my head to take a couple of deep breaths. For the first time since discovering that Valentino was the beaten pulp of a man in the basement, I'm able to relish a moment of composure and clear my thoughts. As far as I know, they've bought the scene I left behind and are more worried now about finding us than they are about substantiating what Valentino said. My best course of action is to get the hell out of these woods and back to some civilization. The only direction I know for certain will take me there is back down the road that leads up the driveway. I know I can't walk along the road itself. One of them will be watching it for sure. But if I can stay parallel to it under the cover of the woods and night, it will lead me to where I need to be.

I carefully begin making my way back in the broad direction of the house, keeping myself far enough in the backwoods to hopefully avoid detection. With the night-visions, I've got a huge advantage over the boys. I can see them but they can't see me. Thank God there's still enough cloud cover from the passing storm to keep the moonlight in check.

My head swivels from side to side, scoping for sudden movements, which isn't easy with the wind blowing. *Everything* is moving. The lights from the house come into view again. Every window is ablaze. I keep my distance, using it only as a lighthouse to navigate my way along the dangerous coastline of a life I should have left behind years ago. I cautiously cross the plane of the side of the house and see both Alvar's Buick and Moretti's Cadillac parked out front.

The sight of Moretti's car reminds me of the ride out from

Vegas. Sitting in the passenger seat of that snow white Cadillac was excruciating, as I was forced to listen to that fat bastard in the backseat suck at Arianna's face while he rubbed his sweaty hands all over her body. It's been merciless enough having to sit through it on short trips up and down the Vegas strip, but Moretti's fear of flying forced me to endure it for two days of travel. I would have rather ridden with Alvar and Tony but the boss . . . *ex-boss* . . . wanted me close to talk business. He always wanted me close to him and Arianna.

It's what ultimately got me caught up in this mess.

Chapter 37

My mind has strained to rationalize the insanity behind my relationship with Arianna a couple thousand times. I've dissected the affinity into pieces, studied the madness and recklessness of it all, and still let myself spiral down the path that brought me to where I am tonight. It's not just about love. Arianna's like crack and I'm an addict. A hopeless, tormented addict who has told himself again and again that he has far more than what he deserves sitting at home and waiting with open arms. Yet, it's the forbidden temptress whose covers I keep slipping back under.

Arianna's always been an awe-inspiring sight. That silky, unblemished bronze skin and that long and straight black hair, with her striking, luminescent yellow eyes—a lethal combination of her half-Greek, half-Chinese pedigree. She has the kind of epic beauty that wars were fought over long ago. Yet, it's not just her looks. At times she has a delectable innocence about her, like when she signed "Good morning" to me the first time we met. It took my breath away.

Arianna has a younger half-brother who's deaf. She left him behind somewhere near Hong Kong when her father brought her to the States. The boy had been born without his hearing, and she'd learned to sign with him in Asia at an early age. She was fluent, though the dialect she used was significantly different than the American one they teach here. At Moretti's urging, we'd occasionally teach each other the differences. The bastard got a kick out of watching us exchange dialogue for some reason. He found it entertaining.

I don't know exactly how Arianna and Moretti came to be. She avoids talking about that part of her past and becomes angry whenever I press her. I think it has something to do with her father. I gathered from a cryptic joke Moretti once made that her father had been indebted to him for some reason. My guess is that Moretti had a hand in smuggling the family into the country, but I can't say for sure. All I know is that her father has been out of the picture for a long time.

Between us, it started out harmless enough—playful, in a way. I think she saw a lot of her brother in me and enjoyed having someone close that didn't treat her in a domineering and repressive way, the way Moretti does.

Playfulness turned into flirting and that eventually led to something far more serious, despite the blaring tornado sirens that blasted a dire warning through my skull the first time she clenched her talons into my shirt and pulled me into her moist lips.

I know I have a good wife; I've never questioned that. She's everything a man could possibly ask for, and that's why I pursued her. But after living a lie for too long—a lie that has been the entire foundation of our marriage—the everyday reminder of how undeserving I am, along with the stress of perpetuating the lie, it's all taken its toll on me. It's broken me.

With Arianna, it's different. We're both broken people. Both tainted with dark, mysterious pasts. Both longing to start over. At least that's how I've managed to rationalize it. Instead, it might just be her exotic touch that won't let me think rationally. Maybe she's my kryptonite, absorbing my strength and unwilling to let me escape. Still, I don't *want* to escape.

I tried to break things off with her shortly after I'd returned to work after recovering from Valentino's beating. I knew I had dodged a bullet and feared for my life if things continued between us. I told her that it needed to end. She saw things differently.

Watching Valentino pummel me that night had done something to her. Changed her. I thought I had seen a glimpse of that change at the time as Valentino wailed on my face. She stood there silently with what appeared to be a smirk of satisfaction across her thick lips as she watched the brutality. Not a single wince from her.

While Moretti and the boys were busy trying to hunt down Valentino to no avail, things between us only heated up. Her aggression and perversions grew. We did things I had never dreamed of, in places I would have never thought of. In some unexplainable way, seeing a man suffer pain for her was an aphrodisiac. I'd lost all capacity to resist her advances. I'm no victim though. I've wanted her every bit as much as she has wanted me.

God, why didn't I get out before the Colorado deal? We would have been spared all of this. My plan had been to move on from Moretti in a month or two. I'd turn in my informal notice and wish the man luck. He'd be disappointed but he'd get over it and wouldn't stand in my way. That wouldn't have always been the case, but our relationship had come a long way from when we first met. He respected me.

After ending things with Lisa, I'd take the next couple of months to finish preparations for my new life in Traverse City with Arianna. Then, I'd come back for Arianna and take her away with me. By then, I'd have enough phony identification for her that Moretti would never be able to find her . . . or me. The IDs are never what consumes the most time. It's the creation of a new individual that does. Getting into Customs computers and state databases; all doable when you know the right people, but still painstaking and time-intensive. With enough time having passed after my departure, Moretti wouldn't suspect it was me who set her free.

It would have been perfect. Moretti has never known about the cottage in Michigan. It's another secret I've managed to keep from him.

My discretion served two purposes. First off, I always thought it would make a good safe house if the DEA ever came down on Moretti's operation. The title's under my name, but under a different social security number and credit history. It's not some exotic location where someone who's looking to hide would typically go. It's a place with seasons. It's a place where you can mingle freely among other people—most of whom spend no more than three months a year there before getting back to their lives. With no one else aware of the cottage, the authorities wouldn't come there looking for me if everything went to shit.

Secondly, with a second property on the side, Moretti might suspect that I've been skimming off him in order to pay for it. He'd be right, but I've been putting away for years, long before I worked for him.

By the age of sixteen, I'd taught myself to count cards. I was good at it. With a fake ID and the right choice of clothes and hairstyles, I managed to live life as full-fledged casino rat.

It's funny how the movies tend to portray such people. It's usually some smug, Matt Damon–looking guy wearing a snap-brim fedora with a hot female accomplice by his side to serve as a lookout for suspicious pit bosses. They build up a huge amount of money before, inevitably, security is notified by a couple of guys watching the table action from a monitor in a dimly lit room, and a chase scene ensues.

The truth is that if you don't pull out too much money all at once and don't draw a lot of attention to your winnings, you never have to worry about such things. Also, you've got to switch casinos often. Don't stick around in one place for too long. I built up an ample savings over time.

It also didn't hurt that I could read the lips of casino security guards who'd occasionally case me out at the direction of some hidden observer. It gave me an extra edge for knowing when to bow out.

As I found out, however, discretion isn't always enough. Moretti himself caught me red-handed at his casino. It was how we met. The fat bastard had been standing right behind me for ten minutes before I noticed he was there, scrutinizing my every move until he was convinced that I was pulling a fast one. He had Frank strong-arm me out back with the promise of me being worked over with a set of brass knuckles. Through dark and smoky corridors, Moretti kept up pace with us, huffing and puffing as he sang me a song about how they used to take care of punks like me in the old days.

I still remember the stunned look on his face when I turned to him with my arms pinned behind my back and said, "If the king is wasting his time sniffing out little league card-sharks, that means his castle's about to crumble."

I don't know why I said what I did. It wasn't a smart move by any stretch of the imagination, especially coming from a nobody like me. Steam practically poured from Moretti's ears, and I half expected him to snatch the knuckles from Frank and slice up my face himself before we even made it outside. He probably would have if I hadn't then told him that I knew how he could get himself into the big leagues.

It had to be a mixture of financial desperation and admiration of someone standing their ground that let him hear me out. It turned out that the big beasts on the new strip were eating his casino alive, just like with many establishments that hugged the old strip. Moretti had made a small fortune over the years, but nostalgia and half-assed theme changes weren't enough to stop his casino's sharp decline in profitability.

I had a few business model ideas for his casino, but what really got his attention were my underground contacts. When your business is creating counterfeit IDs and documents for the shadiest snakes in the desert, you find yourself privy to some pretty remarkable information. There's an intricate flowchart to how the underground works that you'd never know about unless you had the kind of broad view that I did. So many of these people do indirect business with each other and few of them know it. They buy and sell the same guns, drugs, and whores, and even share the same suppliers who let them all think they've got exclusive partnerships. The truth is that just about every outside source is working multiple deals at any one time.

That wasn't the case with a rising Mexican drug cartel out of Chihuahua that had a recent falling out with the LoGrasso family. With the cartel purposely engraining themselves in a culture of tight discretion—tighter than most—the loss of the LoGrassos left an open vacuum that needed filling. It was a timely opportunity for someone to grab control of a runaway train filled with money and steer it right into their depot.

Moretti had been dabbling with the illegal drug scene for some time, but he was a smalltime player, not bringing in nearly enough to subsidize his fledgling casino.

After a couple of days of checking out my story and a hell of a lot of convincing on my part, he let me put him in touch with the right people and the rest became history. Moretti's net worth doubled in the first year, and I became a valued and well-paid member of his crew. I left the counterfeiting business but kept good ties to my former employer.

The transition didn't come without complications, though. It brought Alvar Montoya into our lives—Moretti's fiercely loyal and equally frightening liaison to the cartel. Though my role in Moretti's organization has largely been reduced to that of a traveling accountant over the past couple of years, there are still occasions where I'm forced to work with Alvar, and on each of those occasions, I feel as though I'm working alongside the devil himself—a sadistically evil son of a bitch who's probably never battled with a single moralistic qualm in his life. A man without a conscience. A man without a soul.

If I don't make it out of the forest alive tonight, it will be because he has gotten me. And once Alvar Montoya gets ahold of you, it's best that you pray for a quick death.

Chapter 38

I catch a brief glimmer of light out of the corner of my eye and I immediately stop in my tracks. It's a good distance away but there's definitely something out there in the dark. It vanishes as quickly as it appeared, as if someone lit a cigarette with a lighter or match. I remain still and stoic, emulating the thick tree whose flush limbs are draped broadly beside me. I keep watching. After a few seconds, it appears again in another quick burst. The shape of the light is circular. It's from a flashlight. It can't be coming from Tony and whoever his search buddy is. They went off in the opposite direction. It's someone else, flicking their light on and off in spurts so as not to give away their exact location as they roam through the woods looking for the escapees. Whoever it is, they're standing between me and my way out, and they'll see me if I continue down this way. I'm unarmed. Whoever is out there surely isn't.

I glance back at the house, where the lights are still visible between the silhouettes of timber and brush. It occurs to me that all of Moretti's men are in the woods. With two to the west and someone to the east, that leaves only Moretti and Arianna. With both cars out front and the chances of Moretti huffing and puffing his way across the terrain alongside his crew being slim to none, it's a safe bet that they and they alone are inside the house right now.

I eye Alvar's Buick that's parked behind the Cadillac and picture myself with Arianna by my side in it, racing wildly down that dirt road. If I only have Moretti to contend with, this is doable. Arianna and I can leave together tonight—not three months from now. Not everything's ready. Not everything's prepared. But if I don't leave with her right now, I may never be able to.

By the time the rest of them figure out what's happening, we'll be halfway to town. If someone does get in our way, we'll just stay low and hope the bullets miss.

I cautiously make my way back toward the house, hoping the sound of my heavy breathing is inaudible due to the wind. I stop when I reach a lonely fence post beside the driveway. Most of the drapes inside the windows are open, but from my angle I can only see light fixtures and the top of a floor lamp. No movement. Behind me, I see the hurried flicker of the flashlight again and decide that it's not moving any closer—at least not yet.

I exhale and dash across the dirt path to the Buick's driver's side door that's parked just outside of the lamp light's range above the garage. I know better than to risk opening it before assessing my chances at success. Alvar's self-installed alarm has a hair-trigger, so I poke my head up along the window to check if it's unlocked. I breathe when I see that it is. I peer deeper into the interior, searching for his keys in the ignition and I find them there. Thank God.

There's still no movement from the house but the flashlight in the forest seems to have changed direction and I think it's now getting closer. It's not approaching at a pace that makes me worry I've been seen, but I fear whoever's behind it is slowly returning to the house.

I've known for years that Alvar keeps a piece in his trunk, hidden under the spare tire. I'll use it to snatch Arianna from Moretti. I've already killed tonight. If Moretti makes me pull the trigger, I will. Even if he doesn't make me, pulling the trigger may be the only way of ensuring he'll never come after us.

I'm aware that there's no bulb in the trunk of Alvar's car, just like there's no dome light. Both were disabled to avoid attention during late night transactions back in Vegas. If I commit myself, I'm sure I can pull this off.

Carefully, I raise the handle and let the driver's door glide open for just a few inches before I reach in and flip the trunk lever. I feel a release of tension along the floorboard and close the door as carefully as I can muster, fluctuating my attention between the blustering foyer of the building and the slowly approaching flashlight.

I crawl to the rear of the vehicle and feed the house another glance before I prop up the trunk door with my trembling arm. Inside, the night-visions expose a reflective, dark material that looks like satin. It's draped over the top of something lying along the floorboard. I try to brush the clump aside but there's substantial weight under it. Possibly logs for the fireplace. Earlier in the day, Moretti had talked about starting a fire tonight for Arianna. He said it would be romantic.

When I feel dampness along my wrist, I hold out my hand in front of the lens and see that blood is oozing from the towel wrapped around it. I was sure that I had stopped bleeding, but evidently not.

Before another thought is allowed to cross my mind, something grabs me firmly by the wrist and my body buckles in panic. The back of my head smacks against the edge of the trunk door. I bite my tongue and instinctively yank my hand free. As I do, the momentary, green-tinted image of a delicate, feminine hand decorated with sparkling jewelry freezes in my mind like a still-life picture. My attention snaps to the corner of the trunk where Arianna's sick and frightened eyes are staring back at mine. I gasp at the sight and the blood rushing from my face nearly forces me to faint. Her eyes are filled with confusion and desperation and fine streams of blood are trickling down both sides of her opened mouth. The blood on my hand is not mine. It's hers.

My mortified gaze drops to her chest just below her exposed cleavage where her snug evening dress is soaked. Blood is flowing from a tear in her material and it's draining into a pool below her body.

Oh God . . .

It doesn't take a doctor to tell me that she's been shot or stabbed and that so much blood is present that she hasn't a chance. He's killed my Arianna.

Her hands and head alone are moving, and it's as if she's floating limply on her back in the ocean. I cup the palm of my hand under her head and prop it up slightly as tears freely stream into the eye cups of the goggles strapped to my head. My mouth is gaping open, but I can't manage any words.

She squints her eyes as if a sliver of pain just jolted up her back and her lips move in some sort of intended dialogue, but I can't read what she's saying. I haven't a clue if she knows who I am behind the goggles or if she can even see me at all in the nearly pitch darkness of the trunk.

"Honey . . . Baby," I whisper as I lean forward and peer into her confused eyes.

She doesn't respond. Instead, her skull goes limp under my outstretched hand. Her yellowish, feline eyes that look almost clear under the tint of my sights come to a sudden stop after her eyelids flutter one last time. They lay trained on me, and I feel as though they're either assigning me blame for my inability to help her or succumbing to her first vision of the afterlife.

Time stands still for a few moments before an uncontrollable trembling overtakes me and my body feels loose and off balance. A strong gust of wind presses the trunk door down across my shoulders, urging me to snap out of my glaze and recall where I am.

With my eyes flooded from tears, I lower Arianna's head to the floor and crane my neck outside of the trunk. I see that the flashlight, now steady in its luminance, is getting close, but my attention is quickly drawn to a shadow that emerges along the driveway beside me. I lift my head to check the house.

The front window is no longer bare. The thick silhouette of a stout figure inside is standing at its center. Moretti. His immaculately kept strands of hair, normally slicked back in uniform alignment, are now a frazzled mess as he runs his chubby fingers through them.

My clenched hands shake in rhythm and I can barely catch my breath. All that matters in my mind in that moment is that he has to die.

Moretti turns his head to the side and a lamp in the room exposes that he's visibly agitated—downright irate and screaming under his thick mustache. His other hand is holding a walkie-talkie to his ear so tightly that you'd think he's trying to plug a leak in the portside of a ship. It's one of the same transmitters that Alvar had been fooling with earlier. Moretti's collar under his sports coat is drenched with sweat, as are the sides of his flushed face. He's paying no attention to the scene outside.

My face burns with unbridled hate as I lift back up the trunk door and slide my arm under Arianna's wet, still warm body to feel for the outline of the lid that covers the spare tire. I find it and pull up on it, but it bends from Arianna's weight. I quickly check the forest to find that the proximity of the wandering flashlight has grown closer. I flash Moretti another glance to make certain he's still preoccupied. He is, but only for another second. My heart stops when his rant suddenly halts. The frame of his body snaps to attention and his thick eyebrows are angled upwards as if he's heard a loud noise or had an epiphany.

"What do you mean *right outside*?" I manage to read across his lips.

Without any further contemplation, he whips his head to the window. The transmitter falls from his hand, and he presses his curled fingers up against the window to squelch the obscuring glare from inside. He stares outside.

I don't wait for our eyes to meet. I lift the trunk door up as far as it will go before doing the same to the spare's cover. Arianna's limp body morbidly tumbles forward. My hand is spinning the metal wing nut that secures the tire when a bright flash of light explodes beside me, intensified by the sights of my goggles. I twist my head to see the flashlight in the forest bobbing from side to side. He's running toward me. A sharp flash emits from directly in front of him. He's shooting at me.

I fear I'll be dead before I can get to Alvar's gun, so I turn and sprint into the forest. I dodge between trees and through limbs, taking only a second to twist my head to see the flashlight still in pursuit. Whoever it is must have seen me from the woods and alerted Moretti on the radio.

Dancing sparks bounce off the side of a large, weather-scarred rock beside me right as I weave around it. Within seconds, they'll all be after me.

Chapter 39

It had to have been Frank who shot at me. Alvar wouldn't have missed.

Oh, Arianna . . . How did it happen? Did he not believe your denials, or did you outright admit it to spite him? It's got to be the former. She wouldn't have come clean. Yet, it's clear now that Moretti bought Valentino's story.

By now, they've surely congregated back at the house and are organizing to come after me. A modern day lynch mob. I bet Alvar's licking his chops.

I wonder if they even know who they're chasing. Do they think it's me or Valentino? I'm covered up pretty well so I doubt anyone got a great look. I'm not sure it matters, though. They know one of us is out here, and they've probably figured out that I'm not armed. They'll be coming after me quickly.

If I ever get that close to Moretti again, I swear to God he's dead. How could it have been so easy for him to kill her?

The trees I'm scrambling through with broken breath are gradually thinning out, and I worry that I'll turn into a sitting duck without any places to hide or physical barriers to put between my body and a bullet. When a vast meadow opens up before me, that worry turns to horror. It spreads down a mild slope of short grass for what seems like the length of a football field before leading to another patch of forest.

The trees are still dense to the west, even though that direction leads me further from the road and town. I feel I have no choice, so I scurry back into the woods. The timing is none too soon as at least two beams of flashlights become visible behind me, cutting their way through the night. Town will have to wait. Right now, it's about just staying alive.

My shoes weren't meant for this. I feel every sharp corner of stone and rounded branch with any size beneath them. I keep my legs moving. With the denser timber comes even drier, dead wood along the ground. It's surely crackling as I stomp through it. I do my best to dance around the big stuff, but it's impossible to completely avoid without slowing to a crawl.

I take a crumb of comfort in the knowledge that the others can't keep up with my pace. I've gotten myself in good shape over the past couple of years. Whoever knew that taking up jogging at the urging of my wife would have paid off at a time like this? Frank's gotten slow with age, and Alvar isn't built for speed. Tony's pretty spry, but he doesn't have the balls to lead out too far in front of the pack.

The wind's dying down and what little cloud cover I can see above the thick trees appears to be lifting. Though I can't see it through the walls of the forest, my bet is that it's the glow of a full moon that's illuminating the landscape more than what's comfortable.

I'm keeping well ahead of the flashlights, but they're not deterred. They know which way I'm headed.

The terrain takes a sharp decline and it forces me to be more deliberate in my footing. Before I know it, gravel is shuffling below my heels and the slope turns into a wicked descent. I have no choice but to hustle my way down through the large slabs of rock, gripping my hands along the coarse edges of boulders to keep from losing it. This only works for so long before my momentum won't let me regain control. I slip to my back and slide down the steep embankment, riding unsettled rock as if I were a single grain from a handful of sand being poured down a funnel. The goggles slide down to my mouth and the darkness that surrounds me keeps me from processing the best way to brace myself from an inevitable collision with a solid object. My body goes weightless for a quick eternity but the helpless flaying of my arms and legs are whipped into conformity when I'm yanked to a sudden halt. My chest feels tight, and I realize that the strap of my brief bag has latched me onto something. I taste dirt and grime in my mouth, and am unable to better digest my predicament before the tautness gives way and I tumble forward another ten feet or so before landing awkwardly on a knee and the back of my opposite leg in a collection of rocks and other rubble. I'm lucky I didn't break my neck, but I fear I've pulled something in my leg or hyper extended it. The pain is manageable, but I feel an unnatural give when I bend my knee. My hand is throbbing and the sting along my laceration is intense. I'm sure I've reopened it.

I raise the goggles back to my eyes and find that I've dropped down into a craggy ravine where there are no trees and only frail shrubs. I smell water only a moment before I turn and behold that I'm at the precipitous shore of a raging river erupting through the gulch with breathtaking ferocity. Its spray whips against my face like I'm standing along the bow of a boat in the ocean. It's the river I'd heard about—the one that marked the boundary of the property.

The shore on the other side is probably only twenty-five feet away, but it might as well be a mile because there's no crossing it. The churning, white rapids would sweep me away in a heartbeat if I tried. If I could have heard the roar of the water I never would have come down this way. It's too late to do anything about that, which is made clear when thin beams of light spread out over the granite wall above me. I clench my teeth and lunge down to the amassment of serrated rocks that line the shore and crawl with my elbows digging into the rubble until I reach a nest of three large boulders. I cower behind them, certain by the randomness of the gliding beams that I haven't been spotted. My shoes are partially sunken in a small, shallow pool of overflow from the river. The water is biting cold.

With the sky now free of obstructions, I slide the goggles up to my forehead to confirm that the moon is illuminating the surrounding area enough to make me an easy target if I put myself out in the open. I slide them back down and scope the men above, who look unsure of what to do. The ravine is as much a surprise to them as it was to me. There are three of them. I can tell by the shape of their silhouettes that they're Alvar, Frank, and Tony. The taller men are holding the flashlights and Tony's stuck in between them like an asshole-sandwich.

How in the hell am I going to get out of this? They know I'm down here. Dust, lit up by their flashlights, is still floating in the air from my descent.

The reflection of one of the lights dances off the wakes of the disgruntled water behind me, and I tuck my head down tight. When the beam stops along the top of one of the rocks in front of me and stays there, I hold my breath. There's a flash of light and then shards of rock crumble down along my shoulders and head. I'm being shot at. They must have seen me. I stay put and imagine what sort of strategy they're probably plotting. To my surprise, the light moves to another large rock about twenty feet away. A moment later, sparks fly off the side of it and the beam picks up the resulting particles that spread through the air.

They're uncertain of exactly where I am. The vultures just know their prey is down here somewhere and they're trying to spook him out of his hiding spot so they can pick him off from their perch. They perform the routine a third time, farther up the river. With their attention turned upstream, I crawl to the far side of the rocks to better position myself for a good look.

They're standing up there together talking to each other. I watch one of them, who I think is Frank, hold his hand up to his mouth like a megaphone and yell something out into the night. Interesting. They must think I'm Valentino. They wouldn't waste the breath on a deaf guy. I wonder what they think happened to Kyle Kimble.

The only firearm I can see between them is Alvar's rifle, which he's peering through the sights of as he pans the riverside, but the others are surely packing as well. I'm a sitting duck down here. The second I try to leave the cover of the rocks, I'll be a quick casualty in a shooting gallery. If I was only able to grab the gun from Alvar's trunk, I'd at least stand a fighting chance, even if it was a poor one.

For now, all I can do is sit here, keep quiet, and wait for them to make a move. After a few minutes, that's exactly what they do.

There's some shuffling of flashlights between them and then they spread out. One of the beams hikes upstream and the other one heads down. Alvar remains stationary, like Christ the Redeemer from atop Corcovado Mountain, gazing down with a watchful eye over Rio de Janeiro. That's as far as the comparison goes. Jesus isn't trying to kill Brazilians. They must only have two flashlights between them because Alvar's standing in the dark and relying on the other two to guide his aim.

Whoever's walking downstream is closer to me. I watch their spotlight glide along the shoreline. It illuminates some flatter terrain where a narrow bank of sand and pea gravel resides. A little farther down there's a row of leafy trees whose modest branches dangle above the river. If I can make it to them, I'll at least have a little cover to try and make an escape. Getting there's the tough part. There's practically no cover between here and there.

My feet, especially my toes, are beginning to numb up from the freezing water they're submerged in. I'm concerned that they'll trip me up if I make a run for it.

The circle of light cast from the man downriver flashes up from the shore and it doesn't return. To find out why, I crawl forward and peer from behind the rounded, lower edge of the rock my shoulder is pressed firmly to. The flashlight's still on but it's pointed directly in front of the man holding it. He's lighting up a path. He's found a way down. I force myself not to hyperventilate as he shuffles his way down the ravine, several times grabbing onto the stems of thin but strong shrubbery. I press my back flat up against the rock. Closing my eyes, I strain in desperation to decipher a passage to freedom. A last resort could be to throw myself into the river and let it carry me away, but its force is unreal. My chance of surviving might be even worse than if I put my hands in the air and gave up to Moretti's goons.

He's about to the bottom of the ravine now. I'm out of time to come up with some brilliant maneuver. The best I can hope for is to make a mad dash for my life and hope to God that I don't get shot. My shoes slide in the mud when I plant my heels in preparation to spring and a group of rounded stones, the smallest one just a hair larger than a softball, bumps against my ankles. Without thinking, I grab a hold of one in each hand. I jostle them in my forearms until I've got the larger one in my left hand.

When the man with the light gets within a dozen feet of me, I don't wait for him to guide his beam around the side of my shelter. I backhand the larger stone to the upstream side of the shore to hopefully get his attention elsewhere for just a moment. Almost immediately afterwards, I spring upright and hurl the other stone as hard I can, aiming for directly above the flashlight. I know it connects when I see the outline of the man topple backwards with his flashlight falling from his hand. Under the green tint of the goggles, I watch as something else bounces along the ground beside him. A pistol. If I dash off, there's a good chance he'll snatch the gun and fire a shot in my back before I can get clear. That's not going to happen.

I see now that it's Frank. The glazed look in his eyes tells me that he hasn't a clue what hit him. He scrambles along the rocks, either trying to get to his feet or trying to get to his gun. I nail him in the side of the head with the toe of my shoe. I barely feel the impact, thanks to the temperature of the river. I grab the gun from the rubble beside his neutralized body and take off along the shore, leaping over and between rocks. I beat back the pain jolting through my knee and turn my head and see the other flashlight's beam dashing back to where Alvar had been standing. I'm hoping the altercation caught the big man off guard and he's uncertain who his target is. It doesn't take long for him to figure it out. I see my shadow appear along the rocks in front of me and I know I'm being lined up between sights.

My gut tells me to weave to the left. When I do, sparks bounce off the pile of rocks to my right. My heart's bashing my chest and my eyes are drawing tears with each breath. Without looking, I swing my arm back toward the top of the ravine and fire off a shot, merely meant to give them pause. The recoil nearly knocks the piece from my hand, but I manage to keep hold of it.

The row of trees along the bank is just a few steps away. I haven't sensed any more shots since the one that sent sparks flying. The vision of the helpless rabbit dangling from Tony's branch jolts through my mind and I can't circumvent the notion that I'm being sized up by Alvar, like it was, to lay in the perfect shot. He knows anyone in their right mind would seek the shelter of the trees. I show him that I'm not in my right mind by abruptly weaving in the opposite direction, digging into the muddied pea gravel closer to the river. A sharp breeze whisks by my ear and I'm sure it's the trail of a bullet. A little further to the right and it would have picked me off. Only then do I venture up under the trees.

I latch onto a web of tree roots that stray out from the crumbling earth like a partially buried cargo net. Dirt fills my shoes as I desperately search for footholds. My injured knee buckles every time I try to dig in. I find little solid ground, but I'm able to lift myself upwards with my arms nonetheless.

By the time I find the crest of the hill, a broad beam of light rises above its jagged horizon and I know one of them is close. I fire another stray bullet in that direction to slow them, not recognizing its futility until I'm back on my feet, realizing that a gun with a silencer isn't going to send anyone diving for cover. Hell, they probably didn't even know I shot at them.

Fighting through the hindering pain in my knee, I find that I can run well enough if I keep my leg relatively stiff and lead with my other. I stray away from the river a bit, where the forest is thicker, and I don't look back, barreling between trees like a horse fleeing a fire.

Chapter 40

Countless times throughout the night my weary eyes would define the outline of a tall man standing perfectly still among scores of lanky trunks and branches that swayed with the wind. But with each compliant step forward, his contour would blend back in with the wilderness and convince me that my mind was simply exhausted.

I don't know why they stopped pursuing me. Maybe I got lucky and sunk one of those stray shots inside one of them. Maybe they thought I headed off in a different direction—into the heart of the forest instead of sticking to the shoulder of the river.

My knee is swollen tightly and each painful, unbalanced step feels like it could be my last, but I continue on. My leg buckles when I slip on a large, smooth stone just as I crest a long hill. I grunt and leap forward to keep my balance and stay upright. My arms go horizontal and I scramble down to the bottom of the embankment, slipping and stumbling along the way. I reach the bottom where small rocks and dislodged chunks of earth bang against the backs of my ankles. I take a breath that lingers visibly in the air and continue on, pulling my thin, dirty fingers now clenched into fists back under the dark trench coat sleeves for warmth.

I rested little, merely five or ten minute breaks here and there after collapsing to my knees and letting my chest rise and fall. I didn't want to stay idle for long. Each time I did the image of Arianna's lifeless eyes returned and pried into my soul like a hot spear through my rib cage.

My lips and throat are dry, and when I drink from the river, my thirst only returns a minute or two later.

Still, the rushing river remains my constant companion, encouraging me that signs of civilization will emerge into sight, along with the rising sun. The sun's rays jet through the sky and clouds above in rejuvenation, like the promise of continuing life, though I can't yet feel their heat. It's a beautiful sight but a disheartening one, too, because I know that my life has no purpose without Arianna. She's gone, and I can't fathom a day when that wound in my heart could heal.

I wonder when Moretti did it. If he delivered her the fatal blow before they ever got back to the house, there truly is nothing I could have done to stop it. But if he returned to the house with Arianna still alive, it's possible my absence is what proved to him Valentino's claim, and in a rage, he ended her life. Maybe if I had stuck around, she'd be alive right now.

All of that effort to deceive them into believing that the man who escaped their clutches was Valentino—it could have well been the catalyst for Arianna's death.

If they've figured out by now that it's me and me alone that they have to worry about, I'm uncertain of their next move. What I do know is that they won't stop until they find me—not until my head is a trophy on Moretti's mantel.

I know how Moretti thinks. He'll take whatever revenge he can against me, and that includes coming after Lisa. He'll see it as an eye for an eye. A tooth for a tooth. At least she'll be safe for the moment. They don't know where she is.

I never should have let Moretti know about Lisa at all, but there's no way I could have kept her a secret from him. He's got too many connections in Vegas—too many people who'd recognize me with a mysterious woman. When I built up the nerve to tell him of my second life, he laughed hysterically for ten minutes straight and to my surprise seemed to admire my creativity. From his standpoint, the gimmick was preferable to worrying about a spouse knowing too much about his business. Again, plausible deniability. He probably figured the marriage wouldn't last two months anyway, let alone two years.

Still, Moretti felt compelled, in direct terms, to help me with my charade. That's how he phrased it anyway. He insisted that he take Lisa and me out for dinner one night so he could play the part of a retired colleague at the FBI. It was a terrible idea—an impending disaster—but I had no choice. The anger that began to stew in his eyes when I expressed my reservations told me that he wasn't going to take no for an answer.

Lisa was actually eager to meet my former colleague, Lawrence Falcone. It was an alias Moretti had come up with quickly, as if he'd used it before or knew someone of that name. For Lisa, it was the promise of some much awaited insight into a secretive, exciting career that I avoided talking about. Moretti didn't disappoint. While scarfing down medium-rare steak and wine, he rattled off anecdote after anecdote of fabricated stories—the details of which made the hair on the back of my neck stand up. I was astonished by the amount of preparation he must have done in order to so convincingly deliver such fiction. He'd even turned off what was left of his Italian accent.

Moretti was enjoying himself, and I could sense that he was sending me a message with his performance—a message that he was a puppet master who held my immaculate deception in the palm of his hands. He could cut the strings at the moment of his choosing. He's always liked being in control—of everything.

He told Lisa the tale that his marriage ended because he too often brought the job home with him, making the mistake of exposing the gory details of crimes committed by the worst of humanity to his wife. He spoke of how he burdened her, wore her down, and pushed her away. It was as convincing as hell. I swear I even saw a tear form in his eye. Lisa seemed to take his words to heart. She rarely pressed me on the details of my work after that. I suppose, in that sense, that

Moretti did me a favor, but if I could take any of it back, I'd take it *all* back. I would have never married her. I would have never exposed her to any of this.

I could run to the Feds and turned state's witness, but who would be testifying against whom? I killed a man. I did it in cold blood, and to the Feds, that might not make me any less of a notch on their belt than Moretti. Sure, I've got a lot of dirt on the big guy, but he always insulated me from the worst stuff. I've got his books, which are important. But if the Feds have the paper trail, they don't need me. And without the evidence, how much am I worth to them?

Even in a best case scenario, I'd end up in witness relocation with Lisa by my side, condemned to live with a man she had no idea was a cheating, pathological liar, and now a murderer to boot. She's had no part in any of this.

Valentino Greco weighs heavily on my conscience. The man was no saint, by any means, but did he deserve to die? I killed him for nothing. His death was pointless. As hard as I try to fight the crushing realization that I drained the life from his body—that he died at my hands—I'm unable to absolve myself of the dark, punishing guilt that hangs over me.

God, I've destroyed so many things. Lisa keeps entering my thoughts. Prior to today, it had gotten to the point where our marriage had become nothing but a burden, an obstacle that stood in the way of the clarity I felt whenever I'd fantasize about my future plans with Arianna. She was standing between me and a fresh start. I resented her. I had contempt for her. Now, I can't stop thinking about her. Maybe it's the epiphany that the same lifelessness I saw last night in Arianna's eyes is what Lisa's been seeing in mine for over a year. And now, I've placed a target on her back, too. If I'm to set her free from all of this, and set *myself* free from all of this, there's only one thing left to do.

I glance down at my trench coat that spent the night in my brief bag. Its sharp and clean appearance is a stark contrast from Tony's grimy, muddied jacket that I buried between some rocks upstream. It covers so much of my body that you'd never know I spent the night in the forest. I look like I'm headed to a job interview.

I sense movement out of the corner of my eye and observe a small white blur in the distance. It flickers through the gaps in the sporadically dense wilderness, unhindered by the terrain and moving quickly from east to west. A cloud of dust floats behind it and I realize that it's an automobile along an apparent dirt road. The car doesn't slow down when it reaches the path of the river. It glides on over to the other side. There must be a bridge ahead.

The theory is confirmed when I reach a small clearing along the riverside. The bridge is constructed primarily with wood but has two vertical, cement piers that rise up from the water to support it. There's text branded along its lower wall. It reads "Meyers Bridge – CR 2." I assume that the CR stands for County Road and I pull a ripped piece of newspaper from my bag that I discovered during the night. It had fallen in there along with other items from the top of the desk back at the house when I was in a hurry to grab Moretti's ledger. I had used it as a piece of scratch paper during the meeting in town, earlier in the day. On the backside of the paper is a local map. On it, I see a County Road 1, but no 2. It must be farther south because this is the first bridge I've come to. That would make me close to the town of Winston if the promoters of the 7th Annual Beggar's Basin Fish-Off were true to their representation.

It takes a desperate man to put such faith in the hands of an oversimplified map from a newspaper advertisement, but I believe it has served me well.

Another car comes into view through the trees, traveling in the opposite direction from the first one. It's a dark shade of gray, and

I dart for cover behind a tree with my chest pounding, aware that I no longer wear the cloak of night to help hide me. The car's moving slowly but is not coming to a stop. I peer through a web of leaves and brush as it continues on its way, prowling along methodically like a steel shark in search of food. It's Alvar's Buick. Shit.

I'm exhausted. I no longer have the will or the strength to fight for my life, but I may not have to as they haven't spotted me. They're probably just canvassing the area, hoping to get lucky. Moretti's Cadillac is most likely out somewhere on the same mission. The car's lit headlights tell me that they've been at it for a while.

Exposing as little of my face as I can, I watch them slowly vanish behind a ridge to the east, in front of what I believe at first are fence posts. A concentrated stare divulges them as rural mailboxes. The disappearance of the car is so illusory that I half wonder if its presence was even real or if my exhausted mind was playing a cruel trick on me.

I check my watch. It's nearly six a.m. I don't have a lot of time to make this work. The event starts in just a few minutes.

I'd planned to be farther down the river by now, but it might actually work to my advantage if one of the locals later remembers seeing a gray Buick driving down County Road 2 in the early morning hours. *This* is the place to do it.

I dwelled hard during the night, and I'd succumbed to the notion of letting Lisa find out about me from the police during the investigation. She'll be floored by the raw details. She'll take it hard. Of this I have no doubt. But she'll one day get past it and live the kind of life she's always wanted. Of this, I also have no doubt.

The sight of the mailboxes gives me pause, though. I hadn't expected such an opportunity to present itself. It's as if I'm being sent a message from God himself to both make things right with Lisa and ensure Moretti gets what he deserves.

I sit down on a large, rounded rock that makes a convenient seat. I open my brief bag and spread it across my lap. I yank a couple sheets from the back of Moretti's thick financial ledger and turn them over where they're blank. In my haste, the only writing utensil I managed to sweep into the mouth of the bag was a red ballpoint pen. It doesn't write at first, but some scribbling brings it to life.

One would think that an exhausted man with no soul left in his body would have trouble finding the words to write, but they come effortlessly. I tell Lisa nearly everything—who I really work for, the affair, what happened last night, and why she'll never see me again.

I let her know that when my body is found, the authorities will look at Moretti. All kinds of people saw us together in Lakeland. Our entourage of slick Italians, a hot woman, a giant Mexican, and a blonde-haired pencil-pusher stuck out like a sore thumb. And if that's not enough, the FBI in Vegas will receive a blueprint of my murder, along with details of Moretti's numerous illegal activities on their doorstep in a couple of days. I tell her that she'll be safe, and that Moretti won't bother to seek retribution against the wife of a dead man who wronged him—especially if he thinks that man was murdered by another adversary.

I end the note with, *I'm sorry. I wish I was the man who you deserved.*

I set the note along the forest floor and begin a second one—this one to the FBI office in Las Vegas who knows more about Moretti than pretty much anyone besides me. I quickly scribble a frantic note that I hope to look like it was written under distress, explaining to the Feds that I'm an associate of Moretti and witnessed him murder a woman at a mountain home near Lakeland. I tell them that I also saw them take a man named Kyle Kimble deep into the forest and return without him. I tell them that I fear for my life and am being watched closely by Moretti's men, and that I hope they'll find the enclosed information useful if something happens to me. I sign the letter, "Valentino Greco."

One last mind-fuck to absolve Lisa from any act of revenge if things don't work out this morning as planned.

I dig back into the leather bag and retrieve two legal-sized manila envelopes, one of which I had planned on using to send a signed contract to Moretti's new partner. I write the Las Vegas address for the FBI on one of them, knowing it by heart from the identification I've carried around in my wallet for the past few years. The note and the ledger go inside. The other note goes in the envelope I address to the cottage. I write both as legibly as I can to ensure they get where they need to go. I secure an abundance of postage to each, using up all of the first class stamps that I have.

I seal the envelopes with long licks that are dry from thirst and stack them across a nearby stump, then pull the purple stocking cap from my head. I hold it to my face and inhale, absorbing Arianna's scent as a reminder of what could have been. I shove it into my brief bag and begin raking away at a patch of wet dirt beside an overturned tree, using my fingers as picks to dislodge rocks and earth. Once I've created a hole satisfactory in size, I shove my bag into it and begin refilling the hole with dirt. When I realize that I've still got the page of newspaper in my coat pocket, I add it to the grave, pound it down under the loose dirt, and place a large rock over the disturbed terrain. I thought about just tossing the stuff in the river, but if it's found, it will only prompt questions that will distract from the scenario I've created.

I wash off my hands in the river, then watchfully venture my way across the range toward the mailboxes, alternating my attention between the ridge to the east and the bridge. I keep low, ready to drop behind the tall grass that lines the dirt below me at a moment's notice.

I reach the boxes and survey the road more closely now that I've got a clean view. Nothing. An American flag stems out from the lone mailbox that stands next to a yellow, plastic newspaper box labeled, "The Winston Beacon." I was right. I'm in Winston.

I open the mailbox to find a couple of outgoing letters, which is good. The resident won't check the box again until the mail's been picked up. I add my mail to the pile.

A minute later, I stand alone at the center of the bridge with my hands in my pockets and my shoulders relaxed, feeling totally exposed and unhindered. I've spent the past several hours using the terrain of the forest for protection, but now it's as if it's releasing me from its guard and returning me to the outside world. My concentrated stare switches from one side of the road to the other, assuring that no one else is around to share in the moment. The sun is peaking up above the tranquil mountain range to my left and its greeting warms my face. Just a few hours ago, I wasn't sure I'd see another sunrise. I'm thankful it's such a brilliant one because it will be my last.

Beyond the mountains, lakes, and state lines is Lisa, probably tired after a restless sleep of wondering why I haven't joined her yet. The world as she knew it is about to turn upside down, but she'll pull through. Maybe she'll even find a way to forgive me some day.

I peer down over the guardrail that stems up from the edge and gawk at the power of the rushing water below. Its force is awe-inspiring, and I'm confident it will take me where I need to go. It will also take mercy on me and finish me off if the bullet doesn't.

Again I check for oncomers and see none, but not knowing how well the road is traveled, I decide that I best hurry along. I step over the railing and plop myself down on a post, taking a moment to gander at the dry blood along the palm of my hand—a mixture of mine in Arianna's. I hope I see her soon, both of us now free of her master's grip.

I can't say for sure what's in store for me, though. If there is an afterlife, what will mine be like having killed a man? My letter will fool the Feds, but it won't fool the Man upstairs. I say a quick prayer and ask whoever's listening for forgiveness before I reach into my back pocket for my wallet. I open it and am greeted by a photo of Lisa and me, both wearing stocking caps and standing together, cheek to cheek, in front of a snowy basin. Smiles light up both of our faces, as a reminder of happier times. Ironically, it was taken not all that many miles from where I sit now.

Things might have been so much different if I wasn't me. I'm not a good person. I never have been.

I set down the gun along a post beside me, stand up, and balance myself along the edge of the bridge with my heels firmly planted on solid wood. The wallet goes back in my pocket that I button up to make sure there's an easy way of identifying me after the screams of children downriver announce my arrival.

I retrieve the gun and raise it carefully up behind my head. My arms tremble, and I fight back the impulse to drop the piece from my hands and climb back to safety. The barrel of the gun is flat against the back of my head, centered where I'm certain it will do the job. I stiffen my body and lean forward like I'm about to engage in a leap of faith, trying to put as much distance between my head and the bridge as possible before I pull the trigger. I feel the spray of the rapids inviting me forward, and I squeeze my finger.

For the briefest of seconds, I find my sight unexpectedly glimpsing back up toward the bridge. It stalls on the peculiar image of a man with his hand reaching down to me. It fades when the biting cold water devours my last breath.

I hope the man was an angel.

Chapter 41

"Y ou've been keeping me very busy, Chief," said Dr. Laura Venegas before diluting a reserved grin from her lips, quickly deeming it inappropriate.

The sun above them hung brightly, though the morning air was still cool down by the shaded bank of the reservoir.

She read no acknowledgment from Lumbergh that he'd even heard her remark. His tired eyes from a sleepless, highly stressful night were transfixed on the contents of the yellow, partially transparent body bag that was sprawled out along the padded stretcher propped up between them at the roped-off crime scene. The corpse inside was barely recognizable from the picture in the corner of the well-preserved driver's license that the chief held in his gloved hand. The wad of gum trapped in Lumbergh's mouth hadn't been gnawed from the moment he'd opened the dead man's wallet handed to him by the doctor's assistant.

Venegas, the county medical examiner, tugged at the zipper, sealing off a short, open section at the top.

"Not by choice, I assure you," replied Lumbergh after a delay long enough that Venegas had nearly forgotten its reference.

From upside down, she glanced at the photo of the thin, blonde-haired man staring straight ahead and asked Lumbergh who he was.

His eyes lifted to meet hers, displaying a level of seriousness that unsettled her. "His name is Kyle Kimble. He appears to work for the Las Vegas branch of the Federal Bureau of Investigation."

"You're kidding."

"No, I'm not. Which means, I probably won't be working this case by the end of the day."

It meant far more than that to Lumbergh, though. It meant that whatever his brother-in-law was mixed up in went way beyond a drunken conflict and a retaliatory act of murder. In all of his years as a crime investigator in Illinois, the chief had never experienced anything close to this. Three dead bodies, one of them a federal agent. A sadistic killer of two of them on the loose, and the man who most likely held all of the answers—his own brother-in-law—missing and probably on the run.

"Any idea how long he was in the water?" he asked before glancing down at his own matted shirt that he'd been wearing for over twelve hours.

"It's hard to say for sure," she answered, pulling back the hood of her white medical examiner's jacket. She brushed a strand of her long, black hair from her eyes. "Two or three days probably, judging by how bloated he is."

"How is that possible?"

"What do you mean?"

The stick of gum in Lumbergh's mouth began churning again. "Let's just say that I have reason to believe that this man went into the river, up by Winston, on Saturday morning."

"And?" she replied with a shrug of her shoulders.

"My point is that . . . that's only a few miles upstream. There was a big event out here that morning. That yearly fishing thing."

"Yes, the contest. I was here with my son. They had a record turnout, I believe."

"Exactly."

He dropped the contents of the dead man's wallet into a Ziploc bag before pointing his finger toward the large and tranquil reservoir that stretched broadly beyond the shoreline laying just a few yards short of where the two of them stood. The grand, inverted image of Beggar's Basin reflected along the rippling water. "There were people everywhere, yet no one found this man until this morning."

"There's a simple answer for that," said the doctor with a knowing twinkle in her eye. "His body got hung up somewhere. The way his limbs are mangled, and the way his clothes are all torn and stretched out . . . He probably got snagged on a downed tree or something and was tossed around like a hooked bobber that someone cut loose from their line. He probably broke free after a couple of days and ended up here last night or this morning."

The chief nodded his head in deference to her expertise.

"I'm glad his trip was delayed," she added. "I don't think there would have been enough money in the county budget to cover the counseling expenses for a few hundred children if one of them had reeled him into shore."

He let himself chuckle before his expression went eerily blank. She noticed the alteration of his disposition and wondered if she had just said something that had led him adrift or if the stress of the past twelve hours was taking its toll on the lawman.

It was the realization that the body, in all likelihood, *should* have been carried to Beggar's Basin right around the time of the highly publicized event. The revelation invited a fresh perspective worth contemplating. Up until just then, it had made absolutely no sense to the chief why a man would commit suicide by shooting himself in the back of the head. However, an explanation was suddenly unwinding and emerging, just as the body itself had done that morning. *What if he wanted to be found that morning, and wanted it to look like he had been executed by someone else?* In Illinois, Lumbergh had investigated more than one murder in which the body had been disposed of somewhere away from the location where the actual killing had taken place. Never, in any of those cases, was there ever identification left on the body. A murderer didn't typically want his victim to be easily identified. In this case, however, it was as if the discovery of the man's I.D. was the desired result.

"I'm going to head on out, if you don't mind, Chief," Venegas said, robbing back his attention for a moment. "I've got a lot of work to do, as you know. How's your wife doing?"

He nodded. The arch of his eyebrows suggested that he was being genuine when he told her that Diana was taking things better than one could expect.

"Any word on her brother?"

With a deep sigh, he answered, "Not yet."

"He'll turn up."

He noticed her attention shift to something over his shoulder.

"Meagher's back," she announced.

Lumbergh thanked the doctor and helped her and her assistant wheel the body into the back of their van before turning his attention to the approaching pickup truck with turret lights attached to its roof. In the driver's seat was Chief Pete Meagher, the one and only member of the Rinkshaw police department. The nearby town of Rinkshaw was dwarfed even by Winston in population, and Meagher's title as police chief was a part-time position. He also ran a hardware store in town. Technically, he had jurisdiction over the Beggar's Basin area.

Lumbergh liked Meagher, mainly because the man knew his weaknesses. They were close in age. Meagher was a bit older, but far less experienced. His duties were primarily confined to addressing the occasional domestic dispute or managing traffic in and out of the reservoir area for events.

He'd worked with Lumbergh on a couple of occasions and was always more than happy to cede the leadership role to him. When a body turned up in the water that morning, however, something he'd recently read in the Lakeland paper triggered the belief that he might actually be able to play a useful purpose in the investigation.

He'd left the reservoir for his house to retrieve the paper shortly after Lumbergh had arrived on the scene.

Lumbergh watched Meagher's head twist back and forth between him and the medical examiner's van that he'd noticed was on its way out.

"Hold up! Hold up!" he yelled out his open truck window after skidding to a stop. He waved his hand in the air. The van slowed down.

"Pete!" shouted Lumbergh. "It's okay! I've got an I.D!"

Meagher nodded that he understood and let the van pass him by. After parking beside Lumbergh's Jeep, he hustled on out of his truck and jogged over to his Winston counterpart. Meagher hadn't a uniform, just a red flannel shirt with jeans, cowboy boots, and a badge. A Colorado Rockies baseball cap sat high on his head. He quickly unfolded the newspaper he'd shuffled between his hands when sliding his truck keys into his front pocket.

"Is it him?" asked Meagher.

He held up a page with a decent-sized black and white picture. It was a close-up, candid shot of a man with short, brown hair and wearing a white t-shirt. The headline above the picture read, Local Shop Owner Missing Since Friday.

"No, it sure isn't, Pete," answered Lumbergh. He held up the identification card of Kyle Kimble so Meagher could see it. Meagher squinted and gave it a close look. His eyes quickly widened.

"FBI?" he yelped before taking a step back. "He was a G-Man?"

"It looks like it. I haven't called it in yet."

"Should we have moved him? Shouldn't we have talked to the Feds before letting Doc Laura take him away? They might have wanted to look over the crime scene first."

Lumbergh shook his head. "He wasn't killed here. I'm sure they'll check him out at the examiner's office. Mind if I see that?" He pointed to the newspaper.

Meagher handed it over.

"I'm surprised I hadn't heard about this," said Lumbergh with a wrinkle in his face that resembled a wince.

"The guy's girlfriend didn't report him missing until Sunday. Seems they were going through a rough patch. They hadn't talked in a couple of days."

Lumbergh skimmed the article.

"Chad Grimes. That's an interesting name." After reaching the bottom of the page, he looked up at Meagher. "It doesn't say anything in here about him and the girlfriend being in a fight?"

Meagher clarified: "I gave them a call up there in Lakeland before I left the house, you know, to let him know we found someone. I guess I jumped the gun."

"Don't worry about it. Do they have any leads?"

Meagher snickered and shook his head. "What? You don't think you've got enough on your plate right now?"

A gasp of air left Lumbergh's lips, and he said, "I suppose you've got a point there, Pete. The sheriff's office is taking over on the two from yesterday, though. I'm too close to it. They said I should take some time to grieve with my family. I guess that will have to hold off until tomorrow. So, *do* they have any leads in Lakeland?"

"There's a kid. A teenager who busses tables up at the Elk-Horn Grill. It's just a couple doors down from Grimes's shop."

"Yeah, I've eaten there. Good salmon."

"Oh yeah, the best. Anyway, he was hauling some trash out back Friday night. He saw a dark gray, maybe a black sedan speeding down the back alley and onto the main street. Lakeland's finest believe it went down not long after Grimes was last seen closing down his store."

"What kind of sedan?"

"The kid didn't know," Meagher answered. He removed his hat for a moment to scratch his forehead before continuing. "Kids don't know their cars anymore, do they? They just ain't interested in that stuff these days. All they care about are video games."

"Probably no license plate then either, right?"

"No number. The kid didn't think it was all that suspicious at the time, but he did notice that it had out-of-state plates."

"Where from?"

"Nevada. Blue mountains under an orange sky."

Lumbergh's heart skipped a beat. "Nevada? The dead agent, Kyle Kimble . . . He's from Las Vegas."

Meagher stood back and watched the gears in Lumbergh's head grind for a few seconds, then asked, "Are you thinking they're related somehow? Do you think the FBI is here in Summit, maybe helping to search for Grimes?"

"No. They wouldn't be part of a missing person's case this early unless they suspected a kidnapping. I'm sure the boys in Lakeland would have mentioned that to you if that was the case. Besides, Kimble was killed before Grimes was reported missing."

"You're sure of that?" Meagher asked.

In answering yes, Lumbergh recognized that he'd taken full ownership of being wrong in his dismissal of the claims made to him Saturday morning by his brother-in-law. It was a bitter pill to swallow.

Sean's whereabouts were still unknown, but at least Lumbergh had a lead now in the form of the dead agent, and he was sure the FBI in Las Vegas would be able to shed a bright light over everything that was going on in his town.

Chapter 42

Until Monday night, Ron Oldhorse hadn't been privy to Sean Coleman's story of the mysterious man who'd shot himself on Meyers Bridge. He didn't make it into town all that often and never read the newspaper, for he had no interest in the local gossip. But after a double murder occurred in the mountains that he considered his backyard and he was asked to help find a lost child who was chased into the woods by a maniac, he grew concerned by the evil that had come to Winston.

He'd planned to spend the morning bow hunting along the eastern ridge of Aimes Pass, but felt compelled to begin the crisp, bright day at Meyers Bridge. He went there unsure of what he was looking for or hoped to find.

Oldhorse never had much use for Sean Coleman and didn't believe him to be an honorable man. Still, the security guard's account that he'd overheard from the chief and his officer during the night's search triggered his curiosity. Like Jefferson, Oldhorse wondered if it had some relevance to the arrival of the murderer—that is, if there was any truth to what Coleman had said.

There was a personal stake in his interest as well. He'd liked Zed Hansen. Oldhorse didn't really consider Zed a friend. The tribesman had no friends. However, he respected the kind gentleman who'd always kept his word in their dealings. While most of Winston was uneasy with Oldhorse's solitary, naturalistic lifestyle and was skeptical of his past, Zed was different. He showed reverence to Oldhorse and treated the man as an equal rather than as an eccentric novelty.

If Sean was telling the truth, three days and one heavy rainstorm had passed through since the mystery man's dead body had fallen to the river. If there was any trail of where the man had come from, it was far from fresh. Oldhorse, however, relished the challenge.

There wasn't much to find by the bridge itself other than some prints from a small person who Oldhorse deemed the same as those left the night before by Toby Parker. North of the bridge, however, there were plentiful signs of human activity. On the east side of the river, the moist earth was littered with the footprints created by a large man. Their depth suggested that they were left during or shortly after the rainstorm on Saturday night, which was after Sean had already brought his claim to the police station. This led Oldhorse to deduct that they were left by Coleman himself, who was most likely pillaging the area in hopes of finding the same type of trace evidence that Oldhorse was now in search of. By Oldhorse's assessment, Coleman had indeed found something.

An object had been exhumed from under the moist earth. A crater in the soil and a few rocks were the focus of a lot of attention.

The tip of a large, compound hunting bow jetted out from the unzipped flap of a customized camouflage backpack that Oldhorse wore across his shoulders. The top of the bow lurked high above his mane of scraggly hair that was loosely tied back in a ponytail. He scrutinized the crater and noticed something small and shiny resting at its center. He dropped to a knee to investigate.

He dug his fingers inside and pulled out a couple of metal paperclips, the standard kind used for bundling papers. His hawkish eyes inspected them closely before he stood back up and shoved them in the front pocket of his jeans.

When widening out his search, he found a trail of trampled and broken grass that led to the southeast. A few trace footprints were small enough for Oldhorse to determine that they belonged to someone other than Sean, but larger than Toby. This got his juices flowing, but they appeared to lead back in the direction of the road. This implied that the origin of whoever left them lay to the north, upriver.

Chapter 43

S ean found it nearly impossible to take his eyes off the widow's expressionless gaze while she sat quietly in his car across the parking lot, sheltered by a shade tree. Lisa hadn't uttered a word since finishing the letter. In his hand, Sean held the well-used receiver from a pay phone outside of a convenience store, having just confirmed a collect call to the Winston Police Department.

He could only imagine the confusion and pain that Lisa must be experiencing, having found out in the same day not only that her husband had killed himself, but that their whole marriage was a lie—one that had nearly gotten her killed less than an hour ago.

The somberness that surrounded her displayed a stark contrast to the typical summer action of an upper-scale, carefree community in northern Michigan. The area was flush with people—a mix of midlife crises driving convertibles and vacationing tourists toting their families around in minivans and SUVs—all seemingly happy in their lives.

Sean watched her hold a damp rag against her raw eye. Cradled inside it were cubes of ice he had stolen from a plastic bag inside the machine beside where he stood. Even with her beaten face and her defeated spirit, she hadn't lost the remarkable beauty he had earlier witnessed from the forest. The fact that her asshole husband couldn't keep his pants on for that struck him as total idiocy.

"Where the fuck are you?" Jefferson yelled into the receiver so loudly that Sean nearly dropped the phone.

Sean's eyes narrowed. He was taken back by the officer's unexpected verbal assault.

"What the hell's your problem, Jefferson?" he quickly replied.

"Put Lumbergh on the phone! I need to talk to an adult!"

"The chief's not here, Sean! He's down at Beggar's Basin where they found the guy you shot!"

Back in Winston, Jefferson's eyes bulged from behind his sloppy, paper-riddled desk at the sound of his own words. He hastily covered the phone receiver with his meaty hand and silently mouthed an obscenity over his shoulder before checking to see if anyone else in the office had heard him. The theory that Sean Coleman was behind the death of the man dragged from the river that morning was his own. His suspicions and eagerness to stick it to Sean had gotten the better of him, and he knew immediately that he had screwed up. Sean needed to come back to Winston where things could be sorted out. In a thoughtless moment, Jefferson feared that he had just scared off the man who surely held the answers to everything that had gone on over the past few days. He held the phone back to his ear and timidly listened for Sean's response. He could have never predicted what it would be.

"What in the hell are you talking about? The guy I shot isn't even in Colorado!"

"What?" Jefferson shouted as he leapt to his feet. "You *did* shoot somebody?!"

He could almost hear Sean scowl into the receiver. "Sean, listen to me," he said in a careful and much more restrained tone, as if he was trying to talk Sean down off the ledge of a tall building. "You need to turn yourself in. Tell me where you are."

He placed his hand over the phone and snapped to attention the office secretary who had just approached the copy machine beside his cubicle. "Was there a caller ID number for this call?" he asked in a hushed spurt. "Does one show up on that little screen for a collect call?"

"Turn myself in?" Sean snarled over the phone line. "What the hell for? What's going on?"

318 Frorm a Dead Sleep

"Sean, I'm sure there's a good explanation for whatever happened," Jefferson said. "We can talk about it here. We'll get the chief in on this and just sort everything out."

Sean was having none of it. He winced and slammed the receiver down on the payphone's metal hook.

"Idiot!" he shouted into the air before glancing at Lisa who was still seated in the car. His outburst went unnoticed by her.

Under heavy breath, he picked up the phone and placed a second collect call to the person he wished he had tried first. He could hear the alarm in his sister's voice when the operator asked her if she would accept the call.

"Yes. Thank God," Diana stated over the line.

Sean was still burning. "D, I just talked to Jefferson and—"

"Sean, where the hell have you been?" she broke in before he could finish. "Someone killed Uncle Zed!"

His stomach sank and his legs went wobbly. His sister continued on, but he heard little of what she said. He fell to a knee and placed the palm of his hand on the sidewalk underneath him. Keeping the phone to his ear, he looked across the parking lot where he noticed an expression of concern on Lisa's face. She was staring back at him. She quickly climbed out of the car and ran to his side.

She asked him repeatedly if he was alright, but he didn't answer.

"Do you have any clue what's been going on here for the past couple of days?" Diana asked.

After a few seconds more of processing, he finally answered, "No."

He listened as she launched into a breathless summary of the double murder that went down at his apartment and how Toby survived with the help of their uncle. She relayed the description Toby had given from the hospital of a tall, silver-haired man with ugly teeth who had come looking for Sean. She told him of Rocco.

"This morning, they found a body downriver, Sean," she added. "He was wearing a black trench coat. He had blonde hair. A hole in the back of his head, just like you told Gary. Sean, what happened on that bridge? Who is this man who came looking for you?"

He said nothing. The despair depicted in his eyes steadily corroded into anger. After a few seconds, he muttered in a tone that his sister couldn't recognize, "How did they know to come looking for me?"

"What?" Lisa and Diana asked him at the same time.

"The newspaper!" he answered to his own question before slamming his fist into the brick wall of the building behind him. "Roy Hughes. He wrote about what I saw in the *Beacon!*"

His eyes transcended into recollection of what Toby had told him the morning he'd left. The boy had known about what had gone down at Meyers Bridge from a piece Roy Hughes had written in *The Winston Beacon*. The article was only printed for entertainment purposes, to make Sean look like a lunatic for once again wasting the police chief's time. Yet, the headline clearly captured the attention of Moretti's crew who were looking for Kyle Kimble. The article let them know that Kimble had died at his own hand.

The gears in Sean's head ground away and he remained unresponsive to the querying voices around him. He imagined how the large man who Toby described as having silver hair had seen Sean's name in the paper and came to his home to find out what more Sean had seen or knew. And once that man had gotten inside Sean's apartment, he would have found Kyle Kimble's bag and concluded that it was Sean Coleman who had possession of Moretti's ledger—the one that should now be in the hands of the FBI. Zed, Bailey, and Toby were all in the wrong place at the wrong time.

"I led them right to you," Sean said to Lisa without looking at her.

Kyle Kimble had made it clear in the letter to his wife that she would be safe at the cottage in Michigan because Moretti knew nothing of it. With an address turning up in Sean's apartment, however, they were probably able to look up the property information somehow and see who owned it. When Kimble's name came up, they most likely figured it was worth their time to check out what was there. Maybe something that could incriminate them. Maybe even the ledger.

Sean sat down on the sidewalk, resting his back against the building with the phone still glued to his ear. He lowered his head.

"And if I hadn't passed out at Meyers Bridge Friday night, none of this would have happened," he said to no one in particular. "It would have ended that morning. I gave those sons of bitches a trail and they followed it, and people are dead because of it." His eyes finally rose to meet hers. "And they nearly killed you."

"Sean, what are you talking about?" he heard his sister's voice say through the receiver. "Are you there with someone?"

"Diana, listen to me," he said into the phone. "The man behind all of this . . . his name is Moretti. He's some kind of Las Vegas big shot. The dead man in the river . . . his name is Kyle Kimble. I'm here with his wife. Moretti's people tried to kill her." He took a second to catch his breath before continuing. "I stopped them. I need to talk to Gary."

"Oh shit! Oh shit!" he heard Lisa suddenly shout.

He glanced to her; her attention was turned to the nearby street. She dropped to a knee beside him, covering the side of her face with her hand. There was a crippling fear in her eyes.

He frowned. "What is it?"

"The guard!" She spoke with her face wrenched in a grimace. "Josh Jones! He just drove by!"

He scrambled to his feet and peered over the tops of cars parked in front of a row of gas pumps. Out of the corner of his eye, he caught the backend of a fast-moving, beige Volvo disappearing behind the corner of the building with a river of other cars trailing behind it. The rental sticker along the back window looked to be the same one

Sean had seen in the cottage driveway. There was no indication that
the driver had seen either one of them.

"Are you sure it was him?" he asked, his jaw set in determination.

She nodded. "I never forget a face."

He turned back to the phone. "Sis, have Gary call the Traverse
City Police Department. In Michigan. They'll find a dead body at
One-Fourteen Bluff Walk Road. He's one of Moretti's guys. They're
the same people who shot Uncle Zed."

"A dead person? In Michigan?" Diana's tone was incredulous.
"You're in *Michigan*?"

"Yes, write it down. One-Fourteen Bluff Walk Road. I'll call you
back when I can! There's a lot more, but I have to go!"

"Sean, wait! Just stay on the phone! Let me try and get Gary on
the radio."

"No time! Just tell him!" He slammed down the phone and
darted in the direction of his Nova. His eyes were ablaze with anger
and reckoning. Josh Jones was with the people that killed his uncle—
that killed Rocco—and he wasn't about to let him get away.

"What are you doing?" screamed Lisa, who jogged after him with
her hands in the air.

He opened the driver's side door and already had a foot on the
floorboard before he turned to acknowledge her. "Those bastards
shot and killed my uncle! The same people that were after your
husband and are now after you. Josh Jones is one of them."

"Just call the police!" she pleaded. "Describe the car to them! Tell
them the direction he's headed in! Let *them* take care of it!"

The Nova groaned in dissent when Sean's weight crashed down
across the front seat. The ignition cranked, and the engine roared
with the trademark soundness that Uncle Zed had helped Sean
maintain from the car over the years.

The door slammed shut and Sean draped his head outside the
open window. "I don't have time to explain it all to them! The police
never believe me anyway! He's getting away!"

Her eyelids fluttered like a butterfly's wings. She shook her head and asked, "What about me?"

"Stay here and call the police yourself if you want, or come with me! I don't give a shit, but I need to leave now!"

The tires pealed when he shifted into reverse and slammed onto the gas pedal. He turned his car in the direction of the road. Lisa stood in front of him. She looked like a deer frozen in front of a pair of headlights. By the expression on her face, it looked like her heart was beating faster than his.

"Make a decision!" he snarled out the window.

A second later, the passenger side door sprung open and she was inside. As tires screeched again, she cursed under her breath, mumbling something about whether or not she had made the right choice.

He could understand her dilemma. She barely knew him, this gritty man who sat an arm's length away from her, but she had to be convinced he was on her side. With all they'd been through, she had to know. It had been a sign of trust when she'd opened that door and gotten in.

And as the Nova barreled down the street, Sean figured that with no one else in the world left to trust, Lisa's trust in him had to mean something.

Chapter 44

"Was there anyone else with him?" asked Sean before he sped up and cut off a yellow Volkswagen Bug who honked in objection.

"In the car?"

"Yeah."

Lisa shook her head. "I don't think so. It didn't look like it."

Sean grunted in annoyance at the thickness of traffic that had seemingly come out of nowhere and was hindering him from catching up with the beige Volvo. They could still see Josh Jones's car from a distance, far in front of them, but he was clearly in as much of a hurry as they were, weaving in and out of a clog of other cars.

For the first time since they'd met, Lisa found herself closely studying the appearance of the man whose introduction had changed her world. His short but scraggly beard only partially covered the rough complexion of his skin. His yellowed teeth and unkempt hair added no positive accentuation. Sprawled along his shirt were several small holes from years of wear and tear that would have forced most people to retire it to a trashcan or pile of rags somewhere in a garage long ago. His boots were nearly threads at the toes.

An empty beer can along with an assortment of flattened candy wrappers and other trash decorated the backseat and the floorboards.

"Are you homeless?" she asked.

His strained eyes that had been narrowed on the road slightly widened as he turned to the woman who sat beside him. "Homeless?"

His reaction brought embarrassment to her battered face.

"I'm sorry," she quickly stated before letting her gaze return to the road. "It's just that you had said before that you'd watched my husband fall from a bridge, and that no one had believed what you'd seen."

"So, what? You thought I *lived* under that bridge?

She didn't reply.

He shook his head and returned his attention to the road. "No. I'm not homeless," he said before taking a second to further ponder the question. "Well, hell, maybe I am now. My landlord's dead."

Her head titled back to him with concern etched across the delicate features of her face.

"You lived with your uncle?"

He shook his head. "No. I *worked* for my uncle . . . which means I'm probably homeless *and* jobless. Jesus Christ . . ."

She had more questions, but it didn't seem the moment to ask for clarification.

"These assholes took a lot from me," he said as she was deliberating asking another question. "When we catch up to that little fucker, I'm gonna make him feel some pain."

"Is that what we're doing?" she said. "We're just going to, what? Run him off the road so you can kick his ass again?"

"At least."

"I don't think that's a good idea. These people are dangerous."

"As Josh's buddy found out, so am I."

She sighed and shook her head. "Kyle sent the ledger to the FBI. They have what they need to put Moretti away. They'll take care of him."

"Don't count on it," he barked. "If there's such good shit in that ledger, he wouldn't have needed to blow his own brains out to try and frame Moretti for murder."

Her hand went to her mouth and her shoulders fell forward, fighting back the urge to cry at his insensitive remarks.

She didn't look at him, but heard him grunt and then add in a more restrained tone, "Listen, I'm just saying that if he felt so hopeless that the only way out of his situation was to kill himself," he said more carefully, "and pin his murder on Moretti, it's a pretty safe bet that there aren't enough goodies in that book alone to put the man in prison. I saw your husband's face as he sat on that bridge. He wasn't confident. He was desperate."

She nodded subtly, acknowledging that he had a point.

"Besides, I've ruined your husband's plan. I told the cops it was suicide. Moretti's off the hook for his murder."

She dwelled on his words, wiping her face, her eyes threatening tears.

His attention returned to the road and he immediately stomped on the brake.

"Come on!" he roared at an SUV hauling a boat trailer that continually padded its brakes in front of them. The larger speed-boat that rested across its prongs stood high enough to obstruct his view of the Volvo.

When he asked her if she could still see Jones from her side, she gave a quick glimpse ahead from her vantage point and nodded. "He's in the right lane."

He tapped the steering wheel in annoyance and scratched at the back of his head, where she'd seen the bald patch, seeming to consider trying to pass the traffic from the opposite lane once he had an opening.

"No, I'd better not," he said out loud. "Boats on trailers make for good cover."

He turned to Lisa, seemingly feeling the need to elaborate on his remark. "I don't want to give anything away in case Jones is checking his mirrors," he said with a smirk. "A little something I picked up from an episode of *Hardcastle and McCormick*."

She looked at him with confusion.

He glowered at the boat in front of them. "Guess that's lost on you . . ."

". . . I guess." She shook her head slightly.

Despite the cluster between them and the Volvo, they seemed to be slowly catching up.

"Where the hell's he going?" he mused aloud.

"Back to Vegas?" she speculated.

"Not directly. That's a rental car with Michigan plates. They got it locally."

"Do you think there are more of them here? Maybe he's meeting someone."

"Josh Jones is no seasoned professional," he said. "I'm sure of that. Unless, is it possible that Moretti or the silver-haired man Toby mentioned are here in Michigan?"

He seemed to be talking more to himself than her, so she waited for him to answer himself.

"Let's follow him for now," he declared, nodding to convince himself. "We'll see where he stops."

"And then we'll call the police? Right?" she asked hopefully.

"Sure."

She suspected the man next to her wasn't being sincere, but she found a morsel of comfort in the notion that ramming Josh Jones's car was off the table.

Sean seemed to force himself to breathe moderately and settled into a more discreet posture among the transit.

Minutes of silence passed that felt awkward in the tight quarters.

Lisa felt compelled to say something. "What do you do for a living, Mr. Coleman?"

He chuckled at the attempt at small talk under the circumstances.

"I'm a security guard . . . At least I was."

It explained some of his mannerisms. "What kind of security guard?"

"Property mainly. Not a ton of responsibility, I guess. Just keeping things safe." He shook his head, seemingly at his own unimpassioned description of the job, as if it seemed completely insignificant.

"Well, you kept *me* safe, Mr. Coleman," she said with a timid grin, seeing through his attempt to downplay his modest livelihood. "Thank you."

He gave her a quick grin, showing appreciation for the honest gratitude coming from her. She could see he was more accustomed to receiving praise delivered under a veil of sarcasm. He tried to hide it behind the stony set of his jaw, but she could see through the tough façade. She didn't like to think of what could have happened to her if she'd faced her assailant alone. Her gaze dropped to her hands knotted in her lap.

"You're welcome."

He seemed to mull something over, but settled for: "I wish I could have saved him."

Her sad eyes rose to his, and she felt as though she was witnessing a rare moment of genuine compassion from a man who seemed seldom ready to offer any.

"I tried everything that morning," he explained, not looking to her. "I yelled my ass off and waved my arms in the air. I ran across that bridge as fast as I could. If I had gotten to him a couple seconds faster, I might have been able to stop him."

She fought back a tear and found a way to curl the sides of her mouth in a display of graciousness. "Kyle was never an easy person to get the attention of," she said. "God, I guess I wasn't either. How could I have been so stupid?"

"What do you mean?" he asked.

She suspected he already knew what she meant with the statement.

"Our marriage. Everything. It was all a lie. I honest to God believed that he worked for the FBI. I thought I was married to a federal agent who was doing something noble for a living." She shook her head before continuing. "My whole life, I've battled this notion people have about me that I'm naïve, and the truth is that I'm the biggest idiot on the planet!"

He kept his eyes on the road, sensing either venting or ranting brewing.

"The lengths he went to!" she continued. "I mean, there were times when I dropped him off at work, for God's sake. I met his coworkers! And this whole time, he worked for some kind of gangster!"

She gazed out her window, not wanting to meet his eyes in her raw openness. She watched a layer of tall and thin leafy trees glide by. They wove in the light breeze as if they were trying to offer her some comfort.

"And he was sleeping with another woman," she added with bitterness in her voice, still not looking to him. "I suppose I should have at least suspected *that*. He'd been so distant for so long. I attributed it to his job. Another woman . . . Why . . .?"

"He's getting off!" he interrupted.

"Excuse me?" she replied, her face twisted in disgust. She was unsure if she'd heard him right.

"Up ahead. He's turning. Highway 31. Do you know where that goes?"

She wondered if the man next to her had heard a thing she'd just said. "It leads over to the west coastline. South of here," she answered with the frown still etched across her lips.

"Is anything down there?"

"Some towns . . . Honor, Benzonia. A couple of lakes."

"Is there an airport?"

"Yes. There's one a little further down in Manistee. I've come through it before."

He nodded and rubbed the back of his head with his thumb. "Can you rent cars at that airport?"

She now turned to him. "Yes, you can."

His stare tightened on the road as he flipped on his turn signal. "I think Josh Jones is looking to catch a flight."

She looked ahead. *A flight?*

Chapter 45

He found early on that his venture up the river was not a fruitless effort. Ron Oldhorse discovered a plethora of manmade blemishes along the terrain that would have gone completely unnoticed by most people. Sporadic footprints, overturned rocks along the damp earth of the riverside, and trampled vegetation. Oldhorse determined that they were left by a single individual who'd shuffled his pace back and forth between a brisk jog and a tired walk.

After he took a moment to scoop up a splash of cold river water into a leather canteen given to him by an elder tribesman, he lifted his head to the steep and rocky shoreline. Far ahead from where he stood at a ravine base, several sizable and mostly round rocks rested in an angled clump along a sheer section of the gorge. They seemed to piggyback each other, with the larger rocks on the bottom. Something artificial drew his attention to the bottom of the rubble; it appeared to be a dark fabric.

He jogged up through the natural quarry, skipping gracefully from rock to rock until he reached it. The fabric had some elastic on the end that emerged from a narrow crevice between the rocks. When he tugged on it, he found a sleeve. He jostled the rocks and stones and let them tumble to the shore so he could free more of the garment. It was a man's jacket—black in color and made of vinyl. It wasn't particularly large.

It had been there a couple of days, as established from its dampness from the recent weather, but it was in decent shape. It hadn't been snagged by the rocks; it had been purposefully concealed between them and probably only became visible due to the unsteadiness of the pile.

Oldhorse inspected the jacket closely. Along with some dirt and grime smudged into the fabric, he found dark red stains across one of the sleeves. He held the sleeve to his broad nose and determined it to be blood. He carefully folded the garment and found some space for it in one of the pockets of his backpack.

A sharp breeze cut through the gully. The air felt cooler to him than it should have with the sun still hovering unhindered high above. It was as if nature was warning him of what he would find ahead if he kept searching.

The wad of gum in Lumbergh's mouth was clamped tightly in his jaw as the radial tires that propped up the left side of his Jeep hugged the edge of Pine View Road. It was a narrow, dirt road that he typically avoided due to his queasiness over its long and steep drop to the river that lay a couple hundred feet below.

It was an obscure route in getting back to Winston, but the trail followed the cold, raging water the dead body had been swept away in before it poured into the reservoir at Beggar's Basin. He felt compelled to trace its path back as far as he could, even though the road stuck to the mountain range that veered northwest which would take him away from Meyers Bridge.

He had no expectations of finding anything of note, especially from such a height. However, he hoped that positioning himself in the proximity of where the ghastly series of events had begun would somehow give him a fresh perspective of the questions he was struggling to answer in his mind.

He peered down the long and winding trail of water, watching from afar the white foam churn and crash against large boulders that looked like stones from such a distance.

He took a breath and reached for his radio when the sound of blaring static belched out from its speaker. It was followed promptly with Jefferson's voice calling out the chief's name.

"I was just getting ready to call you, Jefferson," he spoke into the speaker. "What's up?"

"Sean just called into the office."

Lumbergh sat up straight in his seat. His pulse accelerated. "Good. Where is he?"

"Well, I'm not sure."

"You're not sure?"

"No. He called collect so his caller I.D. information didn't show up on that little screen."

Lumbergh scowled into his speaker. "Well, what did he say?"

"Not much really."

The chief waited for him to continue, but nothing followed. "You still there, Jefferson?"

"I think he said that he killed someone."

Lumbergh's head jerked backward. "Killed someone?"

"Yeah."

"The man we found in the river?"

"I don't think so."

The chief was quickly losing patience with his officer. "Jefferson, this is ridiculous. What the hell's going on?"

The officer told him of the conversation, and the chief could sense that he was bracing for a scathing indictment of his own incompetence. Instead, Lumbergh clenched his steering wheel until his knuckles turned white and took a deep breath. He then pushed in the button on his radio transceiver. "If he calls back, ask him where he is before saying anything else, got it? It's important."

"Yes, sir."

"Now I've got something else for you. I need you to call the FBI office in Las Vegas, Nevada. Look up the number. The guy we pulled out of the river was one of their agents. His name is Kyle Kimble." He relayed Kimble's identification number along with additional details to his astounded officer who struggled to keep up with the unraveling onslaught of new information. He ended with: "Tell them that we think his death might have something to do with the double murder from yesterday. Tell them everything we know, got it?"

"Yes," Jefferson answered with noticeable shakiness in his voice. After a brief pause, he asked, "How do you think the FBI is mixed up in all of this?"

"I don't know, Jefferson. We'll hopefully find out soon. Get going on it."

Once his handheld transmitter went back to its base, Lumbergh leaned across his seat to take a gander down at the raging water again. A sense of neglect sputtered off the walls of his stomach. He could have had a search and recovery team at the river by late morning on Saturday to scour its path. If Dr. Venegas was right and the body had been snagged up somewhere, there'd have been a good chance that it would have been found. He fought the urge to place the blame squarely on Sean Coleman's shoulders as the boy who cried wolf one too many times, but Sean was not the chief of police. It was Lumbergh's own inaction that had prolonged the exposure of the truth of what happened that morning. He even worried that his dereliction may have led to the additional events of violence transpiring in his town.

A burst of CB static interrupted his thoughts. A familiar voice that was not Jefferson's poured through the speaker.

In an accelerated tone, he heard his wife broadcast, "Gary, Sean called here. He needs your help!"

Chapter 46

When the man he knew as Josh Jones strayed off of the main highway and headed west onto Platte Road, Sean found himself questioning whether the airport in Manistee was his destination after all. He hoped he'd just been wrong, but feared that Jones had realized that he was being followed and was now leading them God knows where.

The traffic was much thinner along the two-lane road, which made him uneasy. There were no automobiles in between him and Jones, so Sean was careful to keep his distance. Adding to the unsettling sensation Sean felt in his gut, Jones had slowed down his pace to that of the speed limit.

"I don't like this," stated Lisa, leaning forward a little in her seat. She had lowered her sun visor in front of her in an act of discretion. She worried that if they got too close, Jones might make out her face and blonde hair in his mirror. "What if he recognizes your car?"

"He's never seen my car," he quickly rebuked.

"You don't know that for sure. This is a mistake! What if he's leading us into some type of trap or back to more of Moretti's men? We should just pull over to the side of the road at the next gas station and call the *local* cops this time."

He said nothing, but he was sure she could read the irritation in his eyes.

"Why is that such a bad idea? I'm certain your brother has contacted them by now. They know what's going on."

"He's my brother-*in-law*, and I'm not letting this guy out of my sight."

She let her back drop against her seat. She closed her eyes and her fingers went to her forehead as if she were battling a migraine. She whispered under her breath, "What was I thinking?"

Sean bit down on his lower lip before subtly nodding his head and saying, "A lot of chicks fall for the wrong guys."

She twisted her body toward him and cocked her head to the side with an expression on her face that exemplified her displeasure with the remark. "I meant what was I thinking *when I got back into this car?* I should have stayed at that gas station back in Traverse City and waited for the police."

He threw a hand into the air. "I told you that you could have!"

Her eyes drifted back to the road. She obviously didn't have the strength or will to argue. Instead, she mumbled something to herself about not thinking to grab her cellphone when Sean whisked her out of the cottage. If she had, Josh Jones most likely would have been in custody by then.

"That Marty guy, from back at the guard station . . . I think there's a good chance he's all right."

It was a completely unexpected and quite miraculous remark, and considering the look he saw cross her face, not far from the thoughts flashing through her mind. Her lips lifted open a bit and her eyelids flickered.

"I thought you might want to know that," he added.

She silently scrutinized his demeanor, but his stoic expression was unreadable. "Why do you think that?"

"Well, there wasn't any blood on the uniform that the asshole in front of us was wearing. He may have just stolen it from a locker or something."

"But Josh Jones knew his name."

"I know, but he kept saying Martin, while you called him Marty. My guess is that people that know him call him Marty. Right?"

She nodded her head.

"Yeah, our boy in the Volvo probably just read Martin off of a name badge. I don't think he and the guy in your kitchen knew exactly what they'd find at your house. They wouldn't risk a murder beat just to get inside the wall and look around. I think the old guy was as surprised to find you there as you were to have him show up at your door."

She absorbed his logic, then brushed her hair over her shoulder and glanced out her window at an old, abandoned drive-in movie theater that rested along a large lot of dirt. The speakers and their poles were missing, but the large, peeling screen still towered above the flat, open land.

"Are you guys pretty tight?" he asked.

"Who?"

"You and Marty."

Her face soured. "Why would you ask that?"

Sean kept his eyes to the road and shrugged his shoulders. "Well, I'm pretty sure that if I worked from that guard station where Marty worked, and didn't get very close to the people driving in and out through my gate, I can't imagine any of them would be able to identify my uniform when I'm not the one wearing it."

He noticed the rise in her eyebrows when he flashed her a quick glance. Before she could respond, he continued. "I've worked a few guard stations in my time, you know," he said in a way that implied he was bragging about the experience.

"No, I didn't know that," she said with an eye roll.

He continued. "Plus, I noticed two mostly empty wine glasses on your kitchen counter. With your husband out of the state . . ."

"Yes, Mr. Coleman," she interrupted in annoyance. "I know him a little better than the other residents. Okay? But it's not what you think."

Sean pursed his lips and he fought back the urge to smirk. "I wasn't thinking anything. I just thought you might want to know that he's probably okay."

Lisa felt embarrassed, but at the same time a little impressed. If she had judged Sean by his appearance and demeanor alone, she wouldn't have concluded him to be particularly intellectual. Contrarily, he seemed brighter than how he presented himself. At the very least, he was a keen observer. He'd known almost immediately back at the cottage that something wasn't right about Josh Jones. And despite no one believing him in his own town, he was able to figure out the identity of the man he'd seen on the bridge, even if it meant driving halfway across the country to confirm it.

"I think you might be selling yourself short as a security guard, Mr. Coleman. You'd make a good investigator."

For the first time since she'd met him, she noticed the man's mouth curl into a smile—a dopey smile that he clearly wasn't comfortable displaying. It seemed to her that he'd just heard what might have been the most flattering compliment anyone had ever paid him. He twisted his head away from her a bit in nonchalant fashion, like a young student who had just been praised by a teacher he had a crush on.

Or maybe that was just her impression, being a teacher. Her attention eased back to the car they were following. Its speed didn't seem to fluctuate. It was as if the man behind the wheel was on a casual Sunday drive. A thought tickled her mind of how they'd left Josh Jones sprawled out on the floor, unconscious in her hallway, as well as the pandemonium that led up to that moment.

"Wait a minute," she said out loud. "When we turned on the radio that Josh Jones was wearing, the guard we heard said that Marty wasn't at his post and that the gate was left open. Doesn't that mean that they *did* do something to him?"

His eyebrows arched. "You've got a point . . ."

She wasn't sure what about his expression changed, but it seemed to, even if minutely. Perhaps he had considered the idea as well, but he didn't want to lend credence to it because he was sure the thought would worry her.

She sighed, looking back out the side window. If there had been a confrontation, maybe Sean's hope was that Marty had just gotten beat up and not killed. It was certainly her hope.

———

When the first police car screeched to a halt at the gated entrance in front of Bluff Walk Road, the officer found a pale, hunched over figure with short, blonde hair that was partially stained red, stumbling his way out to the road from behind an assemblage of trees. Clad only in a t-shirt and plaid boxer shorts, he'd been beaten, gagged, and still had twisted and torn strips of thick duct tape wrapped around his wrists.

Minutes later, sirens blasted their way up through the winding, flush hills of the upscale community, causing scores of birds to flee the tops of thick trees. Marty Rutt told an attentive, stout female officer the story of a seemingly kind older man wearing a hat who'd asked for directions from his Volvo at the front gate. Marty described how their conversation was cut short when he happened to glance over his shoulder and notice some movement across the screen of one of the security monitors inside the window of his guard station. Someone was scaling their way over the front wall, just about fifty yards down, out of view from the front of the station. Marty quickly apologized to the misplaced traveler and took off on foot, in pursuit of the intruder.

The athletic guard quickly caught up with who he believed to be a teenager and tackled him to the ground. The kid had brown hair, spiked in the front, and repeatedly shouted during their tussle that he was just there to see his girlfriend.

After Marty had gotten the boy pinned chest-down in the grass with a knee lodged into his back, he held up his radio to his mouth when he'd heard rapid footsteps approaching from behind him. It was the older man from the front gate.

"It's okay. I've got this!" he'd shouted to the man who he'd believed had come to help him.

The man wasn't there to assist the guard, but rather to come to the aid of the captive. Marty saw something black and shiny clasped in the fist of the man a mere second before it was smashed down along the crest of his skull.

Marty remembered little after that, other than taking some stomps to his face and ribs, and the angered voice of the older man scolding the younger one. When he awoke with a fierce, throbbing headache and gasping for breath from under a couple of cracked ribs, he found himself stripped and his arms hugging a large elm tree with his wrists bound together on the opposite side.

Chapter 47

"What do you mean he doesn't work for them?"

"That's what they're telling me, Chief," answered Jefferson. "They don't have a Kyle Kimble that works for them. The government employee number is bogus. They're sure the ID is a fake."

Lumbergh's jaw tightened. "Well the man's not fake!" he barked in frustration. "He's got a wallet full of credit cards, a Nevada driver's license, and a picture of him beside his wife—who's also very real because she's with Sean right now." Listening to the words coming out of his own mouth was fueling his frustration. What Diana had told him about Sean only added to the fire. "And now someone *else* is dead!"

The chief was barely able to keep up with his breath. His hand was clenched so tightly to the transmitter of his Jeep's radio that he nearly cracked its frame. He bit down on his lip and used the back of his hand to clear strands of spit from the sides of his mouth. With his teeth tightened, he brought the transmitter back to his face.

"Chief?" Jefferson said with some anxiety in his voice.

"The second you hear back from the Traverse City P.D., you get back to me! Do you understand?"

"Chief, there's more."

"Spit it out, Jefferson."

"I've been trying to. The Feds didn't know Kimble, but they knew the name Moretti. It really got their attention. They want to talk to you about him, the man in charge. They wouldn't give me the skinny."

Lumbergh's eyes softened and he nodded his head. "Okay, I'll be back soon."

Moments later, he'd made it to the end of Pine View Road and it felt good to leave the self-imposed detour of dirt and gravel and be back on a paved street where he could push the accelerator down. Speeding along Colorado Road 1007, the RPM gauge steadily rose along with the chief's anxiety. A deficiency of modern technology at his disposal left him feeling irritated and naked. Back in Chicago, streaming a landline call through a police radio would have been as simple as pressing a button. Out of his Winston office, it just wasn't an option. So, his eagerness to sync up with the Feds and learn of the man his brother-in-law referred to as Moretti was pulling at his chest.

"A Las Vegas big shot," he muttered through clenched teeth as he shook his head. It was the phrase Sean had used with Diana. "What the hell does that mean?"

Whoever the individual was, the FBI in Las Vegas was aware of him, which meant he was a man of importance—most likely not in a good way.

Lumbergh experienced torment caused by the growingly familiar feeling of being left completely out of the loop, leaving him to frolic around in his own aimless speculation. He was used to being the man in the know—the man in charge. But at that very moment, the best he could do to serve any practical purpose was to get back to town as quickly as he could while he listened for updates from Jefferson. Sean, on the other hand, was right in the middle of something big and consequential, and Lumbergh prayed that whatever it was, it wouldn't lead to anyone else getting killed.

The chief quickly passed up a slow-moving, rust-red pickup only to get stuck behind a beige Dodge moving at an even slower pace while a caravan of vehicles approached from the oncoming lane. He swore in frustration and longed for the police cruiser and its siren. For now, the horn would have to do, and he laid on it hard. When the

Dodge began veering onto the shoulder to let him pass, Lumbergh accelerated and flew around a blind curve that had quickly presented itself. He was driving at a speed he knew was reckless while edging across two yellow lines. When a range of thick spruce gave way to the horrifying sight of an oncoming car that blared its own horn in panic, he yelled and cranked his steering wheel far to the right. His Jeep skidded across the shoulder and onto an uneven, downward slope. The decline was masked with tall grass and unattended weeds. His foot cranked down on the brake pedal, and every mundane object inside the car that wasn't bolted down flew forward and onto the floorboard. The vehicle came to an abrupt dead stop that left his damp, clenched fingers cemented to the steering wheel and his heart bemoaning his poor decision.

With enlarged eyes, he swallowed some bile and uttered aloud the phrase, "To serve and protect." It was a reminder of the key responsibilities of his job—responsibilities that seemed at that moment to warrant reciting.

A stream of sweat ran down his brow as he rolled down his window to fire out an overchewed wad of gum that he released from his clamped jaw. He took a few short breaths and let his pulse normalize. As he did, the image of the white car he'd nearly collided with hovered in his glazed vision like a single, subliminal frame from an art film. Below its tinted windshield and gleaming, silver grill hung a frame of blue mountains under an orange sky. A Nevada state license plate.

By geographical standards, Nevada and Colorado were only separated by a single state, but Utah was a large state and close to six hundred miles, and numerous mountain ranges separated the region from the Nevada state line. Aside from that, Colorado Road 1007 was an obscure route. It marked the rural, sparsely populated boundary between Lakeland and Winston, and was normally only used by local commuters and a few ranchers. While the appearance of a Nevada plate was by no means a foreign sight within Colorado, it was highly unusual and perhaps unheard of for one to turn up there in the backwoods, far away from the action of the downtown area in northern Lakeland.

A long, white car would have never been mistaken for a dark sedan, even by a teenage busboy who didn't know his automobile makes. Still, Kyle Kimble, Moretti The Big Shot, and even the disappearance of Chad Grimes—the shop owner from Lakeland—appeared to have ties to Nevada. Though the significance felt thin, Lumbergh's refined law enforcement instincts weren't quite prepared to treat the unusual finding as an absolute coincidence.

He reached into his pocket and pulled out a fresh stick of gum that he unwrapped in what would have appeared to a casual observer as one quick motion. He flung it into his mouth and checked for oncoming traffic before flipping a U-turn across the road and setting off in the direction of the white Cadillac.

The man who'd made it as far as Meyers Bridge was not alone before he ended his life. That was the conclusion that Oldhorse made after spending the better part of the morning tracking his trail up the long and lofty ravine. The markings of a single man had been joined by those of at least three others who looked to have been in pursuit of him. A pack of wolves chasing a deer.

Oldhorse was now on private land, but he cared little. He was engrossed in tracing the split nerve back to its root.

As two aggressive squirrels spiraled their way up a tall pine's trunk high above the rocky terrace that loomed above him, Oldhorse imagined that the prey had either fallen or been thrown off of the jagged ledge above. The impact of his body had left an obvious trail of disruption with its rapid decent, all the way down the steep wall. He'd survived the fall though, only to get into an altercation with one of his pursuers along the shore.

Oldhorse scaled his way up the gorge at a pace that would have rivaled expert climbers, effortlessly digging his fingers and the toes of his moccasins into every delicate wedge and crevice. When he reached the top and examined the surface of the plateau, he found not only tracks but a family of .30-30 rifle shells. Their nestling together along the ground attested that their owner had fired shots down toward the river from his perched position.

All four sets of tracks congregated at that point, having emerged from the thick forest that lay to the east.

Oldhorse dipped one of his coarse and weathered hands into a pouch on the side of his pack and retrieved a dark strip of elk jerky that he'd dried himself. He gnawed on it with the back of his teeth before tearing a chunk off, devouring its taste and letting it slide down his throat.

His tapered eyes pierced through the maze of tall stalks of chipped bark and their thick crowns of intertwined branches. A deep breath filtered out through his nose before he entered into a corridor of the forest that seemed darker than it had any right to be.

Chapter 48

"What is that?" Lisa asked.

"What's what?"

"That welt, or whatever it is on the back of your head. You keep touching it. Did you hurt yourself back at the house?"

Sean rolled his eyes and shook his head. "It's nothing. It's been there forever."

"Forever?" she said with a mark of confusion in her tone and inquisitiveness in her eyes. It didn't take long for her to recognize that he'd rather not continue with the topic, so she was surprised after a few seconds when he did.

"I don't mean *forever*, forever. I wasn't born with it. It just . . . Well, I don't know how long it's been there. My head just started itching one day and it's never really stopped." His eyes lowered to the circular gauges along the dashboard of his car.

"That doesn't sound healthy," she said with her eyes blinking in thought. "You should probably get that looked at."

"Yeah, probably." His forehead formed ripples and his eyes angled toward her. "Do you always ask this many questions?"

She let her gaze drift back to the road in front of them and she shrugged her shoulders a bit. "No. Not really. Maybe if I did, I would have figured out who my husband really was."

He said nothing.

Peering above some trees on the side of the road ahead was a large, sky-blue metal canopy with multicolored stripes jetting diagonally down its wide edge. Beside it, the tall price sign of a gas station came into view.

He let up on the gas pedal while keeping a steady eye on the car they'd been following. Lisa sat up in her seat and turned to him.

"You're stopping?" she asked with some zest.

"Yeah."

"Thank you," she said, with her lips hinting at a grin. She placed her hand on his large shoulder to demonstrate to him her appreciation. "You're doing the right thing."

He grunted and shook his head in disappointment before whipping the car sharply into the parking lot. "Don't thank me. I only stopped because we're out of gas."

She leaned forward and peered between the spokes of the steering wheel. Under the dashboard, the needle drooped well below the letter "E" and the low-gas indicator was brightly lit.

"It's been on for the last five miles," he said when he quickly pulled up to the nearest pump and jammed on the brakes. "Which means we probably only have another two. We've got to make this fast!"

He cranked the gearshift into park and turned off the ignition. The door flew open with a loud creak and he was out in no time, fumbling for the hooked gas nozzle on the side of the pump.

Lisa watched the Volvo glide farther and farther away, and part of her wanted it to keep going so that the she and the man she'd come to know throughout the day would be cut loose from their foolhardy pursuit.

"Oh, you got to be kidding me!" Sean snarled from outside the car. "Prepay?"

He lowered his head through the open driver's side window and asked her in an almost timid manner if she had a credit card.

With a dispirited sigh, she answered, "Back at the cottage."

"Dammit!" he moaned before snapping straight and pounding a fist on top of the roof of his car.

"Sean, we need to let this go," she said, mostly to his torso that she could see through the window. "We'll go inside, call the police, and tell them which direction he's headed in. They'll take over from here."

She watched him briskly pace back and forth beside the car with his hand rubbing the nagging spot along the back of his head.

She came to a conclusion. "Sean, this is the end of the road for me either way. I'm staying here. Please stay with me."

Sean was riddled with frustration as he paced. He noticed a teenage girl working the register inside. She was taking a moment from servicing a line of customers to glare at him from behind a dirty window, most likely wondering what in the hell he was doing. The heady odor of gasoline surrounded him and taunted him with its candor. The Volvo was shrinking off into the distance.

"Let's just make the call," he heard Lisa say.

He sent her a glare through the car window.

"Please?" she said.

Despite the overwhelming frustration he felt, he couldn't escape the tenderness in her eyes. Her gaze was sincere and captivating, and for the first time in many years, he felt as if someone other than those obligated by a family tree was concerned about his well-being. The gleam in her bright blue eyes was like the promise of something new. Something different. He had a spur of the moment, consequential decision to make—the kind he typically made off of pure impulse. This time, he found himself more carefully deliberating possible outcomes.

Part of him wanted to adhere to her judgment, but Sean tasted defeat in his mouth and its sourness spoiled the moment. He thought about his uncle and the ultimate sacrifice he had made to stop the same people that were about to vanish from his view.

"Get on out and make the call," he snapped. "I've got two miles of gas left in this baby and I'm gonna use it to take down that son of a bitch."

She buckled forward in the seat like her strings had been cut, lowering her head and closing her eyes. She felt his returning weight depress the seat of the car. Without extending as much as a glance in his direction, she spun on the vinyl and pulled up on the door handle just as the engine cranked and blazed in fury.

She lifted herself up from the security of the Nova and stood in the dirt parking lot with her shoulders at half-mast. One of her fists was clenched and depicted her dissatisfaction. Raising her head to meet the horizon of the road that Sean would soon disappear down, she perused the abstracted Volvo that was little more than a beige blip at the center of an open sliver of space between green and yellowish clumps of distant trees. Her mind led her to believe that it would dematerialize in mere seconds, but to her wonder, she saw two red lights illuminate at the back of the car. Soon after, the left one began to blink and moments later, the blip changed directions.

Her attention shot to Sean. "He pulled off the highway!"

Chapter 49

Tony Fabrizio's spinning head nearly collapsed to his steering wheel in a heap of its own sweat and relief once the blue, older model Chevy vanished from sight in his rearview mirror.

"Thank you God," he whispered twice while recoiling from the salted sting of the open gash along the back of his head.

His trembling hand tossed a lit cigarette that had been burned to the filter outside his open window. He retrieved his cellphone from the center console and brought the undersized gadget back to his ear.

"It was a false alarm, yo," he sputtered into the phone. "It pulled off the road. Whoever it was, they weren't following me."

He could smell the rank odor of his own armpits rising up from the dampness at the base of his sleeves. The blue, oversized uniform he'd stripped from the guard clung to his chest and was no longer light in shade.

"Are you sure?" a cold, dark voice on the other end berated.

"Yeah, man. I just . . . I just gotta chill out."

"No. You've *just gotta* finish cleaning up your mess and get back here."

"I know, man . . . I know," Tony said with a gulp in his throat. "Do you have a location for me yet?"

"It won't be at the house. We don't know what all Kimble sent his wife in that envelope. If he put this address in there, the cops could show up at any minute. We're packed up. Once Moretti gets back, he and I will be leaving."

Nodding his head, Tony replied, "Should I just call you once I land?"

"No. I'll call you. And, kid, don't waste any more of my time. You're on your own until you get back."

The call went dead.

Tony pressed a button on the face of the cell and let it fall to the passenger seat where it flopped upside down on the tight upholstery.

He took some limited comfort from the tone of the man's voice on the other end of the line. As ghoulish as it was, it was the most composed he'd heard it in days. A far cry from the rage that poured from the man's lungs after he'd lost his footing along the top of that ravine back at the river and dropped his rifle over the ledge. If it wasn't for that misstep, they would have all caught their prey Friday night—whether it was Kimble or Greco that was running from them.

Today hadn't fared much better for Tony Fabrizio. What was supposed to be an uncomplicated task and a colossal waste of time as far as he and his colleague, Frank, were convinced, had turned into another major shit-storm.

It hadn't taken long for Moretti to figure out who owned the property at the hand-scribbled address Alvar retrieved from Sean Coleman's kitchen. What required some more delving into was why Coleman had that address in his possession. According to the Winston newspaper, Coleman had been a mere witness to Kyle Kimble's suicide. But, the fact that he had Kimble's belongings and information with him posed questions of what all else the security guard knew. With the ledger missing and Coleman AWOL, Moretti feared that Coleman realized he possessed multiple bank account numbers of a very wealthy man. He theorized that Coleman was trying to figure out how to make a withdrawal from one of those accounts.

Soon after reading of Kimble's death in the paper, Moretti had a couple of his boys check out his deceased employee's home in Vegas. The place was neat and his wife was gone, but they had no reason to believe she was out of the state. They checked his computer and file cabinets and found nothing to tie him back to Moretti. It made sense considering the ruse Kimble was pulling with his wife.

Frank and Tony had been sent to Michigan only to cover all bases. With the address turning up, Moretti wanted to know what was there and delivered orders to destroy anything that needed to be destroyed. They never expected to find Kimble's wife stashed out there, and especially not Sean Coleman.

The series of blunders in Michigan began with the guard at the gate. Frank was supposed to keep him distracted while Tony jumped the wall and checked out the address on Bluff Walk Road. The plan was for him to only call Frank if he needed assistance or guidance. That call to arms came far sooner than expected when Tony scaled the wall about thirty yards short of where Frank had instructed him to. He was nabbed almost instantly.

As penance for his major blunder, Frank took point and coroneted Tony as the beaten security guard's replacement until he returned back down the hill with the car.

"Just let people in and out, asshole," Frank had barked. "A child could do it."

While Frank might have been correct, it was ironically Tony's youthful appearance that drew undesired attention from a handful of residents that commuted in and out of the enclosure during his watch. Their scrutinizing eyes rattled the less experienced Tony, who cowered in worry over the amount of time Frank had been gone. He became unnerved and abandoned his post to catch up with Frank on foot.

He'd made it to the bottom of the long driveway when he heard a barrage of gunfire erupt from within the house. He'd hoped it was from Frank's gun, but found out otherwise when he got to the front door.

When he came to after the large man from Colorado had laid him out, he found himself in a heap of battered defeat with a pulsing headache. Stumbling through an empty house with his dead partner sprawled out on a hallway floor, he knew he needed direction.

He caught Alvar on his cell, who worked him through what he needed to do.

Minutes later, he was exiting the gate he'd left opened and following Alvar's instructions precisely—only one planned stop on his way back to the airport. He was halfway around Platte Lake before he noticed that the blue car that had exited the highway behind him was still there. When he altered his speed, he was sure the car had mirrored the change, and he'd become convinced that he was being followed. It wasn't until it pulled off the road that he felt comfortable enough to carry out Alvar's instructions.

An unmarked dirt road that entered a thickly wooded area on his left looked like as good a place as any. It didn't seem particularly well traveled, which was good.

With his window rolled down, the smell of seaweed and dead fish that poured in seemed like a fitting burial place for the crotchety, old Vegas thug who had often worn thin on Tony's nerves with his numerous stories about the town's golden era.

Twigs and some assorted stones crackled beneath the tires of the slow-moving Volvo whose quiet engine let him hear the cries of seagulls in the distance. He scouted for a sufficient spot and found one after a quarter of a mile.

A fence of tall, thick foliage hugged a patch of flatland about twenty yards off the road, and he found that he could easily drive around to the opposite side of it as long as he took things slow and didn't bottom out.

There was broad daylight above him, but he was certain he and his car were concealed well from any remote chance of a passerby catching a glimpse. He lit up a fresh cigarette that he pulled from a pack on the dash and took a deep drag. He then popped the hatchback and exited the vehicle. He took a moment to leer at the eerie sight of a man's filled shoes protruding out of a large green, rolled-up poly tarp with two stands of multicolored bungee cords. Tony had pillaged the items, along with the digging shovel that lay beside the body.

He pulled out the shovel by its wooden shaft and winced when the back of the blade inadvertently smacked against the side of Frank's head. The low buzzing of the ensuing vibration of metal lasted only a second or two. He flipped the shovel over his shoulder and took another comforting drag of his cigarette before scouting the area for a raw patch of dirt. He found one where the earth was soft and the edge of the shovel sunk in easily.

He mused over how he'd graduated from a flunky entrusted with relatively menial duties to playing a role in burying his second dead body in twice as many days. He was certain the size of the hole he was digging would need to be larger than the one used for Arianna.

The sight of the fire in Moretti's eyes Friday night was something Tony would never forget. He'd thought he'd seen Moretti angry before, but it was nothing compared to the pure rage that fumed through the veins in his head after Alvar had pulled him aside after dinner. If Arianna hadn't been in the ladies' room at the time, she would have seen it herself and at least have had a clue of what was about to happen to her.

Tony didn't know if it was Alvar or Moretti himself that offed her. He and Frank were told to drive ahead and wait for them at the edge of town. The Buick caught up in just a minute or two with only two heads visible through the windshield.

It wasn't until the next morning that Alvar let it slip in not so many words that she'd supposedly been carrying on an affair with Kyle Kimble, and for some time. If Valentino Greco hadn't killed Kimble and dumped his body somewhere during his escape, Moretti had fully intended on finishing the job. In the end, Kimble had died at his own hand, which deprived Moretti of the pleasure.

Tony wiped sweat from his brow and planted the blade of the shovel into the ground to admire the sizable grave he'd carved into the woodsy ground. The shovel handle stood behind him and waddled in the light breeze as he walked back to his car. He leaned in through the open window and padded the tip of what was left of his stout cigarette on the metal dish of the ashtray drawer. He then leaned forward and again popped open the backdoor of the car. With a labored groan, he wrapped his forearms around Frank's feet, pressed the sole of his own shoe along the bumper, and heaved the lifeless body out along the coarse but thin carpet. When Frank's head reached the head of the bumper, his body found nothing but air beneath it and dropped to the ground with a sick sounding thud. Tony closed the hatchback and leaned forward to get a grip on the tarp that blanketed the body.

The penetrating ripple of a gunshot suddenly sliced open a tear in the tranquility that had surrounded Tony only a moment earlier. The rupture of glass from the back windshield of the car sent shards down across his body as he fell to his rear.

"Holy fuck!" he bellowed.

He hadn't a clue where the shot had come from. Frank's gun was in the glove compartment and it seemed a mile away at that very moment. He instinctively crawled for the nearest cover, which was the underside of the Volvo. His elbows dug into the clammy ground as he pulled himself farther under and his heart pounded the hard earth below him. He remembered that he had a butterfly knife in his pants that he had inherited from Frank when it fell from the dead man's pocket while wrapping his body back at the cottage. However, the quarters underneath the car were too tight for him to retrieve it.

He wailed in terror when he felt a large pair of hands fasten onto his bony ankles. The tips of his fingers clawed the dirt desperately as he was dragged savagely along the ground. A second later, the cover of the car gave way to the unobstructed brightness of the sun. He was yanked up by the back of his collar and felt the underside of the bumper bat the top of his skull. His arms and legs flailed wildly under the barbaric manhandling, and he screamed in protest a mere instant before his head was forced forward into the spiderweb of shattered glass of the back windshield. Excruciating pain radiated from his nose to his chin, and his teeth shook inside his mouth as he was thrown to the ground like a sandbag in the midst of a flood.

"Enjoy the scenic drive, asshole?" he heard a man's voice say before the heel of a boot slammed into his stomach.

Tony's body folded and his eyes bulged, but he didn't see the follow-up roundhouse punch that devastated the side of his head and sent a stream of blood from his mouth across the ground like a wild paint stroke.

"Remember the man that you left on the floor of my apartment? That man was like a father to me!"

Tony flopped around on his back like an overturned turtle before the stiff point of the same boot jolted his ribs and sent him to his side.

"That old, blind dog whose throat you slit had more balls than every one of you!"

Tony shrieked from the biting pain as his body was yanked up by the roots of his hair. Some blood streamed from his mouth, but most of it drained down his throat, forcing him to gag and cough as he was unwillingly guided on unsteady legs away from the car.

He clawed at Sean Coleman's wrist with one hand while the other jammed into his front pocket to search for the butterfly knife.

"It wasn't me!" he howled. "I wasn't even there!"

"Who did it then?" Sean demanded.

"His name is Alvar! He's one sick mother-fucker, yo! He . . . He does shit like that you know . . . It wasn't me!"

When Tony found the knife in his pocket, the curl of his wrist snapped it open and he swung it wildly at the shoulder at the large man. He felt it sink into flesh, but there was no sound or recoil from his assailant who grabbed his thin wrist and twisted it backwards until the sound of a sharp snap filled the air. Tony bawled like a sea lion being attacked by a killer whale.

A colossal head-butt caused Tony's neck to buckle before Sean released his grip on the smaller man and let his body fall backwards into the gaping grave that he had dug in the earth just minutes earlier.

Tony fell in a heap, and Sean watched his wrenched and bloodied face with twisted delight. He sneered at the man lying before him before yanking the impaling knife from his shoulder and dropping it to his side. Blood oozed steadily from the wound.

Sean's hand disappeared behind his back and it returned with his silver Colt Python whose muzzle he pointed directly at the uniformed thug.

"Where were you headed after this, Josh?" he asked. "Where can I find Alvar and his boss, Moretti?"

He noticed the angst heighten in the kid's eyes at the mention of Moretti's name. "That's right, dickhead. I know who you work for."

"Don't kill me, man," Tony pleaded. "I had nothing to do with any of it. Just don't kill me."

"Where are they?" Sean growled.

Tony shook his head in defeat. His head drooped to his shoulder. "Colorado, man. We were gonna meet them back in Colorado."

"They're still there? Why?"

Tony said nothing.

"Why?" Sean roared.

"They're looking for someone. Some guy named Valentino. He stole money from Moretti."

"Where? What's the address?"

"I don't know, man!"

"Where!" Sean snarled.

Tears rolled down Tony's face over his own uncertainty until his eyes enlarged. "The guy who owns the place!" he yelped out. "I know his name. It's Ray Sarno! The place is south of Lakeland!"

The name was familiar to Sean. He'd read his name in the paper. A wealthy businessman who owned at least one Lakeland casino.

The distant blare of a police siren filtered its way in through the tension of the exchange. Wincing through sun, sweat, and blood, Tony looked as though he couldn't tell if the man standing over him even heard the clamor. There was no acknowledgment in the lines of Sean's face, and his dark, deadpan eyes were glued to Tony's without a hint of emotion. When Sean's arm raised a little and Tony's gaze crept down to the gun, he found himself digging his elbows into the dirt and edging backwards.

"Don't," Tony whispered with a resigned plea.

Sean held the gun steadily, making it clear to the man sprawled out before him that his life was in his hands. The sirens grew louder and were accompanied by the coarse screech of a set of tires before the grumble of movement along the dirt road could be heard homing in. Sean was unfazed and lifted his thumb onto the hammer. The click sound that emanated compelled a twitch of Tony's body.

"Don't," he said again, shaking his head.

A growing wet spot was spreading out quickly from the crotch of Tony's pants.

A monochrome blue Michigan Highway Patrol car with a sapphire shield painted proudly across the driver's side door screeched to a halt behind the Volvo.

Sean heard a door quickly open and the brisk shuffle of feet before a loud male voice shouted the words, "Freeze! Drop the gun!"

It was a dangerous game for Sean to play, but he wanted the Vegas hood to question up until the very last second whether he would comply with the officer's command. He ignored the lawman's repeated calls until another car of the same make pulled up. Only then did Sean let his piece drop from his hand and to the ground. With his eyes still on Tony, Sean's lips curled and he slowly placed his hands behind his head and interlaced his fingers.

Lisa was with the officers. Sean could hear her impassioned defense of him and her calls for calmness as he was drawn down to his chest by two men in uniforms with a third barking commands at Tony.

"They're still in Colorado, Lisa!" Sean yelled over his rights being read to him. "Call Lumbergh! Tell him they're with Ray Sarno!"

Oldhorse raised his calloused hand to his forehead, which beaded with shimmering sweat under the relentless sun. A passing shadow from above had drawn his attention from the trace evidence of the four men who'd frenziedly raced through the woods days earlier. The shadow had been cast by a hovering bird whose wide wingspan and posture had deemed it significant among the others that meandered in and out of the treetops. It was a turkey vulture that he had quickly identified by its bald, red head. He watched it glide from sight behind a rummage of needled treetops. He kept his gaze trained on the sky, watching for any company. He quickly found it in the appearance of a second vulture of the same species. They were low, and they were circling.

He hurried in the direction of the scavengers, weaving in and out of imposing trees whose low branches he ducked. In patches that were less dense with growth, he looked to the sky and spotted a third vulture in tow. Something had certainly caught their attention.

He leaped over a downed tree and found himself in an area of open ground that was bone dry from its unobstructed exposure. A fourth vulture was consumed with a pile of detached branches along the forest floor. The forager poked and prodded at something beneath it with its sharp, cone-like beak. When he approached, the bird danced away but didn't take flight. He understood why when the rank stench of death filled his nose. It was strong, and he was expecting to uncover the decaying carcass of a deer until the peeling back of the branches revealed a more familiar, distinguishing odor that he had experienced a couple times overseas.

It poured out from between the wooden planks that covered an old, brick water well. The planks had already been pried loose from the frame of the well so they came up without much effort. The reeking stench intensified greatly at the removal of the wood, and Oldhorse breathed through his mouth. The inside of the well was deep and dark, and the bottom could not be seen.

He dug into his pack for a book of matches and found one. He pulled a single match loose and lit the heads of the remaining matches before dropping the entire book into the shaft. He watched the flickering flame float slowly downward in a soft, spiraling motion before it eventually came to rest on the bottom.

He knelt down and adjusted his eyes while the distant flame lit up the sides of the well's brick walls. After a moment or two, the exposed tips of a set of human fingers revealed themselves, and the vultures above cackled with envy.

Chapter 50

Lumbergh allowed a great deal of distance between himself and the Cadillac. Even though his Jeep didn't bear any obvious markings to identify himself as a law enforcement officer, he didn't want the presence of the large spotlight mounted on the side of his car to invite any suspicions. He continually reminded himself that in all likelihood, the person behind the wheel hadn't a thing to do with any of the crimes that had plagued the area in recent days, but a nagging fluttering at the pit of his gut told him that his pursuit was worth the effort. That feeling was the same fire in his belly that drove him to great achievements when he worked in Chicago. It wasn't something he could easily verbalize, but its presence was unmistakable.

While his controlling nature pled with him to return to his office in Winston and sync up with the FBI, his old-school investigative instincts urged him on. From his glove box, he snagged a compact pair of binoculars given to him by Diana as a gift shortly after they moved to Winston. A straight stretch of road had given him the opportunity for a closer look without closing the gap between the two cars. The strap from the binoculars dangled against his chin as he gleamed through its eye-cups. His aim bobbled until he had his sights set on the license plate. He mouthed the combination of three digits and three letters repeatedly to remember them, then lowered the binoculars to the side console and pulled his radio receiver to his lips. It took him only a few seconds to get Jefferson responding.

"Jefferson, when you were talking to the Feds, did you get the sense that they were inclined to be helpful on this matter?"

"I think so, Chief," the officer replied. "I don't think they were taking too kindly to someone posing as one of them."

"Good. Call them back. Get the same person you talked to before. Ask them to run a Nevada plate for me: 742-GFA. You got that?"

"Yep. Will do."

"Anything more from Sean or the Traverse City police?"

"Nothing from Sean. The police have been dispatched to the address, but they haven't gotten back to me with any info yet."

Lumbergh shook his head. "You've got to stay on those people, Jefferson. If you don't hear back from them in fifteen minutes, you call them. It's important."

"I will. Are you gonna be back soon?"

Lumbergh hesitated before answering. "In a little bit. I just need to check on something first. Let me know as soon as you hear back from anybody, okay?"

Jefferson acknowledged the request before signing off. No sooner did Lumbergh get off the broadcast with his officer than the white Cadillac flipped on its right blinker. Lumbergh tapped on his brakes until he watched the car disappear down a dirt side road. Temple Trail. Lumbergh had never been up the road as it fell outside of his jurisdiction, but he knew that a lot of the mountainous property it crossed was owned by a couple of Lakeland's more successful businessmen. He wasn't familiar with the men personally, but he'd heard people in town talking about how the two had been smart enough to snatch the land up at a time when nearby Lakeland was struggling financially, back before the legalized gambling boom launched off some major economic growth. They apparently got it at a steal. It wasn't clear if the two were associates or just like-minded opportunists.

The Cadillac's change in direction discouraged Lumbergh a bit. If there was any reasonable explanation for an expensive, out-of-state car to be passing through these parts, it would have been as a visiting guest of one of the rich businessmen. Still, the pursuit was worth following. He slowed down and made the same turn.

It wasn't hard for him to keep out of sight of the Cadillac. There wasn't much in the form of wind, so the lingering dust trail left by the car hovered long enough to make it the only visual he required. Every quarter mile or so, he would see a black and orange "No Trespassing" sign protruding from the bark of a tree. They served as reminders of how remote and isolated the surrounding area was. A few miles in, he noticed that the dust trail was beginning to thin out, and he feared the Cadillac was pulling away from him at a faster pace.

He narrowed the distance between his gas pedal and the floor to try and keep up. His decision proved detrimental when he rounded the crest of some low-hanging birch trees and suddenly found himself cast into a totally exposed, large clearing of open land. Greenery and timber no longer provided concealment, and the sight of a broad, stately home made mostly of wood stood proudly along the slope of a mild hill. Its gravel driveway proved to be the only outlet of the long, winding road he'd traveled. The Cadillac was pulling up toward the open garage door when it slid to a halt just shy of the overhanging archway above the building. The driver had apparently taken notice of the unfamiliar Jeep and wasn't sure what to make of the unexpected visitor.

"Shit," moaned Lumbergh who eased his speed and reached for his radio. "Jefferson? Do you have a make on that license plate yet?"

His answer was nothing but faint static. "Jefferson, this is the chief, come back."

Still no response.

He sighed in annoyance and decided that the best course of action was to play things cool. After all, he had little to go on besides curiosity and his gut. There was no sense in jumping any further toward a conclusion until he got a feel for who was driving the Cadillac. He was also out of his jurisdiction. He technically had no claim to conduct town business there without the permission of the Lakeland P.D., although he was certain he could get it if needed. For now, he would play things casual.

He pulled over to the edge of the road, stopping short of the driveway. He was careful not to block the driveway so as not to appear threatening. He sat in his car for a moment, taking notice that the driver had not yet exited his car, nor had he even turned off the engine. Lumbergh found it suspicious but not enough to alter his approach. He watched through the deeply shaded back window of the Cadillac and was sure he could make out only the outline of the driver and no one else. The brake lights were still illuminated. The driver had yet to put the car in park.

Lumbergh twisted his key in the ignition and let the Jeep's engine die. He stepped outside, with the cuffs of his pleated pants falling below his ankles when he stood up straight. His holster and its firearm were exposed for the driver to see along with the police badge that hung confidently from his shirt pocket. He raised his open hand in the air in greeting and managed to form a wide, inviting grin.

He wasn't but a few steps up the driveway before he noticed a second car nestled under the shade of the interior of the garage. It was a late '90s Buick. A dark sedan. Nevada plates as well.

His grin dissipated. His body froze. Just then, a door along the wall that bordered the rest of the house swung open loudly from inside the garage and a large, dark figure of a man emerged. He walked purposefully out into the driveway with the boldness of a military tank, his broad shoulders resembling two turrets. When the sunlight fell on his glasses and his thick head of sinuous, silver hair, Lumbergh's heart stopped. The chief immediately reached for his sidearm, but just as his hand clasped the grip of his Glock, the giant man's arm raised stiffly and steadily like an opening security gate, and with it an AK-47 machine gun. Its controlled blast screamed out a hail of bullet fire that shattered the tranquility of the surrounding forest along with Lumbergh's upper chest and shoulder.

He howled from the wrenching pain that tore through his body and fell awkwardly backwards to the unforgiving gravel road. Through some miracle, he managed to hold onto his gun. His uninjured limb clung to it out of pure impulse. Wincing through dust from his fall, he spewed a sick grunt between his numb lips and raised his arm, squeezing off two rounds toward his attacker. He didn't wait to see if they connected, and instead spun his body along the ground so he was facing his Jeep. He was grossly outgunned, but fierce adrenaline pushed him forward on his knees. He scrambled to the other side of the Jeep before his dead arm collapsed under him and he fell to his chest. He rolled again to escape his attacker's line of fire but a second barrage of automatic gunfire pummeled the hood and grill of the Cherokee. Shards of splintering metal sprayed into the air. A sharp gust of pressure jetted into his waist before the frame of the Jeep drooped cockeyed from a blown-out tire.

Lumbergh could hear the roar of an engine and punching of rock on dirt before the Cadillac rammed the front of the Jeep in reverse. The fender from the passenger side of the Jeep smashed against his decimated shoulder and his skull, sending his body barreling into the center of the road. His head buzzed like a fire-drill siren and his tight stomach nearly forced him to vomit. The wild move from the driver of the Cadillac didn't seem intended to take out Lumbergh, but was a desperate means of escaping from the ensuing fire fight. The driver popped the transmission and sped past Lumbergh who was left with barely enough awareness to crawl out of the car's way.

Lumbergh found himself at the backside of his Jeep. With a moment of temporary cover from the man with the silver hair, he fired a couple of rounds into the backside of the Cadillac, leaving a charred hole at the center of its back window along its trunk. It continued back down the road it had driven up just a minute earlier, weaving wildly at the hands of the panicked driver.

Lumbergh knew to let it escape. Saving his own ass was the only effort that mattered.

His mangled shoulder was coated with blood, and the small rocks and dirt that clung to it resembled the sprinkled nuts on a caramel apple. He didn't know the extent of his injury, only that the ripped flesh around it felt like it was on fire. By the way his shoulder drooped at a sharp angle, he was sure it was dislocated. It was the least of his problems at that very moment.

He went as flat as possible to the ground, sprawling out on his chest and peering out from under his Jeep the best he could. He didn't see the feet of his attacker. He craned his head around the taillight closest to the house and immediately saw flames of gunfire spreading out from behind the cobblestone corner of the garage. He dropped down to his butt and the imploding sound of incoming lead rippled across the land while his Jeep bore the brunt of more punishment.

Almost hyperventilating through a grimace of fear and agony, he verbally calmed himself down to clear his head. He dropped to his side and awkwardly pulled himself along the ground toward the passenger side of the car. With his knees and a single forearm propping him up as he crawled, he resembled a miller moth with a missing wing trying unsuccessfully to take flight.

He desperately needed backup, and he knew if he could get to his radio, he could call for help. It was a tall order. The garage of the house was on an incline, overlooking his Jeep. The man with silver hair could fire through the driver's side window if he saw Lumbergh try to slide in along the passenger seat. The chief was pinned down.

"Just one of you?" he heard his assailant yell out, almost in morbid amusement. The attacker's voice was deep and hollow above Lumbergh's heavy breathing and a hint of an accent could be heard. "I know you hillbilly hicks aren't used to a lot of action, but this is a goddamned insult!"

Lumbergh knew what the man was capable of, as evidenced by the two dead men he'd left behind at Sean's place. But this twisted taunt proved to the chief the man was a pure sadist—someone who enjoyed violence and relished his participation in it.

"Who gave it up?" the man yelled. "Was it Valentino? Is that prick even alive? If he is, I lost fifty bucks!"

Lumbergh rested his head against the Jeep door and peered into the passenger mirror. He could see the distant image of the corner of the garage where the tall man had his back pressed up against it. He wore a dark blue jacket that deviated enough from the color of the forest to keep him from camouflaging in with the brushwood behind him.

When he noticed the man's arms working in feverish movement, he realized that he was in the process of reloading his weapon. The rhetoric coming from the man with the silver hair was a distraction to buy some time.

Lumbergh managed to swallow through his dry throat and pulled himself up to his tottering feet before laying his arm across the warm hood of the Jeep. He took aim and fired at his assailant. Four rounds were let loose, but the man saw the offense coming and pivoted around the corner of the wall before the first one ever reached him. Gray dust clouded the air as a couple of the bullets ricocheted off of the wall where he took refuge.

Lumbergh tucked himself back down as a hail of gunfire was returned. Glass shattered above him from the demolition of the side window and much of the jagged shards dropped across his thin shoulders. The offense was overwhelming and he knew that if he couldn't get inside his Jeep to retrieve a second magazine for his Glock, he had only six or seven rounds left. His heart pounded his chest and his mind raced in a thousand directions, searching for an idea that would get him through this alive.

A break in the gunfire let the chief hear an abrupt flash of static from his radio inside the Jeep. It was Jefferson trying to reach him, calling the chief's handle. A few seconds later, he tried again.

"Just heard back from Sean, Chief. Got a lot of news. Come back."

The cursory though excited tone in the officer's voice signaled that he hadn't a clue of the dire situation his boss was in, which made sense, but drew a discouraged exhale from Lumbergh. With a sweat-laced wince folded across his face, he knew that with Jefferson in front of the radio back at the office, all it would take was a quick transmission to let him know where he was and that he needed help. In a mere minute his officer could have Lakeland officers on route. Without more ammo though, he wouldn't last that long.

He checked the mirror again and saw that the man with the silver hair was perched up on one knee beside the garage, lying in wait for him to make a move. He noticed what looked like a blood stain along the man's thigh and realized that one of his initial shots had connected. It explained why the man hadn't been able to finish him off from the onset.

"Are you Moretti?" he yelled in hopes of breaking some of his attacker's focus. "Or is he the pussy who took off in the Cadillac?"

While he spoke, he stuck his Glock between his knees and raised his good arm to pry his fingers under the handle of the passenger door. He carefully lifted up on it and felt the hinges give.

"He's the pussy who took off in the Cadillac," the man with the silver hair freely answered after dwelling only a couple of seconds on the question. Though the man tried to hide it, Lumbergh detected bitterness in his voice. Obviously he hadn't expected his apparent boss to leave him behind.

"Well, it doesn't really matter!" Lumbergh shouted. His voice trembled from the adrenaline bouncing through his veins. "We'll get him after we take you down!"

A string of deep, hollow laughter echoed down from the top of the driveway. Lumbergh took the opportunity to scoot forward a little and let the door hang open no more than an inch, hoping the man with the silver hair wouldn't notice. He didn't seem to.

"Who's *we*, hillbilly? You're out here all alone, unless you're hoping for the forest animals to come save you!" He ended the statement with bellowing laughter.

Little more than an arm's length sat between Lumbergh and what he needed from the Jeep: The radio receiver, whose cord could be stretched outside to where he sat, and the spare clips for his gun. If he could rattle the man who had him pinned down, if only for a second or two, he could lay down some quick fire and snag what he needed from the Jeep. He relaxed his breathing and let his mind piece together the earlier words of his assailant along with what little he knew of Moretti. Though he wasn't nearly as seasoned of a bullshitter as his brother-in-law, desperation urged him to give it a shot.

"Valentino gave you up, asshole!" he shouted, praying that his words had more meaning to the man than they had to him. "He gave it *all* up! Everything! You've got the FBI coming after you—the Las Vegas office working with the Denver bureau. Bringing your shit across state lines wasn't the brightest of moves."

He waited for a response but received none. He hoped he had struck a nerve of some kind. He continued. "A fleet of agents started pouring through these mountains this morning! They're on to you, man! None of you are getting away!"

Without raising his arm into view, he pointed his gun to the sky and squeezed off two quick rounds, hoping the sudden shots and the echoes they'd create would force the assailant to take cover long enough to make his move. He swung open the Jeep's door and lunged for his radio receiver. Without hesitation, an onslaught of bullet fire shredded through the windshield and side window. He felt the collision of bullets stream into his underarm. The high-pitched, agonizing cry that he heard didn't seem to have come from him, but it did. His body crashed down along the running board of the Jeep before he fell to the dirt. He no longer felt his gun in his hand. Only incredible pain.

The deep cackling of the man who'd served him that pain replaced the sound of gunfire, but it was no less terrifying. Both of the moth's wings had been clipped, and Lumbergh's twisted face released groans and snarls of frustration and utter helplessness.

"I think you're full of shit, hillbilly," spoke the man whose voice now sounded closer.

Lumbergh knew he was being approached. He painfully twisted his neck from side to side as warm blood further dampened his shirt. He couldn't find his gun.

The edge of the man's imposing shadow advanced into Lumbergh's view along the road and he tried his best to dig his heels into the dirt and gravel to slide along his back in the opposite direction. His lack of mobility heightened the sense of hopelessness that already accompanied his panicked state.

His mind darted straight to Diana and he knew that there would be no greater test of her steadfastness among crisis than his death. He saw her long, wavy hair dangling above him and smelled her scent through his own sweat. When the wide, crooked, and sadistic smile of the man with the silver hair rose above the hood of his Jeep, he felt as though he had been hit by another bullet, not of lead but of punishing angst.

The lenses of the man's thinly framed glasses failed to shield his demonic eyes that seemed to read Lumbergh's every thought with their glaring imposition. Lumbergh held his breath and waited for the man to raise his automatic. Instead he watched the impulsive widening of the man's eyes and the eerie transition from his large grin to an awkward grimace. His shoulders slumped and he winced as he gracelessly spun around on the toes of his boots, lending his attention toward the front of the house.

The lodged shaft of a long and dark metallic arrow protruded squarely from between the man's shoulder blades. Deep red fletchings that matched the color of the small but growing stain of blood from the arrow's entry flared out its tail like flames.

An enraged, animalistic snarl filtered out through the man's clenched teeth and he raised his automatic rifle and took quick aim before firing into the forest north of the house.

From that forest, Ron Oldhorse let the thick trunk of the tall pine he'd taken cover behind bear the brunt of the rapid bullet fire. Though his face remained characteristically stoic and emotionless, his mind couldn't fathom how the man with the silver hair was still standing. He'd hit him dead center.

From the scene Oldhorse had come upon after running in the direction of the noisy barrage of gunfire that had erupted through the forest, he feared he'd arrived too late. The chief's Jeep had been turned into Swiss cheese, and a trail of bloodstained earth leading around to its hidden side was all he could see of the lawman. But if there was any chance Lumbergh was still breathing, he wasn't about to leave him. Abandonment was not an option.

It shouldn't have been an option years ago, the day a younger Ronald Wilson accidentally struck a young Bosnian Serb with a US military Jeep during an overseas peacekeeping operation. An angry mob in the town of Brčko in northern Bosnia kept him from attending to the woman's severe wounds. Wilson was forced to speed away to protect himself and the men he was responsible for. He learned later that the woman had died without receiving treatment quickly enough. A mother of two. The fear of dying and the hopelessness he read in her eyes was a dark, persistent memory that Oldhorse hadn't been able to move on from. It transformed him into the spiritual yet misunderstood man that he now was.

As he told Toby's mother, Joan Parker, last night as she sat under a blanket that provided her no comfort, he would die before he left a lost and battered soul behind.

Keeping his shoulders tight to his sides, Oldhorse lifted an arm up and snagged a fresh arrow from his pack. He lowered its nock to the center of his bow's taut string and breathed in through his nose.

He waited for the intermittent discharges of the rifle to stop before he stole a glance around the splintered edge of the tree to see the man. He had moved in closer than Oldhorse had guessed, limping noticeably from a shot he had taken to his thigh. Only about twenty yards away. A used magazine dropped from the man's hand to the ground and he quickly pulled a new one from his jacket pocket. Before he could shove it into the base of his rifle, Oldhorse was on the move.

Like a whisper in the wind, he wove through dense trees and scrub with the weaving locks of his long hair chasing him. He hoped to draw the man's attention further away from the chief.

The man with the silver hair howled and shouted unintelligibly as he unloaded his rifle. The sweeping movement of his arm from side to side sent lead through the surrounding terrain like an enraged swarm of bees chasing a predator from its nest. From his lips poured incessant rage that sounded of a mixture of foreign tongue and unleashed fury. His face, contorted in anguish, glistened from sweat. Wheezing gusts of air escaped his flared nostrils.

His compressed gaze had lost track of the spry man who'd gotten the jump on him, but he knew he was close. He mouthed a silent promise to finish that quarrel. When he swung his body back toward the Jeep—off-balance and fatigued from the metal tip of the arrow wedged between his lungs—his eyes bulged in a display of perhaps the first grain of fear Alvar Montoya had ever experienced in his life.

"Hillbilly?" he muttered.

A half second later, his forehead imploded just above the bridge of his nose. Smoke drifted out from the hollow trail of the bullet nested in his cranium and he stumbled forward on random footing before collapsing to his knees and then his chest. Yards in front of him lay Chief Gary Lumbergh sprawled out along the bloodstained dirt road, his Glock held tightly at the end of his shaking, outstretched arm. Smoke rose from the barrel before his grip loosened and the gun fell from his hand.

"I'm from Chicago, asshole!" he groaned before his eyes squinted shut and he collapsed.

Chapter 51

"Just getting off the plane now, D," he spoke into the receiver as he stepped in front of an obese, curly haired woman who was being pushed up the gateway carpet in a wheelchair.

"Hey! How 'bout a little patience," the woman barked in protest at the large man who had crippled the momentum of the struggling flight attendant who was doing her best to guide the chariot forward.

Sean didn't even hear her.

With his face cleanly shaven, his hair combed, and his large body clad in fresh clothes that let him resemble a vacationing tourist, he continued, "Yeah, I'm on a cellphone. A friend let me borrow it."

Sean's thick neck swiveled and he glanced back at Lisa who offered him a smile from down the jet bridge where she was stuck along with other passengers behind the slow-moving woman in the wheelchair. She was dressed in dark blue jeans that fit her well and a white shirt that was partially covered by an unbuttoned, ecru jacket. The strap of a small, red purse hung over her shoulder. From where Sean stood, the welt given to her from her attacker at the cottage was far less noticeable.

He stepped off into the terminal and continued his conversation with his sister.

"You know, when I told Mom that you saved a woman's life, she said she was proud of you."

"Bullshit," he answered at a volume that compelled a mother waiting for a departing flight to cup her young son's ears with her hands and reprimand Sean with a disapproving scowl. He didn't notice it.

Diana chuckled and insisted that she was telling the truth. A half-grin developed across his coarse lips.

"I've got someone here who wants to talk to you," she said. "Hold on."

From a small Lakeland hospital room decorated with vases of flowers and a couple of gift baskets, Diana kept a hand firmly wrapped around her husband's while she held the corded phone receiver to his ear. Gary sat up in a reclined position as best he could with an arrangement of shoulder cast, thick bandages, and IV tubes constraining him.

"Hello, Sean," he said with some dryness in his voice. "Welcome back."

"Hollywood!" Sean shouted over the phone in near jubilation.

Diana watched a lighthearted sneer form across her husband's face.

"How are the nurses treating you? I bet they love having a real-life celebrity under their care!"

Diana could hear her brother's remark through the phone. She grinned at her husband as she watched him shake his head.

Gary said, "Yeah. Diana told me it's been all over the news."

"*National* news, Hollywood," Sean interjected. "Your ugly mug was on CNN this morning. I saw it at the airport in Michigan."

"It looks like you weren't kidding about Vincenzo Moretti being a big shot," said Gary. "Not just in the casino world, but also in drug trafficking. I guess the DEA's been onto him for some time, building a case. With Tony Fabrizio singing like a bird, they're getting more than they ever could have hoped for."

"Yeah, Fabrizio's soft. I've never seen a grown man cry like that. Have they found Moretti?"

"No. Not yet. A guy from the bureau thinks he may be on his way to Mexico. Maybe Canada."

"Why do they think that?"

"They found his passport in Alvar Montoya's car. They think he might have had someone FedEx it to them from Vegas," Gary said. "Whatever's in that ledger had him scared enough to want to leave the country. Without his passport, only the landlocked ones are going to let him in. Speaking of Alvar Montoya, it turns out that he's got a rap sheet four pages long."

"Big surprise," Sean grumbled.

Gary let his wife hold a large cup of water with a straw in front of him. He took a sip before continuing. "Most notably, he was wanted in connection with the murder of two US border agents down in Texas. Seems he'd been under the radar for the past couple of years, going by the name of Alvar Sanchez. The Feds didn't know he was the same guy. He dyed his hair silver, wore glasses he probably didn't need, and carried a plethora of phony identification."

"Well, he won't hurt anybody else from the grave," asserted Sean. "And *you* finally got to fire your gun."

Gary's tongue formed a ball and pressed it against the inside of his cheek. "In the line of duty, Sean," he said with some annoyance. "I've fired all kinds of guns."

He knew Sean would feel compelled to get in at least one dig.

Diana squeezed her husband's hand while he spoke, grateful to God that he was alive and that surgeons told him he'd recover from his injuries over time with the right rehabilitation. Maybe never one hundred percent, but enough to return to work as Winston's police chief. The irony of it all, though, was tough to digest. They had left Chicago, in part, because she worried for her husband's safety there. She would have never thought in a hundred years that Winston would prove to be more dangerous. Still, the look in her face admitted she enjoyed watching the pride in his eyes when he spoke of his involvement in his first serious case since leaving the big city. She also saw some rare vulnerability from him since she arrived in the hospital. A sincere appreciation for her companionship and love. She was looking forward to having him home for a few months to rest and heal, and had already tossed every pack of chewing gum in the house into the trash. She mused at the comical image of him sharing the television with her mother.

At that airport, Lisa had seen Sean's grimace of pain when he leaned his knife shoulder to the post beside him while on the phone with his brother-in-law. She was at his side in seconds.

"Ask him if the FBI has the ledger," she whispered to him.

He almost grinned at the hint of perfume that met his nostrils as she leaned in to him. "Do the Feds have the ledger?" he asked into the phone.

"They do," Lumbergh said. "It turned up in a mail room at the Las Vegas branch. Unopened until we let them know they should have it. They haven't told me what's in it. I doubt they will."

"They were probably just happy to have someone do their jobs for them," said Sean.

No one spoke for a few seconds as each waited for the other to say something.

"I should have believed you, Sean," Lumbergh eventually said.

Sean could imagine Diana's surprise in reaction to her husband's words.

Lumbergh added, "You were right."

There was only silence on Sean's end until he finally responded with, "I bet that hurt to say."

"Yes," Lumbergh replied. "But you did good detective work. You didn't give up. That's commendable."

Sean grinned. "You know, I think I was right about Tariq being a terrorist too."

"No, you weren't."

Both men could hear each other smile through the phone. It was the first time the two of them had held a civil conversation. Respect had been earned.

"How long are you going to be out of commission?" Sean asked.

Lumbergh sighed. "Oh, I'll be back before anyone misses me."

"Who's in charge until then?" Sean asked eagerly.

"Of the office? Jefferson, of course."

"Jesus," Sean bemoaned. "You'd be better off just handing your badge over to Toby."

Lumbergh belched out an abrupt laugh that Sean figured had awakened his injuries because Diana took over the conversation.

"Joan says that Toby put together a really nice photo collage for Uncle Zed's funeral service, Sean," came her voice.

Sean's shoulders lowered, and Lisa noticed his smile deflate a little.

"He's really looking forward to seeing you back," she continued. "He feels terrible about Rocco though. He feels like he let you down, because you put him in charge and all."

Sean sighed and said, "He didn't let me down. I owe him."

He wished his sister well with the promise that he would be back home to Winston in a few hours. He then handed Lisa her phone back. She ended the call, snapped it shut, and dropped it into her purse.

The two strolled down the wide airport terminal as others walked faster around them, reflecting back on some of the conversations they'd had on the plane and over the past forty-eight hours. Sean was cognizant to the looks he received, having such an attractive woman by his side. Lisa needed to catch a connecting flight back to Nevada where her late husband's body was to be shipped, so the two stopped when they reached the center of the terminal.

"Have you figured out when you're going to make it back to Michigan to get your car?" she asked him with a grin.

"I'm not sure. Once the funeral's over, I'll figure it out. I'm not planning on leaving it behind. We've been through too much together."

She nodded and reached into her purse. She pulled out a small white, rectangular box with a shiny red ribbon wrapped tightly around it. She held it up to him in the palm of her delicate hand.

"What's this?" he asked, suspicion lacing his voice.

She smiled brightly. "A gift."

Some reluctance to accept it was apparent in his gaze, but she insisted, watching his large fingers toy with the ribbon.

"You just have to slide it off," she said.

He smirked and tugged off the ribbon before peeling up the lid. His lips pursed at the sight of a black, sleek-looking cellphone that was nestled inside in red tissue paper, matching the color of the ribbon. His eyes lifted to meet hers. She grinned again. The radiance of her face produced a fluttering sensation deep in his gut.

"It's time to embrace the twenty-first century, Mr. Coleman. You should never leave home without one. It will save you a heck of a lot of trouble in the future."

The small phone resembled a child's toy at the center of his excessive hand. He studied the gadget so intently that he looked like an archeologist trying to determine what kind of fossil he'd just discovered.

"The buttons are so tiny," he muttered. "I'll be lucky if I can punch in a number."

"You'll get used to it. I promise," she said with a giggle. "I made my phone number easy for you. I added myself as your number one contact."

She pointed to a larger button in the upper left portion of the phone's keypad and added, "Just push this one and then the number one."

"Sounds easy enough," he conveyed with a touch of uncertainty.

The two gazed at each other for a strained moment before Lisa let her eyes flow to the row of large television monitors that hovered at an angle above the wide and busy hallway they stood in.

"Well, I'd better be moving onto the next concourse," she said. "My flight should start boarding in about fifteen minutes."

He nodded as large herds of people shuffled their way around them in both directions. Only bits and pieces of other conversations lingered in the air while he struggled to come up with the words to offer as a parting farewell.

"I hope you have a good flight," he eventually blurted out, instantly regretting his choice.

He took a breath and extended his hand to her. She ignored the hand and swept her body in close, delivering a tight embrace around his large frame. The side of her face pressed against his chest and he wondered if she could hear his elevated heart rate as he breathed in her fresh scent. He hadn't expected such a sign of affection, but he timidly returned the hug.

"Thank you," she whispered before her arms slipped from his back.

He noticed her eyes shift and narrow before she craned her neck over his shoulder. "What?"

"That sore, or whatever it is on your head," she noted. "It's healing."

Only then did Sean Coleman realize that the itch at the back of his skull that had persistently nagged him for longer than he could remember had escaped his notice for two straight days. His hand went to the back of his head where a solid scab marked its mending.

"I'll be damned," he muttered under his breath.

She wiped a misty eye with the side of her soft hand and then latched onto the elevated handle of the leather carry-on suitcase that stood behind her. Its wheels strolled on thin, gray carpet and then linoleum as she made her way toward the escalator that would take her down one floor to the tram. She only turned back once, waving goodbye to the man from Colorado who hadn't yet moved.

He waved back, a hint of sadness in his face.

She held a finger and thumb to the side of her face in the shape of a phone and mouthed the words, "I'll call you."

He nodded and took a breath, watching her body and then the top of her head float down below the floor until she had disappeared from sight.

She leaped off the last step of the escalator before it disappeared into the floor at the bottom of its metal track. It was a habit that had formed from her childhood when she used to travel with her parents—one that she'd never given up for whatever reason.

While waiting for the interterminal train to arrive, she watched in amusement as a handsome man, probably in his later thirties and wearing khakis and a polo shirt, dragged his young daughter across the pale, linoleum floor. The little girl was probably only three years old with long and curly blonde hair. She had wrapped her arms and legs tightly around her father's larger leg, and he made funny faces, much to her delight, as he walked around in circles to tote her along. Her sister, who looked a couple of years older, joined in her laughter, and their pretty mother watched on, displaying a pleasant smile.

It occurred to Lisa at that very moment that she was no longer shackled by disappointment and false hope. There was a new life out there for her somewhere—a fresh start toward the things she wanted and often dreamed of. Once her old life was sorted out in Las Vegas, a new chapter would begin and maybe her story would unfold somewhere other than Nevada.

When she reached her concourse and made her way down to her departing terminal, she learned that her flight had been delayed by twenty minutes. To kill time, she meandered her way over to the terminal's small food court where she purchased a poppy seed bagel and glass of orange juice. She sat with her legs crossed in a seat along an empty row that faced the walkway and enjoyed her snack. A couple of pilots, clad in short-sleeved, white uniform shirts with dark ties, took notice of her as they walked briskly by, pulling their luggage behind them. She offered a polite smile before glancing down at her watch.

The news that her flight's delay had been increased to thirty minutes was delivered by a woman's voice over a loudspeaker. The news didn't faze her. *What's an extra ten minutes?* she thought to herself. Moments later, another announcement was broadcast through the intercom. This time, it was a man's voice, requesting that a passenger return to Gate 27. Had it not been for the name of the passenger, the page would have completely escaped her notice. Its familiarity however, triggered her attention.

She knew that name—Lawrence Falcone. It belonged to the man who she'd met one night long ago at a restaurant back in Las Vegas. Kyle had presented him as a retired coworker from the FBI. She shook her head with an abandoning sigh, appraising again the lengths her late husband had gone to in order to prolong his sham. She wondered who that man had really been. Probably a blackjack dealer or some bartender Kyle had paid off.

Lisa finished up her bagel and juice and disposed of her plastic cup in a tall, metal trashcan that stood in front of a bathroom entrance that she passed by.

Her wandering eye evaluated the lit-up destinations displayed on digital signs that hovered above each gate as she made her way back. The flight at Gate 23 was headed for Phoenix. The one at 25, for Miami.

Lisa had never been to Miami. She almost flew there a year and a half ago when some teacher friends of hers and their spouses invited her and Kyle on a Caribbean cruise that departed from a port in the city. However, a last minute assignment—or so she'd been told by her husband—came up a week beforehand and their plans were cancelled. She wondered now what the real story had been.

When she passed a gate with the destination of Newark, she glanced over at a stout, broad-shouldered man with a shiny, bald head and wearing a cream-colored suit. His back was toward her as he stood at the flight desk, speaking quietly to the middle-aged woman who worked the counter. If it wasn't for the excessive amount of sweat running along the sides of his neck and the base of his skull, she'd have probably not noticed him at all.

His feverish nodding at whatever instructions the airline employee was giving him sent out a signal that the man was deathly afraid of flying.

When the man turned his head to point his pudgy finger in the direction of the nearby gate, Lisa slowed to a near stop. With his profile exposed, she realized that she somehow knew him. The shape of his face, the placement of his eyes, the curl of his mouth. Wherever she recognized him from, he looked different than before. He had hair before, not just on his head but also on his face. A goatee or perhaps just a mustache. Her mind strained to picture him as he was at that time. She never forgot a face and knew she wasn't mistaken.

She'd only been to Colorado once before—a weekend trip with Kyle to Copper Mountain a while back. Perhaps he was someone who'd stayed at the same lodge or who worked there.

Her breath left her when she noticed the gate number above his head: 27. Her eyes gaped open before she carefully turned her face away from the desk and picked up her pace until she was safely concealed from view behind a large support pillar. She pressed her back against it, feeling her own pulse tap her chest. She twisted her neck and peered around the edge of the pillar to catch a closer look at the man she had known as Lawrence Falcone from that enlightening night out with her husband in Vegas. His hair and mustache were both now gone, but it was undoubtedly him.

She tucked her head back between her raised shoulders like a turtle preparing for a predator and noticed that her suspicious demeanor had caught the eye of an elderly woman, sitting in a chair across from her who was knitting what looked to be a scarf. While the woman's fingers didn't flinch from her needlework, her invasive, judging eyes peered up through gold-framed spectacles and advertised her interest in the odd behavior she was witnessing.

Lisa stole a breath and forced herself to appear relaxed. She smiled politely at the woman to diffuse the conjecture but the woman's gaze was trained on Lisa like that of an astute owl that was instinctively aware of its surroundings.

Lisa's pleasant grin morphed into an annoyed scowl, and she reached into her purse to pull out her cellphone. She held it to her ear and shuffled out from behind the pillar and closer to the flight desk, careful to keep her back to the man who stood in front of it. She pretended as if she was engaged in a casual conversation while she discreetly weaved in and out through fellow travelers until she stood just mere feet away from the man.

She was confident he wouldn't recognize her as long as she didn't make eye contact with him, but she wondered how he'd react if she did. Part of her wanted to confront and castigate the imposter for playing a role in her husband's deception, even if that role was quite small. Yet, it was her grim curiosity that kept her as a mere observer. She managed to eavesdrop on bits and pieces of Lawrence Falcone's conversation with the airline employee. It sounded as if the man who had once posed as her husband's partner at the FBI was being granted an upgrade to first class.

If there was any doubt left in her mind that she indeed had the right man, it was erased when the sound of his raspy voice fell within earshot. There was a touch of an accent that hadn't been there before, but otherwise, its distinctiveness was so identifiable that it brought back vivid memories of the discussion she'd had with him over steak and cocktails that night.

He had portrayed the role of a retired agent flawlessly, primarily due to his convincing presentation as a man of authority. He seemed to hold a nearly parental influence over her husband and the way he began to command results from the airline employee again projected that persona.

Falcone padded his beading head with a handkerchief before returning it to his jacket.

"You'll be in seat 3C, Mr. Falcone," said the woman from behind the counter. "The first-class section will board first. That should be in about thirty minutes."

"What about on the second leg of the flight?" he inquired. "Can we go ahead and upgrade on it too?"

"You'll have to check with the gate in Newark for your continued service to Rome. We can't guarantee a seat in first class at this time."

Falcone scoffed and snatched his freshly printed boarding pass from the woman's hand and grabbed the handle of a small, camel suitcase beside him. The woman's professional grin vanished as he stormed off. When his head spun during the about-face, Lisa turned away from him and mumbled some pleasantry nonsense into her phone. She kept a subtle eye on him as he lumbered out into the hallway, around a young couple engaged in a deep kiss and onto the moving walkway headed toward the central area of the terminal.

The way he carried himself generated suspicion in Lisa that this man wasn't just some schmuck who her husband had once paid off to fool his wife. He was a man of importance, who she had just learned was on his way out of the country.

"Moretti," she whispered into her powered-off phone.

Her husband's former boss hadn't yet made it out of the state. If he made it out of the country, he'd most likely avoid justice for good.

She waited until the bulky fugitive was nearly at the end of the escalated walkway and about to step onto the next platform before she began following him. She kept the phone to her ear as an excuse for her lowered head not to draw suspicion if he somehow took notice of her. Her eyes darted through the terminal for anyone dressed in a security uniform, but she spotted only civilians and a short, dark-skinned man who was part of a clean-up crew. She lowered her cell only long enough to punch in a couple of numbers before it returned to her ear.

Sean Coleman stood just inside the closed doorway of the tram shuttle that was rapidly decreasing in speed. His hand tightly gripped a vertical support bar for balance while the intrusive banter of cheesy, departure-safety instructions blasted through an intercom positioned above his head.

When the instructions concluded, he could hear a low, pulsing noise from somewhere near him. It repeated itself twice before the man next to him pulled out a small, silver cellphone from his pocket and announced, "It's not me."

Sean's eyebrows arched and he reached into his pants pocket to retrieve his own phone. Its display screen was lit up with Lisa's name.

"Oh crap," he grumbled while trying to figure out how to accept the call.

The ringing continued, unhindered, and Sean grew angry. "Come on, you piece of shit."

"Just press the 'talk' button, man," said a teenage girl with purple hair and a nose ring who poked her head around Sean's shoulder. "It's the red one."

Sean complied just as the sliding doors of the train were preparing to open.

"Hello!" Sean shouted.

"Sean, he's here!" came Lisa's voice.

"What?"

He could barely hear Lisa's whispering over the noisy crowd of people pushing their way to the side of the train.

"He's here!" she repeated, this time as forcefully as her discretion would allow her.

Sean noticed from the glares of those around him that they could all hear Lisa's voice as well as he could, at ample volume.

"You turned on the speaker phone, dude," said the same ratty-looking girl who had helped him before.

The doors slid open and a ripple of travelers pushed their way into Sean. He staggered backwards and out of the train as they herded him toward a pair of upward-bound escalators.

"Who's where?" he shouted over the commotion.

"Moretti! He's here in the terminal. He's trying to leave the country!"

His skeptical eyes tapered and he shook his head. "What do you mean? How can you know? You told me you never even met the guy."

"It's a long story, but I know it's him. This is for real. Believe me."

"Okay, okay!" he said before pushing his way back against the oncoming crowd.

Clusters of travelers were already entering the train from the opposite side, and Sean feared the doors would close before he reached them. He shoved and forced his way against the tide, ignoring the angry protests of others as he did. Just as the doors began to close, he slid back inside.

"Listen, I'm back on the train. I'll be there soon! Terminal C, right?"

"You're still in the airport?" she said. "Good! Yes, it's Terminal C. I'm going to try and find airport security."

Lisa's voice through the cellphone's open speaker was attracting attention, this time from a new group of travelers. Sean ignored their glares and kept the phone to his ear.

When she didn't speak for a few seconds, he frowned. "Lisa?"

Silence.

"Hello? Hello!" he snarled to no avail, other than commanding the attention of everyone seated and standing around him. "Lisa?"

Lisa watched Moretti use the sleeve of his jacket to repeatedly brush sweat from his forehead. He continued the action about every eight seconds or so, resembling a car's windshield wipers on an intermittent setting. He continually twisted his head in different directions to assess his surroundings. She believed he was keeping an eye out for people in uniforms, just as she was, but for different reasons.

She remained in the distance, merging her way in with families and other clusters of people to avoid sticking out.

"He's a short, heavy man in a cream-colored suit," she spoke into the receiver. "He's bald."

When Sean didn't respond, she realized that the call had been dropped.

"Dammit," Lisa muttered before dropping the phone into her purse.

She watched Moretti approach a newsstand and dig through his wide pants pocket. He snatched out some change and grabbed a folded newspaper from the countertop after the vendor acknowledged him with a nod and took his money.

Lisa slowed her stride and huddled herself next to a tall terminal directory. He rifled through the tall pages of the paper with his suitcase at his feet. She kept a close eye on him, wondering what could be running through his mind at that very moment. Maybe he was looking for some mention of himself in the headlines.

She wondered if he believed he was about to get away with murder or if he feared being caught before he landed on Italian soil. She hoped he was afraid. She hoped he felt at least a little bit of the same fear that her husband must have felt as he stood on that bridge with a gun pointed to his head. She hoped he felt an inkling of the fear that the others had felt—the ones who lost their lives in the mountains because of him.

She was staring down an evil man who had bestowed pain on more people than he probably ever bothered to consider. Yet, the man probably knew her husband far better than she ever did.

A rumble of static lightly echoed off the walls of the terminal. The sound hooked her attention, as it did Moretti, who quickly lifted his newspaper in front of his face to subtly conceal himself. The noise had come from a radio attached to the side of an older, bearded man wearing a sky-blue uniform with dark pants and matching tie. A gold badge was pinned just above his left shirt pocket. Airport security. He was walking casually toward the area where Moretti was standing, though the relaxed mannerisms revealed that he had no interest in anything or anyone in particular. Just sweeping the perimeter. He wore a gun holstered on the opposite hip as his radio.

Lisa made certain Moretti wasn't watching and discreetly waved her hand at the guard, careful not to lift it high enough to capture the notice of unwanted eyes.

The guard was oblivious. His gaze seemed to be centralized on the foreheads of people taller than her, who swam back and forth between them. She wove her arm more deliberately to compensate, but it did no good. The guard was inching closer to Moretti. Lisa decided she would let him wander on past the outlaw where she could then pull him aside, out of sight of Moretti.

She entered the stream of travelers and let herself be whisked away with the flow.

———

I've always hated that fucking picture. Sure, no one's mug shot is ever worth a frame, but it makes me look like a fucking degenerate. Some homeless guy who they dragged in off a park bench. Vincenzo Moretti ain't no degenerate. With my hair long and stringy and all mopped to the side, though, I ain't surprised that security gropers didn't give me two looks. They're looking for Ron Jeremy, not Telly Savalas.

So, according to *The Denver Post*, the cops pinned me for offing Valentino. Give me a fucking break. I didn't even get a chance to lay a mitt on the prick. Hell, I didn't jack with any of these people. Zed

Hansen? Harold Bailey? They were Alvar's baggage. The stupid ape stuck around to wait for that idiot security guard and half the town showed up on his doorstep.

Nothing in this article about Arianna. I wouldn't expect there to be. They'll never nail me for her. They'll never even find her body. Alvar promised me that. He even blindfolded Tony before taking him to the spot where they dug her grave. Alvar never quite trusted the kid but liked to make him get his hands dirty. Alvar may have been a fucking nutcase but at least he was thorough. And unlike Kimble, he was loyal.

One less lying whore in the world, and the only mope who gave two shits about her is gone too. She begged me to spare his life before she died. I didn't see that coming. Good riddance to both of 'em. They can have each other now.

Kimble fucked me good before he died. He saved himself a far nastier death by taking himself out. If I had gotten ahold of him, I would have peeled his skin off his bones and made him watch me wear it as a scarf. He got my ledger to the Feds somehow, but they didn't start freezing my bank accounts until it was too late. By then, most everything had been wired to Switzerland and the Caymans.

I'm gonna miss Vegas. The king may have been forced into early retirement, but he's leaving with his ransom.

What a week. Who would have thought I would have spotted a clean-cut Valentino Greco from across a crowded intersection, two states away, after the son of a bitch stole from me and disappeared? I should have known the idiot was too dumb to have done it on his own. I never thought Kimble would cross me. He not only crossed me, but he swept away my doll—my compensation. Still, no broad is worth dying over. What a weak and pathetic little punk he was.

There's a security guard waddling his old ass over this way. Some schmuck probably six months away from starting his pension. Pure window dressing. An empty uniform to make travelers feel at ease.

No sense giving him a good look at this mug, though. I'll lift up my newspaper and let him pass on by.

I hear the tune of a song, blaring for just a second or two before it's cut short. It came from somewhere across the terminal's lobby. I know that song. It's familiarity steals my breath. I lower my newspaper and look for its source. I don't remember the name of the song, as it was only told to me once. Something by that blind black guy, Ray Charles. I just know that it played on Kimble's phone whenever his clueless wife was trying to reach him.

My eyes shoot back and forth across the hall, looking for anyone holding a phone. They stop when they find a cute, blonde woman with long hair, wearing jeans and a tan jacket. Her head is lowered as she speaks intently into her phone. There's a sober look of worry on her face. I hear a gasp slip from my mouth when I realize who she is. It's Kimble's wife. What in the holy hell is she doing here? She was in Michigan two days ago, or so Tony said before he was nabbed.

When she lifts her eyes to meet mine, I turn away. We're far enough apart that she shouldn't recognize me at a mere glance, not with how I look now. I find out quickly that I'm wrong.

"He's a fugitive!" I hear her scream. "Him in the suit! He's wanted by the police!"

I spin to see the old security guard's head swinging back and forth in confusion, like he just woke up from a nap. He hasn't a clue who she's ratting out, but he fumbles for his holster anyway. The rest of the travelers around us are every bit as mystified, but I know the fog won't last long. I rush the guard and make him eat the corner of my suitcase with a roundhouse swing that nearly takes me off of my feet. He goes down hard, and I pry his pistol from his holster.

Screams and shouting spread through the corridor, and people scatter in every direction. Parents are picking up their children and running. A threesome of flight attendants disappears around a corner with the heels of their scampering shoes sending echoes off the floor. A businessman holds his briefcase in front of his face while he cowers behind a bench. I lose track of Kimble's wife in the chaos. She has to have fled with the rest. I release the pistol's safety and hold it out in front of me while I put a death grip on the handle of my suitcase. In it is enough cash to get me out of the country—large bills shoved inside my rolled socks—but I won't be leaving from here anymore.

A gray door with no handle flies open across the concourse from me where another security guard suddenly appears. This one's much younger and he's armed. He probably watched the bedlam unfold from a television monitor somewhere. I fire a couple of shots at him and break for the escalator behind me. It leads down to the tram. More screams fill the area, and I nearly level an old man with his wife and an oxygen tank before I grab onto the escalator's moving railing. I scramble down the steel steps. My chest is tight and my breath is thin by the time I falter back onto stationary flooring.

The train has just pulled up to its last stop, and there are droves of people exiting out on the side opposite from me. They're clueless to the panic upstairs.

"Get the fuck out of my way!" I snarl at a group of grungy teenagers who are playing hacky sack in front of the train doors, which I expect to open at any moment.

After catching sight of my gun, they scatter like a school of fish that spotted an incoming sea predator. I leap over one of their bags that they left behind on the floor. Sweat is draining from every pore in my skin, and I fight to breathe. I hope to God I ain't having another heart attack. I try my best to control my breathing.

I know security will be informed and waiting for me at Terminal B. It doesn't matter. I plan on getting off before then. The tram tunnel's concrete walls are lined with emergency exits. I saw two or three doors outside the train window on my way over. I'll pop the emergency brake. If I can get outside before the airport is locked down, I shouldn't have much trouble finding a cab. Maybe I'll need to fly out from Mexico. I'll figure that out later.

The train is still emptying on the other side. Any second now and I'll be allowed in. I twist my neck back toward the escalator and see Kimble's wife poke her head up above the railing near the top of the steps. She's still blabbing into the phone, probably talking to the police. The stupid bitch. If I could pick her off from here, I would. I know better than anyone, though, that I can't shoot for shit, and I don't know how many bullets I've got.

"The train doors are about to open," I hear a computerized voice announce. "Please watch your step upon entering."

When the thick steel cab invites me in, I hear a second voice—a woman's voice. It sounds somewhat digitized and it's unnaturally loud, as if it's being broadcast over a P.A. system.

"Fat guy in a cream suit!" shouts the voice. "Bald! Sweaty!"

The moment I step inside, I catch the mere glimpse of a hulking man with untamed eyes and a face filled with intensity swing forward at me with a fist the size of a football. A locomotive of knuckles collides wickedly with the bridge of my nose and my head is snapped backwards like the recoil of a mortar round. For a second I feel as if I'm floating outside of my body and watching myself cartwheeling through the air before collapsing to the floor in a pain-wrenched clump of my own limbs.

The overhead lights of the train are a blur through my flickering eyes. I'm barely able to move and the back of my head feels like it's welded to the floor. The man who leveled me is silhouetted in front of the glare like a mammoth eclipse. He leans his head forward above me and examines my mug with a wince stretched across his face. He then lifts his head toward the door and places his arm along the doorway to keep the portal open.

He leans his head outside of the train and he holds a black cellphone up to his mouth before taking notice of something or someone across the train's boarding platform. The phone drops to his side and he points a finger down at me.

I hear him shout with grim uncertainty through the open doorway: "This is the guy, right?"

Chapter 52

"Why hadn't you left the airport?" Lisa asked with her thin hand caressing the side of his adherently smooth face, her deep blue eyes penetrating his.

He pretended not to know what she was talking about as the police officer who'd just finished questioning them paced back and forth among the medley of uniformed officers and paramedics. One spoke to someone on his radio.

"Come on," she pressed. "You know what I'm asking. I left you back there at the gate a good thirty minutes before I called you and you were still here in the terminals. I figured you'd be long gone. Not even in the building."

Sean nodded and let a hesitant smirk escape from his lips. He was lost in her eyes and feared his tongue would twist into knots if he tried to answer with anything other than the truth. "I guess, uh . . . I just stood there at the gate for a while . . . I thought you might come back."

Her dainty eyebrows raised and the hint of a grin formed along her glossed lips. "You thought I might come back?"

He let some air escape his lungs as he looked away. His eyes fell in the direction of the floor. He shook his head and then his eyes widened. "I'm sorry," he said with a nervous chuckle. "I think I've just watched too many movies. Too many TV shows."

She tugged his chin back in her direction and gazed into his eyes with such intimacy that his stomach felt hollow.

"You want to hear something funny?" she asked.

"Sure," he answered with a shrug. "Why not?"

"I used to have a dog," she began, which invited instant

befuddlement from Sean. His face contorted in response. "His name was Cletus. God, he was a great dog. He died about a year ago. I brought him up to the cottage a few times, up in Traverse City."

He nodded.

"I loved Cletus. He was loyal, and he was reliable. Those were two things I really needed in my marriage to Kyle, because with him, they just weren't there. That's even more apparent now that I know the truth. So, it was good to have that in my life." She chuckled, then continued. "Even if it was from a German Shepherd."

"So . . . do you want another dog then?" he asked, which brought a broad grin to her face.

"No. Listen. Cletus also made me feel safe. He protected me. I never worried about someone breaking into our house and hurting me because I had him. After he died, I guess I stopped feeling that. I stopped feeling like I had a constant in my life that would protect me."

She read the bewilderment in his face and watched the reflection of her slightly teary-eyed face in his eyes.

"When the man with the gun, back at the cottage, came chasing after me . . . When I tried to get out through the backdoor, I saw that dog-flap flip up and I thought just for a second that Cletus was going to dash right through it, like I knew he would have if he was still alive, and come to my rescue. But it was you. It was you who saved me. It was you who came to my rescue. You were there for me when I needed it the most."

Sean's mouth opened but nothing came out. He, for the life of him, couldn't make out whatever point she was trying to convey.

"Ever since that moment, I've been thinking of you as a human abstract of Cletus," she continued with a lighthearted smile.

Now he fought back the urge to grimace.

"Rough-looking and diligent, with a loud bark, but also with a kind heart that just a few people saw. Most importantly, an inherent instinct to protect those people, whether it be the guy you told me about on the plane who you thought was a terrorist, or the lady you thought was dealing drugs . . . It's all done in the interest of protecting others. And that's a very admirable and attractive quality to have, Mr. Coleman."

"Why are you telling me this?" he finally asked.

Her smile slowly widened until she was gleaming from ear to ear.

"I'm telling you this because the fact that I've been thinking of you as a reincarnation of my dead dog is a far more embarrassing admission than you thinking you'd get the lady at the end of the movie, and that she'd do this."

She cupped his face between her hands and guided his jaw down to hers, standing on tiptoe to meet him with her lips.

He was taken back by her directness and the tenderness of her touch, but willingly bent to her face. In her kiss he felt a deep desire for the same, honest affection that agonizingly reflected his own. He thought she could feel it too. He didn't care if she tasted the pain and loneliness of a man who had all but given up on ever finding someone whose time and patience was so desperately needed to understand who he was and accept him.

The way her body molded to his and the contact of her lips on his, he felt no reservations from her; no judgment, no intolerance, no fear.

Whatever else life had in store for him, Sean knew he could look it square in the eye.

She approved of him, and that's all that seemed to matter at that very moment.

He'd been needed and had been there to fill the need, just as he was. Yet, in her touch he also felt the promise of something new— something profound and worth striving for that couldn't be found inside a beer bottle or hiding behind an armory of bitterness. He felt free of the hardened binds of a broken man, and for the first time in his life, saw his future as a blank canvas primed for the masterstroke of an exciting creation.